Praise for W. P. Kinsella

"Kinsella defines a world in which magic and reality combine to make us laugh and think about the perceptions we take for granted."
—*New York Times*

"He has learned from Twain, has studied Hemingway. . . . The talent that lifts up off these pages is special."
—*Village Voice*

"Kinsella is a brilliant writer."
—*Edmonton Sun*

"His characters are both big and small as life, neither romanticized nor patronized. . . . Kinsella respects their integrity and humanity. . . ."
—*Publishers Weekly*

"We're reading a writer here, a real writer."
—Roger Kahn, author of *The Boys of Summer*

"[Kinsella is] Canada's answer to fabulists like Gabriel García Márquez."
—*Globe and Mail*

"Kinsella's style is fresh, poetic, and delightful; he gently creates a fictional world so intimate and natural we've been there before."
—*Saturday Night*

"Kinsella takes ordinary people and makes them extra ordinary through a compassionate telling of their stories and their lives."
—*Vancouver Sun*

"W. P. Kinsella is a protean writer . . . an important literary figure."
—*Detroit News*

"Kinsella has a wild sense of humor that makes him one of the best of today's fiction writers."
—*The Leader Post*

Cover art copyright © 2015 by Thomas Canty
Cover and interior design by Elizabeth Story
Author photo copyright © 2015 Laura Sawchuk

Tachyon Publications
1459 18th Street #139
San Francisco, CA 94107
www.tachyonpublications.com
tachyon@tachyonpublications.com

Series Editor: Jacob Weisman
Project Editor: Jill Roberts

ISBN 13: 978-1-61696-187-9
ISBN 10: 1-61696-187-2

Printed in the United States by Worzalla

First Edition: 2015
9 8 7 6 5 4 3 2 1

THE ESSENTIAL
W. P. KINSELLA

Tachyon | San Francisco

Also By W. P. Kinsella

Novels
Shoeless Joe (1982)
The Iowa Baseball Confederacy (1986)
Box Socials (1991)
The Winter Helen Dropped By (1994)
If Wishes Were Horses (1996)
Magic Time (1998)
Butterfly Winter (2011)

Short Story Collections
Dance Me Outside (1977)
Scars (1978)
Shoeless Joe Jackson Comes to Iowa (1980)
Born Indian (1981)
Moccasin Telegraph and Other Tales (1983)
The Thrill of the Grass (1984)
Five Stories (1985)
The Alligator Report (1985)
The Fencepost Chronicles (1986)
Red Wolf, Red Wolf (1987)
The Further Adventures of Slugger McBatt (1988)
The Miss Hobbema Pageant (1989)
The Dixon Cornbelt League and Other Baseball Stories (1993)
Brother Frank's Gospel Hour and Other Stories (1994)
The Secret of the Northern Lights (1998)
Japanese Baseball and Other Stories (2000)

Nonfiction
*Two Spirits Soar: The Art of Allen Sapp,
the Inspiration of Allan Gonor* (1990)
Ichiro Dreams: Ichiro Suzuki and the Seattle Mariners (2002)

Poetry
The Rainbow Warehouse (1989, with Ann Knight)
Even at This Distance (1994, with Ann Knight)

CONTENTS

INTRODUCTION
Rick Wilber

I t takes considerable nerve to call a collection of twenty-seven stories the "Essential" short stories of a writer as prolific as W. P. Kinsella. After all, Kinsella has published, by some accounts, more than two hundred short stories and gathered them in sixteen different collections, starting in 1977 with *Dance Me Outside*. That's a lot of excellence to narrow down to a little more than two dozen stories.

But if any collection of the prolific Kinsella's work could safely assume to truly be offering his essential short fiction, this is it. Kinsella himself has taken part in the selection process, editor Jacob Weisman is a deep admirer of the Kinsella *oeuvre* (and familiar with everything Kinsella has written), and Tachyon Publications has an outstanding reputation for finding and gathering the top material for just this kind of book.

So have some faith, dear reader, this is it, *the* must-read compilation that will show you, story by story, how W. P. Kinsella has become famous in two literary arenas, attracting a loyal readership that loves and admires his work, whether there's baseball involved or not.

It's true, Kinsella is most famous for his merging of baseball and the fantastic. Other notable writers have found success here, as well, but it is Kinsella who brought the quiet little subgenre to vibrant life with his "Shoeless Joe Jackson Comes to Iowa" story (reprinted in this collection), which led, over time, to the terrific novel *Shoeless Joe*, which led, over time, to the famous Kevin Costner movie *Field of Dreams,* which led to an entire generation of grown men weeping in theaters across North America before going home to call their fathers or their sons to tell them how much they loved them.

But for all of its cultural impact and import, "Shoeless Joe Comes to Iowa" is just one of several dozen excellent baseball-influenced stories that Kinsella has published. The best of those are reprinted here, including my personal favorite, the very charming "How I Got My Nickname," which is, I happen to know, editor Jacob Weisman's favorite as well, and the story that, for me, holds the purest magic realism you will find in a baseball story, "Searching for January," with a tragic, ghostly Roberto Clemente trapped in his own memories.

And there is an important other side of Kinsella's fiction represented here, too, one that is often overlooked in the love affair so many readers have with an Iowa baseball field busy with mythic ballplayers come back to play the game. A Canadian, Kinsella is equally famous in certain (mostly Canadian) circles for his Hobbema Indian Reserve stories, which are set on a Canadian reservation and feature several recurrent characters who are wise and funny and honest and deserve your attention. It is absolutely fitting that "Truth," one of the most famous of the Hobbema stories, leads off this collection with a witty, rollicking, important story of a reservation hockey team and a riot.

There are other stories here that stand alone, far away from baseball and the reservation. I recommend them all to you, though the touching and honest "The Last Surviving Member of the Japanese Victory Society" is my personal favorite. The sharply satiric "Lieberman in Love" is a close second, with its portrayal of a man in an unusual relationship with a prostitute. The film adaptation of "Lieberman" won the "Best Short Subject" Academy Award in 1996.

In every instance, from the baseball field to the Hobbema Reserve, from hired lovers to ghostly baseball players, from Iowa to Alberta to Hawaii and elsewhere, what you will find in this fine collection is the magic, the compassion, the humor, the power, and the sheer brilliance of storytelling that have made W. P. Kinsella one of the very best writers we have. It's about time that the very best of his many stories are gathered into one collection. This is that collection. Enjoy.

Rick Wilber
October 2014

Dr. Rick Wilber is a journalism and mass-media professor at the University of South Florida. He has published several novels and dozens of short stories, many of which contain elements of baseball and the fantastic. One of his baseball-themed short stories, "Something Real," won the 2013 Sidewise Award for Best Short-Form Alternate History. He is the editor of several anthologies, including *Field of Fantasies: Baseball Stories of the Strange and Supernatural* (Night Shade, 2014), which collects classic and contemporary reprints of stories by W. P. Kinsella, Stephen King and Stewart O'Nan, Karen Joy Fowler, Jack Kerouac, Rod Serling, Robert Coover, Louise Marley, and many more.

TRUTH

No matter what they say it wasn't us that started the riot at St. Edouard Hockey Arena. The story made quite a few newspapers and even got on the Edmonton television, the camera showing how chairs been ripped out of the stands and thrown onto the ice. There was also a worried-looking RCMP saying something about public safety, and how they had to take some of the 25 arrested people all the way to St. Paul to store them in jail. Then the station manager read an editorial about violence in amateur hockey. None of them come right out and say us Indians was to blame for the riot; they just present what they think are the facts and leave people to make their own minds up. How many do you think decide the white men was at fault?

There was also a rumor that the town of St. Edouard was going to sue the town of Hobbema for the damages to the arena. But nothing ever come of that.

Another story have that the trouble come about because my friend Frank Fencepost own a dog named Guy Lafleur. Not true either. Frank do own a dog named Guy Lafleur, a yellow and white mostly-collie with a question mark for a tail. And Guy Lafleur the dog *was* sitting on a

1

seat right behind our team players' box. That dog he bark whenever our team, the Hobbema Wagonburners, get the puck. And every time he bark Frank would shout the same thing, "Shut up, Guy Lafleur you son of a bitch." A lot of heads would turn every time he said it, because, as you maybe guessed, St. Edouard was a French Canadian town. But it was something else that started the riot.

We never would of been there anyway if Frank hadn't learned to read and write. Someday, I'm going to write a story about the time Frank go to an adult literacy class. Now, just to show off, he read everything in the *Wetaskiwin Times* every week, even the ads. One day he seen a notice about a small town hockey tournament that offer a $1000 first prize.

"I think we should enter a team, Silas," he say to me.

"What do we know about hockey?" I say back. Neither me nor Frank skate. I played a little shinny when I was a kid, but I don't much like ice and snow up my nose, or for that matter, hockey sticks.

"Let's go see Jasper Deer," say Frank, "there's a $200 entry fee to be raised."

Jasper is employed by Sports Canada. All the strings on Sports Canada are pulled from Ottawa. Jasper he have an office with a gray desk big as a whale, in the Consolidated School building. About fifteen years ago Jasper was a good hockey player. I'm not sure what Sports Canada is, but I know they figure if they give all us Indians enough hockey sticks, basketballs and volleyballs, we forget our land claims, quit drinking too much, get good jobs so we can have the weekends off to play games.

Jasper is glad to have anybody come to see him. He was Chief Tom's friend, was how he come to get this cushy job, though he would rather be trapping, or cutting brush than sit in an office. He is already bleary-eyed at ten o'clock in the morning.

"You want to enter a team in a tournament, eh?" he say to us, pushing his desk drawer shut with his knee, the bottles rattling.

Hobbema has a team in the Western Canada Junior Hockey League, so once guys turn 21 and don't get signed by any NHL team, they got no place to play.

"It'll be easy to get some good players together," Frank say, "and playing hockey keep us young people sober, honest and religious."

By the time we leave Jasper is anxious to put his head down have a little sleep on his desk, but he agree to pay for uniforms, loan us equipment, and rent us a school bus to travel in. I write down all those promises and get him to sign them.

Trouble is, even though a thousand dollars sound like a lot of money to me and Frank, the guys we approach to play for us point out it don't even come to $100 each for a decent sized team. So the players we end up with is the guys who sit in the Alice Hotel bar bragging how they turned down NHL contracts ten years ago, plus a few of our friends who can stand up on skates, and a goalie who just got new glasses last week.

The uniforms are white as bathroom tile, with a bright red burning wagon on the front, with HOBBEMA in red letters on the back. Some people complain the team name is bad for our Indian image, but they just ain't got no sense of humor.

Frank is team manager. I am his assistant. Mad Etta, our 400 lb. medicine lady, is doctor and trainer, and Guy Lafleur is our mascot.

St. Edouard is way up in northeast Alberta, a place most of us never been before. Gorman Carry-the-kettle drive the bus for us. We have a pretty rowdy trip once we get Etta all attended to. She squeeze sideways down the aisle and sit on the whole back seat.

"I'm surprised the bus didn't tip up with its front wheels about three feet off the ground," say Gorman.

"Don't worry, you'll balance things out," we tell Gorman. He is about 280 lbs. himself, wear a red cap with a yellow unicorn horn growing out of the crown.

We stop for lunch in a town called Elk Point, actually we stop at the bar, and since most of the team is serious drinkers, it is 3:00 P.M. before we get on the road again. I have to drive because Gorman is a little worse for wear. When we get to St. Edouard, a town that have only about ten houses and a little frame hotel gathered around a wine-colored elevator as if they was bowing down to it, we find we already an hour late for our first game. They was just about to forfeit us.

The game played in a hoop-roofed building what is a combination curling rink and hockey arena. It sit like a huge haystack out in a field half a mile from town. Being February it is already dark. All I can see in any direction is snow drifts, a little stubble, and lines of scratchy-looking trees wherever there's a road allowance. The countryside is not too different from Hobbema.

Soon as our team start to warm up, everybody, except maybe Frank, can see we is outclassed. We playing the St. Edouard Bashers. Their players all look as if they drove down on their combines. And they each look like they could lift a combine out of a ditch if it was to get stuck. Most of our players are hung over. And though most of them used to be hockey players, it easy to tell they ain't been on skates for years.

The St. Edouard Bashers is young, fast and tough. Someone mention that they ain't lost a tournament game in two years. There must be 4,000 people in the arena, and they all go "Booooo," when our team show itself.

"I wonder where they all come from," says Frank. "There can't be more than fifty people in the town; sure must be some big families on these here farms."

They sing the national anthem in French, and after they done with that they sing the French national anthem. Then about a half a dozen priests, and what must be a bishop; he got a white robe and an embroidered quilt over his shoulder, come to center ice where they bless a box of pucks. The priests shake holy water in each goal crease. The players all cross themselves.

"We should of brought a thunder dancer with us," says Frank. "Make a note of that, Silas. We do it next time."

I don't bother to write it down. I'm already guessing there won't be a next time.

Right after the puck is dropped St. Edouard take hold of it, carry it right in on our goal. They shoot. Our goalie don't have any idea where the puck is; by pure luck it hit him on the chest and fall to the ice. The goalie, Ferd Tailfeathers, lose his balance fall forward on the puck.

About that time a half-ton St. Edouard defenceman land with a knee on Ferd's head, smash his mask, his face and his glasses about an inch deep into the ice.

Guy Lafleur stand up on his seat and bark like a fire alarm.

"Shut up, Guy Lafleur you son of a bitch," says Frank. Then looking out at the rink where Ferd lay still as if he been dead for a week or so, he say, "That fat sucker probably broke his knee on Ferd's head."

But the St. Edouard defenceman already skating around like he scored a goal, his stick raised up in the air, his skates making slashing sounds.

It is Ferd Tailfeathers get carried from the ice.

"Who's buying the next round?" he ask the referee, as we haul him over the boards.

"They take their hockey pretty seriously up here, eh?" says Frank to a long-faced man sit next to Guy Lafleur. That man wear a Montreal Canadiens toque and sweater, and he have only four teeth in front, two top, two bottom, all stained yellow, and none quite matching. I notice now that almost everybody in the arena, from old people, like the guy next to Guy Lafleur, to tiny babies in arms, wear Montreal Canadiens sweaters. Somewhere there must be a store sell nothing but Montreal uniforms.

"You think this is serious," the old man say, "you ought to see a wedding in St. Edouard. The aisle of the Catholic Church is covered in artificial ice, at least in the summer, in winter it freeze up of its own accord. The priest wear goal pads and the groom is the defenceman," he go on in a heavy French accent.

"I didn't see no church," says Frank, "only big building I seen was the elevator."

"You seen the church," say the old man, "elevator got torn down years ago. You guys should stick around there supposed to be a wedding tomorrow. The bride and bridesmaids stickhandle down the aisle, careful not to be off-side at the blue line; they get three shots on goal to score on the priest. If they don't the wedding get put off for a week."

Another old man in a felt hat and cigarette-yellowed mustache speak up, "We had one priest was such a good goal-tender there were no weddings in St. Edouard for over two years. Some of the waiting couples had two, three kids already—so the bishop come down from Edmonton and perform a group ceremony."

Knocking Ferd out of the game was a real unlucky thing for them to do. I'm sure they would of scored ten goals each period if they'd just been patient. In the dressing room we strip off Ferd's pads, look for somebody to take his place.

Frank tell first one and then another player to put on the equipment.

"Put them on yourself," they say to Frank, only not in such polite language.

"You're gonna have to go in goal," Frank say to me.

"Not me," I say. "I got some regard for my life."

"Put your goddamned dog in the goal," say the caretaker of the dressing room. We can hear the fans getting restless. They are chanting something sound like "Alley, alley, les Bashers," and stomping their feet until the whole building shake.

"You guys should go home now," the old caretaker say. "They just looking for a bad team to beat up on. The way you guys skate it will be like tossing raw meat to hungry dogs."

"I think he's right," I say. "Let's sneak out. We can fend off the fans with hockey sticks if we have to."

We are just about to do that when Frank get his idea.

"It's why I'm manager and you're not," Frank say modestly to me that night when we driving back toward Hobbema.

We hold up the game for another fifteen minutes while we try to find skates big enough to fit Mad Etta.

Etta been sitting in the corner of the dressing room having a beer. Her and Frank do some fast bargaining. End up Frank have to promise her $900 of the thousand-dollar prize money before she'll agree to play. Frank he plunk a mask on Etta's face right then and there.

"Not bad," say Etta, stare into a mirror. The mask is mean looking, with a red diamond drawed around each eye and red shark teeth where the mouth should be.

When we ask the Bashers to loan us a pair of BIG skates, they tell us to get lost.

"We've got to default the game then," we tell them, "guess you'll have to refund all those fans their money."

That make them nicer to know.

"Yeah, we didn't bring them all the way up here not to get in a few good licks."

"Besides the fans are in a mean mood. They want to see some blood. We're going to get even for what happened to Custer," say their biggest defenceman, who is about the size of a jeep and almost as smart. He give us his extra skates for Etta, then say, "We'll score four or five goals, then we'll trash you guys for a full hour. Get ready to bleed a lot."

We set Etta on a bench with her back to the wall. Me and Frank get one on each side of her and we push like we was trying to put a skate on a ten-pound sack of sugar.

"I'm too old for this," puffs Etta. "What is it I'm supposed to do again anyway?"

"Just think how you'll spend the $900," says Frank, tie her laces in a big knot, "and everything else will take care of itself."

Three of us have to walk beside, behind, and in front, in order to steer Etta from the bench to the goal. The fans are all going "Oooh," and "Ahhhh."

I get to walk behind.

"If she falls back I'm a goner," I say.

"So keep her on her feet," huffs Frank. "I figure you value your life more than most, that's why I put you back there."

"That's one big mother of a goaltender," say one of the Bashers.

"More than you know," says Etta, but in Cree.

"Alley, alley, les Bashers," go the audience.

Once we get Etta to the net she grab onto the iron rail and stomp the ice, send chips flying in all directions, kick and kick until she get right down to the floorboards. Once she got footing she stand with an arm on each goal post, glare fierce from behind that mean mask what painted like a punk rock album cover.

Soon as the game start again the Bashers get the puck, pass it about three ways from Sunday, while our players busy falling down, skate right in on Mad Etta and shoot . . . and shoot . . . and shoot. Don't matter where they poke the puck, or how often, there is always some part of Mad Etta blocking the goal.

After maybe ten shots, a little player zoom in like a mosquito, fire point blank; the puck hit Etta's shoulder and go up in the crowd.

"That hurt," shout Etta, slap with her goal stick, knock that little player head over heels as he buzz by the net. She get a penalty for that. Goalies can't serve penalties, but someone else have to. The Bashers take about twenty more shots in the next two minutes.

"You're doin' great," Frank yell from the bench.

"How come our team never shoot the biscuit at their goal?" Etta call back.

"We're workin' on it," says Frank, "trust your manager."

Things don't improve though, so Etta just turn her back on the game, lean on the net and let the Bashers shoot at her backside. There is more Etta than there is goal; even some shots that miss the goal hit Etta. I think it is a law of physics that you can't add to something that is already full.

There is no score at the end of the first period. Trouble is Etta assume the game is only one period long.

"I got to stay out there how long?" she yell at Frank. "I already earn more than $900. That little black biscuit hurt like hell," she go on. "And how come none of you guys know how to play this game but me?"

The players is all glassy-eyed, gasp for air, nurse their bruises, cuts, and hangovers.

As we guide Etta out for the second period, Guy Lafleur go to barking like a fire siren again. He always hated Mad Etta ever since one day he nipped at her heels while she huffing up the hill from Hobbema General

Store, and Etta punted him about forty yards deep into the mud and bulrushes of the slough at the foot of the hill.

When she hear the dog Etta spin around knock a couple of us to the ice, make Frank afraid for his life, and go "Bow-wow-wow," at Guy Lafleur, sound so much like a real dog that he jump off his seat and don't show his nose again until after the riot.

The way we dressed Etta for the game was to put the shoulder pads on, then her five-flour-sack dress, then tape one sweater to her chest and another to her back.

Soon as she get to the goal she have to guard for the second period, she don't even stomp the ice, just fumble in the pocket of her dress, take out a baggie with some greenish-looking sandy stuff in it, sprinkle that green stuff all across the goal line. Frank rush off the bench, fall twice on the way 'cause he wearing slippery-soled cowboy boots.

"What are you doin'?" he yell at Etta, who is waddling real slow, force each skate about an inch into the ice every step, and is heading for the face-off circle to the left of her goal.

"If I stay in front of that little closet I'm gonna be so bruised I'll look polka-dotted. I've had enough of this foolishness."

"But the goal," cries Frank.

"Hey, you manage the team. I'll do what I do best," and Etta give Frank a shove propel him on his belly all the way to the players' gate by our bench.

As the referee call the players to center ice, Etta sit down cross-legged in that face-off circle, light up a cigarette, blow smoke at the fans who stomping their feet.

The St. Edouard team steal the puck on the face-off, sweep right over the defence and fire at the empty goal. But the puck just zap off to the corner as if there was a real good goalie there. After about ten shots like that the Bashers get pretty mad and the fans even more so. It is like Etta bricked up the front of the goal with invisible bricks.

The St. Edouard Bashers gather around the referee and scream at him in both of Canada's official languages, and all of Canada's swear words.

The referee skate to the net, test with his hand, but there is nothing to block it. He stick one skate into the net. He throw the puck into the net. Then he borrow a stick from one of the Bashers and shoot the puck in, several times.

"Stop your bitchin' and play hockey," he say to the St. Edouard players.

"I bet I could sell that stuff to Peter Pocklington and the Edmonton Oilers for a million dollars an ounce," Frank hiss into my ear. "You're her assistant, Silas. What do you think the chances are of getting hold of a bag of that stuff?"

"It would only work when Etta stare at it the right way," I say.

"Hey, Edmonton Oilers could afford to buy Etta too. She's more valuable than Wayne Gretzky. And we'd be her agents . . ."

"Forget it," I say. "You can't buy medicine."

Les Bashers keep shooting at our goal all through the second period and into the third, with no better luck.

It a fact of hockey that no matter how bad a team you got you going to score a goal sooner or later. At about fifteen minutes into the third period, Rufus Firstrider, who skate mainly on his ankles, carry the puck over the St. Edouard blue line, try to pass to Gorman Carry-the-kettle, who been wheezing down the right wing.

The goalie see the pass coming up and move across the goal mouth to cover it, and there's a Mack truck of a defenceman ready to cream Gorman if the puck even gets close to him. But Rufus miss the pass entirely, fall down and accidentally hit the puck toward the net and score. That is all the goals there is: Hobbema Wagonburners 1, St. Edouard Bashers 0.

It was them and their fans what started the riot. We all headed for the dressing room, except for Frank, who jump into the stands looking for Guy Lafleur, and suffer a certain amount of damage as a result.

After the RCMP cooled everyone off and escorted us to our bus, Frank show up with a black eye and blood on his shirt, while Guy Lafleur have a notch out of one ear but a big mouthful of Basher hockey sweater to make up for it.

They got carpenters screwing the seats back in place and men busy resurfacing the ice. The Bashers decide to start the tournament over the next day, playing against teams they can beat. They agree to pay us $2500 to go home and never enter their tournament again.

And that's the truth.

HOW I GOT MY NICKNAME

In the summer of 1951, the summer before I was to start Grade 12, my polled Hereford calf, Simon Bolivar, won Reserve Grand Champion at the Des Moines, All-Iowa Cattle Show and Summer Exposition. My family lived on a hobby-farm near Iowa City. My father who taught classics at Coe College in Cedar Rapids, and in spite of that was still the world's number one baseball fan, said I deserved a reward—I also had a straight A average in Grade 11 and had published my first short story that spring. My father phoned his friend Robert Fitzgerald (Fitzgerald, an eminent translator, sometimes phoned my father late at night and they talked about various ways of interpreting the tougher parts of the *Iliad*) and two weeks later I found myself in Fitzgerald's spacious country home outside of New York City, sharing the lovely old house with the Fitzgeralds, their endless supply of children, and a young writer from Georgia named Flannery O'Connor. Miss O'Connor was charming, and humorous in an understated way, and I wish I had talked with her more. About the third day I was there I admitted to being a published writer and Miss O'Connor said, "You must show me some of your stories." I never did. I was seventeen, overweight, diabetic, and bad-complexioned. I alternated between being terminally shy and obnoxiously brazen. I was nearly always shy around the Fitzgeralds and Miss O'Connor. I was also terribly homesick, which made me appear more silent and outlandish than I knew I was. I suspect I am the model for Enoch Emery, the odd, lonely country boy in Miss O'Connor's novel *Wise Blood*. But that is another story.

On a muggy August morning, the first day of a Giants home stand at the Polo Grounds, I prepared to travel in to New York. I politely invited Miss O'Connor to accompany me, but she, even at that early date, had to avoid sunlight and often wore her wide-brimmed straw hat, even indoors. I set off much too early and, though terrified of the grimy city and shadows that seemed to lurk in every doorway, arrived at the Polo Grounds over two hours before game time. It was raining gently and I was one of about two dozen fans in the ballpark. A few players were lethargically playing catch, a coach was hitting fungoes to three players in right field. I kept edging my way down the rows of seats until I was right behind the Giants dugout.

The Giants were thirteen games behind the Dodgers and the pennant race appeared all but over. A weasel-faced bat boy, probably some executive's nephew, I thought, noticed me staring wide-eyed at the players and the playing field. He curled his lip at me, then stuck out his tongue. He mouthed the words "Take a picture, it'll last longer," adding something at the end that I could only assume to be uncomplimentary.

Fired by the insult I suddenly mustered all my bravado and called out, "Hey, Mr. Durocher?" Leo Durocher, the Giants manager, had been standing in the third base coach's box not looking at anything in particular. I was really impressed. That's the grand thing about baseball, I thought. Even a manager in a pennant race can take time to daydream. He didn't hear me. But the bat boy did, and stuck out his tongue again.

I was overpowered by my surroundings. Though I'd seen a lot of major league baseball I'd never been in the Polo Grounds before. The history of the place . . . "Hey, Mr. Durocher," I shouted.

Leo looked up at me with a baleful eye. He needed a shave, and the lines around the corners of his mouth looked like ruts.

"What is it, Kid?"

"Could I hit a few?" I asked hopefully, as if I was begging to stay up an extra half hour. "You know, take a little batting practice?"

"Sure, Kid. Why not?" and Leo smiled with one corner of his mouth. "We want all our fans to feel like part of the team."

From the box seat where I'd been standing, I climbed up on the roof of the dugout and Leo helped me down onto the field.

Leo looked down into the dugout. The rain was stopping. On the other side of the park a few of the Phillies were wandering onto the field. "Hey, George," said Leo, staring into the dugout, "throw the kid here a few pitches. Where are you from, son?"

It took me a few minutes to answer because I experienced this strange, lightheaded feeling, as if I had too much sun. "Near to Iowa City, Iowa," I managed to say in a small voice. Then "You're going to win the pennant, Mr. Durocher. I just know you are."

"Well, thanks, Kid," said Leo modestly, "we'll give it our best shot."

George was George Bamberger, a stocky rookie who had seen limited action. "Bring the kid a bat, Andy," Leo said to the bat boy. The bat boy curled his lip at me but slumped into the dugout, as Bamberger and Sal Yvars tossed the ball back and forth.

The bat boy brought me a black bat. I was totally unprepared for how heavy it was. I lugged it to the plate and stepped into the right-hand batter's box. Bamberger delivered an easy, looping, batting-practice pitch. I drilled it back up the middle.

"Pretty good, Kid," I heard Durocher say.

Bamberger threw another easy one and I fouled it off. The third pitch was a little harder. I hammered it to left.

"Curve him," said Durocher.

He curved me. Even through my thick glasses the ball looked as big as a grapefruit, illuminated like a small moon. I whacked it and it hit the right field wall on one bounce.

"You weren't supposed to hit that one," said Sal Yvars.

"You're pretty good, Kid," shouted Durocher from the third base box. "Give him your best stuff, George."

Over the next fifteen minutes I batted about .400 against George Bamberger, and Roger Bowman, including a home run into the left centrefield stands. The players on the Giants bench were watching me with mild interest often looking up from the books most of them were reading.

"I'm gonna put the infield out now," said Durocher. "I want you to run out some of your hits."

Boy, here I was batting against the real New York Giants. I wished I'd worn a new shirt instead of the horizontally striped red and white one I had on, which made me look heftier than I really was. Bowman threw a sidearm curve and I almost broke my back swinging at it. But he made the mistake of coming right back with the same pitch. I looped it behind third where it landed soft as a sponge, and trickled off toward the stands—I'd seen the play hundreds of times—a stand-up double. But when I was still twenty feet from second base Eddie Stanky was waiting with the ball. "Slide!" somebody yelled, but I just skidded to a stop, stepping out of the baseline to avoid the tag. Stanky whapped me anyway, a glove to the ribs that would have made Rocky Marciano or Ezzard Charles proud.

When I got my wind back Durocher was standing, hands on hips, staring down at me.

"Why the hell didn't you slide, Kid?"

"I can't," I said, a little indignantly. "I'm diabetic, I have to avoid stuff like that. If I cut myself, or even bruise badly, it takes forever to heal."

"Oh," said Durocher. "Well, I guess that's okay then."

"You shouldn't tag people so hard," I said to Stanky. "Somebody could get hurt."

"Sorry, Kid," said Stanky. I don't think he apologized very often. I noticed that his spikes were filed. But I found later that he knew a lot about F. Scott Fitzgerald. His favourite story was "Babylon Revisited" so that gave us a lot in common; I was a real Fitzgerald fan; Stanky and I became friends even though both he and Durocher argued against reading *The Great Gatsby* as an allegory.

"Where'd you learn your baseball?" an overweight coach who smelled strongly of snuff, and bourbon, said to me.

"I live near Iowa City, Iowa," I said in reply.

Everyone wore question marks on their faces. I saw I'd have to elaborate. "Iowa City is within driving distance of Chicago, St. Louis, Milwaukee, and there's minor league ball in Cedar Rapids, Omaha, Kansas City. Why there's barely a weekend my dad and I don't go somewhere to watch professional baseball."

"Watch?" said Durocher.

"Well, we talk about it some too. My father is a real student of the game. Of course we only talk in Latin when we're on the road, it's a family custom."

"Latin?" said Durocher.

"Say something in Latin," said Whitey Lockman, who had wandered over from first base.

"The Etruscans have invaded all of Gaul," I said in Latin.

"Their fortress is on the banks of the river," said Bill Rigney, who had been filling in at third base.

"Velle est posse," I said.

"Where there's a will there's a way," translated Durocher.

"Drink Agri Cola . . ." I began.

"The farmer's drink," said Sal Yvars, slapping me on the back, but gently enough not to bruise me. I guess I looked a little surprised.

"Most of us are more than ballplayers," said Alvin Dark, who had joined us. "In fact the average player on this squad is fluent in three languages."

"*Watch?*" said Durocher, getting us back to baseball. "You *watch* a lot of baseball, but where do you play?"

"I've never played in my life," I replied. "But I have a photographic memory. I just watch how different players hold their bat, how they stand. I try to emulate Enos Slaughter and Joe DiMaggio."

"Can you field?" said Durocher.

"No."

"No?"

"I've always just watched the hitters. I've never paid much attention to the fielders."

He stared at me as if I had spoken to him in an unfamiliar foreign language.

"Everybody fields," he said. "What position do you play?"

"I've never played," I reiterated. "My health is not very good."

"Cripes," he said, addressing the sky. "You drop a second Ted Williams on me and he tells me he can't field." Then to Alvin Dark: "Hey, Darky, throw a few with the kid here. Get him warmed up."

In the dugout Durocher pulled a thin, black glove from an equipment bag and tossed it to me. I dropped it. The glove had no discernable padding in it. The balls Dark threw hit directly on my hand, when I caught them, which was about one out of three. "Ouch!" I cried. "Don't throw so hard."

"Sorry, Kid," said Alvin Dark, and threw the next one a little easier. If I really heaved I could just get the ball back to him. I have always thrown like a non-athletic girl. I could feel my hand bloating inside the thin glove. After about ten pitches, I pulled my hand out. It looked as though it had been scalded.

"Don't go away, Kid," said Leo. "In fact why don't you sit in the dugout with me. What's your name anyway?"

"W. P. Kinsella," I said.

"Your friends call you W?"

"My father calls me William, and my mother . . ." but I let my voice trail off. I didn't think Leo Durocher would want to know my mother still called me Bunny.

"Jeez," said Durocher. "You need a nickname, Kid. Bad."

"I'll work on it," I said.

I sat right beside Leo Durocher all that stifling afternoon in the Polo Grounds as the Giants swept a doubleheader from the Phils, the start of a sixteen-game streak that was to lead to the October 3, 1951, Miracle of Coogan's Bluff. I noticed right away that the Giants were all avid readers. In fact, the *New York Times* Best Seller Lists, and the *Time* and *Newsweek* lists of readable books and an occasional review were taped to the walls of the dugout. When the Giants were in the field I peeked at the covers of the books the players sometimes read between innings. Willie Mays was reading *The Cruel Sea* by Nicholas Monsarrat. Between innings Sal Maglie was deeply involved in Carson McCullers's new novel *The Ballad of the Sad Café*. "I sure wish we could get that Cousin Lymon to be our mascot," he said to me when he saw me eyeing the bookjacket, referring to the hunchbacked dwarf who was the main character in the novel. "We need something to inspire us," he added. Alvin Dark slammed down his copy of *Requiem for a Nun* and headed for the on-deck circle.

When the second game ended, a sweaty and sagging Leo Durocher took me by the arm. "There's somebody I want you to meet, Kid," he said. Horace Stoneham's office was furnished in wine-coloured leather sofas and overstuffed horsehair chairs. Stoneham sat behind an oak desk as big as the dugout, enveloped in cigar smoke.

"I've got a young fellow here I think we should sign for the stretch drive," Durocher said. "He can't field or run, but he's as pure a hitter as I've ever seen. He'll make a hell of a pinch hitter."

"I suppose you'll want a bonus?" growled Stoneham.

"I do have something in mind," I said. Even Durocher was not nearly so jovial as he had been. Both men stared coldly at me. Durocher leaned over and whispered something to Stoneham.

"How about $6,000," Stoneham said.

"What I'd really like . . ." I began.

"Alright, $10,000, but not a penny more."

"Actually, I'd like to meet Bernard Malamud. I thought you could maybe invite him down to the park. Maybe get him to sign a book for me?" They both looked tremendously relieved.

"Bernie and me and this kid Salinger are having supper this evening," said Durocher. "Why don't you join us?"

"You mean J. D. Salinger?" I said.

"Jerry's a big Giant fan," he said. "The team Literary Society read *Catcher in the Rye* last month. We had a panel discussion on it for eight hours on the train to St. Louis."

Before I signed the contract I phoned my father.

"No reason you can't postpone your studies until the end of the season," he said. "It'll be good experience for you. You'll gather a lot of material you can write about later. Besides, baseball players are the real readers of America."

I got my first hit off Warren Spahn, a solid single up the middle. Durocher immediately replaced me with a pinch runner. I touched Ralph Branca for a double, the ball went over Duke Snider's head, hit the wall and bounced halfway back to the infield. Anyone else would have had an inside the park homer. I wheezed into second and was replaced. I got into 38 of the final 42 games. I hit 11 for 33, and was walked four times. And hit once. That was the second time I faced Warren Spahn. He threw a swishing curve that would have gone behind me if I hadn't backed into it. I slouched off toward first holding my ribs.

"You shouldn't throw at batters like that," I shouted, "someone could get seriously hurt. I'm diabetic, you know." I'd heard that Spahn was into medical texts and interested in both human and veterinary medicine.

"Sorry," he shouted back. "If I'd known I wouldn't have thrown at you. I've got some good liniment in the clubhouse. Come see me after the game. By the way I hear you're trying to say that *The Great Gatsby* is an allegory."

"The way I see it, it is," I said. "You see the eyes of the optometrist on the billboard are really the eyes of God looking down on a fallen world . . ."

"Alright, alright," said the umpire, Beans Reardon, "let's get on with the game. By the way, Kid, I don't think it's an allegory either. A statement on the human condition, perhaps. But not an allegory."

The players wanted to give me some nickname other than "Kid." Someone suggested "Ducky" in honour of my running style. "Fats" said somebody else. I made a note to remove his bookmark between innings. Several other suggestions were downright obscene. Baseball players, in spite of their obsession with literature and the arts, often have a bawdy sense of humour.

"How about 'Moonlight,'" I suggested. I'd read about an old-time player who stopped for a cup of coffee with the Giants half a century before, who had that nickname.

"What the hell for?" said Monte Irvin, who in spite of the nickname preferred to be called Monford or even by his second name Merrill. "You got to have a reason for a nickname. You got to earn it. Still, anything's better than W. P."

"It was only a suggestion," I said. I made a mental note not to tell Monford what I knew about *his* favourite author, Erskine Caldwell.

As it turned out I didn't earn a nickname until the day we won the pennant.

As every baseball fan knows the Giants went into the bottom of the ninth in the deciding game of the pennant playoff trailing the Dodgers 4–1.

"Don't worry," I said to Durocher, "everything's going to work out." If he heard me he didn't let on.

But was everything going to work out? And what part was I going to play in it? Even though I'd contributed to the Giants' amazing stretch drive, I didn't belong. Why am I here? I kept asking myself. I had some vague premonition that I was about to change history. I mean I wasn't a ballplayer. I was a writer. Here I was about to go into Grade 12 and I was already planning to do my master's thesis on F. Scott Fitzgerald.

I didn't have time to worry further as Alvin Dark singled. Don Mueller, in his excitement, had carried his copy of *The Mill on the Floss* out to the on-deck circle. He set the resin bag on top of it, stalked to the plate and singled, moving Dark to second.

I was flabbergasted when Durocher called Monford Irvin back and said to me, "Get in there, Kid."

It was at that moment that I knew why I was there. I would indeed change history. One stroke of the bat and the score would be tied. I eyed the left field stands as I nervously swung two bats to warm up. I was nervous but not scared. I never doubted my prowess for one moment. Years later Johnny Bench summed it up for both athletes and writers when he talked about a successful person having to have an *inner conceit*. It never occurred to me until days later that I might have hit into a double or triple play, thus ending it and *really* changing history.

When I did take my place in the batter's box, I pounded the plate and glared out at Don Newcombe. I wished that I shaved so I could give him a stubble-faced stare of contempt. He curved me and I let it go by for a ball. I fouled the next pitch high into the first base stands. A fastball was low. I fouled the next one outside third. I knew he didn't want to go to a full count: I crowded the plate a little looking for the fastball. He curved me. Nervy. But the curveball hung, sat out over the plate like a cantaloupe. I waited an extra millisecond before lambasting it. In that instant the ball broke in on my hands; it hit the bat right next to my right hand. It has been over thirty years but I still wake deep in the night, my hands vibrating, burning from Newcombe's pitch. The bat shattered into kindling. The ball flew in a polite loop as if it had been tossed by a five-year-old; it landed soft as a creampuff in Pee Wee Reese's glove. One out.

I slumped back to the bench.

"Tough luck, Kid," said Durocher, patting my shoulder. "There'll be other chances to be a hero."

"Thanks, Leo," I said.

Whitey Lockman doubled. Dark scored. Mueller hurt himself sliding into third. Rafael Noble went in to run for Mueller. Charlie Dressen replaced Newcombe with Ralph Branca. Bobby Thomson swung bats in the on-deck circle.

As soon as umpire Jorda called time-in, Durocher leapt to his feet, and before Bobby Thomson could take one step toward the plate, Durocher called him back.

"Don't do that!" I yelled, suddenly knowing why I was *really* there. But Durocher ignored me. He was beckoning with a big-knuckled finger to another reserve player, a big outfielder who was tearing up the American Association when they brought him up late in the year. He was 5 for 8 as a pinch hitter.

Durocher was already up the dugout steps heading toward the umpire to announce the change. The outfielder from the American Association was making his way down the dugout, hopping along over feet and ankles. He'd be at the top of the step by the time Durocher reached the umpire.

As he skipped by me, the last person between Bobby Thomson and immortality, I stuck out my foot. The outfielder from the American Association went down like he'd been poleaxed. He hit his face on the top step of the dugout, crying out loud enough to attract Durocher's attention.

The trainer hustled the damaged player to the clubhouse. Durocher waved Bobby Thomson to the batter's box. And the rest is history. After the victory celebration I announced my retirement blaming it on a damaged wrist. I went back to Iowa and listened to the World Series on the radio.

All I have to show that I ever played in the major leagues is my one-line entry in *The Baseball Encyclopedia*:

	G	AB	H	2B	3B	HR	HR %	R	RBI	BB	SO	EA	BA	Pinch Hit AB H
W. P. Kinsella				KINSELLA, WILLIAM PATRICK "TRIPPER" R TR 5'9" 185 lbs. B. Apr. 14, 1934 Onamata, Ia.										
1951 NY N	38	33	11	2	0	2	6.0	0	8	4	4	0	.333	33 11

I got my outright release in the mail the week after the World Series ended. Durocher had scrawled across the bottom: "Good luck, Kid. By the way, *The Great Gatsby* is *not* an allegory."

For Brian Fawcett,
whose story "My Career with the Leafs"
inspired this story.

THE NIGHT MANNY MOTA
TIED THE RECORD

August 7, 1979: Dodger Stadium, Los Angeles, California. Dodgers are playing Houston Astros. I am seated high above the field, just to the third-base side of home plate. Pregame presentations are being made. It is Mormon Family Night. The stadium is nearly full. It is five days since Thurman Munson died.

I spend my time people-watching. In front of me are a number of co-workers from an office of some kind, probably a food company, I decide, noting the size of the women. Every one of them is overweight, the one directly in front of me by about two hundred pounds. These women cram their sweating faces with every variety of concession food. The one in front of me has purchased a tray of six hotdogs. Several of them have whole trays of beer, six cups, each slopping foam over its waxy edge.

To my left, I watch an old man standing in the aisle staring at his ticket as if trying to decide where his seat should be. Eventually he chooses my aisle and makes his way to the seat next to me. He looks like a retired bank manager: iron-grey hair carefully styled, a blue pin-stripe suit, vest, and tie. He carries a zippered leather binder. What fascinates me is the ticket he holds in his left hand. As he stands in the aisle it appears to blink like a tiny computer making calculations. It flashes all the way down the row of seats, stopping as he slides into the chair next to mine.

Our eyes meet as he adjusts the small brown leather case in his lap, and I can see the same sense of tragedy floating in his eyes as I have viewed on my own the past five mornings.

"A terrible thing," I say.

He nods gravely. "Did you watch the funeral coverage on TV?"

It is my turn to nod. He has a sincere, fatherly voice that, my mind being preoccupied with the death of Thurman Munson, reminds me of the unseen baseball executive who talks to Munson in a widely shown commercial for a shaving product.

In the commercial, Munson knocks, then enters the executive's office, saying, "What's the problem? I'm playing good ball."

"You certainly are," the unseen executive says. "In my opinion, Thurman Munson is the finest catcher in the game."

As if reading my mind, the dapper old man beside me looks straight into my face and says, "Yes, a terrible loss, to the game and to the fans. In my opinion, Thurman Munson *is* the finest catcher in the game."

I feel like an egg with a finger-painted happy-face on it as I register my surprise.

"Is?" I say.

He leans towards me, smiling wryly, and speaks in a confidential manner. "Death," he says, "need not be as final as many of us are used to believing."

We are interrupted by the playing of the National Anthem. The old man stands at attention with his right hand over his heart. I look around me: everything appears to be normal, the palm trees beyond the left-field fence sway ever so slightly. I can discern nothing out of the ordinary except the presence next to me. When the anthem finishes I remain silent; whatever kind of game we are playing, it is his move.

"What would you say," the old man continues, "if I told you that it might just be possible to move time back, like a newsreel being played in reverse, and undo what has been done?" He stares at me, half smiling, giving me the chance to joke his statement away if I choose.

"You're talking about Thurman Munson?"

"More or less."

"Are you suggesting that if time were turned back, Munson's plane would have landed safely at the Canton Airport last week? That none of this would have happened?"

He nods.

"But at what price?" I say. "There has to be a catch."

"You're right, of course. As they say, there is no free lunch." He looks long at me, his kindly grey eyes on my face, and I'm sure at that instant we recognize each other for what we are, above and beyond business, family, or religion—baseball fans. The true word is fanciers. Fans of the game itself. Men having favourites, but not blind prejudices, here because we love the game. Not Sunday fathers dragging young sons after us, or college kids guzzling beer and cheering ourselves hoarse, but steady, long-term, win-or-lose fans. I can tell by looking at him that he has seen Mike Marshall work on a sleety April night in Bloomington; that he has endured the arctic cross-winds of Candlestick Park in San Francisco and Exhibition Stadium in Toronto; that he has been jellied in his seat by the steam-cabinet humidity of Busch Stadium in August. I feel towards that old man the camaraderie that soldiers must feel for their fellows as they travel home after a long campaign.

"My name is Revere," he says, extending a manicured hand that is solid as a ham, a baseball player's hand. "I caught a little myself at one time," he says, knowing I can feel the outsize fingers, like plump, scarred sausage. "I think we should have a serious talk."

"The price," I say. "What is the price of tampering with time?"

The game had begun. Jerry Reuss, pitching for the Dodgers, set Houston down in the first without a murmur.

"I'll explain the situation to you exactly as it is. No deception. I'll always be candid with you. Don't feel badly if you don't believe me. In fact, most people don't."

"Go on," I say.

He talks for a full inning. Explaining to me as if I were a child attending his first baseball game and he were a benevolent grandfather outlining the rules between hotdogs and orange drinks.

"What you're saying is . . ." but I am interrupted by the rising roar of the crowd as Joe Ferguson of the Dodgers strokes a home run to right field. I was not involved with what was happening and have to stare around the buffalo-like woman in front of me to see if there are runners on base. Revere and I applaud politely, sit down while the people around us are still standing; it is like sliding into the shade of a fence on a summer's day. As the buzz of the crowd subsides I continue:

"What you're saying is that everyone has someone, somewhere, who if contacted and agreeable, could replace them in death."

"Badly put but basically accurate," says Mr. Revere. "Limited, of course, to people who have achieved fame or made an outstanding contribution to society, and who still have an outstanding contribution left to make if given a second chance."

"And you're suggesting to me that I might be able to sacrifice myself in order to give Thurman Munson a longer life."

"At this point I am only acquainting you with the situation. I want to make that very clear. There are many of us at locations throughout the world. Our search is rather like a game: we have a few days to find the one person in the world who can, if he or she desires, make the event—in this case Thurman Munson's death—unhappen, so to speak. Experience teaches us that the natural places to be looking are ballparks, taverns, and assembly lines . . ."

"My case would be a little different," I say. "It would be like a chain of command, if I replaced Munson why there would be someone out there who could, if you found him, replace me."

"I'm afraid I don't understand," Mr. Revere says, looking genuinely puzzled.

I introduce myself. "I'm a writer," I say. "I've published four books. Have dozens left to write."

"Really?"

"Short stories, too. Over a hundred of them. I've had very good reviews."

"It's embarrassing," Mr. Revere says, "but I would have known if you were on the protected list. Something we never do is ask one protected person to replace another. And it isn't like we didn't know your name. We have ways of knowing things like that," and he taps the side pocket of his suit where he had deposited what may or may not have been a ticket stub that winked and blinked.

"But I'm relatively famous," I protest. "I've made a contribution. I'm at least well known." Mr. Revere remains silent. "I *do* have a following."

"I'm sure you do. But you must understand, our list is small. Few writers." He smiles as if reminiscing. "Hemingway was there."

"But you couldn't find his . . ."

"Oh, but we did. Even as a young man he contemplated suicide. Used his service revolver one night. There was a retired bullfighter who replaced him."

Houston goes scoreless in the third. There are a couple of hits but I scarcely notice. Usually I keep a score card. Use a green or purple felt pen and have the card woven over with patterns as if it were a square of afghan. Tonight my program lays whitely on my knee.

"If you're totally appalled at the idea, you must let me know," says Mr. Revere. "If you feel that I'm senile, or crazy, or if you know that you could never do such a thing, don't take up my time. There was a certain magic about you or I wouldn't be here."

Thurman Munson: I have never been a fan of his, though I recognized his greatness. It was the Yankees. They have always been like the rich kid on the block who could afford real baseballs and a bat that wasn't cracked. You played him, you tolerated him, but you were never sorry when he got spiked.

"No," I hear myself saying, "tell me more. Still, dying . . ."

"Ceasing to exist," corrects Mr. Revere.

"Dying," I insist. "Euphemisms don't change the nature of the beast. It is definitely, ah, quite final?" I ask.

"I'm afraid it would be, as we say, terminal."

Mr. Revere settles back to watch the game, a rather sly smile playing at the corners of his mouth.

Ferguson and Yeager hit back-to-back homers for the Dodgers in the fourth. The fans in front of us, whom I have mentally named the Buffalo Brigade, all stand, blocking my vision. The largest woman has made two trips to the concession since the game started. She applauds with half a hotdog protruding obscenely from her mouth. I remain in my seat as each of the home-run hitters circles the bases.

Die. The word rings through me as if it were a bolt rattling in my hollow metal interior. Who would I die for? My wife? I like to think that we are beyond that kind of emotional self-sacrifice. I would, in a split-second situation, endanger myself, say, to push her from the path of a speeding car, but, given a thoughtful choice like this, of quietly dying so the other might live, I suspect we might each choose to save ourselves. My daughters? Yes. In effect I would be saving my own life by saving them. My grandchildren? The blood ties thin. I think not. Is there anyone else? I have never had a friend for whom I would even consider such a sacrifice. A stranger? As unlikely as it seems, there are probably several.

I look over at Mr. Revere; he appears engrossed in the game. "Take your time," he says, still looking at the emerald infield. "Feel free to ask questions."

What would motivate someone to make the supreme sacrifice so that a stranger might live? Heroism is the only word I can muster. Heroism, I believe, is something basic to human nature. I have often fantasized delivering my wife or daughters from some holocaust, or walking steely-eyed into the jaws of death to rescue one or more of them, perhaps, afterwards, expiring in their grateful arms, my mission accomplished, the cheers of the crowd fading slowly as my life ebbed.

An idea begins to form. I inch forward on my seat.

"I'm afraid not," Mr. Revere says. I look at him harshly.

"Couldn't I rescue him from the plane?" I suggest.

I could see myself racing across the tarmac of that airport near Canton, Ohio, tearing open the door of the plane and dragging Thurman Munson's body to safety, gripping him under the arms like a two-hundred-and-twenty-five-pound sack of flour and backing away from the flaming wreckage. Later, when I was interviewed by television and newspaper reporters, I would speak modestly of my accomplishment, displaying my bandaged hands. I would be known as The Man Who Rescued Thurman Munson.

"Our operatives are always quite anonymous," says Mr. Revere.

"No possibility of recognition. It makes the choice harder," I say.

"It eliminates the insincere," says Mr. Revere, returning his attention to the game.

I am silent for a few moments. "What would happen to me?" I say to Mr. Revere's neatly trimmed, white, right sideburn. He is intent on the game; Houston has a bit of a rally going.

"You needn't have any fear of pain," he replies, sounding, I think, suspiciously like a dentist. "You might, after the game, decide to sleep for a few moments in your car before driving home. It would be peaceful, like sinking into a warm comforter."

"What guarantee do I have?"

"None at all. You would have to sense that I'm telling the truth. You would have to feel the magic, see the world from a slightly different angle, like batting while lying prone."

"Who have you saved? How many?"

"Not as many as we'd like. Our business can be compared to searching for the proverbial needle in the haystack. We have many more failures than successes. The rather sad fact is that no one ever hears of our successes."

"Who?" I insist. "Name names."

He unzippers the leather binder in his lap and produces a front page from the *New York Times*. The headline reads: PRESIDENT FORD ASSASSINATED IN SACRAMENTO. Below it is a large photograph of Squeaky Fromme holding a smoking gun.

"We went through four hectic days in 1975, the days after Miss Fromme's gun didn't misfire. Gerald Ford's body was lying in state in Washington when we found the party."

"Of course, there is no way to verify that!"

"Absolutely none." Enos Cabell ends the Astros' fifth but not before they score two runs to cut the Dodger lead to 4–2.

"What about John Kennedy?" I cry. "Half the world would have given their lives for him. I would have. Still would . . ."

"There is only one chance for each person on our list. We saved him once, during the PT-109 sinking. It was a young black woman from Memphis who . . ." and his voice trails off.

I think about Thurman Munson, remember how I heard of his death. I didn't listen to TV or radio the night of August second. Mornings I write. My wife, who teaches at a nearby university, brings a newspaper home at lunchtime. On August third she brought me ice cream to soften the blow. When I'm troubled or disturbed or can't write, I often head for the nearest Baskin-Robbins. At noon on August third, my wife walked into my study without knocking and handed me a cardboard cup overflowing with chocolate and coconut ice cream, my favourites. There was a fuchsia-coloured plastic spoon stabbed into the middle of it.

"There's bad news in the paper," she said.

"Did the Twins lose again?" I replied.

"I'm serious," she added.

I was going to say, "So am I," but didn't as I caught the inflection in her voice.

"Bobby Kennedy?" I say to Mr. Revere. "Martin Luther King?"

The Houston Astros, as ragtag a crew of ballplayers as ever held first place in August, are running wild in the sixth inning, forcing errors, blooping hits, stealing bases. In front of us, the Buffalo Brigade are shuffling in and out with new armloads of food. It is very difficult for two fat people to pass in the narrow space between rows.

"We should be thankful they are sitting in front of us rather than behind," says Mr. Revere. "If one of them should fall forward, I'm afraid it could be fatal."

I repeat my previous question.

"We were unable to find the party representing Dr. King."

"Then he's still out there. You could still . . ."

"We have only a short period. Even now the time for Mr. Munson runs low. We did find the man representing Robert Kennedy. In fact I found him myself. He was an Eastern philosopher, a man of great religious piety. He refused to cooperate. He had no qualms about his own fate, but his belief was that death is the highest attainable state; therefore he felt it would be a tremendous disservice to bring any man back to this world after he had experienced the next."

"How do the people feel who come back?"

"They never know they've been away," Mr. Revere says. "Gerald Ford thinks that Miss Fromme's gun misfired. Hemingway thought he changed his mind about suicide in 1918. We are able to be of service sometimes, but our odds of success are rather like hitting eighteen in blackjack. Not very high."

"Who is the 'We' you keep referring to? You make it sound like a corporation. Who are you?"

"Perhaps we should watch the baseball game for a while," suggests Mr. Revere, smiling kindly.

I look at the scoreboard. The Astros have put up six runs in the sixth inning with my hardly noticing, and now lead 8–4.

I wonder about Thurman Munson. Would he want to come back? I picture Thurman Munson dead, his spine splintered like a bat hit on the trademark. Tentative cause of death, asphyxiation, caused by breathing in toxic chemicals from the burning craft. I understand now why I couldn't be rescuer, why his friends couldn't move his body from the wreckage. His spine shattered; he wouldn't have wanted to be rescued.

Would he want to come back now? For all his short life he did what he loved best. He died with the smell of the grass still in his nostrils. The crack of the bat and the rising roar of the crowd never had to fade away and become muted memories like distant thunder. He never lived to hear some fresh kid say, "Who was Thurman Munson?" He left a beautiful wife and a young family he loved very much. I suppose that would be the best argument for granting him a second chance, and I recall a picture in the newspaper of his young son, Michael, wearing a baseball uniform with Munson's number fifteen, and the story of his asking why everyone was sad and saying that they should be happy that Munson was with God. "God has taken Daddy to heaven because He needs good people there."

Still, I wonder, would that be such a bad way to remember your father . . . having him taken when you were still young enough not to realize that he was only a very ordinary mortal?

Some athletes can't adjust to retirement; relationships disintegrate. There are many old baseball players who sell cars or insurance, drink too much, and wish that they had gone out in their prime while they were still adored by the fans. I recall the emotionally exhausting scene at Yankee Stadium as the crowd cheered for nine minutes when Thurman Munson's picture was flashed on the scoreboard. Many fans, tears streaming down their cheeks, cheered themselves into exhaustion, somehow exorcising the grief that hung in their chests like concrete.

Perhaps, I consider, no one is meant to tamper with time.

I try to concentrate on the game but can't.

"There is magic," Mr. Revere says. "It is close by. I can tell when someone feels it."

"It is the game," I say. "Not you."

"We all have to claim some game as magic," he says and takes from the inside pocket of his jacket a thick sheaf of paper that looks like a half-dozen sheets of foolscap folded over. I strain to get a look at what is written on them. I can't distinguish the letterhead, but there appears to be long lists of questions with little boxes after each, places for Mr. Revere to make Xs or check marks.

"Name?" and he reads my full name for me to verify. "A writer, you say. I'm afraid I haven't read anything of yours. My job keeps me quite busy, as you can imagine."

During the next inning Mr. Revere plies me with more irrelevant questions than a tax return and loan application combined. There are questions about ancestry, employment, family, hobbies; it is as though I am being interviewed by a very thorough reporter. I am reminded that I once underwent, in connection with an employment application, the MMPI (Minnesota Multiphasic Personality Inventory), a series of several hundred questions designed to supply a detailed personality profile. Mr. Revere's questions are equally probing but do not include such MMPI gems as: *Are you a messenger of God?* and *Has your pet died recently?*

As I answer the questions my mind is working at three levels, with the baseball game being relegated to the lowest, Mr. Revere's questions to the second level, while my top priority becomes: What will I do if I am chosen?

I am forty-eight years old; I am not ready to die.

"Thurman Munson was only thirty-two and he wasn't ready to die either," says Mr. Revere between questions.

In my time, given this opportunity, who would I die for? The names flash past me like calendar pages blown in the wind: FDR, Dr. Tom Dooley, Bobby Greenlease, Perry Smith, Bogart, Jim Reeves, Elvis, Lyman Bostock, Martin Luther King, Gandhi, James Dean, Amelia Earhart, Lou Gehrig . . .

"Given the choice, would you rather be an aeronautical engineer, a sign painter, or a dishwasher?"

My head feels as though a dealer is shuffling cards inside it, his thumbs have slipped, and I'm inundated in an avalanche of playing cards. "What on earth do you care for? I have zero mechanical ability. I can't draw. I would rather be a dishwasher."

"I'm sorry," Mr. Revere says, giving me his grandfatherly smile. "Everything used to be much simpler. We are experimenting with some rather advanced concepts in hopes of increasing our success rate. I'm sure you understand."

I recall Sydney Carton's words from *A Tale of Two Cities*, something to the effect that "'Tis a far, far better thing I do than ever I have done before." It is only the hero complex again, rising out of the crowd in front of me like the Loch Ness monster.

"Why me?" I almost shout, causing several people to glance my way briefly, annoyed that I have distracted them from the excitement of a Dodger rally in the eighth.

"Because you love the game for the sake of the game. There aren't many of us left. It is rather like finding a genuinely religious person . . ."

"I'm not exactly unprejudiced," I say. "To put it mildly, I have never been a Yankee fan. I resent a team that buys its winning percentage."

"You disapprove of the management, but do you hate the players?"

"Hate is a word that has no place in sports. I've never cheered for Thurman Munson, except in all-star games, but I don't hang over railings with a red face and hair in my eyes screaming insults either."

"And you stay until the last out, even if one team is winning 12–0." I nod. But the question remains: What will I do if he chooses me? I feel like the thirteenth at table. A chance to be either a god or a devil.

The crowd suddenly breaks into a chant: "Manny! Manny! Manny!" Rhythmic, ritualistic, the voice of the crowd rises like a monstrous choir as the leather-faced veteran Manny Mota appears from the dugout to swing his bat in the on-deck circle.

Manny Mota has 143 pinch hits in his career and needs one to tie and two to break the record held by Smoky Burgess.

"Manny! Manny! Manny!" the crowd rhapsodizes as he approaches the plate.

The largest of the Buffalo Brigade, built to resemble a chest of drawers with an encyclopaedia set on top of it, stunned by copious amounts of beer, remains standing even after Mota has stepped into the batter's box, completely blocking my view. Shouts of "Down in front," come from other people whose view is also obstructed. She ignores the shouts, if she hears them. She stands sturdy and dark as a pillar, a container of beer raised in her cupcake hand.

On a two-strike count Mota slashes a hard grounder to the right side. Landestoy, the Houston second baseman, gets in front of it, but the force of the ball turns him around. He regains his balance and fires to first but the split-second delay was all Mota needed: he is safe on a very close play. The fans roar their approval. Mota tips his hat to the crowd. When he is replaced by a pinch runner the crowd stands again to cheer him back to the dugout.

Mr. Revere, apparently through with his interrogation, folds the legal-size pages of questions and, unzipping his leather binder, places them carefully in the bottom between what look like sheets of cardboard or black plastic that may have been blinking golden like a night sky.

The briefcase seems to be making a whirring sound as if thousands and thousands of tiny impulses are perhaps processing the information just fed to it.

I look around at the ecstatic crowd. I look at the fat lady, still standing. "I've decided to do it," I say to Mr. Revere.

"I know," and he smiles in his most kindly manner and I somehow picture a sweet-pea- and petunia-scented evening on the veranda of a square, white, two-storey house somewhere in Middle America where a grandfather and a child sit in the luminous dusk and talk of baseball and love and living. A feeling of comfort surrounds and calms me and I feel an all-encompassing love for my fellow man, so strong that I must be experiencing what others who have found religious faith have experienced. I love all mankind. I love the fat lady.

Mr. Revere reopens his zippered case and takes out the question-naire. He studies it closely. I recognize that it is subtly different but I cannot say how. Perhaps only my perceptions are different.

Mr. Revere smiles again, a smile of infinite sadness, and patience and love. "I'm sorry," he says. "You're not the one."

"But I've decided," I say.

"I'm aware of that. I appreciate . . . we appreciate that you want to help. I'm afraid I may have spoiled a very good ball game for you . . ."

"But I want to . . ." my voice rises like a whining child's.

"I'm sorry." Mr. Revere is extending his hand to me.

"I'm not good enough," I flare. People are staring at me. The ballpark is very quiet. Houston is batting in the ninth, going out with a whimper. "I warn you, I'm a writer. I intend to write about this."

"Suit yourself," says Mr. Revere calmly. "In fact, feel free. If we find the right party in the next few days, everything that transpired tonight will be obliterated from every memory. But if we don't . . ." he smiles again. "Why, who would believe you? If someone actually tracked me down, I'd plead innocence or senility or both. I'm just a retired gentleman from Iowa who came to Los Angeles for a few baseball games and sat beside a strange and rather disturbed young man. You'd end up looking rather foolish, I suspect. Anyway, no one should believe a silly old man who goes around baseball stadiums talking about resurrecting the dead," and he chuckles.

The game ends. Mr. Revere makes his way briskly to the aisle and disappears in the crowd. I eventually edge my way to the aisle and down the steps for ten or fifteen rows. The Buffalo Brigade are now behind me. I turn to look at them. I scrunch myself against the railing and wait for them to catch up with me. There is something I have to know.

The fat lady huffs down the stairs towards me. I turn and face her in all her grossness. Her forehead and cheeks are blotched and somewhat out of focus, as though her face is covered by an inch or two of water.

"It was you I was going to do it for," I say. The fat lady stops in mid-waddle, puffs her cheeks like a child, and belches. "It was you that Manny Mota made the hit for. If you'd only realize it. Why don't you realize it?" I stand in the middle of the aisle facing up towards her. She is close enough for her sweetish odours of beer and perspiration to envelop me.

"Are you all right, fella?" a man behind her directs the words my way.

"Move along," somebody else shouts.

"Thurman Munson died for you," I say to the fat lady, who, three steps above me, glares down in bloodshot indignation.

"Oh, Jesus," says a voice behind her, a voice that is somewhere between an oath and a prayer.

First Names and Empty Pockets

A doll is a witness
who cannot die
with a doll you are never alone.
—Margaret Atwood

Fact, fiction, fantasy, folklore, swirl in a haze of colour, like a hammer-thrower tossing a rainbow. And always, I am haunted by images of broken dolls. Old dolls, lying, arms and legs askew, as if dropped from a great height; dolls with painted, staring eyes, faces full of eggshell cracks, powdered with dust, smelling of abandonment.

JOPLIN TOPS CHARTS!
SPLASHERS MAKES A SPLASH!

The headlines are from *Billboard* and *Cashbox,* publications which have become my main reading fare over the past two decades. We've been married for nearly fifteen years, Janis and I. *Splashers* is her seventeenth album.

The idea for the album cover was mine: Janis seated sidesaddle on a chromed Harley. Two views: one, she is facing the camera, her carrot-coloured hair below her shoulders, less frizzed, but wild and windblown as always; she is wearing jeans, pale-blue platform shoes, rhinestones embedded in the criss-cross straps that disappear under her cuffs, a denim jacket, open, showing a white T-shirt with SPLASHERS! in bold red capitals. She looks scarcely a day older than when I met her. The cosmetics of the years, the lines around the corners of her mouth, eyes, and at the bridge of her nose, have been airbrushed away and she grins, eyes flashing. She is smoking a cigarette, looking tough and sexy.

The flip side of the album features Janis' back and spotlights the cycle-gang colours: a golden patch on the faded denim in the shape of a guitar, again with the word *Splashers* only this time in black script.

Before I discovered Janis my life was peopled by antiseptic women with short hair and cool dresses, sexless as dolls. Always they lurk like ghosts just out of my vision. I smell their coolness, hear their measured voices, see their shapes when I close my eyes. I shudder them away and think of Janis crooning her love for me alone, our bodies tangled and wet. I think of her and of our mouths overflowing with the taste of each other, and I recall the San Francisco street where I first told her my name. My whole name.

"Man, you got something nobody else on the street has."

"Huh?"

"A last name, man. Around here it's all first names and empty pockets. Beer and hard times. Watching the streets turn blue at 4 A.M. while you cadge quarters at a bus stop or outside a bar. Do they have freaky chicks like me where you come from?"

Also, on the back of the album, there is an inset photo of the band, Saturday Night Swindle. *Splashers* is their sixth album with us. It was my idea to change bands—Big Brother and the Holding Company were never much—but Janis started with them and we stuck with them for eleven albums.

"This is what I do instead of having kids," Janis jokes. And it is true that she has averaged an album every nine months for nearly ten years.

I know little about music, even after all these years. *Janis* is my job, my life. "Like holding a lid on a pressure cooker with bare hands," is how I described my life with Janis to *Time* magazine, the last time they did a cover story. Generally, I trust the judgement of record producers when it comes to music, though recording the Tanya Tucker song, "What's Your Mama's Name?" was my idea. The album, our unlucky thirteenth, has sold nearly two million. I chose the musicians for Saturday Night Swindle. I had an agent I trusted send me résumés of five musicians for each position. Musically there was little to choose, but I had their backgrounds investigated and chose with endurance in mind. There are no heavy drinkers and no hard drug users in this band. The less temptation available the better.

While they were photographing Janis for the album cover, redoing the front scene for the twentieth time, I crossed the set to her, knelt down and turned up the left cuff of her jeans about three one-inch turns: the way you see it on the album cover.

"What the fuck are you doing?" Janis demanded.

"It's just a touch. It's the way you were when we first met. Do you remember?"

"Nah. My memory don't go that far back. That's all ancient fucking history."

I raise my head and look at her. She grins and her eyes tell me that she does indeed remember.

I straighten up. "I'd kiss you, but the makeup man would hemorrhage."

"Later, Sugar," and she purses her lips in an imitation kiss. One of the photographers looks quizzically at the rolled-up denim and then at me.

"Trust me," I say.

She sidled up to me, plump, wide-waisted, a sunset of hair in a frizzy rainbow around her face. Her hand hooked at the sleeve of my jacket.

"Looking for a girl?"

"How much?" There was a long pause as if she was genuinely surprised that I was interested. Her eyes flashed on my face, instantly retreated to the sidewalk. Then she uttered a single, almost inaudible word, like a solitary note of music that hung in the silence of the soft San Francisco night.

"Five."

I almost laughed it was so pitiful. Would have if she had resembled the whores I'd seen downtown: booted, bra-less, hard as bullets, whores who asked for $30, sometimes $40, plus the room. I took a quick look at her, a husky, big-boned girl, with a wide face and squarish jaw, anything but pretty, but I found her appealing, vulnerable, in need.

There was another long pause before I said, "Okay." Her fingers still gripped the sleeve of my jacket. We were on a dark street a mile or more from downtown San Francisco, a street full of ghostly old houses and occasional small shops. The houses were three-storey, some with balconies, all with latticework, and cast eerie shadows over the street. It was my first of three days in San Francisco. I had never been there before.

"Where do we go?" she said and looked around the deserted street as if hoping that a hotel might suddenly materialize.

"I'm a stranger here," I said. "I thought you'd know of a place."

"Yeah, well I'm kind of lost myself. Just got to walking. I don't usually leave the downtown. Business hasn't been very good tonight," and she made an effort at a smile. She was wearing faded jeans, one cuff rolled up about four inches as if she had recently ridden a bicycle.

The Iowa town where I come from, where I've lived all my life, is a white-siding and verandah town of 20,000 souls, of old but newly painted houses on tree-lined streets, lilacs, American flags, one-pump service stations, and good neighbours.

I work framing buildings, sawing, pounding nails, bare to the waist in the humid summers, bronzed as maple, sweat blinding my eyes, my hands scarred. I will likely never leave this town except for a brief holiday to San Francisco, and possibly a honeymoon trip; later, we will take our daughters to Disneyland.

The house where I live with my parents is square and white, so perfect it might have been built with a child's blocks. There are marigolds, asters and bachelor buttons growing in a kaleidoscope of colour between the sidewalk and the soft, manicured lawn. On a porch pillar, just above the black metal mailbox, is a sign, black on white, about a foot square that reads: DOLL HOSPITAL.

In my workshop I make dolls as well as repair them. I show them to no one for they are always incomplete. Broken dolls: fat pink arms that end at shredded wrists, sightless eyes, a twisted leg, a scar on a maligned cheek like an apple cut by a thumbnail. There is a balance to be kept. I make the unwhole whole, but . . .

The dolls are my way of being different. A delicate rebellion. They are my way of handling energies that I don't understand, electric energies which course like wine and neon through me, wailing like trains in my arms and chest.

"There are hotels," she said, and laughed, a stuttering sound like a bird trapped in a box. "Maybe if we walk down to . . ." She named a street unfamiliar to me. She wore a man's blue-and-red-checkered work shirt with the cuffs open, jeans and unisex loafers worn down at the sides.

We walked for a couple of blocks. She scuffed one of her feet, a sound that magnified and made the late evening silence almost ominous. We both, I'm certain, felt ridiculous in the company of the other. I was wearing brown slacks, freshly cleaned and creased, a pastel shirt and a brown corduroy jacket. Nondescript, straight, I have always felt that pastels provided me with anonymity, a privacy that I craved as much as Janis feasted on spotlights and crowds. We fought about my image. Slowly I have let go. I have let my hair grow; had it styled. I wear faded jeans and a Pierre Cardin shirt, and hand-tooled boots and belt of leather, soft and warm as sundrenched moss.

"Do you think we're getting closer to downtown or farther away?" I asked.

"I don't know." There was an ice-cream store across the street, closed of course, a pink neon cone blinked in the window.

"I have a room."

"Where?"

I named the hotel.

"I don't know it." I fished the key out of my jacket pocket. We checked the address on the oxblood tag, our heads together under a streetlight. Neither of us knew where it was. It was there that we exchanged names. Close to her, I discovered about her the odour of peaches ripe in the sun. I remembered visiting my grandmother in summer, walking in a peach orchard near Wenatchee in the Willamette Valley in Washington where the peaches lay like copper coins on the grass, where the distant-engine drone of wasps filled the air as they sucked away the flesh from the fallen fruit. As they did, the peach scent thickened making the air soft and sweet as a first kiss. Walking in San Francisco that night was like stepping among peach petals.

"Perhaps if I get a taxi," I said, looking around. The street was dark in all directions.

"I've never done this before," Janis said, and leaned against me, taking my hand, hers rough and dry as cardboard.

"I believe you," I said. We both laughed then. Hers less nervous now, coarse and throaty, full of barrooms and stale beer.

"I mean, I've propositioned guys before, but no one ever took me up on it. They practically walked right through me like I was fucking invisible."

"Everyone has to start someplace," I said inanely.

"When we get to the top of the hill we'll be able to tell by the lights where downtown is," Janis said.

"Or we could look for moss on the north side of utility poles?"

"You're weird," she said, and I could see, as the golden tines of street-light touched her face that she had thousands of freckles. "Gimme a cigarette."

"I don't have any . . . I don't smoke."

"I don't suppose you'd have a drink on you either?"

"No."

"You're sure you want a girl?" and her mouth widened into a beautiful grin as she held my hand tighter and we both laughed. "Where you from?"

"Iowa."

"They grow corn there don't they? A state full of corn farmers. Are you a corn farmer?"

"No. I repair dolls." I looked quizzically at her to see how she'd react.

"No shit? That's weird, man. You're funny. I don't mean queer funny. Well, maybe I do. No, I think funny, funny. You are, aren't you?"

"And you," I said, "where do you come from?"

"About fifteen miles from Louisiana," she said, and it was her turn to look at me with lifted eyebrows.

"I don't understand," I said.

"You don't need to. It's a private joke," and she paused. "I sing a little." We had reached the top of the hill. "Hey, we are going in the right direc-tion. When we get down to the lights we can ask somebody how to get to that hotel of yours."

But before we went to the hotel she wanted to go to a bar. "There's this joint I know. It's downstairs and there isn't a window in the place. I love it. It's always the same time there . . . no night or day . . . it's like being closed up in a bottle of water . . . time just stands still . . ."

I looked at her, scruffy as a tomcat, but radiating the same kind of pride.

It was a forlorn bar, a dozen stools and a few wooden tables. A place that looked as if it had endured a century of continuous Monday nights. There was a red exit sign above a bandstand where a lonely guitar leaned against a yellowed set of drums.

Old men dozed at the tables, a woman with straight grey hair, dressed in a man's tweed topcoat, glared angrily into a beer. A black man, looking like a failed basketball player, drunk or drugged, lolled crazily on a bar stool. A sampling of Janis' favourite people.

"I understand them," she says.

She has infinite patience with drunks. She'll listen to their stupid convoluted ramblings as they whine about how badly the world has treated them.

"I've been there. I'd be there now if I hadn't met you."

Janis, when she was drunk, had her own sad story. "The Famous Story of the Saturday Night Swindle," she called it, and depending upon her mood the story could take up to an hour to tell. Condensed, it was simply that all our lives we are conditioned to expect a good time Saturday night, we look forward to it and plan for it. And almost always we are disappointed. Yet we keep on trying for there will always be another Saturday night.

In the winter, her freckles become pale, seem to sink just below the surface of her skin like trout in a shallow stream. In summer they multiply: dandelions on a spring lawn. "Fuck, look at me; I look like I've been dipped in Rice Krispies."

"I love your freckles," I say. "Each and every one of them. I am turned on by freckles," and I hold her, kissing slowly across her cheeks and nose.

I love to watch the light in the eyes of little girls as they retrieve their dolls from me. In my workroom I have a row of shoe-box hospital beds. I have painted brown bed-ends on the apple-green wall above each box. On the front of each box is a make-believe medical chart. The wall glows with flowered decals and sunny happy-faces. Sometimes, if I have to order parts all the way from Baltimore, I let the children visit their dolls for a while on Saturday afternoons.

My own children are like dolls, girls, all angel eyes and soft little kisses. Cory, my wife, makes their clothes. We walk to church each Sunday down the heavily treed streets of white houses. Our home is surrounded and overpowered by lilacs. There is a groaning porch swing where we sit in the liquid summer dusk. Even in the humid summers Cory always wears a sweater, usually a pale pink or blue, pulled tight across her shoulders as if it were a shield that might protect her.

"What'll it be?" the bartender asked as we settled on the stools.

"Kentucky Red," said Janis.

"The same," I shrugged. I had no idea what I was ordering. The bartender had a flat face with a permanent case of razor burn, and short hair that he might have cut himself with a bowl and a mirror.

"I'm afraid I'm gonna turn out like that," Janis said, inching closer to me by shifting her weight on the bar stool. She nodded toward the shaggy old woman sitting alone and hostile, a cigarette burning toward her fingers. "I'm afraid I'm gonna be one of them loud old women who wear heavy stockings all year and slop from bar to bar getting drunker and more cantankerous by the minute. I don't want to, but the writing's on the fucking wall," she said, hefting her glass.

I moved myself closer to her. I have an abiding fear of old men who sit in bars and hotel lobbies, brittle and dry as insects mounted under glass. I thought of my hotel, decaying on a sidehill, an ancient facade decorated like a fancy wedding cake, a brown linoleum floor in a lobby full of old men and dying ferns.

Janis tossed back her second drink. I pushed mine toward her, barely touched.

"You ain't a juicer?" she said and grinned.

"Should we go look for the hotel?" I said. I was feeling edgy. Perhaps she only wanted a mark to buy her drinks and cigarettes.

"You mean you still want to?" she said, surprised. She eyed me warily, like a dog that had been kicked too many times. "I mean, man, you seen me in some light, and you've been with me long enough to make up your mind . . ."

"I still want to."

———————

Deep in the night I turned over, away from Janis, but with no intention of leaving the bed. She grasped at my arm, much the same as she had grasped at my sleeve earlier in the evening.

"Don't fucking leave me, man." I moved back closer to her. "You any idea what it's like to wake up in the middle of the night alone and know that there ain't a person in the whole fucking world who cares if you live or die? You feel so useless. . . ." And she held me fiercely, crying, kissing, trying to pull me close enough to heal her wounds—fuse me to her—store my presence for the lonely nights she anticipated.

Years later, Janis at Woodstock, blue her favourite colour, blue her chosen mood—anxiety nibbling at her like rats before she went on stage. But the magical change in her as she did: like throwing an electric switch in her back; she pranced on stage stoned in mind and body by whatever evil she could stab into her veins or gulp into her stomach. Footwork like a boxer, waving the microphone phallically in front of her mouth—blue shades, blue jacket, blue toreador pants, sweating booze, blind, barefoot, she spun like an airplane. She made history on stage. She collapsed into my arms as she came off.

"Sweet Jesus, but I was awful."

"You were a wonder."

"I'll never be able to appear in public again." She holds me like the end of the world. She is wet with sweat and pants into my shoulder while I tell her again and again how great she was. Finally she relaxes. I have done my job.

"Yeah? You really want to? How about that," and she smiled like a kid. "Harry?" she said to the bartender. "Is it okay?" and she nodded toward the tiny, dark stage.

"Sure, Janis," he replied. "You know you're welcome any time."

Her music: like a woman making a declaration of love with a fishbone caught in her throat. All the eerie beauty and loneliness of the Northern Lights. Like getting laid, lovingly and well. That is what the critics said about her.

How to explain her success? Voyeurism? Vicarious living? The world likes to watch people bleed, suffer and die. Janis stands up on stage and metaphorically slits her wrists while the audience says, "Yeah! Man, that's the way I feel. That's what I want to do, but don't have the nerve."

She opens her chest and exposes her heartbeat like a bloody strobe light, and they watch and they scream and they stomp and have wet dreams and climax as they stand on their chairs and say, "Man, that was wonderful. But I'm glad it's her and not me."

"Why on earth do you want to go to San Francisco?" my mother said to me when I told her of my decision to holiday on the west coast. "Why go way out there? California is full of strange people." She was wearing a grey-hen-coloured housedress, a kerchief on her hair, her gold-rimmed glasses sparking in the bright kitchen light.

"I'd like to see some strange people."

"Well, your daddy and I went to St. Louis on our honeymoon. Saw the site of the World's Fair and your daddy went to see the St. Louis Browns play baseball, though I'll never understand why. Goodness knows that team never won a game to my recollection."

In the bar again the next evening, Janis a little drunk. "Jesus, don't keep looking at me like that."

"I'm sorry."

"You're a gawker. They're the worst kind. You must spend your life looking over fences and through windows. What's the matter with me? You look like the creeps I went to school with. What the fuck are you doing with a sleazy chick like me?"

"I like you," I said lamely.

"Cheap thrills . . . you can go back to . . . wherever, and tell your fucking dolls about the weird chick you balled in San Francisco. Everybody who looks weird gets fucked over . . . did you know that? I been fucked over so many times. Mostly by guys I don't want. But by the ones I want to. Shit, I been turned down more times than the bedspread in a short-time room."

And on and on, and I listen and shrug it off, for I understand her, and I sense that when she goes after me with words sharp as a gutting knife, that she is really slashing at herself. If she can make me hate her, then I'll leave her and she'll be alone, the way she feels she deserves to be.

She is so unlike Cory. Janis protects herself with loud words, loud music, loud colours, clouds of feathers and jangling bracelets, but they could be twins; each of their bodies is riddled with fear.

Cory: tiny and gentle. Afraid of the world. Cory loves me. I love her as carefully as if she were flower petals or fine china. Our loving is silent, unlike with Janis who screams and moans and thrashes and tries to absorb my very body into hers. Cory is a broken doll, an abused child, battered, raped, bartered, reviled. She clings to me in her silence. Her climax is barely a shiver. That first night in the hotel Janis shrieked as if she were on stage, a note, clear and sharp as a tuning fork, hung in the air of that sad hotel room as her body fairly exploded beneath me.

The only place Janis is not afraid is on the stage. Bracelets splashing lights like diamonds, she high-steps to the microphone and begins her cooing, growling, guttural delivery. She is the spirit of Bessie Smith, Billie Holiday, and every gritty, gutsy blues singer who ever wailed. There is a sensuality, a sexuality, in the primeval sounds she emits. There is terror, love, sex, passion, pain, but mainly sex.

"I sound like I'm in heat," she said to an interviewer once, "and baby, I am. Sometimes I go right from the stage and I pick up my honey here," she said, referring to me, "and we go right to the hotel and ball, and ball, and ball."

"I sing right from my pussy," she said another time, then pulled her blue sunglasses down on her nose so she could peek over them to get the full shocked reaction.

"Why did you choose to sing?" an interviewer once asked her.

"It was a way out," she replied. "Where I come from a girl works at catching a man—then has a lot of kids and keeps her mouth shut. I'm hyper . . . I've always been like a pan of boiling water."

"Do you know what the difference is?" I asked Janis as she clung to me after a concert, sobbing, repeating over and over how awful she had been . . . *awful,* after 15,000 people had danced in the aisles and screamed out their love for her. "The difference between what you do and what I used to do is that mine, and almost everyone else's work, is tangible. I'd build a house or a garage, or even repair a doll and when I was finished I could say, 'There is the house I built or the doll I've repainted.' You have to wait to be evaluated. You sing a song or record an album but it means nothing until the fans buy or the critics say, 'Yes, this is good.'"

It takes very special people to bare their souls for mere humans to evaluate. Not many can stand up to it. I have always tried to remember that when I find Janis drunk or stoned—when she rages and accuses and smashes, and vomits, and lies in a fitful sleep, sweat on her upper lip and forehead, her mouth agape.

My assignment, as I sometimes look upon it, has been to protect Janis from herself and from people: those who would tap her veins and draw the life from her like so many vampires with straws. I am known as the most protective manager in the business. We hardly ever tour anymore. There are the albums and Janis plays Vegas for twelve weeks a year.

Has it been worth it? Has what I've gone through been worth it to prolong a career for a few more years? In just a month or two it's going to happen. I will go home to Iowa, alone, "for a holiday," I'll say. But I'll know differently. Janis will be left alone in the house near Las Vegas: that desert house, arid and dry as Janis' hands the night we met. A $20,000 boat stands, like the mythical, mystical ark, on a trailer in the back driveway. The nearest lake is 60 miles away and artificially created. Janis bought the boat like anyone else would buy a Tonka toy as a gift for a child. We have never used it. I stare at it and shudder.

While I am away, the mouse will play, and play, and play. And she will finish doing what I interrupted in San Francisco, what she has been trying to do all her life, not maliciously, or viciously, or violently, but with that lack of care, of restraint, that has always characterized her.

Fog is heavy in my life, dimensions of time telescope—I have been called. I have given nearly twenty years of my life for ten of hers. But no one knows. Really knows. There are other dimensions where Janis no longer exists, where I never left Iowa, where I sit tonight on a white front porch in the humid dusk and string my dolls.

"Nobody ever stays with me," Janis said in the grey morning light of my creaking hotel room.

"I'll stay as long as I can," I said.

"How long is that?" And I couldn't bring myself to answer. My flight home was booked for the next afternoon.

"You know, just the sound of your voice, even if you're talking about dolls, is more to me than solid food. I just get so fucking lonely."

"Nobody likes to be alone."

"Was I crying last night?"

"A little."

"More than that wasn't it? I do that when I get drunk. I cried on your shoulder, right?"

"You weren't any trouble."

"Thanks for staying with me. I mean, really."

We walked the warm morning streets for a while, small clouds were low enough to touch, still as the foggy gulls perched on posts along the piers. We breakfasted at a squalid café. Again we sat on stools at the counter. An oriental, wrapped tight as a mummy in a filthy white apron, was cook and waiter. I ordered bacon and eggs. Good, solid, nutritious North American food. Janis had pecan pie, ice cream and a Coke. Junkie food I was to learn later as my education progressed. She grinned at me through the widening haze of her Marlboro.

"I'm sorry you're not staying."

"So am I."

"Well, I'll move on," she said, sliding off the stool. "Maybe I'll see you around . . ."

"You're not going to leave," I said. "I don't have to go until tomorrow."

"You mean you *want* to stay with me? I'm grateful you stayed last night . . . you don't have to put yourself out."

"I want to stay with you."

"But you have to go back to . . . Iowa."

"I have a job to get back to . . . and my dolls."

"F'chrissakes."

"I have to . . . I'm sorry."

"Still, it's weird though, a big man like you messing with dolls."

An eight-inch steel implement that looks like a large crochet hook is the main tool of my trade; accessories consist of a supply of sturdy elastics, glue, a tea kettle, a set of pastel paints. Exposure to a steaming tea kettle allows me to soften joints and remove arms, legs, and heads. Like Dr. Christiaan Barnard I perform transplants. Like the good Dr. Frankenstein, I have a box of leftover parts from which I often extract a leg or an eye to make a broken doll good as new.

When we reached the room, we were both perilously shy, Janis even slightly reluctant. The exchange of money was forgotten. "Are you sure?" Janis asked several times, still expecting to be rejected.

"I am," I reassured, though I wondered why. She was so opposite to the girls I knew at home. I couldn't explain my excitement, my desire for this plain, shoddily dressed, rather vulgar girl. Perhaps even then I felt the charisma. I never confused her with her singing. I wanted her before she ever sang to me. But there was that power about her. She has the ability to stand on stage and hold the audience as if she were whispering in the ear of a lover, or lead them to dance in the aisles, or stand on the tables and stomp out her rhythms like a biker putting boots to a cop.

"You know what they did to me? At the university I was voted 'Ugliest Man on Campus.' You any idea what that did to me? Those straight chicks in angora sweaters and skirts, lipstick, and about a ton of hairspray, and the guys in cords and sweaters, or even shirts and ties . . . and just because I was different . . ."

I had asked about her former life. Sometimes I try to learn the why of her, but gently, like unwinding gauze from a wound. Years have passed and she trusts me now, as much as she ever trusts anyone. I never made my flight back to Iowa. Have never left her. I paid for my parents to visit us once. Only once.

"Your workshop's just as you left it," my mother said. "I just closed up the door. Had to take the sign down eventually . . . Little girls kept coming to the house."

"Oh, they thought they were so fucking righteous. But I'll show them. I can buy and sell them all now. I showed them once. I'm gonna show them for the rest of my life. They all married each other and live in the city and have split-level plastic houses, and plastic kids, and cars, and cocks, and cunts . . ." and she broke off amid a mixture of laughter and tears. "I suppose I should be happy just not to be part of them anymore . . . be happy being different . . . shit, it was only fifteen miles to Louisiana, and that was where the real people were, and real music. That was where I did my first gigs, and learned how to drink, and yeah, that too. God, did I ever tell you about high school? What they did to me? You don't want to hear, Sugar. It was too awful to even talk about."

"Are you sorry?" Janis once asked me, in a strange, soft voice, as if she had suddenly had a glimpse through the veil at what could have been: at what life would have been like if we hadn't met.

"I miss handling nails in the sunshine—the raw strength in my arms. My hands would blister now if I really worked."

"And your dolls."

"I miss them too."

"You know, I've never seen you fix a doll. I bet you were good. I've told you you could . . ."

"It wouldn't be the same."

"Maybe when we're old?"

"Maybe."

The third morning. The same café. Our going there a fragile attempt at ritual.

"Do you need anything?" I was reaching for my wallet.

"Hell, no. I'll get by. I always do. I'm just as tough as I look. Tougher." We walked out of the café hand in hand.

She turned to me then to be kissed. A shy, hurried brushing of lips, our bodies barely touching. About us, the beautiful scent of peaches.

"Be cool. Maybe I'll see you around," and she gave me the peace sign, something I'd never seen before, and shambled away among the moving crowd.

Here, on the lazy verandah in the Iowa dusk, as my children sleep, as my dolls sleep, as my wife waits with her delicate love, I dream. Am haunted by the spirit of a dead girl. A dead singer who died a broken doll, pitched face-first onto a blond wood night table in a Los Angeles motel. Nose broken, spewing blood, she wedged between the table and the bed, her life ebbing while the needle grinned silver in the darkness. I remember her in my arms in that sad hotel in San Francisco, wild, enveloping, raucous as her songs, her tongue like a wet, sweet butterfly in my mouth. I am haunted by her death and by what might have been. And what I might have done to prevent her rendezvous with the needle: surrogate cock. Evil little silver dildo. A sexual partner she didn't have to fear. The needle never left her alone in the middle of the night. I sometimes look at my hands, marvelling that there are no wounds, so many times have I pushed the needle away.

"If you can't get love one way—in the physical way—then you get it in another," she said to me during those fine days we spent together before it all began. During the few gigs she'd done she had discovered that the applause, screams, cheers, wails, were enough for then. "I'm only somebody when I sing, but God, the gigs are so few and far between." Of course, that was to change, and soon.

Friends were visiting Cory and me the night that Janis' death was announced. It was an afterthought item at the end of the news, between weed killer and fertilizer commercials.

"Oh," was all Cory said.

"Who?" said my parents.

"Who?" said our friends, noting my consternation. *She* watches the soap operas in the afternoons. *He* collects records of marching bands.

After our first breakfast we walked all day, looked at the ocean, the terraced houses frosty white as splashes of tropic sun. The day was full of spring—all San Francisco tasted and smelled of peaches.

The magic of her—whirling onto the stage—a white girl singing black music—the trills, the shrieks, the croaks, the moans, as she made love through her music. "The only love I know is with the audience—that's my whole life," she told an interviewer once, as I shrank into the shadows. But the gods of music would have been pleased with her, "a whirling dervish with blue nail polish, a wall of hair closing over her face like drapes," is how *Rolling Stone* described her recently. "The biggest, wildest, roughest, most flawed diamond in show business." We have sold more records than anyone but Elvis.

The picture-taking session over, Janis, exhausted, rests her head on my shoulder. "Sweet Jesus, but I need a drink."

"Just one," I say, and she makes a face at me, shaking her head.

"Aw, Sugar, after a session like that Mama needs to cut loose."

"We'll see," I say as we walk off the set.

I think of all the people that her life touched in the sixties and until her death: all those people whose lives are different in countless tiny and not so tiny ways because I appeared to Janis on a dark San Francisco street on a spring night.

I can't help but wonder how much of history I have personally changed. I know what is going to happen soon but am powerless to stop it, not even sure that I would if I could. In my workshop a few swatches of blue satin, a dozen lion-coloured hairs, a few feathers and rhine-stones . . .

SEARCHING FOR JANUARY

On December 31, 1972, Pittsburgh's all-star outfielder Roberto Clemente took off on a mercy flight taking clothing and medical supplies to Nicaraguan earthquake victims. Some time that night his plane went down in the ocean. His body was never recovered.

The sand is white as salt but powdery as icing sugar, cool on my bare feet, although if I push my toes down a few inches, yesterday's heat lurks, waiting to surface with the sun.

It is 6:00 A.M. and I am alone on a tropical beach a mile down from our hotel. The calm ocean is a clear, heart-breaking blue. Fifty yards out a few tendrils of sweet, gray fog laze above the water; farther out the mist, water, and pale morning sky merge.

It appears slowly out of the mist, like something from an Arthurian legend, a large, inflatable life raft, the depressing khaki and olive-drab of military camouflage. A man kneeling in the front directs the raft with a paddle. He waves when he sees me, stands up and calls out in an urgent voice, but I can't make it out. As the raft drifts closer I can see that the lone occupant is tall and athletic-looking, dark-skinned, with a long jaw and flashing eyes.

"Clemente!" is the first word I hear clearly. "I am Clemente! The baseball player. My plane went down. Days ago! Everyone must think I am dead."

What he says registers slowly. Clemente! It has been fifteen years. Is this some local fisherman playing a cruel joke on a tourist?

"Yes," I call back, after pausing too long, scanning his features again. There is no question: it is Roberto Clemente. "I believe everyone does think you're dead."

"We crashed on New Year's Eve," he said. "I'm the only one who survived."

He steps lithely into the water, pulls the raft up on the beach, tosses the paddle back into the raft.

"Five days I've been out there," he says. "Give or take a day. I sliced up the other paddle with my pocket knife, made a spear. Caught three fish. Never thought I'd enjoy eating raw fish. But I was so hungry they tasted like they were cooked. By the way, where am I?"

I tell him.

He thinks a minute.

"It's possible. We crashed at night on the way to Managua. The plane was carrying three times the weight it should have, but the need was so great. Supplies for the earthquake victims.

"You look so surprised," he says after a pause. "Have they called off the air search already, given us up for dead?" When I remain silent he continues. "Which way is your hotel? I must call my wife, she'll be so worried."

"I am surprised. More than surprised. You are Roberto Clemente, the baseball player?"

"Of course."

"You were lost at sea?"

"Until now."

"There's something not quite right."

"Like what?" says Clemente.

"Like what year do you think this is?"

"When we took off it was 1972, but New Year's Eve. We crashed in the ocean. It must be January fifth or sixth, maybe even the seventh, 1973. I haven't been gone so long that I'd lose track of the year."

"What if I told you that it was March 1987?"

"I'd laugh. Look at me! I'd be an old man in 1987. I'd be . . ."

"Fifty-two. Fifty-three in August."

"How do you know that?"

"I know a little about baseball. I was a fan of yours."

He smiles in spite of himself.

"Thank you. But 1987? Ha! And I don't like the way you said *was*. *Was* a fan of mine." He touches spread fingers to his chest. "These are the clothes I wore the night we crashed. Do I look like I've been wearing them for fifteen years? Is this a fifteen-year growth of beard?" he asks, rubbing a hand across his stubbly chin. "A six-day beard would be my guess."

His eyes study me as if I were an umpire who just called an outside pitch strike three: my pale, tourist's skin, the slight stoop as if the weight of paradise is too much for me.

"Say, what are you doing out here alone at dawn?" Clemente says skeptically. "Are you escaped from somewhere?"

"No. But I think you may be. Believe me, it is 1987."

"Can't be. I can tell. I'm thirty-eight years old. I play baseball. See my World Series ring." He thrusts his hand toward me, the gold and diamonds glitter as the sun blushes above the horizon.

I dig frantically in my wallet. "Look!" I cry. "I'm from Seattle. Here's the 1987 Seattle Mariners schedule." I hold the pocket-sized schedule out for him to look at.

"Seattle doesn't have a team."

"They have a new franchise, since 1977. Toronto came in the same year. Read the schedule."

He studies it for a moment.

"It's crazy, man. I've only been gone a few days."

We sit down on the sand, and I show him everything in my wallet: my credit cards, an uncashed check, my driver's license, coins, and bills.

"Try to remember when your plane went down. Maybe there's a clue there."

We walk slowly in the direction of the hotel, but at the edge of the bay, where we would turn inland, Clemente stops. We retrace our steps.

"It was late in the night. The plane was old. It groaned and creaked like a haunted house. I was sitting back with the cargo—bales of clothes, medical supplies—when the pilot started yelling that we were losing altitude. We must have practically been in the water before he noticed. We hit the ocean a few seconds later, and I was buried under boxes and bales as the cargo shifted. A wooden box bounced off my head, and I was out for . . . a few seconds or a few minutes." He rubs the top of his head.

"See, I still got the lump. And I bled some, too." He bends toward me so I can see the small swelling, the residue of dried blood clinging around the roots of his sleek, black hair.

"When I woke up I was in front of the emergency door, the cargo had rolled over me and I was snug against the exit. The plane must have been more than half submerged. There was this frightening slurping, gurgling sound. Then I realized my clothes were wet. The raft was on the wall right next to the door. I pulled the door open and the ocean flooded in. I set out the raft, inflated it, and took the paddles and the big water canteen off the wall. I yelled for the others but I don't know if they were alive or if they heard me. There was a mountain of cargo between me and the front of the plane.

"I climbed into the raft, paddled a few yards, and when I looked back the plane was gone. I've been drifting for five or six days, and here I am."

"I don't know where you've been, but you went missing New Year's Eve 1972. They elected you to the Baseball Hall of Fame in 1973, waived the five-year waiting period because you'd died a hero."

"Died?" Clemente begins a laugh, then thinks better of it. "What if I go back with you and call in?"

"You'll create one of the greatest sensations of all time."

"But my wife, my family. Will they all be fifteen years older?"

"I'm afraid so."

"My kids grown up?"

"Yes."

"Maybe my wife has remarried?"

"I don't know, but it's certainly a possibility."

"But, look at me, I'm thirty-eight years old, strong as a bull. The Pirates need me in the outfield."

"I know."

"My teammates?"

"All retired."

"No."

"If I remember right, Bruce Kison was the last to go, retired last year."

"Willie Stargell?"

"Retired in 1982. He's still in baseball but not playing."

"Then I suppose everyone that played at the same time, they're gone too? Marichal? Seaver? Bench? McCovey? Brock? McCarver? Carlton?"

"Carlton's won over three hundred games, but he doesn't know when to quit. He's a marginal player in the American League. So is Don Sutton, though he's also won three hundred. Jerry Reuss is still hanging on, maybe one or two others. Hank Aaron broke Babe Ruth's home-run record, then a guy from Japan named Sadaharu Oh broke Hank Aaron's record."

"And my Pirates?"

"Gone to hell in a handbasket. They won the World Series in '78, Willie Stargell's last hurrah. They've been doormats for several seasons, will be again this year. Attendance is down to nothing; there's talk of moving the franchise out of Pittsburgh."

"They need Roberto Clemente."

"Indeed they do."

"And Nicaragua? The earthquake?"

"The earth wills out," I said. "The will of the people to survive is so strong. . . . The earthquake is history now."

"And Puerto Rico? Is my home a state yet?"

"Not yet."

He looks longingly toward the path that leads to the hotel and town. We sit for a long time in that sand white as a bridal gown. He studies the artifacts of my life. Finally he speaks.

"If I walk up that path, and if the world is as you say—and I think I believe you—I will become a curiosity. The media will swarm over me unlike anything I've ever known. Religious fanatics will picnic on my blood. If I see one more person, I'll have no choice but to stay here."

"What are your alternatives?"

"I could try to pass as an ordinary citizen who just happens to look like Roberto Clemente did fifteen years ago. But if I become real to the world I may suddenly find myself white-haired and in rags, fifty-three years old."

"What about baseball?"

"I could never play again, I would give myself away. No one plays the game like Clemente."

"I remember watching you play. When you ran for a fly ball it was like you traveled three feet above the grass, your feet never touching. 'He has invisible pillows of angel hair attached to his feet,' my wife said one night, 'that's how he glides across the outfield.'

"Perhaps you could go to the Mexican Leagues," I suggest. "Remember George Brunet, the pitcher? He's still pitching in the badlands and he's nearly fifty."

"I suffer from greed, my friend, from wanting to claim what is mine: my family, my home, my wealth. My choice is all or nothing."

"The nothing being?"

"To continue the search."

"But how?"

"I've searched a few days and already I've found 1987. Time has tricked me some way. Perhaps if I continue searching for January 1973, I'll find it."

"And if you don't?"

"Something closer then, a time I could accept, that would accept me."

"But what if this is all there is? What if you drift forever? What if you drift until you die?"

"I can't leap ahead in time. It's unnatural. I just can't."

"If you came back to baseball, Three Rivers Stadium would be full every night. You could make Pittsburgh a baseball city again. You'd have to put up with the media, the curious, the fanatics. But perhaps it's what you're destined to do."

"I am destined to be found, maybe even on this beach, but fifteen years in your past. I intend to be found. I'll keep searching for January."

He walked a few steps in the direction of the raft.

"Wait. I'll go and bring you supplies. I can be back in twenty minutes."

"No. I don't want to carry anything away from this time. I have five gallons of water, a bale of blankets to warm me at night, the ingenuity to catch food. Perhaps my footprints in the sand are already too much, who knows?"

He is wading in the clear water, already pushing the raft back into the ocean.

"If you find January . . . if the history I know is suddenly altered, I hope I went to see you play a few times. With you in the lineup the Pirates probably made it into the World Series in '74 and '75. They won their division those years, you know . . . you would have been the difference . . ."

I watch him drift. Trapped. Or am I trapped, here in 1987, while he, through some malfunction of the universe, is borne into timelessness? What if I were to accompany him?

"Wait!" I call. "There's something . . ."

But Clemente has already drifted beyond hearing. I watch as he paddles, his back broad and strong. Just as the mist is about to engulf him, as ocean, fog, and sky merge, he waves his oar once, holding it like a baseball bat, thrusting it at the soft, white sky.

LIEBERMAN IN LOVE

As soon as he entered the airport terminal, a beautiful Hawaiian girl appeared and slipped a lei of waxen orchids over the head of Lieberman, age 52, a land developer from Denver, Colorado, a widower for almost two years, lonely unto death. As he accepted the lei, Lieberman bent his long form to allow the girl to kiss him on the cheek, all the time thinking that Honolulu had to be one of the loneliest cities in the world.

Across the whole island of Oahu brightly dressed tourists fluttered like flags in a breeze. But, thought Lieberman, flags are lonely objects, bright though they may be, always separated from their contemporaries, each snapping briskly in the wind, each alone. Alliances formed in Hawaii were of necessity short, often both harried and hurried. Women who lived in the islands permanently did not want to be bothered with tourists; other tourists were, like Lieberman, desperate for contact of any kind. But there were always planes to catch; one-week tours were ending. You could only stand to visit the Polynesian Cultural Center or take a moonlight cruise so many times, he thought.

Lieberman was a good-looking man with a full head of iron-gray hair. He golfed, swam and jogged regularly; he traveled sufficiently to keep a dark summer tan all year round. His trimmed beard and deep-set eyes were black and contrasted sharply with his almost white hair. Lieberman fancied that he looked like a magician.

His life since his wife's death had been miserable. She had always worked beside him, was as responsible for their financial success as he was. He had lost not only his lover of 25 years, but his best friend and business partner. His sons, both of whom worked in the business—actually they had made all the major decisions since his wife died—appeared to have written him off, acted as if he had suddenly become untrustworthy, seemed to expect him to join their mother in death momentarily.

After observing an appropriate period of mourning, Lieberman had not lacked for female company. But what he longed for was to be in love. His friends' wives introduced him to their friends; he found himself being asked out to dinner three and four times a week. But his dates were usually wilted women with squeezed, bitter faces and thin hands—women who drank too much and spent most of the evening maligning, rightly or wrongly, the husbands who had abandoned them to the world. Or else they were widows who spent the entire night extolling the virtues of their dead spouse. These types usually had a large studio portrait of the deceased beside their bed. More than once while making love, Lieberman looked up to catch the eye of the corpse. "Oy, Harry never did *that*," one of them might say. Or, "I wish you had known Harry, you could have taught him a few tricks."

He occasionally dated one of the younger women who worked for his company or one that he met at one of the several private clubs he belonged to, but younger women, at least these upwardly mobile ones, wanted to go dancing, or skiing, or wanted to eat in restaurants that didn't serve real food, but supposedly healthful concoctions at 20 dollars a plate that looked like algae and tasted like bicycle tires. Lieberman wanted an intelligent, attractive younger woman who liked steak and candlelight, quiet music and sex.

He got so tired of the chase, of boring evenings rehashing his life story for the twentieth time in a month, that he settled for satisfying his sexual needs with prostitutes, both in Denver and when he was traveling. In Honolulu, after a number of failures, he discontinued contact with any of the numerous escort services, which took up a whole small section in the Yellow Pages. He liked to walk the Kalakaua strip, breathing the soft, late-evening air, and make his choice from the many young women who discreetly and not so discreetly offered their services. Lieberman often talked to several women before selecting one, negotiating a price, then hailing a taxi to take them to his hotel.

His experiences with the escort services were that they seemed to send whatever girl happened to be available, paying no attention to the height, weight, or coloring he had specifically requested. He had a number of unpleasant experiences—women appeared at his door, who, though young and attractive, were not sexually appealing to *him*. He had particular difficulty with a tall, toothsome Filipino girl, who was insulted even after Lieberman paid her full fee and tipped her handsomely.

"I earn my money, okay?" she said several times, leaning against the inside of his hotel room door. "Why you no like me? I'm clean. See doctor alla time. You no have to look at me. Lie down, think about girlfriend. I do you good, okay?"

Another time a combative Samoan woman made serious threats against his person after he declined her services, though he paid her in full.

On other occasions he made love to women who displeased him in some minor way. They were too thin, or had scratchy voices, or had shaved their pubic hair, something he particularly disliked.

It took him two weeks to make what he considered a suitable contact. He spotted her standing on the sidewalk in front of a Mrs. Fields cookie shop, on Kaiulani Street. She was staring boldly at passersby, nibbling a chocolate-fudge cookie, wearing a knee-length brown leather skirt, a white haltertop, and white high heels; she was blue-eyed with reddish-blond hair expertly styled. She has a mind of her own, Lieberman thought, and she radiates sexuality.

"Hi," said Lieberman, stopping directly in front of her.

The girl, Shaleen, eyed him up and down, licked cookie crumbs from her lips, said nothing.

"So how's business?" asked Lieberman.

"How do you know I'm not somebody's expensive wife who just walked around the corner from her suite at the Hyatt to buy a cookie and take in some night air?"

"That's exactly who I assumed you were," said Lieberman, bowing slightly. "I also assumed you were a woman looking for excitement."

"And you're a man looking for excitement?"

Lieberman nodded.

"Do you have any idea how I hate being cutesy like this?" said Shaleen.

Lieberman smiled. "So do I," he said.

"The kind of excitement you have in mind, with the kind of woman you have in mind, costs," said Shaleen.

"It costs what it costs," said Lieberman.

"We can get a cab at the Princess Kaiulani. We'll go to your hotel," said Shaleen.

Shaleen was what Lieberman was looking for, an accomplished lover, an intelligent companion, a woman with both common and business sense.

Early in their acquaintance, as soon as Shaleen decided that she would allow Lieberman to become a steady customer, Shaleen set down guidelines.

"I don't think you're the type to get all foolish over a working girl, but let's get a few things straight just in case. First of all, I don't have a heart of gold. I'm a businesswoman. I'm not a lesbian and I was never sexually abused. I come from a perfectly normal, middle-class family. I do what I do for the money, and for the excitement.

"You know what I did after my first month on the street? I flew to Switzerland and opened myself a bank account—pretty smart for an

18-year-old, wouldn't you say? I've sent a little envelope of cash off in the mail every few days ever since. I'm 27 years old, Lieberman, I don't do drugs, I don't have an old man, I don't drink myself senseless like most chicks in this business. Most whores give away their money because they feel guilty about how they earned it, well not me. I don't feel guilty and I bet I'm worth more than you were at 27, maybe even more than you are now."

"You probably are. I have something called taxes that bleed me white. Perhaps you should be paying me."

"I'm gonna retire on my thirtieth birthday. Maybe I'll just live off interest, or maybe I'll buy a hotel, or maybe I'll go into land development. Need a partner?" said Shaleen, laughing.

During his third week in Honolulu, more out of boredom than anything else, Lieberman decided to rent an apartment instead of living out the winter in a hotel. He chose a rental office within walking distance of his hotel. It was the moment that he was introduced to the rental agent that he fell in love.

How could anyone *not* love a face like that? he thought. That she was special to Lieberman only, he knew to be true, but who else was he shopping for? Her name was Kate Mc*Something*. He didn't assimilate her last name, but he could tell from her drawl that she was from either Texas or Oklahoma. She was redheaded with green eyes and freckles, and the twang in her speech made Lieberman's knees weak.

Lieberman had trouble keeping his agitation under control. He asked her numerous unnecessary questions, discovered by looking at her left hand that she was married, was able to establish through questioning that her husband was an officer at nearby Fort DeRussy. In spite of the fact that the young woman was very busy, Lieberman tried to make the interview last forever. He was disappointed that she could not take him around Waikiki to view apartments; her job kept her at her desk. She was wearing a white peasant blouse that exposed her tanned and freckled shoulders. While Lieberman questioned and salivated, Kate got on the phone and set up appointments with apartment owners or tenants, or set aside a number of keys to vacant units. Her phones were ringing constantly, making it difficult for Lieberman to pry personal information from her. He accepted the keys and a paper with his list of appointments. He loved her large, looping handwriting. He held the paper to his nose when he reached the street hoping some brief scent of her had remained behind. He wanted to rent all her available apartment units, leaving her free to deal only with him. Over the next two days he viewed nearly every apartment her firm had available. When an appointment had been made, he felt he had to keep it, and did. He would report back to Kate after each one. If she just gave him keys he often did not view the apartment at all, simply going to a nearby restaurant for coffee until sufficient time had passed that he could return the key and stare at the face of his loved one again.

On the second day he waited for over an hour outside the office, but out of view from the window, planning to intercept her when she emerged to go to lunch. But she did not emerge. Finally he went back in and returned the last key he had been given. The remains of a sandwich and salad tray were in her wastebasket, a can of Diet 7UP on the edge of her desk.

On the third day he invited her to lunch. She refused.

"I work right through," she said. "That way I can go home a half hour earlier."

The next day Lieberman tried a new tack.

"I've taken up so much of your time," he said, smiling with as much charm as he could muster, "I'd like to repay you." He waved off her objection and continued. "Tomorrow I'll make reservations for lunch," and he named a revolving restaurant at the top of a 45-storey building.

Kate smiled and Lieberman could feel his heart melt with desire.

"I'll have to dress up," Kate said. "Usually, since I don't go out of the office, I just wear jeans.

Lieberman shaved twice, changed his shirt three times in preparation for the date. Kate wore a white dress with a single palm frond patterned near her right shoulder, and matching green shoes. As they walked among the tourists on Kalakaua Avenue, Lieberman was ecstatic. He made pointless conversation, tried to conjure up ways of making contact with Kate. He managed to guide her by the arm across a couple of streets, into and out of the elevator at the restaurant. As his fingers touched her, he tried to will her to thrill to the contact the same way he did. The lunch was pleasant, but Kate didn't give him any hint of being infatuated with him. He told her his life story, heavy on the widowhood and loneliness, short on his age, the fact that he had a son nearly as old as she, long on his financial success, without appearing ostentatious.

He found out a little about her. She *was* from Oklahoma, had been in Hawaii for a year; her husband's name was Larry, and he was stationed at Fort DeRussy.

Lieberman was cautious not to make any sexual overtures that might frighten her away. He would take his time. He watched her eating a sliced papaya for dessert. The succulent yellow fruit disappearing into her mouth made Lieberman faint with desire.

"I'd be honored if we could do this again, soon," Lieberman said, when he returned her to her office.

"There's no reason," the girl said, staring at him frankly.

"To make an old man happy," he said. "I hadn't realized how lonely I've been," he said. "Friendship only," he added quickly. "You're so young, and married. I'm not making a pass."

"I enjoyed myself, too," she said. "I don't see why not then, in a couple of days. While I think of it, I've got a new listing you may want to look at."

The next week, Lieberman rented an apartment from her, a beautiful, furnished one-bedroom in Discovery Bay Tower, on Ala Moana Boulevard, with an unobstructed view of both the ocean and Diamond Head.

"I'd invite you to my housewarming," he said to Kate, "you and your husband, except I don't know anyone else here in Honolulu; that would be kind of a small crowd."

Kate smiled at him. She wrinkled her nose when she smiled. Lieberman thought he would die of happiness each time she did that.

"I don't suppose," he went on quickly, "that you'd be able to have dinner with me? Just a friendly celebration, you understand. Is there an evening you'd be free?"

To his surprise Kate allowed it as her husband bowled in a league Thursday evenings. Lieberman hired a limousine, picked her up at the apartment on Date Street where she lived, took her to Nick's Fishmarket, probably the most exciting restaurant in Honolulu, the place where visiting celebrities visited or were entertained. Cheryl Tiegs was there, as was film critic Gene Siskel. Kate had hoped to see Sylvester Stallone, or Bette Midler, both of whom were in the islands, and had been sighted at Nick's on previous evenings.

"It must be wonderful to live this way all the time," Kate sighed.

"Only when you have someone you love to share it with," said Lieberman, fearing for an instant that he had said too much.

But Kate smiled sweetly and said, "You really should be looking around, not wasting your time with someone like me."

"If I don't have a sweetheart, at least I have a friend," said Lieberman, forcing a cheerful smile.

At Nick's, Lieberman danced with her for the first time, held her in his arms, smelled her hair, explored the contours of her body, running his hand up and down her back as they danced. Lieberman was in heaven. He controlled his desires carefully. At the end of the evening, when he walked her to her door, he took both of her hands in his, leaned in and kissed her cheek. She didn't mind. In fact she stood on tiptoes and kissed him on the mouth, a non-sexual kiss of thanks.

Lieberman floated back to the limousine. When he got home he called Shaleen's answering service and left a message. She arrived at his apartment a little after midnight.

"This is my busy time, Lieberman. It's gonna cost you."

He handed her a signed check. "Fill in the blanks," he said. "It costs what it costs."

Lieberman, wanting to know everything about Kate and her husband, called in a private detective. His name was Mr. Woo. He looked like a busboy, Lieberman thought. He reminded himself that the detective came highly recommended by a reputable lawyer. Mr. Woo wore a cheap Panama hat, a cheap Hawaiian shirt, baggy black trousers and sandals. He was about five feet tall, and so thin he might have recently escaped from a country with a food shortage.

Lieberman explained what he wanted to know.

"Involves surveillance," said Mr. Woo. "Time is expensive."

"It costs what it costs," said Lieberman. "Money I've got, information I don't."

He gave Mr. Woo their names, Larry and Kate McInally, their address, the name of the rental agency she worked for and his rank at Fort DeRussy.

"They must never know. You must be certain that anyone you talk to won't report back to them."

Woo bowed slightly, opened his mouth as if to speak.

"I know," said Lieberman, "expensive." He took out his checkbook. "As I'm sure you know, everyone has a price for silence. Neither this man nor his wife must ever know they've been investigated."

Woo smiled as he folded the check and placed it in his shirt pocket.

Six days later the report was delivered by messenger. After reading it, Lieberman felt he probably knew more about Larry McInally than Kate did.

He had lunch with Kate as usual; he explained his excess energy, his edginess, by saying he was waiting for a phone call to confirm a very important business deal. He was so tempted to let slip some of the information he knew about Larry, even some of the things he had found out about Kate that he didn't know. Lieberman felt full to overflowing with terrible secrets.

"I've never seen you like this before," said Kate, laughing.

"Business can be very stimulating," said Lieberman. "A little like hunting, the excitement of the chase, the thrill of closing in for the kill."

He had to wait until mid-afternoon to get through to Shaleen; she left her phone unplugged until she was ready to start her day.

They had finished making love. Shaleen was sitting up, three pillows behind her, smoking a cigarette; her short blond hair was only slightly dishevelled.

"How long are you planning on staying?" she had asked Lieberman earlier, almost as soon as he had arrived. Shaleen's condo was in Yacht Harbor Towers, only a block from where Lieberman rented. Worth $300,000 if it's worth a dime, thought Lieberman.

"All night, if it's okay," he replied.

"It'll cost," said Shaleen.

Lieberman tossed his wallet on the coffee table in front of the velvet chair he was sitting in.

"Help yourself. It costs what it costs," he said.

"Never trust a whore, Lieberman. You'll get burned."

"You just don't want me to know you're honest. Tell me the amount, I'll count it out myself."

She did, and he did.

"For an old guy, you're a great fuck," Shaleen said now, exhaling smoke.

"You're not bad yourself, for a hooker," said Lieberman.

Lieberman and Shaleen were spending three or four nights a week together at either his place or hers. From the day it began he told her about his courting of Kate McInally.

———

"Still not making any progress with your lady love?" asked Shaleen. Lieberman had come to Shaleen's after his third Thursday evening dinner date with Kate.

Lieberman sighed. "Three lunches a week, dinner every Thursday. What else can I do?"

"Offer her money. Shit, Lieberman, some of these little sex-rataries are just dying to turn an extra buck, especially if their husbands are in low-paying jobs like the military. Offer her a thousand dollars to go to bed with you."

"What if she accepts? I'd have to pay her a thousand each time. It would be the same as what we do."

"It costs what it costs," said Shaleen mockingly. "You pay me. You get a good lay. It would be the *same*. Except you're soft at the center, Lieberman. You're in love. You have the mistaken idea that one woman is different from another. It's alright. My business would drop 80% if men realized women are essentially all the same."

"That's ridiculous," shouted Lieberman. "There's love and there's sex, and there's mutual respect and companionship and caring."

"Sure," said Shaleen. "So how are you gonna get into her pants?"

"I don't know. She loves her husband."

"Kill him," said Shaleen. "Or have him killed. Out of sight out of mind, you know the old saying."

"I couldn't."

"Hell, Lieberman, I *know* people. For $25,000 I could arrange to get anybody knocked off."

"That means if I paid you $25,000, you'd only spend $10,000. Is life that cheap?"

"Cheaper. You underestimate my greed, Lieberman. I'd only spend $2,500. For that price the guy would leave a terrible mess and probably his fingerprints, but he'd never know who hired him or why."

"I couldn't," Lieberman repeated. "He's an innocent man. Probably a decent one. From what she says, he loves her too."

"You're all heart, Lieberman. Why don't you fall in love with me? I'll fall in love with you. Just dig out your fucking checkbook, write down the number five and keep adding zeroes; I'll peek over your shoulder and let you know when I'm in love."

"Wait," said Lieberman. "Maybe there is something you could do. What would make it the easiest for me to win Kate over? If Larry wasn't in love with her, right? If *he* dumped *her,* why I could be the dear, patient, long-suffering friend there to comfort her in her time of need. She'd slowly come to love me."

"Oh, God," said Shaleen, "get me a violin."

"Ridicule from someone who would think nothing of having a man killed does not move me," said Lieberman. "The problem is *how* to get Larry to dump his wife. And what more logical way than for him to fall in love with another woman?" He smiled at Shaleen. "And that's where you come in."

"If you thought offering her a thousand a trick was expensive . . ."

"It costs what it costs," said Lieberman. "Money is not the object. I'm in love."

"How nice," said Shaleen. "So, how do you want me to handle the situation?"

"Remember the report I ordered from the detective? I'll get it for you. It's full of photographs. It details his every move, gives the complete history of his life. It tells everything but the length of his peter."

"I'll check it out and let you know," said Shaleen. "Maybe there's a reason why she likes him. Maybe he's well hung. Now, do I tell him I'm a hooker?"

"What do you think?"

"I'll play it by ear. Some guys would be real excited to think a hooker has fallen in love with them, that they're getting free what everybody else has to pay for. Then again, some guys would be mortally offended to find out the sweet girl they think they're in love with is available to anybody with the money. By the end of the first evening I'll know which kind he is."

———————

"It will be easier than stealing sand off Waikiki," said Shaleen. She had stopped by Lieberman's condominium after her first evening with Larry McInally. "He's a nice, pleasant, boring kid from Creede, Colorado, who went to college on an ROTC scholarship, married a cheerleader, and thinks he's a great lover."

"Is he?"

"Are you kidding? He's 28 years old, was probably laid three times in his life in the back of someone's car at a drive-in movie before he married what's-her-name? He equates being a good lover to banging me all the way through the mattress to the floor. If he was mine, I'd give him his own fucking manhole cover to play with so he could leave me alone. He thinks pussy is made out of steel."

"You're seeing him again?"

"Of course. When do you want me to move him in with me, tomorrow or the next day?"

"A couple of weeks at least, but keep him overnight next time. I want Kate to know she has a problem."

"I can't imagine it, Lieberman, you're in love with a fucking cheer-leader."

The next time they met for lunch, Kate was distracted. No matter what Lieberman said, he couldn't make her laugh. She picked at her food. What made it worse for Lieberman was that he knew exactly what was wrong: Larry McInally had spent the two previous nights with Shaleen.

"It really hurts me to see her suffer," Lieberman told Shaleen over the phone, late that afternoon. "What if I break them up and then Kate doesn't fall in love with me? I don't think I could live with that."

"Developing a conscience, are we? What do you want me to do, feel sorry for you, Lieberman? By the way, dear little Larry is thrilled to death about my being a hooker. He's already planning to get out of the service as soon as his hitch is up; while I will continue to earn my living on my back. I think he sees himself in a ruffled shirt, wearing mirrored sunglasses and spending my trick money on stretch limousines and co-caine. He wonders why I burst out laughing for no reason while we're getting it on."

"Don't frighten him off," said Lieberman.

"You know I don't think I've ever frightened a trick off. I know at least 30 other ways to make a john come, but never by fright."

"Just remember how much I'm paying you," said Lieberman. "That should help you to control your laughter."

"I wouldn't ask you for help if I wasn't desperate," Kate said at lunch a few days later. She was wearing the white dress with the green palm frond, the one Lieberman found so attractive. She reached across the table and took Lieberman's hands in hers. "I don't know what else to do, where else to turn," she went on, her voice breaking. Her eyes were red from crying, her cheeks blotchy. Lieberman had never loved her more.

"I know you like me . . . maybe more . . . ," Kate said.

"Much more," said Lieberman.

"That's why what I'm going to ask you is so awful. If you say no, I'll understand."

"Try me," said Lieberman.

"I followed him," Kate said. "I hired a taxi and followed him to her building. I asked the security guard what unit he went to, and he told me. That was at five o'clock last night. I waited outside for seven hours. At midnight I decided he wasn't going to be leaving, so I got the phone number from the security guard. She has a silent listing. I phoned, but all I got was her answering service. So I rang the apartment on the intercom, and when she answered I told her who I was and asked her to send Larry home so I could talk to her. The security man let me sit in his office until Larry left. Then I went upstairs.

"I can never compete with her," Kate cried. "She's beautiful and rich and one of her dresses is worth more than everything I own. She was very nice to me. Her name is Shaleen Berger. She owns her own investment business. Larry's madly in love with her. He's planning on moving in with her next week. And she's going to let him. But she's not as crazy for him as he is for her. She hinted around, intimated that if I had some money, or if I had a rich friend who would help me out, that she could be bought off."

Kate held tightly to Lieberman's hands. Her green eyes had a wildness in them.

"I don't have any money. I thought maybe you could loan me enough to pay her off. I really love him. I don't care if that sounds dumb. I just do. I'd pay you back," she rushed on. "And—I'll do anything for you. You know what I mean. I'll go back to your place with you right now, if you'll promise to help me. I know how cruel this must seem, but if you love me, will you talk to Shaleen? Will you pay her what she wants to stay away from Larry?"

"I'll do whatever I can to help you out," Lieberman said. "And you won't owe me a thing. I appreciate your offer, but I'd never take advantage of such a situation. I only hope Larry knows what a lucky young man he is."

Though he didn't need to, Lieberman copied down Shaleen's name, address, and phone number.

"Why didn't you tell me?" Lieberman screamed into the phone.

"I wanted it to be a surprise," said Shaleen coyly. "I didn't want to spoil your fun. I thought you'd be in bed with her, instead of spoiling my afternoon."

"You've ruined everything," roared Lieberman. "I'm coming over, now!"

"You do that, it sounds as if you need somebody to talk to. Whores are always good listeners."

On the way to her apartment, Lieberman considered ways of killing Shaleen. No hired killer for her. He visualized killing her himself, strangling her slowly, shooting her, using a knife. He discarded the methods one by one. He was not, and never had been, a violent man. Was that true? he wondered. He remembered a time years before, when his business was new. Union thugs had demanded a hefty percentage of his profits from a highrise he was building in return for keeping the site free of labor strife. He arranged to meet them at the construction site. As their car drove up, he'd dropped a concrete block from the fifth floor of the skeletal building. He could still see the glass of the windshield rising like water into the midnight air.

"I don't know why you're so upset," Shaleen said, after Lieberman rumbled into her apartment. "If there's anybody who knows I can be bought, it should be you."

"Why didn't you send her away? Why didn't you tell her you were taking her husband, like it or not? It would have sent her straight into my arms."

"But she was so nice," said Shaleen. "The sacrifices some people are willing to make for love just got the better of me. If she'd come in with her claws out, screeching, I'd have been hard as nails, but she was just so sweet. She could see she was outclassed. I wanted to give her some hope. I suggested she might have a rich friend she could turn to for help. It was just a thought. How was I to know? I'd never seen her before," and she smiled at Lieberman, pursing her lips in an exaggerated manner.

"How much are you supposedly asking to send her husband back to her?"

Shaleen named a figure that caused Lieberman's eyebrows to involuntarily lift nearly half an inch.

"There's a condo two floors up that's for sale for just that amount. I need a little security for my old age," said Shaleen.

"You don't think I'm actually going to pay you. You were working for me. You've already double-crossed me."

"Think how good it'll feel to help young love triumph, Lieberman. Besides, you wouldn't want me to tell poor little Kate that you paid me to seduce her husband. Your little cheerleader is going to get misty-eyed every time she thinks of you for the next 40 years; she'll tell her grandchildren the story of how this wonderful man loved her so much he paid off the evil woman who was taking her husband away from her. You're too much of a romantic to pass up a chance to make the noble gesture of the century."

Lieberman, trapped like an insect on flypaper, wrote Shaleen the check.

"You'll be sorry," he said hollowly as he passed it to her.

"Told you never to trust a whore," said Shaleen.

He met Kate for lunch the next day.

"It's all arranged," he told her.

"I know," said Kate. "She broke off with Larry last night. He came crawling home begging for forgiveness."

"And you forgave him?"

Kate smiled sadly.

"I'll pay you back," she whispered. "I'm flying home to Oklahoma City for a few weeks, kind of to get my head together, you know. Then I'll start paying you back. And the other still applies."

Lieberman declined graciously. A tear oozed out of one of Kate's green eyes and sat on her cheek like a jewel. Lieberman kissed her goodbye, his heart breaking. He wondered what Shaleen had told her. Kate seemed to think there was only a few thousand dollars involved. He was tempted to tell her the truth; she knew the value of a condo on one of the top floors of Yacht Harbor Towers. But Lieberman was too much of a gentleman. He wished Kate well and assured her she need not pay back the money.

Lieberman felt very old in the mornings. He did not open the blinds. He thought of flying back to Denver. He again turned to an escort service for company. The results were most unsatisfactory.

It was during the third week of his mourning that Shaleen phoned.

"I'm coming over," she said.

"I didn't call you," said Lieberman. "What you cost I can't afford."

"Tonight is free," said Shaleen. "I owe you that much."

"And perhaps an invitation to your housewarming?" said Lieberman.

Shaleen arrived all in white, the tips of her golden hair, frosted; several thousand dollars in gold chains circled her neck and wrists. "I saved you a lot of grief," said Shaleen.

"Did I ask to be saved?" glowered Lieberman.

"You didn't want to be married to a cheerleader. Incidentally, I didn't buy the condo. I used the money to pay Kate off."

"For what?" said Lieberman.

"To go home to the mainland and forget about you."

"Me?"

"Aw, Lieberman, somebody had to look after your best interests. Your cheerleader might not be an intellectual, but everything you did was so obvious you might as well have carried flashcards. Actually it wasn't Kate who came to see me, it was me who went to see her."

"Why?"

"Look, Larry McInally is a jerk. She was delighted to get rid of him. You could have had her anytime from the second lunch on, but you were just too backward to see it. She decided, since there was so much at stake, to play things your way, not frighten you off."

"Then she really cared for me."

"She thought she did. But, as we've both always said, Lieberman, everybody has their price."

"You really paid her off?"

Shaleen nodded.

"You paid her off with *my* money!"

"I'm only willing to go so far. What do you want from me, Lieberman, a declaration of love?"

"How much of my money did you give her? How much did you pocket?"

"Does it make a difference?"

"It would be interesting to know how much I'm worth to you."

"Fraid not," said Shaleen. "A working girl's got to have some secrets."

"I suppose you think I'm not in love with her, that I was never in love with her," Lieberman said. It was almost a cry.

"That's what I think," said Shaleen.

"I suppose you think I'm in love with you," wailed Lieberman.

"That's what I think," said Shaleen.

Lieberman sighed.

"We deserve each other, Lieberman. We're both interested in ourselves first. We're ambitious, and we don't give a fuck for ethics. You don't have any business messing around with sad little cheerleaders from Oklahoma City. You'll thank me for what I did, again and again, as the years go by. But tell me, Lieberman, what happens when two people who care mainly for themselves get together? One of them is going to have the upper hand."

"I know," said Lieberman.

"I wonder if you do? Remember, Lieberman, I don't have a heart of gold. I'm interested in gold."

"I understand," said Lieberman.

"I'll spend your money. There'll be a premarital agreement. What's yours is mine, what's mine's my own."

"I understand."

"I'll keep my trick book. There'll be other lovers . . . whoever and whenever I say. I only have to go to Denver once a year, in the summer, and for no more than 14 days. There'll be times when I'll embarrass you, Lieberman. I'll dress like a whore when I meet your relatives. You'll look like a foolish old man . . ."

"I understand."

"I'll sleep with your sons."

Lieberman crossed the room, reached out his hand to Shaleen, pulled her to her feet and into his arms.

"I've been widowed once," he said into her golden hair. "It could happen again."

Shaleen laughed into his shoulder. Lieberman thrilled to the sound.

The Grecian Urn

CHAPTER ONE
A Japanese red herring

The mail slot in the door to my house is taped open. It measures 9½" x 1¼" and is 11" above the step. There is an empty Japanese orange box on the front step, and a three-inch-thick foam pillow on the floor just inside the door. I have placed food and water on the floor at strategic locations throughout the house, in red plastic dishes that once belonged to our cat.

My son argues that with winter fast approaching it is uneconomical to have the mail slot taped open. He is nineteen, in second year university, majoring in civil engineering and doing very well. He has a very attractive girlfriend named Tanya, with a dark red, pouty mouth and exceedingly large breasts. My son often asks just exactly what it is that I expect to come through the slot. I tell him to trust his father.

Recently, and inexplicably to everyone but myself, I have committed some rather bizarre little crimes. To explain to the authorities the perfectly logical reasons for my criminal activity would, as I see it, be far worse than simply accepting the consequences. Explanation would cause me to reveal a story far too ludicrous to be believed. It is, I contend, far better to let everyone concerned assume that for reasons unknown, I, Charles Bristow, age 49, have gone a little, no, more than a little, strange. I am, I must admit, a particularly inept criminal. It is, I suppose, because I have had no practice. Until very recently I was a most average member of the community.

Suddenly becoming a criminal, and an inept one at that, is to say the least a traumatic experience. As a sort of last resort, perhaps in the way of therapy, although I am not at all sure about that, I am doing my best to convince everyone except my son that I am mentally deranged. I think I am going to try to blame my misfortune on the male menopause, about which I read a very interesting article in a back issue of the *Reader's Digest*.

A few weeks ago, if anyone had told me that I would be attempting to convince people that I am insane, I would have laughed at them. Widowed for some two years, I lived quietly in my own home, mortgage-free, with my son. I was employed as a minor bureaucrat in the city civil service, and had held my position for some 30 years. I am currently under suspension without pay, pending disposition of the criminal charges against me. I gardened, bowled Tuesday nights, attended a church-sponsored friendship gathering on Saturday evenings, and subscribed to a book of the month club.

As yet I have refused to discuss Allan or the urn while I am being held for psychiatric evaluation here at the J. Walter Ives Institute for the Emotionally Disturbed. Everyone knows about the urn. No one knows about Allan. The first time I was arrested, the night I broke the Grecian Urn, I was let out on bail, charged with wilful damage and possession of burglar tools, to wit: a hammer and chisel. The next time the charge was trespassing by night, followed by loitering, followed by a second trespassing by night charge, at which time my bail was rescinded and I was remanded in custody for fourteen days for psychiatric evaluation. Seven of those days have passed.

I have submitted to a battery of tests: described my feelings toward my parents, tried to remember if I was bottle- or breast-fed, played with blocks and looked at ink blots.

Unthinkingly, I chose to use the hospital phone to call my son and plead with him to leave the mail slot open. When all rational arguments failed I ordered him to leave it open, reminding him that I paid his tuition to university as well as the utility bills.

My son complains that Tanya won't come to the house since she learned of my strange behaviour. I sympathize with him. She used to come over Tuesdays and Saturdays, my nights out. It was seldom mentioned between us, but I could always tell because the air would be heavy with her perfume when I arrived home. Soon after Tanya began visiting our home regularly, my son took to washing his own sheets. I am quite proud of him.

The phone was apparently tapped. The doctors were smiling like slit throats the next day. They must also have talked to my son, for they were inordinately interested in the Japanese orange box on the front step. I denied everything, even phoning my son. However, during the interview I doodled a number of Japanese flags on the paper in front of me and also wrote, *Remember Pearl Harbor*, in a tiny, cramped hand, quite unlike my own. As I left the room, nonchalantly whistling "Over There," they converged on the paper like baying hounds.

At supper that evening, when a Toyota commercial came on the television, I began flipping carrots at the TV.

CHAPTER TWO
The All-Blue streetcar

I suppose it was logical that Allan should have come to me for help. Outside of Viveca I was probably the only living person who knew. Beatrice may have suspected but we never discussed the matter.

Allan's secret. What exactly is it that I know? That seems to be a real point of contention. I really only know what Allan has told me and what I think I have seen.

I never liked Allan. I didn't like him in 1943 and I don't like him today. I do like Viveca. I would do anything for Viveca. She was the only reason I tried to help Allan.

I have lived in this city all my life. I joined the Army on my sixteenth birthday, 3 October, 1942. Two months later I met Allan, or rather Allan sought me out as a friend. He was lonely. I have never liked to be unkind to anyone. I tolerated him. He had the look of an English schoolboy, cheeks like two apples floating in a pail of white paint, very blond hair, pale blue eyes, a mouth that looked like he was wearing lipstick.

"My parents came over when the war started. Money, you know. Horrified that I joined up."

I was noncommittal.

"I can do some rather unusual things," he said.

I started to tell him I was not interested but instead remained silent.

"My family is unique," he persisted. "We all have powers. They begin at puberty, reach full potential by about 30, then decline to nothing by 50."

"So what?" I said. My father fought with the IRA, claimed to have killed seven Black and Tans. "There'll Always Be an England" was not my favourite song. Allan was somehow insulted that he could not rouse my curiosity, but it didn't keep him at bay for long. He offered no demonstration of his uniqueness. I continued to reluctantly accept him as my friend. It was a few weeks later, on top of a railway trestle, in a streetcar that had jumped the tracks, that I got to observe Allan in action.

The All-Blue streetcar was not, as the name may suggest, painted blue. Instead of having names and destinations the streetcars bore a small metal plate about a foot square on the front and rear. If one wished to get around the city, one learned quickly that the All-Blue streetcar travelled west to south, the Red-and-White streetcar went east to south, while the Green-and-Red went east to west.

On a dismal March night in 1943 we were travelling to a movie on the south side of the city. The All-Blue streetcar had to cross the river valley on top of a railway bridge. Halfway across the car bucked and pitched sideways. We were seated, Allan and I, at about the middle of the car, the only other passengers two girls about our age who were sitting at the very back. I thought we were certainly going to die. I could already feel the streetcar hurtling the 400 feet toward the ice of the river below. The lights went out as the car swung sideways, the rear of the car hanging out over the water. At the last instant the front wheels caught on the outside track and the car hung, balancing like a poorly constructed teeter-totter. The conductor scrambled to safety. Allan and I edged toward the front. I looked back. The two girls were huddled together in the back corner. An instant later they were beside us and the four of us climbed from the front of the car, the white-faced motorman helping us down onto the deck of the bridge.

There is documentation of the incident, if not of Allan's act of moving the girls to safety. On the front page of the 15 March, 1943, issue of a long-extinct daily newspaper is a photograph of two servicemen and two girls. My copy, yellow with age, is framed and hangs on the wall of my bedroom. The photograph was captioned The Survivors. The short blond youth with the chipmunk cheeks is Allan, the taller, raw-boned young man is me. The girls! If I could produce even one of them to document the events of that night. One person in the world who could testify that my recent actions are not those of a madman. The girl beside me in the photo, the pale, blondish girl about whose waist I have my arm, protecting her as best I could from the bitter wind, is Beatrice. We were married in 1946. She died in 1974. The girl beside Allan, the one with green eyes and wine-coloured hair spreading over her shoulders, is Viveca.

CHAPTER THREE

J. Walter Ives is a transvestite.

Day nine. I have taken to writing short notes and dropping them around the hospital. The attendants are all spies as are most of the inmates.

Last night, they brought into my room a whimpering drunk who smelled like wet newspaper.

"Why are you here?" he asked me. He had little red eyes like a rat. A spy's question if I ever heard one.

"I go around killing drunks," I said, which ended the conversation.

My first note read: I am capable of great destruction. It was signed with a triangular Japanese flag. Triangles have great significance to the doctors here. At every opportunity I work the conversation around to the male menopause. A black doctor with an Afro moustache and a red-and-yellow caftan listened for some time before saying, "I'm a rat man myself, and rats don't have no male menopause. I don't believe in none of that jive."

Beware the Ides of March, I left taped to my pillow. That afternoon one of the doctors carried a copy of *Julius Caesar* with many little bookmarks in it.

Isn't everybody a chipmunk? I wrote that on a piece of cardboard and slipped it into a deck of playing cards in the recreation room, in place of the jack of diamonds which I cleverly concealed in the toe of my slipper.

A large, jolly-looking man with bushy eyebrows and eyes as blue as bachelor buttons sits beside me in the recreation room. "I am a latent homosexual," he says, placing his hand on my knee.

CHAPTER FOUR
Cosmo perfume

Neither Allan nor I ever saw any action during the war. We spent our entire time stationed in our own city, although those who joined up both before and after us were shipped off to Europe, many never to return. Perhaps Allan had something to do with it. I never asked him. I am not a very curious person.

After the adventure on the All-Blue streetcar, the four of us became friends. I must reluctantly admit that of the two girls I preferred Viveca. That, of course, was all it was, a preference. Allan and Viveca became inseparable. Like Allan, Viveca was an outgoing person. Besides being beautiful she had enormous vitality. Beatrice was the quiet one. On the assumption that likes attract we were paired together.

A significant, I believe that is the word Allan used to describe Viveca, no powers of her own, but extremely susceptible to his. Once or twice, when we were alone in barracks, Allan gave small demonstrations of his abilities. He made objects fall from shelves, stopped and started my pocket watch several times while seated in a chair across the room. Once he shattered the glass in my shaving mirror simply by staring at it. I was not particularly impressed. I asked if he could make money. He said he couldn't. He said he could, if he wished, dematerialize and inhabit inanimate objects. He said he could live inside a silver dollar, or a tree, or the fender of a bus. He said that because of Viveca's susceptibility to his powers, he could allow her to experience the same phenomena. It seemed to me to be an extremely silly thing to do and I told him so.

Allan tried his best to convert me to his point of view. He said that he and Viveca would travel the world, being able to inhabit great works of art. He had, he said, the command of a dimension of which ordinary mortals were unaware. He could step not only into paintings or sculpture, but could come alive in the time and place that the work represented. It seemed like a lot of trouble to me. I envied Allan only Viveca. Once, at a dance hall, I took Viveca's hand to lead her to the dance floor. I could feel her pulse throbbing like something alive. She placed herself extraordinarily close to me as we danced. I could feel her breasts against the front of my uniform. Her perfume had the odour of cosmos, those tall pale pink and mauve flowers that sway beautifully in gardens like delicate children. I thought of kissing her. I'm certain she wouldn't have minded. But Allan would have, and Beatrice. I don't mean to belittle Beatrice. She was a good and faithful wife to me and as loving as her fragile health would permit. She gave me a fine son and many years of devotion.

"I wish things were different," I said to Viveca as we danced. "I wish that you and I might . . ."

She moved back slightly to look into my face. Her laugh was joyful, like wind chimes, and I remember her words, but I remember more the liquid green of her eyes and the pink tip of her tongue peeking between her lips.

"Dear Charles," she said. "You are of another world."

After the war ended we saw less and less of Allan and Viveca. Sometime late in 1945 they left and we never heard from them again. That is, until the night before I was first arrested.

CHAPTER FIVE
Only you Dick daring . . .

It was Viveca who came to the door. She was 18 when I had last seen her, she looked no more than 25 now; 26, she told me later. It was, she had decided, the ideal age. She held her hand out to me. The pulse was there, throbbing like a bird between us.

It embarrassed me to see her looking so young. I have not aged particularly gracefully. It would be a kindness to say that I have the average appearance of a man dramatically close to 50.

Viveca spent little time on amenities. Allan was in trouble, she told me, and because Allan was in trouble so was she. They needed the help of a third party. Would I be it?

I am sure that Allan, with his inordinate perceptions, knew how I felt about Viveca. That was why he sent her ahead. He knew I could refuse her nothing. It was quite extraordinary, her reappearance after some 30 years. In recent times, and especially since my wife passed away, I have been fantasizing more and more about Viveca. I remember Allan once describing to me certain, to say the least, avant-garde, sexual practices, and intimating rather strongly that he and Viveca . . .

"Allan must talk with you," Viveca said.

I agreed. Allan was like Dorian Gray; he looked scarcely older than when I last saw him. Side by side we could be mistaken for father and son. There was a desperate tone in his voice as he talked to me, a sense of urgency with just a hint of panic. I found great pleasure in Allan's distress. I tried to remain very calm and feign disinterest, but secretly I was greatly stimulated. I recalled Viveca in my arms, Allan talking of his uniqueness disappearing at age 50. Perhaps, just perhaps, there was a chance. I would pretend to help but then at the last moment . . . As my father was known to say, a stiff cock knows no conscience. I would have followed Viveca over Niagara Falls in a teacup.

His powers were virtually gone, Allan explained. He and Viveca had spent the last 30 years doing exactly as they said they would. They had passed like needles through the history of the world. They had visited nearly every time and civilization by means of inhabiting paintings and other original works of art. With Allan's time running out they had decided on a final resting place: a Grecian Urn that was the feature exhibit of a travelling display currently showing at our museum. It was, Allan stated, the urn to which John Keats had written his immortal "Ode on a Grecian Urn." I had no reason to doubt him as I had seen it advertised as such in our newspaper.

"Why me?" I asked. "Surely you've made this transfer of dimension thousands of times before?"

It seemed that they had attempted the transfer a few weeks before, in another city, and failed. Allan had been able to send Viveca on her journey but had no energy left to transport himself, and had barely been able to return Viveca to her natural form. They wanted me along as a safeguard in case something went wrong again. A mere precaution, they assured me. Allan had been conserving his energy for several weeks and everything would go well. Both went into ecstasies about the life ahead of them on the urn. The tranquillity, beauty, peace, they sounded to me like acquaintances of mine who had recently taken up organic gardening. They quoted lavishly from Keats' poem, assured me that they both realized that they would be totally unable to cope with the everyday world without Allan's powers, and that the ultimate in nth-dimensional living was waiting for them on the urn.

I was not about to argue with them although my mind was in turmoil. I tried to think of ways that I could trick Allan into leaving Viveca behind. However, I am hardly a devious person, and as I watched Viveca's face as she described the joys that lay ahead of her, her eyes flashed, and she laughed often, the magic bell-like laughter of long ago. Her perfume was the same and my thoughts moved to the rows and rows of gentle cosmos that had graced my garden the last few summers. I would help them both. It would be the last act of love I could ever perform for Viveca.

CHAPTER SIX
The importance of triangles

Day twelve. Had a long session with one of the doctors today. He reviewed the results of my tests.

"You are as sane as I am," he told me.

He is the one with the copy of *Julius Caesar,* who puts great stock in the importance of triangles.

CHAPTER SEVEN
Blue gnats

The three of us visited the museum that same evening. The Grecian Urn was the central exhibit. They pointed out to me the spot they intended to occupy on the urn. They were as happy as if they were merely going on a holiday. I have a scant knowledge of art, but even to my untrained eye the urn was impressive. It stood some four feet high and there were three bands on it, each displaying a number of raised figures in Greek dress, in various postures, among pastoral scenery.

I arranged to accompany them to the museum the following night.

It was difficult to get close to the urn. It was behind crimson ropes and there was a constant line of people filing past. We waited until closing time. The circular hall was empty. Allan shook hands with me and gave me a few last moment instructions. Viveca kissed me, her mouth a swarming thing. Was I wrong to interpret the kiss as much more than one old friend saying good-bye to another?

"Would you check the exit-way, Charles," Allan said to me.

I walked the length of the red carpet to the doorway, looked outside to be certain that we were alone. When I turned Allan and Viveca were gone: all that was left for me to see was a small swarm of bluish stars no larger than gnats disappearing into the side of the urn in a tornado shape. The urn was several feet distant from the restraining ropes. I looked carefully around, crawled under the ropes, and approached the urn. In the area that Allan and Viveca had pointed out to me were two new figures, a boy and a girl, looking as though they had been part of the urn since it was created. The operation appeared to have been a success. I was just bending to inspect them closely when a startled security guard entered the display hall.

"What are you doing?" he demanded.

I stuttered an illogical reply.

"The museum is closed for the night, sir," he said with an air of authority. He looked carefully at me, then all around the exhibit hall. "I thought I heard voices," he said. "Are you sure you're alone?"

"I was checking for gnats," I said, and laughing hysterically, fled from the building.

CHAPTER EIGHT
The limits of psychiatry

Day thirteen. Another session with the doctors. Three listened; one spoke. The spokesman's eyes were small hazel triangles. Their consensus of opinion was that I am trying to con them.

After a long discussion about doctor-patient relationships, I admitted that I was trying to con them, and told them the complete story from start to finish. Then I asked their advice. They suggested that when I go to court I plead temporary insanity and not try to tell the judge my story.

"He might think you're crazy," the spokesman said.

They intend to certify me sane. Something is wrong.

CHAPTER NINE
Meanwhile, back at the museum

Twice the following evening I went through the lineup to view the urn. It was impossible for me to get beyond the restraining ropes. I merely stood and stared at the figures on the third band of the urn until the people behind pushed me on. Allan had given me certain instructions to follow and in order to do my job I had to get very close to Allan and Viveca. I had no choice but to wait until the museum closed. I hid in an alcove, then at the first opportunity rushed to the urn. I looked closely at the new figures. They seemed to fit in well. I traced the outline of Viveca's body with my index finger. As instructed I put my ear close to the figures.

"Help!" hissed Allan in the voice of a movie cartoon mouse.

"What's wrong?"

"Everything. This urn is not genuine. Seventeenth century at the latest. No character. No dimension . . ."

"There's no one around. Come on out."

"I can't."

"Why not?"

"My powers are weak. It may be weeks, even months."

"You'll just have to rest up."

"The urn is being moved to another city day after tomorrow . . . and by the way keep your hands off Viveca, I saw what you did."

"Viveca's being awfully quiet."

As I spoke I touched Viveca again. I could feel her warmth and smell the faint odour of cosmos.

"Remember it is who maintain her in this dimension," he said in an agitated voice, like a tape being played at the wrong speed. Then he told me what I must do. Detailed instructions on how to rescue him and Viveca. He had barely finished when the security guard appeared.

"You again," he said.

"It is such a treasure," I said. "I only wanted to get a close look at it."

"If I catch you around here again I'm going to have to take you in."

I apologized for inconveniencing him and slunk away.

The following evening I hid in the washroom of the museum. Feeling like a fool, I stood on a toilet seat when the security guard checked the washroom at closing time. After waiting a suitable length of time I took the hammer and chisel that Allan had instructed me to bring and made my way to the urn.

Ever so carefully I worked at chipping the two small figurines from the face of the urn. I deliberately released Viveca first, placed her gently in the side pocket of my suit, then went to work to free Allan. As I had his figure nearly liberated, my chisel slipped ever so slightly and the urn cracked and split into a number of pieces. I managed to catch Allan as the urn disintegrated. Remarkably, his only injury was a very small piece broken from his right foot.

Regardless of what the security guard told the police, it was not me who was screaming and cursing incoherently. At the sound of the urn breaking and Allan screaming in his tiny voice, the security guard ran into the exhibit area. He said something original like, "What's going on here?" Then he drew his pistol and pointed it very unsteadily at me. I bent over and placed Allan among the ruins of the urn. "You had better put up your hands," said the guard as he advanced on me. I complied.

"Come over here with me so I can watch you while I call the police," he said, pointing to a desk and chairs a few yards distant. He looked at me closely. "You're the man who was talking to the urn." He was about

60, pink-cheeked, with a military haircut and a small white moustache like a skiff of snow below his nose. On his dark blue uniform he wore a name tag: Charles Stoddard—Security.

"Dear Charles," I said. "You are of another world."

CHAPTER TEN
After the fall

The day after I was first arrested I stayed home from work. It was the first day I had missed in eight years. I told my son I had gotten drunk and fallen against the urn and that I had no idea why I was in the museum. He looked at me skeptically for he knows that I virtually never drink. My lawyer, the one who I called to post bail for me the previous night, insisted at the time I submit to a breath analysis. My blood-alcohol reading was 0.00%.

CHAPTER ELEVEN
Putting a cloud in a suitcase

They are holding Viveca as evidence. I was searched at the police station after my arrest. I'm afraid I made rather a fool of myself.

"It's a religious object," I wailed. "You can't deny me my religion."

"Looks like a piece of the vase he busted," said a young cop. He was built like a middle guard and looked like a teenager. The whole police force was very young.

"Be brave, Viveca," I said to her as I passed her to the police officer. I could feel her pulse beating very rapidly. The middle guard slipped her into an envelope and licked the flap with a beefy tongue.

I demanded that he leave air holes in the envelope. I'm afraid I may have become a little hysterical about it. Reluctantly he took a pen and poked a few holes in the envelope.

"You're not going to put her in a safe! You mustn't put her in an airtight place of any kind." I tried to remain composed, but my voice was quite out of control.

"Trust me, Mr. Bristow," the officer said.

"You can call a lawyer now," the man on the desk informed me, then turning to one of the officers, said, "It must be a full moon. They come out from under their rocks whenever there's a full moon."

The moment I got home I taped open the mail slot and made the other preparations I have described. While the security guard was phoning the police, Allan limped from the display area to the far wall, and while the deceased urn was being examined and I was being handcuffed and led out of the museum he slipped along the baseboard and out the front doors. I can only assume that he will try to make his way back to my home. It doesn't seem reasonable that he will go anywhere else, for it will be very difficult for a four-inch-tall plaster figure about ⅜ of an inch thick to get much attention from anyone who does not believe in him. Allan gave me so many instructions that after my arrest they all seemed to have blurred and merged with the actual conversations I had with Allan and Viveca. I do seem to recall him saying that after his removal from the urn he would require nourishment, but I can't be certain. I put out food and water just in case.

Now that I'm willing to tell the truth I find it would be easier to stuff a cloud into a suitcase than to get anyone to take me seriously. I pleaded with my lawyer to have Viveca returned to me. I told him to have the museum people check and they would find that she was not a part of the broken urn. He promised he would look into it but from the tone of his voice I could tell he was humouring me. From the hospital I phoned the museum director and pleaded with him to view the piece of evidence the police were holding. I insisted that he compare it with photographs of the urn. I'm afraid I may have become a little hysterical again. He took no action, I suppose considering the source of the call. Over the telephone I have become quite friendly with the middle guard at the police station; his name is Rourke and our families come from a similar part of Ireland. He assures me that Viveca is being kept in an airy bottom drawer.

CHAPTER TWELVE
Meanwhile, back at J. W. I.

I keep having a dream. Sometimes I have it in the daytime, therefore I suppose I would have to say it is a fantasy as well as a dream. The water dishes that I left in my house for Allan's use are large red plastic ones. They are some four inches off the ground. Since Allan is only about four inches tall, my calculations indicate that he would have great difficulty getting a drink without falling in. I should phone my son and have him change the dishes for saucers. Yet I do not. My dream is that my son phones me to say that he has found (a) a four-inch plaster figure in Greek dress submerged in the water dish, or (b) a full-grown man of about 50, who must have had an extremely difficult time drowning himself in less than three inches of water.

Assuming that doctors like to hear about dreams I discussed this one with them. They are not concerned because they don't believe my original story. Their professional advice is to try not to think about it.

The night following my first arrest I went back to the museum grounds to look for Allan. My concern was not really for Allan but that he is the only one who can release Viveca. I spent a good deal of time searching the foliage around the building and skulking about the grounds, until a greasy-looking kid with a widow's peak, driving a Toyota with a frothing Doberman in the back seat, shone a spotlight on me. Trespassing by night. The following afternoon I was arrested for loitering about the grounds. I tried to be more careful that night but the kid with the Doberman got me again, hence my banishment to J. Walter Ives.

CHAPTER THIRTEEN
Sayonara

My fourteen days are up. The doctors come to say good-bye. They explain that according to their analysis of my handwriting I am perfectly sane.

"There are other dimensions," I assure them, "of which you are incapable of understanding. In fact . . ."

I am interrupted by the head nurse who advises me that there is a phone call from my son. The head nurse says that he sounds very agitated.

THE FOG

My littlest sister Delores come running through the doorway of our cabin puffing. "Silas, Silas, there's a phone call for you down at the store."

I can tell she has run all the way; her braids are unravelled, her cheeks pink, and she smell of the outdoors. The phone is a half mile down the hill at Ben Stonebreaker's Hobbema General Store. As we walk down, I hold onto Delores' hand, and every once in a while we skip a step or two, Delores all the time talking a mile a minute. "Hurry up!" she say, pulling on my arm. But I ain't expecting a phone call so anybody who needs to talk to me can wait until I get there.

The phone is nailed to one of the back walls of the store. It made of varnished wood, is about a yard tall, and I bet is older than I am. I'm tall enough to talk into the mouth-piece, while most everybody else have to stand on their tiptoes, yell up as if they talking to someone at the top of a hill.

"Mr. Ermineskin," say a man's deep voice, the kind that set plates to rattling on the table if he was at your house. "My name is J. Michael Kirkpatrick and I'm Bureau Chief for Best North American News Service. I've read your books and I'm very impressed. Very impressed."

That means he's going to ask me to do some work for him: interview somebody, write a column or something. The point I have to establish quick is, is he going to pay me, and if so, how much. Lots of people figure they can pay Indians with colored beads like in the old days; others figure that just because I'm an Indian I should be willing to work cheap.

I listen to what Mr. Kirkpatrick have to say, and I go "Ummmmm," and "Uh-huh," at the proper points so he won't figure the phone has gone dead.

"As you are probably aware, the Pope is on a cross-country tour of Canada. One of his stops will be at Fort Simpson in the Northwest Territories, where he will meet with several thousand native people. We would like you to cover that event as a representative of Best North American News Service, and to write about it from a native point of view, so to speak."

"How much?" I ask. I've learned from sad experience not to be shy about taking money. Editors have kept me on the phone for an hour, or I've sat in a carpeted office listening to a long explanation of an assignment, only to find out they expect to pay me twenty dollars or less for the job.

Mr. Kirkpatrick name a figure. I ask for double. He say no way. I say goodbye. He raise his price $250. I say okay.

It is while he is telling me that I going to get to ride on a chartered airplane that I get my idea.

"How would you like to not have to pay me at all?" I say.

"What's the deal?"

"Well, if you were to send two of my friends along with me, we'd settle for expenses. Medicine lady of our tribe was saying just last night how she'd like to meet the Pope. And I got a close friend I want to bring with me."

"Girlfriend, eh?" say Mr. Kirkpatrick.

"No," I say. "It's a man."

"Oh, well, I suppose it's okay." He sound kind of embarrassed.

"Somehow I never thought of you Indians being *that way*. But I suppose you *are* a writer."

Boy, when I tell Mad Etta what I arranged she get as excited as I ever seen her.

"I want to have a talk with this Pope guy," she say. "You know him and me ain't so different. People believe in what he got to hand out—I can't figure out why—but in the long run it don't matter. For me, having people believe in my cures is about 90% of the battle. Maybe I can make a trade with this Mr. Pope. I seen him on the TV the other day and I can tell by the way he holds himself that he still got pains from the time he got shot. I'll take him some cowslip roots to boil up; maybe I'll even boil it for him. If he drinks the tea his pain will go away."

"Yeah, but what can he do for you?"

"I'm not real sure. But he's a nice man. And, if you stop to think about it, he believes in the old ways, just like us. Maybe I can learn from him something about *influence*. I mean we got over 4,000 people, but only about a hundred or so believe in me. I could use the secret of attracting more followers."

Frank's biggest wish is to get Pope John Paul to bless his lottery tickets. "I'll donate 10% of my winnings to his church. And I'd really like to have him get me a part in that *Knight Rider* TV show. I want to drive that superpowered car that talks like a person."

"Those ain't the kinds of miracles the Pope usually get asked for," I say.

"Right. He must get tired of being asked to cure rheumatism and back aches. I figure he'll pay attention to an unusual request."

"But you don't believe."

"Not yet. I will as soon as that car from *Knight Rider* pull on to the reserve and say, 'Come here, Frank Fencepost. I been dying to have you drive me.'"

Though it is the fall season here in Alberta, with the days warm and the trees still covered with pumpkin-colored leaves, we take parkas and sleeping bags with us. We been to the Arctic once, Frank and me, and it was below zero there, in real temperature, even in the summer.

We sit Etta on her tree-trunk chair in the back of Louis Coyote's pickup truck and drive to the little airport in the middle of Edmonton. Like they promised, Best North American News Service have an airplane waiting. It is small, hold four passengers and a pilot, but it is new. I promised myself I'd never fly in a small plane again after I went to Pandemonium Bay in a plane with doors that wouldn't close and windows where the snow blew right in, and an engine about as powerful as a sick Ski-Doo. But this is another time.

The pilot wear a uniform just like he was in the air force.

"Take us to see the Pope, General," Frank say, salute the pilot. "You got champagne and movies on this here flight?"

"But the pilot pay about as much attention to Frank as if he was a fly buzzing around his head; what he *is* staring at is Mad Etta.

"It's alright," I tell him. "She's a medicine lady; you'll never crash with her aboard."

Etta is decked out in a new deerskin dress. "Deer population will be down for years to come," is what Frank said when he first seen it. The dress got about 10 pounds of porcupine quills on it, including a purple circle on Etta's front the size of a garbage can lid.

"Getting her aboard is what I'm worried about," says the pilot. "That door don't expand."

He's right. The little steps up to the door are like toys, and even ordinary people have to duck and turn to get inside.

"Hey, when I want to do something I get it done," say Etta. "Silas, you go inside and pull; Frank, you push."

Moving Etta is kind of like moving furniture. I seen guys get sofas and deepfreezes up twisting stairs and through doors smaller than the things they were moving.

Etta give the directions and we do the work. A couple of times I figure Etta going to get stuck permanent. Then it look like the door-frame gonna split on us, or else Etta is. I think finally Etta just concentrate and shrink herself about four inches all around, for she pop through the door like she been greased.

During the flight Etta sit on one side of the plane, while me, Frank, and the pilot, and all our luggage sit on the other.

"The News Service has a bigger plane waiting in Yellowknife to take you on to Fort Simpson," the pilot tell us.

It is in Yellowknife where the real trouble start. There is hundreds and hundreds of reporters in the tiny airport, waiting to get any kind of aircraft to fly them to the even tinier airport in Fort Simpson. There's also several TV people from Best North American News Service, who is determined to get to Fort Simpson.

"Your friends are gonna have to stay behind," say a cameraman, who is chewing on a cigar, look like Charles Bronson when he been without sleep for two days.

"No way," I say. "I'm working for nothing so my friends can go along."

"Look, no one ever thought of the shortage of transportation. Everything's been cleared with J. Michael Kirkpatrick back in Toronto. You get paid your full fee plus a $500 bonus. Your friends get a hotel room here in Yellowknife and their meals until you get back from Fort Simpson. They're lucky not to be going. It's gonna be a madhouse there."

It don't look like I have no choice. Boy, I sure hate to explain the change to Etta. When she hear what I have to say she rumble deep inside like bad plumbing.

"When Etta get mad she usually get even," I tell the Best North American people. But not knowing Etta, they ain't impressed.

There is more trouble when I get on the plane. Frank has found a seat for himself next to a lady.

"I'm editor of this here Indian newspaper called *The Moccasin Telegraph*," he is telling her as I come down the aisle. I notice he is already touching her body. "Ah, here's my assistant now. His name is Silas Gopher; he's sort of my gofer," and Frank laugh loud and hearty. He also have a jack-handle laid across his lap and when somebody from the airline tell him to move, he suggest he will do a certain amount of damage to anybody who try to take his seat from him. The pilot and his assistant have a quick meeting and decide to leave Frank where he is; instead they let the cameraman sit in the aisle. If only Frank had thought to bring Etta with him.

You know how when a special visitor is coming you clean up your house. You do things you would never ordinarily do, like wash in corners, clean things and places a visitor would never look. Well, that is the way it is with the whole town of Fort Simpson. The town is not very big to start with, only a thousand people they tell us. Fort Simpson is located where the Liard and Mackenzie Rivers meet, it is the trading place for all the native peoples for hundreds of miles. It seem to me every one of them people must have come to Fort Simpson to see the Pope. Boy, I really have never seen so many Indians in one place at one time.

"Where's our hotel?" is the first question Frank ask after we hit the ground.

"Ha," says the cameraman. "See that row of tents down along the riverbank. That's where we stay. There's only one small hotel in town and it's been booked up forever. Shouldn't be any problem for you guys though. Indians are used to living outdoors."

"*Some* Indians," I say.

I should have asked more questions before I took this job. I mean knowing about the outdoors don't come naturally to Indians. Me and Frank aren't campers or hunters or trackers. We like hotel rooms, Kentucky Fried Chicken, video games, riding in taxis, and electric guitars. But it look like we going to have to do without those things for a few days. What *is* here is like a disorganized carnival with no main event.

It is Government money that keep Fort Simpson in business, so it is Government people who organize for the Pope's visit. People who work full time for the Government is there 'cause they ain't competent enough to work anywheres else. All around town they have really spent a lot of money to show how smart they *ain't*.

To start with some bureaucrat must have ordered a thousand gallons of whitewash. All the sad buildings in this little town, what haven't even a memory of a coat of paint, have been sloshed with whitewash. Coming down on the airplane, these buildings looked like extra big, white birds scattered across the barren land.

These same Government people also imported rolls and rolls of fake grass. It is fall and what little grass there is is brown. The town is mostly rock and mud. Now, in all kinds of unlikely places is little blazes of green.

"What harm do you suppose it would do the Pope to see the land the way it really is?" ask Frank.

"If he's got a direct connection to God, then he'll know what he's seeing is phony and it won't matter," I say.

Every rock within eyesight of Fort Simpson also been whitewashed.

"Looks like Limestone City," says a reporter.

"I wonder if they bathe the people as they come into town, wouldn't want the Pope to smell anything bad," says someone else.

"Didn't you hear?" says a CBC cameralady, "night before the visit they're gonna whitewash us. We'll all glow like foxfire the day of the big visit."

"I wonder what we're gonna do to kill time," I say. It is only Saturday. The Pope ain't due until Tuesday. I been at events where the reporters interview each other they get so desperate for news.

All along the riverbank for as far as we can see is square little pup tents in a long row.

"That's the Press Area," somebody tells us. "Better grab yourself a tent before they're all gone."

I'm sure glad we brought heavy clothes. There are little propane heaters and portable cookstoves in the tents, but it easy to see the first arrivals been having trouble with them, 'cause about every tenth tent been burned down.

Frank and that lady TV producer he met on the plane have decided to share a tent. That evening Frank win a fair amount of money in a card game until somebody point out which side of the deck he's dealing from.

"Indians always deal from the bottom of the deck," Frank say in a serious voice, acting as if he is the one been offended. He at least bluff his way out of any broken bones, though after that no one will play cards with him anymore.

Just as I'm afraid of, since I appear to be the only Indian reporter in town, I get interviewed by other reporters for radio, TV and newspapers. They are all disappointed that I'm not excited about being here. "I'm sure this Pope is a nice man, but as I see it the Church and smallpox have done about equal damage to the Indian people over the years," I tell them. I don't think they ever broadcast or print that. Nobody want to say anything negative about anything, especially the Pope.

The natives, or the *Dene,* as the Indians call themselves, have got things pretty well organized in spite of having the Government looking over their shoulders.

"There are over 8,000 visitors here," a Cree chief from near Yellowknife tell us. Later, I heard there was only 4,000 people all told. When that guy from the news service called me he said to expect 40,000. I notice that a lot of people who have come are really old. They come off the roads in pickup trucks as beat up as the one we drive at home, all dusty, rusty and coughing; they come down the rivers in all kinds of boats powered by stuttering outboards.

Out on the flats is a tent city, not the new canvas of the press tents, but canvas stitched and repaired and patched, sun faded to the color of the hills in late fall. Lived-in tents with smoke blackening around the tops where north winds pushed smoke down against the canvas. That field of tents look exactly like pictures and paintings of old-time Indian settlements I've seen at the Glenbow Museum in Calgary.

The women have set up racks of spruce logs for the curing of moose meat, deer, caribou, whitefish and speckled trout.

In the huge tepee that been built to honor the Pope, drums been throbbing day and night, and dancers dance old-time circle dances. A few, but not many of the dancers are in costume. This is real dancing by men in denim and deerskins, women in long skirts and saggy sweaters—real people, not people dressed in plastic beads and feathers made in Korea who practise their dancing on a government grant.

The people here call the Pope *Yahtitah*; it mean priest-father, as near as I can translate.

Lots of the reporters and many of the Indians have transistor radios, listen to what happen in the outside world.

"He's taking off from Edmonton Airport any minute now," someone report on Tuesday morning, his hand holding the tiny black radio close to his ear. "He'll be here right on schedule."

Then about 10 minutes later, "Take-off's been delayed for 15 minutes."

The circle dancing continues. Smoke the same color of the sky drift in the cool, damp air of morning.

"His plane's developed engine trouble," someone say. "Departure from Edmonton is delayed by 45 minutes."

Nobody's worried yet. But I imagine I can hear Etta rumbling in her room in that hotel in Yellowknife. If she got anything to cook on I bet she boiling up mysterious stuff.

After the delay stretch to over two hours people start to get nervous.

"He's gonna change planes," a reporter cry.

Everyone cheer and clap. The drums in the compound get louder, like they applauding too.

"They're switching to a back-up plane; take-off's in 20 minutes."

Frank busy taking bets on the Pope's arrival time. He sit behind a table, in front of a sign he printed himself read, Frank Bank. He offers to bet money that the Pope don't arrive at all, give 2–1 odds. Indians take him up on that and the pile of money in front of him grow.

"He's takin' off!" and a cheer rise over the settlement like slow thunder. First time I ever hear a whole town make, as Pastor Orkin back home would say, "a joyful noise."

The weather been perfect Indian Summer ever since we arrived. That morning it was foggy first thing, but, as it supposed to do, the sun burn that fog off, and it was clear with a high sky when the take-off finally announced.

Over the next few hours, as the Pope fly through the air toward us, the clouds roll in, filmy and white as smoke tendrils at first, then it is like the sky develop a low roof, won't let the campfire smoke out. Fog all of a sudden rise off the river, twist around our ankles like a cat rubbing. For a while the sun look like a red balloon, then get dull as an orange, fade to the color of a grapefruit, disappear altogether.

The drum slow down as if people's hearts beating slower.

"He's due in five minutes," someone shout. The drums stop and those thousands and thousands of people stare up into the fog. It is so thick I have to strain my eyes to see the top of that 55-foot tepee out on the flats. If I get more than a hundred yards away it look like a shadow of a tepee, the real thing hid from me by a gray blanket.

The long drone of an airplane fill the air, but it is very high and going right past us, not landing.

"Too foggy," call the people with the radios attached to their ears. "Pilot gonna try again."

A whisper pass through the crowd like a shiver. The word "pray" is whispered from a few thousand mouths. People all around me bow their heads and move their lips silently. The fog is cold and a mean breeze cut through my clothes like a razor blade.

The plane make another pass over us.

The fog doesn't budge an inch.

There is a kind of keening sound rise from the enclosure of tents. I feel sorry for the old people who come hundreds of miles down river or cross-country to see this man. I'm sorry too that these people have abandoned their own religion out of fear, for something the white man force on them. If it wasn't for guns there wouldn't be but a handful of Indian Christians.

"There's only enough fuel for one more pass," someone say.

"If there was anything to their religion don't you figure their god could move aside a few clouds?" I say to no one in particular, though I got Mad Etta in mind.

The plane make its final pass and buzz away until it is less than a mosquito sound. People are actually weeping.

"We just wanted him to touch us," say an old woman in a sky-blue parka that glazed with dirt.

"They say he's gonna land in Yellowknife instead. He might come here tomorrow if it's clear."

People who come from the Yellowknife area groan with disbelief.

"Why Yellowknife? It's not on his schedule."

"They say the Pope feel a call to stop at Yellowknife and deliver a message."

At the news that he may come to Fort Simpson tomorrow, some people give a small cheer. The drums start up again and people go back to their dancing and hoping.

"That bit about him coming tomorrow is a lie," say a producer from Best North American News Service. "They're gonna wait until late tonight to announce he's not coming. Some bureaucrat in Yellowknife is afraid of a riot."

Frank have to wait hours and hours to collect his bets. But now, people who like lost causes are putting down money that the Pope will show. It is kind of like by betting on the Pope they are showing off their faith.

"I was hoping I'd feel something," a girl about my age say to me, just after she place a five dollar bet. "The old people believed he could change things. I want to believe like them, but I just don't know . . ." and her voice fade away.

Somebody sum it up good when they say, "Same as the church always do; they promise a whole lot and deliver nothing."

Nobody seems very mad, except the press people, who put in four ugly, cold days and now have nothing to write about. Some of them scared up a legend or two, about a church that was burned down, or that a great leader would die at a place where two rivers meet. And somebody else get an old medicine man to say the animals been behaving strangely for the last few days.

But the Chief of the Slaveys state the believers' attitude the next morning when he say, "The *Dene* understand weather," and after long pause, "better than most."

During the Pope's unexpected stop in Yellowknife he record a radio message for all the people in Fort Simpson. He speak strong words about Native Rights and independence. The Yellowknife TV station was there, and early next morning their tape run on the CBC and we get to see it in Fort Simpson.

"There ain't nowhere in the world you can escape from the CBC," is what Frank says, and I guess it is true.

Just like the producer say, at 11:00 P.M. that night they announce that the Pope's visit to Fort Simpson is cancelled forever. The Pope will fly to Ottawa as planned. "Serious consideration was given to a Fort Simpson visit," they say, "but it would have ruined the Ottawa program."

"We all know they wouldn't want to ruin anything for the fat cats in Ottawa," laugh one of the reporters. "Even the Pope can't pass up the bureaucrats. I wonder how many of them came a thousand miles in a canoe down dangerous rivers to see him?"

The words of the cancellation announcement ain't cold in the air before the fog lift like it was being vacuumed, in ten minutes a butter-yellow moon and stars like tinsel light up the night.

The big surprise on the TV show from Yellowknife is that on the balcony of the hotel, where the Pope speak to about 20 microphones, right beside him, the purple circle on the front of her dress pulsing like a strobe light, was Mad Etta. Etta smiling like she know more secrets than the Pope, and, as he wave to his friends, she wave to hers.

BEEF

Sometimes being cheated ain't as bad as it made out to be. Back over a hundred years ago when the Government take the prairies away from the Indians and give us back these little reservations, our Chief Three Eagles make his mark to an agreement that, to help us Indians become farmers, the Government going to give every family two to four cows depend on its size.

But Three Eagles wouldn't accept the gift. I seen picture of Three Eagles wearing a breastplate, decked out in buckskin, feathers, and beaded wampum. He have the proud face of a hunter and warrior, and he wasn't about to be a farmer.

"I am not a tree," is what Three Eagles said. "My people do not root themselves to the land; we are traveling people. Indians soar like the birds. Just as the white man is a pale ghost of the Indian, so cattle are weak ghosts of buffalo. Farms are prisons. You do not put an eagle in a square cage."

It lucky Three Eagles died young.

We didn't know any of this history until I read in a magazine about how some Blackfoot Indians down south of Calgary just last year hit up the Government for the cattle they was supposed to have got in 1877. They got a priest to do the research that prove their Chief Crowfoot refused the cattle, but that the Indians was still entitled.

Biggest surprise though was that it being an election year, the Government coughed up, not cattle but money.

The magazine explain it this way. "Both sides agreed early on that it would be foolish for the government to drive that big a herd onto the reserve: sorting, distributing, branding and fencing would have been virtually impossible."

Instead, every person on the reserve got $25 in cash money, and another 1.6 million dollars went to the tribe's bank account.

I showed the article to Bedelia Coyote.

"If it happened to the Blackfoot, I bet it happen to us Cree, too," I say. "I sure wouldn't mind that $25."

"You think small," says Bedelia. "You should be looking at the 1.6 million. Oh, what I could do with that . . ."

Bedelia is one of a group of young people has started a Back To The Land Movement. They think they can go back in the hills, hunt, trap, and live off the land like the old-time Indians did.

Myself, I'm kind of fond of electricity, cars and televisions. But if that's what they want to do . . .

Bedelia take the case to a priest of our own, Fr. Alphonse up at Blue Quills School. He head right off to Edmonton to check over papers at the Parliament building and Provincial Museum. Guess he's happy to have something to make him feel useful. He don't have much success turning Indians into Christians, and spend most of his time read books in his office and say Mass for two or three old women in babushkas.

To shorten up the story, it turn out we got the same claim as the Blackfoot, only there more people on Hobbema Reserve, so we have more cattle and money due us.

I lose interest after a while, but Bedelia and Fr. Alphonse push right on, even get the story and their pictures in *Alberta Report* magazine one time.

It take two years but the Government offer up something called Treaty 11, which offer the Ermineskin Reserve 4,000 cows and 40 bulls.

"What about the money?" say Bedelia.

"That's just another part of the process," say Fr. Alphonse. "We formally refuse the cattle and ask for money instead. We have to put it all in writing and it will take another year or two to resolve. We'll ask for the value of the cattle, plus compound interest for the last hundred years . . ."

"I'd rather have the cattle," says my friend Frank Fencepost. "If the tribe got a million dollars, you figure Chief Tom and his friends gonna let us get our hands on any of it?"

Frank and his girlfriend Connie Bigcharles has joined this here Back To The Land Movement though I'm not sure why. Only tool Frank really capable with is a bottle opener. As for Connie, she like tight sweaters, white lipstick and her "Powwow Blaster" radio, that all silver, big as a suitcase and can shake leaves off trees when the volume is up. Connie ain't never farmed in her life. She don't even grow houseplants.

I never thought I'd say this, but I think maybe it was a mistake for Frank Fencepost to learn to read and write. Ever since he done that, it open up to him about a hundred more ways to get into trouble.

Frank has learned to read upside down, so just by standing across Fr. Alphonse's desk he can read the name and address of the bureaucrat in Ottawa that the Ermineskin Nation Back To The Land Movement deals with.

Frank he grin like a Japanese general while he write to the Government say we happy to accept their offer of cattle and could they ship 400 a month until we get all of them. And he sign the letter Fr. Alphonse Fencepost, Instrument of God. "*Fr.* could stand for Frank, couldn't it," say Frank. I suggest he send it to the Department of Graft, Patronage and Corruption, but Frank copy out the real return address from the envelope.

"Don't mess with your spiritual adviser," he tell me.

The Government write direct to Frank agree to send us the stock 400 at a time. And it coming in the name of the Ermineskin Nation Back To The Land Movement, Ms. Bedelia Coyote Executive Director. So there's no way Chief Tom can get his greedy hands on the cattle or the money they going to make for us.

"No problems," say Frank. "We just put the cattle to graze in the hills. The bulls make the cows pregnant. Our herd grows. We sell off the calves and yearlings—invest the money in real estate . . ."

"What about Back To The Land?"

"Hey, land is land. I'm gonna build my ranchhouse in Wetaskiwin; it have a three-storey, twelve-suite apartment block attached to it."

But first we have to do a lot of work. We build a corral between Ben Stonebreaker's store and our row of cabins on the hill. We will put the first 400 cattle there, herd them in little groups to the pasture land. When we get the first 400 settled, we order 400 more.

The Bank of Montreal in Wetaskiwin after we show them the letter actually loan us some money to buy fence posts and log poles to make a corral. Out of that money Frank he buy himself a silk western shirt, cowboy boots, a ten-gallon white hat and a string tie.

"Just call me J. 'Tex' Fencepost," he says, and walk around with his chest pushed out, supervise the rest of us as we dig post holes and nail the poles into place with 6" blue spikes.

Fr. Alphonse sure is surprised when he get a letter from the Department of Indian Affairs say they can't honor his refusal of the cattle because they is already on their way to us, and we should try to get our records in order.

Fr. Alphonse and Bedelia do a little investigating and discover what Frank has done.

"How could you do something so stupid?" roar Bedelia. Me and Rufus Firstrider is working on the corral. Frank laying down in the shade, his cowboy hat pulled down until his face don't show at all.

"Show a little respect for your ranch foreman," say Frank. "Besides, what's stupid? We got 400 cattle arriving, and they gonna come 400 a month almost forever. We get to keep the money we make. We all gonna be rich ranchers. Gonna call my spread the Ponderosa."

"We were going to do something positive," say Bedelia with less anger than I expected. "You'll be sorry," she predict before she stomp off.

As usual, Bedelia turn out to be right.

We actually get the corral finished the day before the first cattle due to arrive. I read somewhere about this here guy named Murphy who has a law about *Whatever can go wrong will go wrong.* I bet Murphy was an Ermineskin Indian.

Boy, we sure is excited when that first cattle transport turn off the highway and onto the main street of Hobbema. Little kids and old people are all along the street waving pennants left over from when the Edmonton Oilers won the Stanley Cup for hockey. People toot their car horns and wave.

The truck back up to the corral, let down its end gate and the first Herefords, with wine-colored bodies and square white faces, step down onto the reserve. Eathen Firstrider, Ducky Cardinal, Gerard Many Hands High, and a couple of other guys who worked the rodeo circuit are there on their ponies to guide the cattle into the corral.

The second truck waiting to unload when the first one is empty. Then another one, and another, and another. Each truck hold about 35–40 cattle, and after a while it seem to me there is close to 400 cows in the corral. But when I look toward the highway there are cattle transports lined all the way down the hill and about four deep all along main street.

It seem some clerk in the Government in Ottawa add an extra zero to our order. And there is 4000 cattle arriving instead of 400.

"It ain't our problem," the truck drivers say. "Our orders are to deliver these cattle to Hobbema. This here is Hobbema. If you ain't got a corral, we'll just drop them in the street."

And they do.

By the end of that day there is more white-faced cattle on the Hobbema Reserve than there is Indians. The corral get so full it start to bulge at the seams. Then come a couple of trucks say they carrying the bulls.

"Can't turn these dudes loose," a truck driver say. "They're mean mothers if I ever seen some."

We have to chase a few hundred cattle out onto the street so the bulls can go into the corral.

"They must weigh 5000 lbs. each," says Frank, watching the wide, squat Hereford bulls wobble into the corral on their square, piano-legs. Each one got a bronze ring in his flat pink nose.

"Lookit the equipment on them suckers," says Frank. "I bet that's what I was in a former life."

"In the present one," says Connie, and Frank grin big.

The trucks just keep unloading. I guess word must work back to the end of the line that we ain't got no more corral space. Some of the trucks way out by the highway drop their loads and sneak away. Soon all the trucks are doing that. The main street of Hobbema look like a movie I seen once of a cattle drive somewhere in the Wild West of about a hundred years ago.

The cattle fill up the school grounds and is munching grass among tombstones in the graveyard behind the Catholic church. One step up on the porch of Ben Stonebreaker's Hobbema General Store bite into a gunnysack of chicken feed and scatter it all about. Four or five more climb onto the porch and one get about halfway into the store before Ben's granddaughter Caroline beat it across the nose with a yard stick and make it back up.

My girlfriend's brother David One-wound have himself a still in a poplar grove a few hundred yards back of town. RCMP can't sniff out his business, but it only take the cattle a few minutes to find it.

"They could work for the RCMP, use them as tracking cattle," says Frank. "And they'd be close to being as smart," he say.

The cattle like the sugar in the throwed out mash, and some of them get as close to mean as these docile kind of cattle can.

Ben Stonebreaker has five cattle prods in his hardware department, and he sell them out in about five minutes. Mad Etta our medicine lady was herding three or four half-drunk cows out of her yard when

Ephrem Crookedneck, who decide to put as many cows as he can into his garden, what only fenced with chicken wire, and call them his own, either accidentally, or by mistake jab Mad Etta with his new electric cattle prod.

"Honest to God, I thought she was one of them. You seen her from behind. It was an honest mistake," he say, after the doctor taped up his cracked ribs and put his dislocated arm in a sling.

The cattle push up against the pumps at Fred Crier's Hobbema Texaco Garage, and before long one of the pumps leaning at a 45 degree angle. Old Peter Left Hand's chicken coop kind of sigh and fold up like a paper cut out, ruffled hens running everywhere, some squawking from inside the flattened building.

Traffic on Highway 2A is tied up, and somebody in a pickup truck hit a cow right in front of the Hobbema Pool Hall. Some young guys built a fire in a rusty oil drum and they barbecue the dead cow. Other guys is stripping down the pickup truck while the driver trying to call the RCMP.

"*We* is the law here," Rufus Firstrider tell the truck owner.

Constable Chretien and Constable Bobowski, the lady RCMP, come by, but there is some situations even too big for the RCMP. Constable Bobowski jump out of the patrol car, get shit on her boots, jump back in, then back out to wipe her feet on the grass. They stare through the windshield at the thousands of cattle milling around—some of them cattle bump pretty hard into the patrol car. Finally, they ease away a few feet at a time. I'm told they put detour signs on the highway a mile above and a mile before Hobbema.

It ain't near as much fun as we thought it would be to have 4000 cattle. Turns out nobody like our cattle very much. Cattle is dumb, and determined. They go just about anywhere they want to. They eat grass and gardens and leaves, knock down buildings, and some get in Melvin Dodging-horse's wheatfield, tramp down his crop. Six or seven of them eat until they die. Then they smell up the air on the whole reserve.

White farmers and even some Indians claim they going to sue the Ermineskin Nation Back To The Land Movement. The main street, and the gravel road to the highway, and even the walking paths is covered in cow shit. Seem like everyplace you can name is downwind of our herd.

It is also pretty hard to keep 40 bulls in a corral when there is close to 4000 cows outside the corral.

"Do something," everybody say to Bedelia Coyote and Fr. Alphonse. But there is a point where people get overwhelmed by a situation and Bedelia and Fr. Alphonse is in that position.

People try to get Chief Tom in on the act, but he stay in his apartment in Wetaskiwin with his girlfriend, Samantha Yellowknees, and after they put pressure on him, decide he have serious government business in California for the next month. Chief Tom don't like the smell of cattle no better than the rest of us.

Everybody grumble. But we got what we said we wanted. It pretty hard to complain about that.

Everybody now eat good anyway. Old hunters like William Irons and Dolphus Frying Pan, have a couple of cows skinned and quartered before you can say, "hunting season," and everybody got steak to fry and liver to cook. William and Dolphus have blood up to their elbows and they ain't smiled so broad since they got too old to go big-game hunting.

Next morning a tall cowboy arrive with a cattle transport offer to buy up cows at $400 each. He put down the ramp at the rear of his truck and pay cash money to whoever load an animal up. He load up 40 cows and promise to come back as soon as he can.

"If he's paying $400, these here animals must be worth a lot more," says Frank.

All the time the truck was being loaded, Bedelia was yelling for them to stop, shouting about our heritage and don't sell the future for pocket money. But nobody pays any attention and somebody even shove her out of the way, hard.

Frank get Louis Coyote's pickup truck and using the same ramp we use to load Mad Etta when we want to take her someplace, we get three cows into the truck box rope them in pretty tight.

Frank he head for Weiller and Williams Stockyard in Edmonton.

Most of us don't really have any idea how much a cow is worth. But after Frank make that first trip to Edmonton he report, "They is paying 80¢ a pound and these cows weigh around 1000 to 1200 pounds." The three he crammed in Louis' pickup truck bring $2640 cash money.

When people find that out everybody want to get in on the act.

When the cattle transport come back, David One-wound announce we going to "nationalize" it and the driver just barely get away with his empty truck and ten guys yipping on his heels.

A couple of people load cows into their wagon boxes and start their teams out for the long trip to Edmonton.

Some of the young cowboys like Eathen Firstrider, Robert Coyote and Ducky Cardinal decide to do a real cattle drive and start about fifteen cows in the direction of Edmonton.

Some other people tie a rope to the neck of the tamest cow and lead her, walking in front of her, in the direction of Edmonton.

Bedelia is still yelling at people to stop and is still getting ignored. Fr. Alphonse gone back to his office at the Reserve School, wishing, I bet, that he'd never found out about us being cheated.

It is kind of sad to see all the crazy goings on. If we could just get organized we could make a lot of money for years and years to come. But people ain't ready to listen to Bedelia; they just go on their own way selling cattle here, there, and everywhere. Local white farmers stop people as they walk up the ditches offer less than half what the animal would bring in Edmonton. But people is too greedy to say no. Ogden Coyote trade a cow for a 10-speed bicycle, have bright pink tassels on the handlebars.

I remember reading in, I think it was *Time* magazine about how in Africa, when some little country that been a colony for a thousand years get its independence, the people don't know how to act. They spend foolishly, act like fools and their country end up in a terrible mess.

I wish I was a leader. I can see what should be done, but I don't know how to go about it. I'm a watcher.

"*You* could stop this foolishness," I say to Mad Etta. "People would listen to you. Why don't you do something?"

"Hey, they *are* doing what they want. Water rise to its own level. You put food in front of hungry people they going to eat good before they think about planting seeds for next year. Same with money. I know what should be done, but the people ain't ready for it yet. Maybe, Silas, when you're an old man . . ." and she stop and stare wistful off into the woods behind her cabin. "But in the meantime, I got a bull and six cows tethered in the pines down the hill. How soon you figure we can use Louis' truck to take them to Edmonton?"

The next morning Frank come bounding into my cabin, smiling like he just got it on with a movie star.

"Hey, Silas, our troubles are over," he yell. "I had me a dream last night and these here cattle going to make us rich."

"How are they gonna do that?"

"All we need is some old sheets and some paint."

"For what?"

"Hey, we gonna sell advertising space on our cattle." Frank is grinning so wide I'm afraid he's gonna dislocate his ears.

"That's crazy."

"No it's not," and Frank jump up on a kitchen chair, then jump off quick, run to my bed and pull a sheet off with one hard yank, leave the rest of the blankets and Sadie right where they were. He set two chairs about four feet apart and drape the sheet over the chair backs.

"Pretend that's a cow. We tie a sheet over her, then . . ." and he pull from his pocket a huge magic marker about the size of a shock absorber, and paint on the sheet HOBBEMA TEXACO GARAGE. "We do that on each side of the cow, then we put them to grazing along the highway. They'll be just like billboards."

No matter what I say to Frank, whether I laugh or make fun of his idea, he stick to his guns.

"There's only one thing to do," I say, "let's go make some sales calls."

In Wetaskiwin we get a parking place in front of Mr. Larry's Men's Wear, COUTURIER TO THE DISCRIMINATING GENTLEMAN.

We troop inside.

"We're here to see Mr. Larry," I say to a tall man dressed so fancy he could lay right down in a coffin and feel at home.

"I am Lawrence Oberholtzer, the proprietor."

"I'm Frank Fencepost, ace advertising salesman. How do you like me so far?" and Frank stick out his hand grab one of Mr. Larry's long pale hands that was by his side, and shake hearty.

"I would just as soon not answer that," he say, his voice able to freeze water or shrivel plants.

"I'm gonna show you how to become the richest businessman in Wetaskiwin."

"I already *am* the richest man in Wetaskiwin," say Mr. Larry. "Now please get to the point."

"How would you like to have 4000 cattle with your name on them?"

"Don't tell me; you're cattle rustlers."

Frank explain his idea.

"You can even advertise on more than one cow. Show him, Silas. This is my assistant Silas Running-up-the-riverbank."

Mr. Larry nod at me.

"Picture your cows grazing in a row beside the highway, Mr. Larry."

I take out four sheets I been carrying, unfold them, drape them over racks of suits. When I finished they read like this:

THIS HERE STORE
IS A FANCY PLACE

SHIRTS & SUITS
FOR EVERY RACE

CHINK OR JAP

CHRISTIAN OR JEW

MR. LARRY'S
IS THE STORE FOR YOU.

Frank he look so self-satisfied he just know it is impossible for Mr. Larry to turn him down.

Out on the street we gather up the sheets from where Mr. Larry threw them and decide to call on Union Tractor Company.

Six businesses later, we put the sheets in the truck and head for the Alice Hotel to have a beer.

"They'll be sorry," says Frank. "I can't help it if I fifty years ahead of my time."

The cattle problem solve itself, sort of like flood water recede slow until you never know the water been high at all.

Everybody on the reserve eat good for a few weeks. The old hunters is happy as pigs in a barnyard. A lot of us carry cattle off to sell in Edmonton. Louis Coyote buy twin Ski-Doos for him and Mrs. Blind Louis.

I buy me a new typewriter but it ain't no smarter than my old one, so it get pushed to the back of the kitchen table and my little sister Delores, who claim she going to tell stories just like me, pound on it once in a while.

Frank buy a video recorder and him and Connie pick out about a hundred movies. Frank is working on tapping into the power line to the UGG Elevator so's they can watch movies soon as they get a TV, which Frank is working on too.

Mad Etta was about the only smart one, she corral two of them Hereford bulls, and got them in separate pens behind her cabin. We drive her around to local farms and she sell their services.

"Etta ain't going to go hungry for a while," she says, rocking back and forth on her tree-trunk chair. "It sure nice to be supported by some-body who enjoy their work," she say and laugh and laugh.

"It's back to the drawing board for us," say Bedelia and Fr. Alphonse. "We got a lot of work to do yet," they say. According to them, the Cattle Treaty was only one of 23 claims outstanding. They going after money for land of ours been given away, used for highways, irrigation canals, and Government Experimental Farms.

"Anytime you need help negotiating," says Frank, "the great Fencepost is available, free of charge."

Frank never quite understand why they don't answer him back.

DISTANCES

The Cadillac was the color of thick, rich cream. It pulled up in front of Mrs. Richards's Springtime Café and Ice Cream Parlor. The main street of Onamata was paved, but the pavement was narrow; there was six feet of gravel between the edge of the pavement and the wooden sidewalk. Dust from the gravel whooshed past the car and oozed through the screen door of the café.

My friend Stan Rogalski and I were seated at a tile table, our feet hooked on the insect-legged chairs. We were sharing a dish of vanilla ice cream, savoring each bite, trying to make it outlast the heat of high July.

It was easy to tell the Cadillac owner was a man who cared about his car. He checked his rearview carefully before opening the driver's door. After he got out, or *unwound* would be a better description, for he was six foot five if he was an inch, he closed the door gently but firmly, then wiped something off the sideview mirror. On the way around the Caddy he picked something off the grille and flicked it onto the road.

He took a seat in a corner of the café where he could watch his car and everyone else in the café, which at the moment was me, Stan, and Mrs. Richards. My name is Gideon Clarke.

The stranger looked to be in his mid-thirties; he had rusty hair combed into a high pompadour that accentuated his tall front teeth and made his face look longer than it really was. Across his upper lip was a wide mustache with the corners turned up; the mustache was the same coppery red as the hair on his head. I guessed he'd worn his hair in a spiffy duck-ass cut in the fifties, but now the duck ass was out of style. Elvis was being replaced by Chubby Checker, and it would be a long time before long hair was in fashion in the Midwest. The stranger's hair was combed back at the sides, hiding the top half of his ears. At the back, it covered his collar and turned up a little at the ends.

"I'd like something tall and cool," he said when Mrs. Richards waddled over to his table.

"I have pink lemonade," she said in a tiny voice that belied her 250 pounds.

"I'll have the biggest size you've got," he said.

After Mrs. Richards delivered the lemonade in a sweaty, opaque glass, he took a long drink, stretched his legs, and looked around the room. He was wearing a black suit with fine gray pinstripes, a white-on-white shirt, and shoes that must have cost fifty dollars.

"What do you figure he does?" whispered Stan. When I didn't answer quickly he went on. "A banker, I bet, or an undertaker, maybe."

"He's suntanned," I said. "And look at his hands." The knuckles were scarred, the fingers calloused.

"What then?"

"Howdy, boys," the stranger said, and raised his glass to us. His voice was deep and soft.

"Hi," we said.

"I see you're ballplayers," he said, nodding toward our gloves, which rested on the floor by the chair legs. "Is there much baseball played in these parts?"

The question was like opening a floodgate. Stan and I told him about everything from the Little League to the Onamata High School team we played for to the University of Iowa ball club to the commercial leagues that had teams in Iowa City, Onamata, Lone Tree, West Branch, and other nearby towns.

"How did your team do this year?" he asked us, not in the way most adults have of patronizing young people, but with genuine interest.

"Well," I said, "we were two and nineteen for the season. But we're really a lot better ball club than that," I rushed on before he could interrupt. The stranger didn't laugh as most adults would have. "I kept statistics. We scored more runs than any team in the league. We're good hitters, average fielders, but we didn't have anyone who could pitch. A bad team gets beat seventeen to two. We would get beat seventeen to fourteen, nineteen to twelve, eighteen to sixteen. We're really good hitters, especially Stan here. Stan's gonna make it to the Bigs."

"I practice three hours a day, all year round," said Stan, picking up my enthusiasm. "In winter I throw in the loft of our barn."

"Then you'll probably make it," said the stranger.

"You look like you might be a player yourself," I said.

"I've pitched a few innings in my day," he said with what I recognized as understatement, and he rose from his chair and made his way, with two long strides, to our table.

"The thought struck me that you boys might like another dish of ice cream."

"You've had a good thought," said Stan.

"I notice my lemonade cost twenty-five cents, as does a dish of ice cream. I might be willing to make a small wager."

"What kind?" we both said, staring up at him.

"Well now, I'm willing to bet I can tell you the exact distance in miles between any two major American cities."

"How far is it from Iowa City to Davenport?" said Stan quickly.

"Those are not major American cities," said the stranger, "but I noticed as I was driving in that the distance was sixty-two miles. What I had in mind, though, were large cities. Des Moines would qualify, as would Kansas City, New Orleans, Los Angeles, Seattle, Dallas."

"How far from New York to Chicago?" said Stan.

"Exactly 809 miles," said the stranger.

"How do we know you're not making that up?" I said.

"A good question," said the stranger. "Out in my car I have a road atlas and inside it is a United States mileage chart. If one of you boys would like to get it for me . . ." As he spoke he reached a large hand into a side pocket and withdrew his keys. I grabbed them and was halfway across the room before Stan could untangle his feet from the chair legs.

The interior of the car was still cool from the air conditioning. It smelled of leather and lime aftershave. There was nothing in sight except a State Farm road atlas on the white leather of the front seat. The very neatness of the car told a lot about its owner, I thought: neat, methodical, the type of man who would care about distances.

I carried the atlas into the café, where the stranger was now seated across the table from Stan.

"Let's just check out New York to Chicago," he said. "There's always a chance I could be wrong."

He turned to the United States Mileage Chart, and all three of us studied it for a moment. In groups of five, in alphabetical order, there were eighty cities listed down the side of the chart; sixty names were across the top. Where the two names intersected was the mileage be-tween them.

"Yes, sir, 809 miles, just as I said." The stranger put a big, square finger tip down on the chart at the point where New York and Chicago intersected.

Up close, I noticed the stranger had a lantern jaw. He was also more muscular than I would have guessed, his shoulders square as a robot's. His eyes were golden.

I quickly calculated that there were nearly five thousand squares on the mileage chart. He can't know them all, I thought.

"Would either of you care to test me?" he asked, smiling. "By the way, my name's Roger Cash."

"Gideon Clarke," I said. "My friend, Stan Rogalski."

We both had money in our pockets, but we were saving for a trip to

Chicago. My father had promised to take us up for an entire Cubs home stand.

"Well . . ."

"No bets, then. Just name some places. Distances are my hobby."

"Omaha and New Orleans," I said.

"1026," Roger Cash replied, after an appropriate pause.

We checked it and he was right.

"St. Louis to Los Angeles," said Stan.

"Exactly 1836 miles," said Roger.

Again he was right.

"Milwaukee to Kansas City," I said.

"1779," he replied quickly.

We checked the chart.

"Wrong!" we chorused together. "It's 1797."

"Doggone, I tend to reverse numbers sometimes," he said with a grin. "Seeing as how I couldn't do it three times in a row, I'll buy you men a dish of ice cream each, or something larger if you want. A banana split? You choose."

It wasn't often we could afford top-of-the-line treats. I ordered a banana split with chopped almonds and chocolate sauce on all three scoops of ice cream. Stan ordered a tall chocolate malt, thick as cement. Roger had another lemonade.

"What made you memorize the mileage chart?" I asked between mouthfuls.

"Nothing made me," said Roger, leaning back and stretching out his legs. "I spend a lot of time traveling, a lot of nights alone in hotel rooms. It passes the time, beats drinking or reading the Gideon Bible. No offense," he then said to me. "I don't suppose that book's named after you anyway."

"No, sir, I reckon it wasn't."

"I've been known to gamble," he went on, "on my ability to remember mileages, on the outcome of baseball games in which I am the pitcher. Never gamble unless the odds are on your side."

"Do you pitch for anyone in particular?" I asked.

"I tried to take a team barnstorming one season. Unfortunately that era is long gone. I used to watch the House of David and the Kansas City Monarchs on tour when I was a kid. Costs too much to support a traveling team these days, and television has killed attendance at minor-league parks. No, what I do now is arrange for a pickup team to back me up—play an exhibition game against a well-known local team. . . . Say . . ." he said, and paused as if he had just been struck by a brilliant idea. "Do you suppose you men could round up the rest of your high school team? What did you say the name of this town is?"

"Onamata," we said together. "And sure, most of the players live on farms around here. We could round up a full team with no trouble at all."

"Well, in that case I think we might be able to arrange a business proposition," he said.

For the next few minutes, while Roger Cash outlined his plans, Stan and I nodded at his every suggestion. It was obvious he had done this kind of thing many times before.

All the time he was talking I had been eyeing the mileage chart, searching for an easily reversible number.

"Have you spotted one that will beat me?" Roger said suddenly.

"Maybe."

"You want to put some money on it?"

"A dollar," I said, and gulped; I could feel the pace of my heart pick up.

"Yer on," he said, turning his head away from where the chart lay open on the tabletop. "Name the cities."

"Albuquerque to New York."

Roger laughed. "You picked one of the hardest. A mileage easy to reverse. Now if I wanted to win your dollar I'd say '1997.'" He paused for one beat. I could feel my own heart bump, for the number he gave was right. "But if I wanted to set you up to bet five dollars on the next combination, I'd say '1979.' I might miss the next one, too. People are greedy and they like to take money from a stranger. I might even miss a third or fourth time, and I always leave the chart out where a man

131

with a sharp eye can spot another easily reversible number. You men aren't old enough to go in bars, or I'd show you how it works in actual practice."

I took out my wallet and lifted out a dollar.

"No," said Roger. "Experience. I'll chalk that dollar up to *your* experience. I have a mind for distances. I once read a story about a blind, retarded boy who played the piano like a master. And I heard about another man who can tell you what day of the week any date in history, or future history, was or will be. I have an idiot's talent for distances."

"What's so great about distances?" said Stan. "I think if I was smart I'd choose something else to be an expert on."

"Let me tell you about distances," said Roger, his golden eyes like coins with black shadows at the center. "Six or eight inches doesn't make any difference if the distance is, say, between Des Moines and Los Angeles, right?"

We nodded in agreement.

"Now suppose you're in bed with your girlfriend." He moved forward, hunching over the table, lowering his voice, because over behind the counter Mrs. Richards was doing her best to hear all of our conversation. "Suppose your peter won't do what it's supposed to do. If it won't produce that six or eight inches, no matter how close you are to pussy, you might as well be 1709 miles away, which is how far it is from Des Moines to Los Angeles." We all sat back and laughed. At the counter Mrs. Richards smiled crossly.

"The distances in baseball are perfect," Roger went on, "ninety feet from base to base, sixty feet six inches from the mound to the plate. Not too far, not too close. Change any one of them six or eight inches, the length of your peter, and the whole game would be out of kilter."

We nodded, wide-eyed.

"Well, since we've got a team, all we have to do is find ourselves an opponent," said Roger. "Here's what I have in mind. Who's the best pitcher in these parts?"

"That would be Silas Erb," I said. "Chucks for Procter and Gamble in the Division One Commercial League."

"Is he crafty or a hardball thrower?"

"Ninety miles an hour straight down the middle, dares anybody to hit it."

"Scratch him. I want a guy who's a curve baller, maybe tries to throw a screwball, has a wicked change."

"That'd be McCracken. McCracken Construction have been Division One champs two years in a row."

"And he owns the company?"

"His daddy does."

"Would he be the kind to accept a challenge from an elderly baseball pitcher with a two-and-nineteen high school team on the field in back of him?"

"Who wouldn't?"

"If we were to get posters printed and build up this challenge game, what sort of attendance do you men think we could expect here in Onamata?"

"People are hungry for baseball," I said. "The King and His Court fast-ball team drew over a thousand in Iowa City in June. I think we could get five or six hundred out to Onamata for a game like that."

"At three dollars a head?"

"Sounds fair."

Roger Cash grinned, the right side of his mouth opening up to show his dice-like teeth. I noticed then, even while he had a suit on, that his right bicep was huge, many inches larger than the left one.

"Would you men care to accompany me into Iowa City this evening? You could point out Mr. McCracken's residence to me. We'll discuss our financial situation at the same time."

What he proposed to McCracken that night was a winner-take-all game, the Onamata High School team with Roger Cash pitching against

McCracken Construction, Division One Champs and one of the best commercial league teams in the state.

"'And of course,' I said to him," Cash told us later, "'I'll be happy to cover any wagers you, your teammates, or the good citizens of Iowa City or Onamata might like to make, all in strictest confidence of course.'

"'At what odds?' McCracken said to me.

"'Even odds, of course,' I said. 'Roger Cash is not greedy.' And you should have seen him smile.

"'I'd like to see you work out,' McCracken said to me.

"'Oh no,' I said. 'The element of surprise is all I've got on my side. I hear tell you played in Triple A for a year, so it's not likely anything an old pitcher like me can throw will surprise you. Myself, I played a dozen games one summer for a Class C team in Greensboro, North Carolina, but they didn't pay me enough to keep my mustache waxed so I moved on. Actually they suggested I move on, but that's another story.' I smiled real friendly at him."

Back in Onamata, after the game was set, Roger led us to the trunk of his car. As he opened the trunk of the cream-colored Caddy, Stan and I were on our tiptoes, staring over and around him. The trunk was almost as austere as the car interior. It contained a black valise, very old, almost triangular, with heavy brass latches, and a canvas duffel bag with a pair of worn black baseball cleats tied around the drawstring at its neck. A few garden tools were cast diagonally in the trunk: a rake, a hoe, a small spoon-nosed shovel. There was no spare wheel, and built into the depression where the wheel would ordinarily have been was what looked like a small, black safe, anchored in concrete in the wheel well. There was no dirt or dust, nothing extraneous.

"We're going to need some money to finance the operation," he said, and smiled slowly, lines appearing in the deeply tanned skin around his eyes. "I'll have to ask you gentlemen to turn your backs while I operate on Black Betsy here. I'd also be obliged if you kept the secret of her existence among the three of us."

The final statement was a command, though it wasn't worded like one. Stan and I busied ourselves staring up and down the street and studying the front of the Springtime Café while Roger Cash turned the dial on the safe. It made sounds like a bicycle lock.

"You can turn around now," he said.

The safe was stuffed with money. I have no idea how much, though I did see that most of the bills were hundreds.

The deal was that each of the eight players to back him up were to get twenty dollars for the game. Stan and I got more for distributing 250 posters to businesses in downtown Iowa City and Onamata. We also distributed a thousand handbills to homes, as well as placing them on car windshields. And we were to be paid for selling tickets right up until game time. Roger suggested that we arrange to sell hot dogs, soda, and popcorn, since no one ever bothered to do that at the Onamata Baseball Grounds. He even peeled off a few bills from a collar-sized roll he carried, advancing us enough to buy and rent what supplies we needed, as well as to hire people for the concessions. In return, we were to split the profits. In the next few days Stan and I felt like real business-men, going around hiring women three times our age to work for us the next Sunday.

Roger needed a place to stay. There was no hotel in Onamata, never had been. I was quick to volunteer our home, where my father and I lived alone in an elegant old frame house with a wrought-iron widow's walk. My father was engaged in a peculiar baseball research project, which took up most of his time. He left the operation of Clarke and Son Insurance to his secretary.

"I need to ask you for another favor," Roger said the next morning. "I need a place to work out, a private place. An old dog like me has to have surprise on his side. I don't want McCracken or any of his spies to see me pitch until game time."

"I think I can arrange that," I said. "My friends have a farm a mile from town. Mr. and Mrs. Baron are like grandparents to me. I know we can set up in their pasture."

A quick trip to Barons' and we were able to find a natural pitcher's mound in the pasture below the house. A few minutes with the tools from Roger's trunk, and we imbedded a length of two-by-four in the mound. We dug a small depression and inset two pieces of wood side by side to form a crude plate after Roger had produced a well-worn tape from his duffel bag and measured out the exact distance from home to the pitcher's mound. I held the beginning of the tape on the mound while he measured to the spot where home plate should be.

Roger then dug out his glove and a ball. He gave me the glove and threw a few practice pitches while I crouched behind the newly installed plate. I guess I was expecting Sandy Koufax, because after about fifteen pitches I said, with that terrible candor the young consider honesty, "You're not very good."

"You haven't seen me with an enemy batter at the plate," he replied. "I may not look like much, and I'm no Juan Marichal, but I change speeds, keep the hitters off balance; keeping hitters off balance is a pitcher's most important function."

Since the game was set for the following Sunday afternoon, the preparations kept Stan and me running all week. Tuesday night we scouted McCracken Construction during a league game in Iowa City. McCracken pitched; he was a stocky, barrel-chested man with blue-black hair. He pitched a three-hitter. Roger made notes on the batters he would have to face.

After the game we discussed strategy.

"I'm gonna have you lead off," Roger said to me. I had kept statistics on our team's whole season, and I showed them to Roger. Stan kept track of only his own batting average; I took home scorecards after each game and calculated everyone's batting average, on-base percentage, and fielding average.

"I'm slow on the bases," I said. "I never honestly stole a base all season."

"You get on, though," he said. "You hit singles, and more importantly, you walk. Walks are very important. You need patience to walk. I'm going to put my batters up in the order of their patience."

"I don't understand," I said. "McCracken has great control."

"It's a strategy," said Roger, as he smiled disarmingly.

We had one practice Friday evening. I'm afraid we didn't look very good. Someone from McCracken's team sat in a pickup truck about three blocks down the street, studying us through binoculars. Roger did not pitch. Our regular pitcher, Dusty Swan, threw batting practice.

"I want you guys to lay back and wait for the fast ball," Roger told us. "McCracken's got a killer curve, a mean slider, a big-league change-up you can break your back on, but his fast ball's nothing; he uses it to set up his other pitches. If we can keep from swinging at anything outside the strike zone, he'll give up lots of walks. Then he'll have to throw the fast ball, and when he does we'll hammer it."

All that week Roger worked out at Barons' in the afternoons, but at night he played the mileage game in every bar in Iowa City. According to the stories we heard, he picked up several hundred dollars each night. It was also a way for Roger to become known quickly, assuring a good crowd at the ball game on Sunday. At the end of his third day in town he had a very pretty coed from the University of Iowa on his arm. Her name was Jacqueline, and she spent the rest of the nights that week in Roger's room, except the night before the big game.

"Do you have any objection, Mr. Clarke," Roger said to my father our first night at supper together, "to my having occasional female company in my room?"

My father looked up from the page of statistics he was studying as he ate, stared at Roger, blinking, perhaps trying to remember who he was.

"Oh no," he said, smiling almost shyly. "You can bring a goat to your room as far as I'm concerned, as long as you're quiet."

It was during that same week that I found out a lot about distances myself. Most of my friends had not discovered girls yet. Oh, we talked about them individually and collectively, usually in a disparaging manner, repeating gossip we heard from older boys at the café or the pool hall. Stan went to the movies in Iowa City a few times with a pale blonde girl named Janice, who wore no lipstick or makeup because her family belonged to some fanatical religious splinter group that thought the end of the world imminent, and taught that we all should be in a natural state when the end came.

"I asked her why she wore clothes," said Stan, after his third and final date. The only reason her parents let her go out with Stan was that he appeared to be a likely candidate for conversion.

The third evening, when they arrived back at her house after the show (her father drove them to the theater and picked them up at the Hamburg Inn afterward), their preacher, a Pastor Valentine, and eight members of the congregation were camped in the living room, which Stan said was decorated like a church interior. Pastor Valentine conducted a service where everyone prayed loud and long for Stan's wandering soul. They said many unkind things about the Catholic Church in general and the Pope in particular, having assumed wrongly that Stan was a practicing Roman Catholic. Stan's family were actually lapsed Catholics with no church affiliation.

That summer I was in love for the first time. Her name was Julie Dornhoffer, and I had become enamored of her just at the end of the school year. She was a robust farm girl, almost my height, and a good fifteen pounds heavier. But she had a healthy quality about her and she always looked me in the eye when we talked. She sometimes drove a four-ton grain truck to school. I liked her straightforwardness, her toughness. I have always been repelled by delicate girls in pastels and cosmetics. Julie tolerated my interest, but made it clear she would prefer a more masculine beau. She teased me about my ignorance of farms and was slightly contemptuous of my physical strength. Also, I didn't drive yet. Julie had been driving farm equipment since she was ten.

I called on her about once a week, walking the three miles of unpaved road to the farm. She would entertain me in the dark parlor of the house, or we would walk in the sweet dusk, watching fireflies rising, sparkling, dissolving in our path. We even kissed a few times. But I knew my interest in her was much greater than her interest in me.

A couple of days after Roger Cash arrived in town, I walked out to the Dornhoffer farm. I arrived at midafternoon on a high-skied, blazing day. The farmhouse was tall and sad-looking, badly in need of paint. I knocked at the side door, and a large woman whom I recognized as one of Julie's aunts answered, wiping perspiration from her forehead with the back of her hand.

"Julie and her sister're coiling hay back in the north pasture," she said. I could not see into the house because of the thick screen on the door, but from the dark interior came the smell of pork roast, the fumes mouth-watering, almost tangible.

I walked through a grove of trees, enjoying the coolness in the midst of the fiery day. I picked a bluebell or two, split the bell, and rooted out the teardrop of honey inside the flower.

On the other side of the trees was a small field of red clover. Half of it had recently been swathed. Julie and a younger sister were at work with pitchforks, layering the hay into coils, which when finished resembled giant beehives.

"You townies don't know how good you've got it," Julie said, driving the tines into the earth, stilling the vibrating fork handle, then leaning on it as if it were a tree. She was flushed and perspiring. Her copper-colored hair spilled over her forehead and was flecked with clover seeds. She wore jeans and a short-sleeved blouse the color of wild roses. The back and underarms of the blouse were soaked dark. She wasn't wearing a bra. I realized that even after my three-mile walk I was still cool. I was wearing a white, open-necked shirt and khaki shorts. My own hair was white as vanilla ice cream, and I was hardly tanned at all. Julie's arms and face were sun-blackened, her hair bleached golden in spots.

"Can I help?" I said, hoping somehow to win her favor.

"Sure," she said, smiling too knowingly, as if there was some private joke I was not in on. "Beat it," she said to her sister, and the younger girl stabbed her fork into the ground and raced off, happy to be relieved of an unpleasant job.

I have probably never worked as hard as I did in the next fifteen minutes and accomplished less. I might as well have been trying to coil water with that pitchfork. I babbled on about my friend Roger Cash, the upcoming baseball game, mileages, distances, posters, concessions, all the while accumulating a pitiful pile of clover in front of me. No matter what I did to it, it had no resemblance to the waist-high beehives Julie and her sister had created; in each coil they had made the hay was swirled, the swaths interlocked, impervious to wind, resistant to rain.

While I worked and talked Julie relaxed, sitting back in the shade of a green coil, smoking, a crockery water jug bathed in condensation beside her.

I finally gave up and joined her, red-faced and disheveled.

"It's not as easy as it looks," I said.

Julie grinned with what I hoped was tolerance rather than contempt.

"You people in town live so far away," she said, her tone still not definable.

"It's only three miles," I said stupidly.

Julie crushed out her cigarette in the earth beside her. She looked at me with a close-lipped smile. "At least you tried," she said, and leaned over so her head rested on my shoulder.

We kissed, both our faces damp from the heat of the day. The smell of freshly cut clover was overpowering. Julie slid closer to me, crossed one of my bare legs with her denim one. She radiated heat. Her breasts burned against my chest, only two thin layers of cloth separating us. Her tongue was deep in my mouth, her large right hand gripped hard on my left shoulder. She was forcing me down onto my back, pushing me deep into the sweet clover. I didn't mind that she was stronger than I was; there was nothing I could do about that; it even excited me. I ran my free hand down the thigh of her jeans, let it find its way between her legs.

We stopped kissing and gasped for breath.

"I bet I could take you," Julie said into my neck, and I knew by her tone that she meant in physical strength.

"You probably could," I said, sitting up, gasping for air. "What does it matter? You work hard, I don't—" But she forced me back down, my head going deep into the hay. All the sexuality of the moment was gone. This was a contest. Julie's hands were on my shoulders. Her right leg was between my thighs; she held my back down flat on the stubbly earth.

I had no experience roughhousing with girls. My own sister, a year older than me, had always been a deadly serious child, resentful and threatening, someone I avoided physical contact with.

My worst fear, a fear I was almost certain was a truth, was that Julie would *care* about being able to outwrestle me. How hard should I defend myself? I'd taken a few wrestling lessons in physical education class. If I was to concentrate on one of her arms, get a solid lock on it . . . But I was flat on my back with Julie sitting on my chest. My shoulders were pinned to the earth, my head partially covered with clover, which choked my senses, the tiny red seeds filling my eyes and mouth, spilling down my neck.

I bucked ineffectually a few times.

"Okay, you've proved your point," I said.

Julie threw herself to one side and scrambled to her feet. I stood and brushed the clover seeds from my face and shirt front. I smiled at Julie, hoping to make a joke of my defeat. But what I read in her eyes said that I was never to be forgiven for my weakness. I was walking toward her with the idea of taking her in my arms, in spite of the coldness in her eyes, when her sister reappeared.

"We've got to get back to work," said Julie, dismissing me.

"I'll see you again," I said. Julie didn't reply.

As I walked slowly back toward Onamata, I knew I would never call on her again.

Saturday night, Roger went to bed about ten o'clock.

"Got to rest the old soupbone," he said, flexing his pitching arm, which was muscular and huge, as he headed up the stairs.

I went to bed shortly after him, but I couldn't sleep. My mind was too full of the game the next day; my thoughts were as much on the operation of the concessions as on baseball itself. I eventually dozed fitfully. Late in the night I woke with a start, surprised to hear the stairs creaking. I stretched out my arm and let the rays of moonlight slanting through the window touch the face of my watch. It was three A.M. I went to the window. I heard Roger's keys jingle in the darkness, watched as he opened the trunk to the Caddy and stealthily extracted the garden tools, hoisted them to his shoulder, and set off down the fragrant, moon-struck street.

About four-fifteen, just as the first tines of pink appeared on the horizon, Roger returned, replaced the gardening tools, and reentered the house.

By game time we had sold 511 tickets; I left Margie Smood at the ticket table to sell to latecomers until the fifth inning. The concessions were booming, and the air was riddled with the smell of frying onions, hot dogs, and popcorn. There was no fence around the ballfield. At Roger's suggestion, we constructed a funnel-like gate with pickets joined by flaming orange plastic ribbons. People were generally honest; only a few school kids and a handful of adults skirted the ticket line.

We were all nervous as we warmed up along the first-base side. One thing we forgot to tell Roger was that Onamata High had never been able to afford uniforms, so we wore whatever each of us could scrounge, from jeans, T-shirts, and sneakers to a full Detroit Tiger uniform worn by Lindy Dean, who was a cousin a couple of times removed from Dizzy Trout.

Across the way, McCracken Construction, in black uniforms with gold numbers on their chests and their names in gold letters on their backs, snapped balls back and forth with authority. Baseballs smacking into gloves sounded like balloons breaking.

"Where are the gate receipts?" Roger asked me.

"In a box under the ticket table. You don't need to worry. Margie Smood's honest."

"Go get them. Just leave her enough to change a twenty."

"But—"

"I've got to get down some more bets."

"What if we lose?"

"Never in doubt, Gideon. Never in doubt."

I brought him the money, and while the Onamata High School Music Makers Marching Band, all six of them, were assassinating the national anthem, Roger carried the money around behind the backstop, and held a conference with McCracken and his teammates.

The president of the University of Iowa was seated in the front row and he had apparently agreed to hold the bets. By the time the game started there were bags and boxes, envelopes and cartons, piled at his feet. As near as I could guess, Roger had about ten thousand dollars riding on the game, most of it covered by McCracken and members of his team.

Roger and McCracken continued to talk animatedly for several minutes. It was a long discussion, and finally McCracken went to his equipment bag and counted out more money; he also signed something. Roger dug into the back pocket of his uniform and produced the keys to his Caddy. He held them up and let the sun play on them for an instant, then dropped them in a box with the money and notes, which a bat boy carried over and deposited at the feet of the university president.

I noticed that McCracken seemed uncomfortable as he warmed up on the mound. One of the concessions Roger offered right off the top was, even though we were playing in Onamata, to allow McCracken Construction to be home team. I was right about McCracken being uncomfortable; he pawed the dirt and stalked around kicking at the rubber. The first three pitches he threw were low, one bouncing right on the plate. He threw the fast ball then, right down the heart of the plate for a strike. I was tempted to hammer it, but I held back, telling myself, a walk is as good as a single. McCracken was in trouble, I wasn't. He walked me with another low pitch. He walked Lindy Dean on five pitches. He walked Gussy Pulvermacher on four. As I moved to third, I watched Roger whispering in Stan's ear, a heavy arm around his shoulders.

The first pitch was low. The second broke into the dirt. McCracken kicked furiously at the mound. I could almost see Stan's confidence building as he waited. The fast ball came. He drove it into the gap in left-center. Stan had a standup double. Three of us scored in front of him, as Roger, leaping wildly in the third-base coach's box, waved us in.

McCracken was rattled now. It didn't help him that the crowd were mainly for us. Here was a high school team with a 2-19 season record going against a crack amateur team who were state champions two years before, and finalists the last year.

Our next batter walked on four pitches. Then McCracken settled down to his fast ball and struck out the sixth and seventh batters. Our catcher, Walt Swan, hammered the first pitch he got, about five hundred feet to deep left, nearly to the Iowa River. Fortunately for McCracken, the ball was foul. He reverted to his off-speed pitches and walked Swan.

Roger Cash stepped into the batter's box. He had confided to me that if he had kept a record, his lifetime hitting average would be below .100. But I have to admit he looked formidable in his snow-white uniform with CASH in maroon letters across his shoulders and the large numbers 00 in the middle of his back. The front of his uniform had only crossed baseball bats on it. He held the bat straight up and down and waggled it purposefully.

"Throw your fast ball and I'll put it in the river," yelled Roger, and curled his lip at McCracken.

The first pitch was a curve in the dirt, followed by a change-up low, another curve at the ankles, and something that may have been a screwball, that hit two feet in front of the plate. Roger trotted to first. Stan loped home with our fourth run. The bases were still loaded.

On the first pitch McCracken came right down the middle at me with his fast ball. I swung and got part of it on the end of the bat; a dying quail of a single just beyond the second baseman's reach. Runs five and six scored. Lindy Dean ended the inning.

McCracken's team tried to get all six runs back in the first. They went out one-two-three.

In right field, I trembled. My judgment of fly balls was not sound, and the opponents would soon find out that when any ball was hit to me the base runners could do as they pleased. Not only could I not cut a runner down at third, I had trouble getting the ball to second on two hops.

McCracken walked the first batter of the second inning, but that was it. His curve started snapping over the plate at the last second, pitches that had been breaking into the dirt now crossed the plate as strikes at the knees. We led 6–0 after three innings, but McCracken Construction got a run in the fourth, one in the fifth when I dropped a fly ball with two out, and two in the sixth on a single and a long home run by McCracken himself.

I managed to hit another Texas League single, but grounded into an inning-ending double play in the sixth.

McCracken and his team were finally catching on that Roger was little more than a journeyman pitcher with a lot of guile. He had a screwball that floated up to the plate like a powder puff, only to break in on the batter's hands at the last instant, usually resulting in a polite pop-up to the pitcher or shortstop. His fast ball was nothing, and he usually threw it out of the strike zone. But his change-up was a beauty, like carrying the ball to the plate. Roger's motion never changed an iota; a hitter would be finished with his swing and on his way to the bench shaking his head by the time the ball reached the catcher.

The seventh went scoreless. We got a run in the eighth on a double and a single, but McCracken's team got two in the bottom, again aided by my misjudgment of a fly ball. It was obvious that Roger was tired. His face was streaked with sweat and grime. His bronze hair appeared wet and wild when he took off his cap, which was after almost every pitch now. To compound matters, we went out on four pitches in the ninth, allowing Roger only about two minutes' rest between innings.

The first batter in the last of the ninth hit a clean single up the middle. The next sacrificed him to second. The third batter swung very late on a change-up and hit it like a bullet just to the right of first. Our first baseman, Lindy Dean, lunged for the ball and, completely by accident, it ended up in his glove. He threw to Roger from a sitting position for the second out. The runner advanced to third.

McCracken was at the plate. As he dug in he sent a steady stream of words toward the mound. Though I couldn't hear, I knew he was baiting Roger. If we lost, there would be at least enough profits from the concessions to pay everyone off, and buy Roger a bus ticket for somewhere not too far away. All I hoped was that the ball wouldn't be hit to me. I didn't mind batting in a tight situation, but defense was my weakness.

McCracken, even though he was right-handed, hammered one to right field on a 2-2 count. Right down the foul line. I actually ran in a step or two before I judged it properly. Then I ran frantically down the line, my back to the plate. I almost overran it. The ball nearly hit me on the head as it plunked onto the soft grass a foot outside the foul line.

Surely he won't hit to the opposite field again, I thought.

Roger gave him a fast ball in the strike zone. It was, of course, the last pitch McCracken was expecting. He swung late, but only late enough to send it to right-center field. I gratefully let the center fielder handle it for the final out.

At our bench Roger wiped his face and hair with a towel.

"You get the rest of the gate receipts and the concession money," he said. "One of McCracken's men will count it with you."

"You didn't bet against us, did you?" I stammered.

"Of course not. I bet it all *on* us."

"What if we'd lost?"

"It wouldn't be the first time I've left a town on foot with people throwing things at me."

Roger collected his winnings from the president of the university and stuffed the stacks of bills into his equipment bag. He settled his debts and bought the team supper and unlimited ice cream at the Springtime Café. He tipped Mrs. Richards ten dollars. While Stan and I again turned our backs, he opened the safe and stuffed it full of bills.

"I'll be on the road before daylight," he said. He gave Stan and me an extra twenty each.

Though I was dead tired, I forced myself to only half sleep; I jumped awake every time the old house creaked in the night. I was up and at the window as soon as I heard Roger's steps on the stairs. As I suspected, he did not leave immediately, but again took the tools from the trunk and hoisted them to his shoulder, being careful not to let them rattle. There had been a heavy thundershower about ten o'clock and the air was still pure and sweet as springwater.

I was waiting by the Caddy when Roger returned. His clothes were soiled, his shoes ruined by mud.

"You been in a fight or what?" I said.

"I think you know where I've been," he said, keeping his voice low.

"I know a little about distances," I said.

"When did you suspect?" he asked.

"I measured the distance on your practice field out at Barons," I said. "Sixty-one feet from the rubber to the plate. No wonder your arm's big as a telephone pole."

"You figure on telling McCracken?"

"No"

"I mean, if you feel you have to it's okay. Just wait until morning."

"I'm not going to," I said.

Roger deposited the tools in the trunk. He began to fiddle with the combination of the safe.

"You don't have to give me anything."

"I want to. I've been working this scam for ten years. No one ever cottoned onto it before. I must be getting careless."

He took about an inch of bills off the top of the pile and handed them to me.

"You really don't need to. Money can't buy what I want."

"Which is?"

"I want this girl I know to like me just the way I am."

"No, money can't do that. But it'll buy a hell of a lot of ice cream." His face broke open into that grin of his that could charm a bone out of a hungry dog's mouth.

"It's all a matter of distances," Roger said from inside the Caddy. "Des Moines to Memphis is 623 miles, less about 110 to Onamata is 513. I'll have a late breakfast in Memphis."

Roger smiled again, reached his right hand up and out the window to shake my hand.

"Maybe we'll run into each other again, Gid. Be cool. It's all a matter of distances. Make them work for you." The window purred up and the car eased away. The only sound it made was gravel crunching under the wide tires.

How Manny Embarquadero Overcame and Began His Climb to the Major Leagues

For me, the baseball season ended on a Tuesday night last August at the exact moment that Manny Embarquadero killed the general manager's dog.

In a season scheduled to end August 31, Manny arrived July 15, supposedly the organization's hottest prospect, an import from some tropical island where the gross national product is revolution, and the per capita income $77 a year. A place where, it is rumored, because of heredity and environment, or a diet heavy in papaya juice, young men move with the agility of panthers and can throw a baseball from Denver to Santa Fe on only one hop.

According to what I had read in *USA Today*, there were only two political factions in Courteguay—the government and the insurgents—depending on which one was currently in power. One of the current insurgents was a scout for our organization, reportedly receiving payment in hand grenades and flame-throwers. He spotted Manny Embarquadero in an isolated mountain village (on Manny's island, a mountain is anything more than fifteen feet above sea level) playing shortstop barefoot, fielding a pseudo-baseball supposedly made from a bull's testicle stuffed with papaya seeds.

Even a semi-competent player would have been an improvement over our shortstop, who was batting .211, and was always late covering second base on double-play balls.

"The organization's sending us a phenom," Dave "The Deer" Dearly told us a few days before Manny's arrival. Dearly was a competent manager, pleasant and laid-back with his players. A former all-star second baseman with the Orioles, he knew a lot about baseball and was able to impart that knowledge. But on the field during a game, he was something else.

"Been swallowing Ty Cobb Meanness Pills," was how Mo Chadwick, our center-fielder, described him. Dearly was developing a reputation as an umpire-baiting bastard, who flew off the handle at a called third strike, screamed like a rock singer, kicked dirt on umpires, punted his cap, and heaved water coolers onto the field with little or no provocation.

"Got to have a gimmick," he said out of the side of his mouth one night on the road, as he strutted back to the dugout after arguing a play where a dimwitted pinch runner had been out by thirty feet trying to steal third with two out. Dearly had screamed like a banshee, backed the umpire halfway to the left-field foul pole, and closed out the protest by punting his cap into the third row behind our dugout. The fans love to boo him.

Before Manny Embarquadero arrived, my guess was that Dave Dearly would be the only one on the squad to make the Bigs.

I planned on quitting organized baseball at the end of this season. My fastball was too slow and didn't have enough action; my curve was good when it found the strike zone, which wasn't often enough. I was being relegated to middle relief way down here in A ball—not a positive situation. I could probably make it as far as Triple-A and be a career minor leaguer, but I wasn't that in love with minor-league baseball. I've got one semester to a degree in social work, and I'd enrolled for the fall.

I'm a Canadian, from Tecumseh, Ontario, not far from Windsor, which is connected by bridge to Detroit.

I agreed with Dearly that unless you were Roger Clemens or Ken Griffey, Jr., you needed a gimmick. As it turned out, Manny Embarquadero had a gimmick. If the ball club hadn't been so cheap that we had to bunk two-to-a-room on the road, I never would have found out what it was.

Manny Embarquadero looked like all the rest of those tropical paradise ballplayers, black as a polished bowling ball, head covered in a mass of wet black curls, thin as if he'd only eaten one meal a day all his life, thoroughbred legs, long fingers, buttermilk eyes.

The day Manny arrived, the general manager, Chuck Manion, made a rare appearance in the clubhouse to introduce the hot new prospect.

"Want you boys to take good care of Manny here. Make him feel welcome."

Manny was standing, head bowed, dressed in ghetto-Goodwill-store style: black dress shoes, cheap black slacks and a purple pimp-shirt with most of the glitter worn off.

"Manny not only doesn't speak English," Chuck Manion announced, "he doesn't speak anything. He's mute. But not deaf. He knows no English or Spanish, but follows general instructions in basic sign language.

"The amazing thing is he's hardly played baseball at all. He wandered out of the mountains, was able to communicate to our scout that he was seventeen years old and had never played competitive baseball. He truly is a natural. I've seen video tapes. The way he plays on one month's experience, he'll be in the Bigs after spring training next year."

Chuck Manion was a jerk, about forty, a blond, red-faced guy who looked as if he had just stepped out of a barber's chair, even at eleven o'clock at night. Any time he came to the clubhouse, he wore a four-hundred-dollar monogrammed jogging suit and smelled of fifty-dollar-an-ounce aftershave. His family owned a brewery—and our team. Chuck Manion played at being general manager just for fun.

"I bet he thought he'd get laid a lot, was why he wanted a baseball team as a toy," said my friend Mo Chadwick, one night when Manion, playing the benevolent, slumming employer, accompanied a bunch of players to a bar after a game. He seemed extremely disappointed that there weren't dozens of women in various stages of undress and sexual frustration crawling all over.

"Sucker thought he'd buy one round of drinks and catch the overflow," said Mo.

He was right. Manion hung around just long enough for one drink and a few pointed questions about Baseball Sadies. As soon as he discovered that minor-league ballplayers didn't have to beat off sex-crazed groupies, he vanished into the night.

"Going down to the airport strip to cruise for hookers in his big BMW," said Mo. Again I had to agree.

After we all shook hands with Manny Embarquadero and patted him on the shoulder and welcomed him to the club, Manion made an announcement.

"We're gonna make Crease here"—he placed a hand on my shoulder—"Manny's roommate both at home and on the road. Crease reads all the time so he won't mind that Manny isn't much of a conversationalist." Manion laughed at his own joke.

I did read some. In fact, I'd been involved in a real brouhaha with my coaches because I read in the bullpen until my dubious expertise was needed on the mound. The coaches insisted that reading would ruin my control. I read anyway. I was threatened with unconditional release. I learned to hide my book more carefully.

Management rented housekeeping rooms within walking distance of the ballpark. My last roommate had gone on a home-run-hitting binge and had been promoted directly to Triple-A Calgary.

My nickname, Crease, had come about because ever since Little League I'd creased the bill of my cap right down the middle until it's ridged like a roof above my face. I always imagined I could draw a straight line from the V in the bill of my cap to the catcher's mitt.

"This guy is too good to be true," Mo Chadwick said to me after we'd watched Manny Embarquadero work out. "Something's not right. If he's only played baseball for one month, how come he knows when to back up third base, and how come he knows which way to cheat when the pitcher's going to throw off-speed?"

"Ours not to reason why," I said. "He's certainly a rough diamond."

If Manny Embarquadero hadn't talked in his sleep, I never would have found out what a rough diamond he really was.

On our first night together, I woke up in humid blackness on a sagging bed to the sound of loud whispering. The team had reserved the whole second floor of a very old hotel, so at first I assumed the sounds were in the hallway. But as I became wider awake, I realized the whispering was coming from the next bed.

Apparently no one was certain what language, if any, Manny Embarquadero understood.

"Our scout says he may understand one of the pidgin dialects from Courteguay," Chuck Manion had said the day he introduced Manny. The mountains Manny had wandered out of bordered on Haiti, so there was some speculation that Manny might understand French. Needless to say, we didn't have any French-speaking players on the team.

I raised the tattered blind a few inches to let a little street light into the room, just enough to determine that Manny was alone in bed. What I was hearing was indeed coming from his mouth, but it wasn't Spanish, or French, or even some mysterious Courteguayan dialect. It was ghetto American, inner-city street talk pure and simple.

He mumbled a lot, but also spoke several understandable phrases, as well as the words "Mothah," and "Dude," and "Dee-troit." At one point, he said clearly, "Go ahead girl, it ain't gonna bite you."

At breakfast in the hotel coffee shop, Manny, using basic hand signals and facial expressions, let me know he wanted the same breakfast I was having: eggs, toast, hash browns, large orange juice, large milk, large coffee.

"I think we should have a talk," I said to Manny as soon as we got back to the room after breakfast.

Manny stared at me, his face calm, his eyes defiant.

"You talk in your sleep," I said. "Don't worry, I'm not going to tell anyone, at least not yet. But I think you'd better clue me in on what's going down."

Manny stared a long time, his black-bullet pupils boring right into me, as though he was considering doing me some irreparable physical damage.

"If I was back home, Mon, that stare would have shrivelled your brain to the size of a pea," Manny said in a sing-songy Caribbean dialect.

"Your home, from what I heard, is in Detroit," I said, "somewhere with a close-up view of the Renaissance Center. So don't give me this island peasant shit. When I look closely I can tell you're no more seventeen than I am. You're older than me, and I just turned twenty-three. I don't know why you're running this scam, and I don't particularly care. But if we're gonna room together you're gonna have to play it straight with me."

"Fuck! Why couldn't I draw a roomie who's a heavy sleeper? I really thought I'd trained myself to stop talking in my sleep."

The accent was pure inner-city Detroit, flying past me like debris in the wind.

"So what's the scam? Why a mute, hot-shot child prodigy of a short-stop from the hills of Courteguay?"

"I just want to play baseball."

"That's no explanation."

"Yes, it is. I played high-school ball. I didn't get any invites to play for a college. I went to every tryout camp in the country for three years. Never got a tumble. 'You're too slow, you don't hit for power. Your arm is strong but you don't have enough range.' If you ain't the most talented then you got to play the angles. I seen that all the shortstops were coming from Courteguay, and they're black, and I'm black, so I figured if I went over there and kept my mouth shut and pretended to be an inexperienced kid from the outback, I'd get me a chance to play."

His words went by like bullets, but I've captured the gist of what he said.

"Shows a hell of a lot of desire," I said.

"I even tried the Mexican Leagues, but I couldn't catch on."

"But in a month or so, when you don't improve fast enough, this team is going to send you packing. Back to Courteguay."

"I'm gettin' better every day, man. I'm gonna make it. People perform according to expectations. Everyone figures I'll play my way into the Bigs next spring, and I'm not gonna disappoint them."

"There's a little matter of talent."

"I have more than you can imagine."

"Lots of luck."

The next night, when Manny played his first game, the play-by-play people mentioned that Manny was mute but not deaf. By the eighth inning, there were a dozen people behind our dugout shouting to Manny in every language from Portuguese to Indonesian. Manny shrugged and smiled, displaying a faceful of large, white teeth.

He was a one-hundred-percent improvement on our previous shortstop. I could see what the scouts, believing him to be seventeen and inexperienced, had seen in him. He had an arm that wouldn't quit. He could go deep in the hole to spear a ball on the edge of the outfield grass, straighten effortlessly, brace his back foot on the grass, and fire a rocket to first in time to get the runner. He covered only as much ground as was necessary, never seeming to extend himself, but covering whatever ground was necessary in order to reach the ball.

Of course, his name wasn't Manny Embarquadero.

"I am one anonymous dude. Jimmy, with two m's, if you must know, Williams with two l's. Hell, there must be two thousand guys in Dee-troit, Michigan, with the same name. And all us young black guys look alike, right?

"I had a Gramma, probably my Greatgramma, but she died. I think I was her granddaughter's kid. But that girl went off to North Carolina when I was just a baby and nobody ever heard from her. Once, Gramma and I lived for three years in an abandoned building. We collected cardboard boxes and made the walls about two feet thick. It gets fucking cold in Dee-troit, Michigan. Gramma always saw to it that I went to school."

Two nights later, there was a scout from the Big Show in the stands. Everyone pressed a little, some pressed a lot, and everybody except Manny looked bad at one time or another. Manny was unbelievable. One ball was hit sharply to his right and deep in the hole, a single if there ever was one. The left-fielder had already run in about five steps, expecting to field the grounder, when he saw that Manny had not only fielded the ball, but was directly behind it when he scooped it up and threw the runner out by a step. What he did was humanly impossible.

"How did you do that?" I asked, as he flopped on the bench beside me after the inning. Manny just smiled and pounded his right fist into his left palm.

Later, back at the hotel, I said, "There was something fishy about that play you made in the sixth inning."

"What fishy?"

"You moved about three long strides to your right and managed to get directly behind a ball that was hit like lightning. No Major-League shortstop could have gotten to that ball. You're not a magician, are you?"

"I'm not anything but a shortstop, man." But he looked at me for a long time, and there was a shrewdness in his stare.

What I could not understand was that no one else had noticed that one second he was starting a move to his right to snag a sure base hit, and an instant later he was behind the ball, playing it like a routine grounder. When I carefully broached the subject, no one showed any interest. He had not even been overwhelmed by congratulations when he came in from the field.

I admired his audacity. It troubled me that on one of my many visits to Detroit to see the Tigers, the Pistons, or the Red Wings, I may have passed Manny/Jimmy on the street, in one of those groups of shouting, pushing, swivel-jointed young men who congregated outside the Detroit sports facilities.

The trouble between Chuck Manion and Manny Embarquadero began on a hot Saturday afternoon, before a twi-night doubleheader. Chuck Manion, wearing a sweatsuit worth more than I was getting paid every month, showed up to work out with the team. He was accompanied by his dog, a nasty spotted terrier of some kind, with mean, watery eyes and a red ass. Manion sometimes left the dog in the clubhouse during a game, where it invariably relieved itself on the floor.

"After losing in extra innings, it's a fucking joy to come back to a clubhouse that smells of dog shit," The Deer said one evening.

"Tell him where to stuff his ugly, fucking dog," one of the players suggested. We all applauded.

"Wouldn't I love to," said Dearly. "Unfortunately, Manion's family actually puts money into this club. An owner like that can do no wrong."

On that humid Saturday afternoon, Manion brought the dog out onto the playing field. Dearly spat contemptuously as he hit out fungoes, but said nothing.

Manny and I were tossing the ball on the sidelines, when Manion pointed to Manny and said to me, "Tell Chico to take Conan here for a couple of turns around the outfield."

"His name is Manny," I said. "And he can understand simple sign language. Tell him yourself."

"You're the one who's retiring end of the season, aren't you?" Manion asked me in a snarky voice.

"Right."

"And a goddamned good thing."

He walked over to Manny, put the leash in his hand and pointed to the outfield, indicating two circles around it.

I wondered what Manny Embarquadero would do. I knew what Jimmy Williams would do. But which one was Manion dealing with?

It didn't take long to find out.

Manny Embarquadero let the leash drop to the grass, and gave

THE ESSENTIAL W. P. KINSELLA

Manion the finger, staring at him with as much contempt as I had ever seen pass from one person to another.

Manion snarled at Manny and turned away to hunt down Dave Dearly. At the same moment, Conan nipped at Manny's ankle.

Manny's reaction was so immediate I didn't see it. But I heard the yelp, and saw the dog fly about fifteen feet into left field, his leash trailing after him.

Manion found Dave Dearly, and demanded that Manny be fired, traded, deported, or arrested.

"Goddamnit, Chuck," Dearly responded, "I got enough trouble baby-sitting and handholding twenty-five players, most of them rookies, without having you and your goddamned mutt riling things up."

The mutt, apparently undamaged, was relieving himself on the left-field grass, baring his pearly fangs at any ballplayer who got too close.

Manion continued to froth at the mouth, threatening Dearly with unemployment if he didn't comply.

At that moment, Dearly must have remembered his reputation as an umpire-baiter. His face turned stop-sign red as he breathed his fury onto Chuck Manion, backing him step by step from third base toward the outfield, scuffing dirt on Manion's custom jogging outfit. Manion had only anger on his side.

"Take your ugly fucking dog and get the fuck off my baseball field," Dearly roared, turning away from Manion as suddenly as he had confronted him. Dearly punted his cap six rows into the empty stands, where it landed right side up, sitting like a white gull on a green grandstand seat.

Manion retrieved the dog's leash and headed for the dugout, still raging and finger-pointing.

"From now on walk your own fucking dog on your own fucking lawn," were Dearly's parting words as Manion's back retreated down the tunnel to the dressing room.

The players applauded.

"Way to go, Skip."

"You better watch out," I said to Manny, over a late supper at a Jack in the Box. "Manion's gonna get your ass one way or another."

"Fuck Manion and his ball club," said Manny Embarquadero. "And fuck his dog, too."

Manion didn't show his face on the field all the next week, but he could be seen in the owner's box, a glass wall separating him from the press table, pacing, smoking, often taking or making telephone calls.

Manny continued his extraordinary play.

"Did you see what I did there in the second inning?" Manny asked in our apartment after the game.

"I did."

"I can't figure out how I did it. If anybody but you sees . . . what would they do, bar me from the game?"

In the second inning, Manny Embarquadero had gone up the ladder for a line drive. The ball was far over his head, but I saw a long, licorice-colored arm extend maybe four feet farther than it should have. No one else, it seemed, saw the supernatural extension of the arm. They apparently saw only a very good play.

"Want to tell me how you do what you do?" I said.

Manny had made at least one impossible play in each of the last dozen games. At the plate it was less obvious, but probably magically inspired as well. He was batting over .400.

"Must be because you know who I really am that you can see what I do," said Manny. "Besides, no one would believe you; I'm just a poor, mute, black, immigrant ballplayer."

"I've no intention of spreading your secret around. I'm going to be through with baseball for good in a few weeks."

"If you want a professional career, I might be able to arrange it. It would involve a trip to Courteguay. And I don't know, you being white and all."

"Not interested."

THE ESSENTIAL W. P. KINSELLA

"There's a factory down there. They sing and chant over your body, wrap it in palm fronds, feed you hibiscus petals and lots of other things. After a week or so, you emerge from the factory with an iron arm and the speed of a bullet and the ability to be in more than one place at a time.

"It's just like a magic trick, only the whole ballplayer is quicker than the eye. They send a couple of guys up to the Bigs each year. I just lucked out. I really thought I'd stand a chance of getting a professional contract if I came from a backwater like Courteguay. The reason I got into the factory, got the treatment, was I got caught stealing food that supposedly belonged to this guerrilla leader, Dr. Noir. Looks like Idi Amin, only not so friendly . . ."

"What do you have to do in return?"

"You don't want to know," said Manny.

"Probably not. You're kidding me, right? There's no factory in Courteguay that turns out iron-armed infielders."

"Think whatever you want, man. This Dr. Noir was from Haiti: voodoo, dancing naked all night, cutting out people's spleens and eating them raw. At the moment Dr. Noir leads the insurgents in Courteguay, but some day soon he'll be president again."

"You're right," I said. "I don't want to know."

A week later, after a short road trip, Dave Dearly was fired. We were in first place by a game, thanks mainly to Manny Embarquadero's fielding and hitting.

The grapevine reported that Chuck Manion had been unable to convince the parent club to get rid of Manny. Dave Dearly was another matter. Since Manion and his family put large amounts of their own money into the stadium and the team, the top dogs decided that if keeping him happy meant jettisoning a minor-league manager, so be it.

The third-base coach, a young guy named Wylie Keene, managed the club the next night.

"It was because The Deer went to bat for your Courteguayan friend over there," Keene told me. "Chuck Manion wanted Manny given the bum's rush out of baseball. But The Deer stood up to him.

"He told the parent club that he wouldn't have his players treated that way, and life was too short to work for an asshole like Manion. But, we all know money is the bottom line, so The Deer is gone. He thinks the organization will find another place for him."

"What do you think?"

"I don't know. He's a good man. He'll catch on somewhere, but not likely in this organization."

When we got home I passed all that information to Manny.

"Manion is a son-of-a-bitch," Manny said. "I'd love to get him to Courteguay for a few minutes. I'd like to leave him alone in a room with Dr. Noir. Hey, he's got a degree in chiropractics from a school in Davenport, Iowa. Dr. Lucius Noir. I saw his diploma. According to rumors, he deals personally with political prisoners. Just dislocates joints until they confess to whatever he wants them to confess to. Wouldn't I love to hear Manion scream."

"Look, you're gonna be out of this town in just a couple weeks. You'll never have to see or hear Manion again."

"But there is something I have to do. Come on," he said, heading for the door.

"It's after midnight."

"Right."

We walked the darkened streets for over half an hour. Manion's house overlooked the eighteenth tee of a private golf course. It loomed like a mountain in the darkness.

"Listen," I said, "I'm not going to let you do something you'll be sorry for, or get arrested for . . ."

"Don't worry, I'm not going to touch him. The only way you can hurt rich people is by taking things away from them."

We crawled through a hedge and were creeping across Manion's patio when Conan came sniffing around the corner of the house. He stopped abruptly and stood stiff-legged, fangs bared, a growl deep in his throat.

"Pretty doggie," said Manny Embarquadero, holding a hand out toward the hairless, red-assed mutt. They stood like that for some time, until the dog decided to relax.

Manny struck like a cobra. The dog was dead before it could utter a sound.

"I should have killed Manion. But I've got places to go."

"Somebody's gonna find you out."

"How? Are you gonna tell? In Courteguay they'd barbecue that little fucker. Dogs are a delicacy."

"You're not from Courteguay."

Manny was going to get caught, there was no doubt in my mind. He was going to ruin a promising baseball career, which may or may not have been aided by the supernatural. Personally, I had my doubts about Manny's stories, but I admired his chutzpah, his fearlessness.

"Manny Embarquadero is pure magic. They'll never lay a hand on me," said Jimmy Williams.

"You forget," I said, "There isn't anyone named Manny Embarquadero."

"Oh, yes, there is," he said. "Oh, yes, there is."

As we crawled through the hedge, I let a branch take the creased cap off my head. A bus passed through town at 4:00 A.M., and I'd be on it.

THE INDIAN NATION CULTURAL EXCHANGE PROGRAM

Every once in a while the Government tries to do something nice for us Indians. Usually it is just before an election when that *something nice* is announced. Whether it ever come about or not is another matter. Sometimes they announce a new program, then after the newspapers get tired of writing about it, they file it away, hope no Indian will ever apply.

That is the way it was with the The Indian Nation Cultural Exchange Program.

OTTAWA TO SPEND TEN MILLION
ON WESTERN INDIANS

was how the *Edmonton Journal* headline the story, and right up until the election, whenever some sneaky-looking politician from Ottawa speak within 50 miles of any Indian reserve west of Ontario, he mention the program and the amount but be pretty vague about the details. He know that after the election that program get filed deep in a Government vault somewhere.

That would have happened to the Indian Nation Cultural Exchange

Program if it weren't for Bedelia Coyote. Bedelia is famous for causing the Government grief. Not that they don't deserve it. One time the Government send 52 John Deere manure spreaders to our reserve. Nobody asked for them, and hardly anybody farm enough to want or need one. Some of my friends try to strip them down as if they were cars, but nobody want to buy the loose parts. Eventually a few of them disappear, the way a cattle herd get smaller if it ain't tended. All that happen maybe eight years ago and there are still eight or ten manure spreaders rusting in the slough below our cabins.

"They should have sent us 52 politicians," say Bedelia. "They're all born knowing how to spread manure. It keep them busy and they be doing something useful for the first time in their lives."

"Even crime wouldn't pay if the Government ran it," say our medicine lady, Mad Etta.

It is Bedelia who go to the Wetaskiwin office of our Federal Member of Parliament, a Mr. J. William Oberholtzer.

"The Conservative Party could run a dog here in Alberta and win by 10,000 votes," I say.

"J. William is about two points smarter than most dogs," says Bedelia. "I seen him tie his own shoes one day. Most politicians don't have that much coordination."

Bedelia have to go back to Mr. Oberholtzer's office every day for about three months, and she have to fill out a whole sheaf of forms, but finally they have to give her the details of the Indian Nation Cultural Exchange Program. Turn out that three people, under 25 years old, from each reserve in Western Canada, can visit another reserve at least 250 miles away to learn the other tribe's culture and teach them about their culture.

"I'll teach them how to drink," says my friend Frank Fencepost. "That's part of our culture, ain't it?"

"Unfortunately," say Bedelia.

"I don't know," says Frank, screw up his face. "I can't drink like I used to. Used to be I could really put it away. But now fifteen or twenty beers

and I'm right out of it," and he laugh deep in his chest, sound like someone pounding on a drum. "Maybe I teach them how to have sex appeal
instead."

"And I'll demonstrate brain surgery," says Bedelia.

"Yeah, you're right," says Frank. "Can't teach other people to be sexy—
you either got it or you ain't."

"Bedelia is a little like the wind," our medicine lady, Mad Etta, say,
"she slow but steady—wind wear down even mountains eventually."

Bedelia fill out another ton of forms and finally all the papers arrive
for people from our reserve to apply to go somewhere else. We get out a
map of Canada and try to decide where it is we'd like to go.

"How about California?" says Frank. "I hear they got good weather
and pretty girls down there."

"California ain't in Canada," we say.

"Then we'll go down there and talk them into joining up with us."

We argue for a long time about different places, but we know we going
to where Bedelia decide, because she done all the work so far.

"You guys ever been to the Land of the Midnight Sun?" Bedelia ask.

"We been to Las Vegas," says Frank.

Bedelia's look is so cold it could freeze us both solid.

"I'm talking about the Arctic. There's a place on the map called Pandemonium Bay, only 300 miles from the North Pole. There's an Indian
reserve there and I think that's where we ought to go."

Like Frank, I'd a lot rather go where it's hot. But I smile at Bedelia and
say, "We're with you." I mean, how many times does the Government do
favors for poor Indians?

I remember another time the Government decide to do us Indians a
favor. Someone in Ottawa get the notion that we all need new running
shoes. Everyone on the reserve. Someone must of told them that Indians
like running shoes, or that we all barefoot.

To save money they do the project by mail. Everyone on the reserve
get a letter, a big, brown envelope that have a five-foot-long sheet of
white paper about two feet wide, folded up in it. Instructions are that

everyone is supposed to trace the outline of their right foot on the paper and send it to Indian Affairs Department in Ottawa. Then they supposed to send everyone their running shoes.

We have more fun laughing over the idea than the time we move Ovide Letellier's outhouse forward about ten feet, so when he go to park his brand new Buick behind it, the car fall nose first into the hole.

There are really over twenty people in Louis Coyote's family, and there is hardly enough room to get all the right feet on the paper. The kids draw around feet with pencils, pens, crayons, finger-paint, peanut butter, Roger's Golden Syrup, and 10-40 motor oil. Some people leave their shoes on; others take them off.

Frank Fencepost draw around a foot of Louis Coyote's horse, and of his own dog, Guy Lafleur. When the running shoes come in the mail, Smokey Coyote get four short, fat shoes, and Guy Lafleur Fencepost two pairs of tiny-baby ones.

When the Government give you something, you got to take it. Mad Etta she put that length of paper on the floor to use as a doormat. The Government write her three letters, say she got to trace her foot and send it to them. Finally they send her a letter say she liable to a $500 fine and 60 days in jail if she don't do as she's told. Mad Etta sit down on a sheet of paper, trace one of her cheeks, and mail it off. A month or two later come a letter say they only make shoes up to size 32, and her foot is a size 57.

The kids use running shoes for footballs. We use them for fillers on the corduroy road across the slough. We tie laces together and toss them in the air until the telephone and telegraph lines along the highway decorated pretty good. For years there was faded and rotting running shoes hang from those lines like bird skeletons.

Me, Frank and Bedelia put in applications under the Indian Nation Cultural Exchange Program to visit Pandemonium Bay Reserve, North-west Territories.

"Pandemonium Bay has the worst climate and the worst economy in Canada," say Mr. Nichols, my teacher and counselor at the Tech School in Wetaskiwin, after I tell him where we're going.

He go on to tell me it is almost always below zero there, and in real temperature too, not this phony Celsius nobody understands. And he say it snow in July and August, which is their nicest weather of the year.

"The ground never thaws, ever," say Mr. Nichols.

"But I bet the nights is six months long," say Frank. "I don't mind that at all. In that country when you talk a girl into staying the night, she stays the night."

It is the better part of a year before the money comes through. We are the only people ever apply under the Indian Nation Cultural Exchange Program, so everybody make a big deal out of it. There is a picture in the *Wetaskiwin Times* of some suits from the Department of Indian Affairs, present Bedelia with the check. Me and Frank are there, me looking worried, my black hat pulled low, my braids touching my shoulders. Frank grin big for the camera. And of course Chief Tom is there, stick his big face in the picture. He discourage Bedelia every step of the way, but when the time come he take as much credit for what she done as he dare to.

Bedelia is serious about almost everything. She belong to so many organizations I don't know if she can keep track. There is Save the Whales, Free the Prisoners, Stop the Missiles, Help the Seals, Stop Acid Rain, and I bet ten more. If there is anything to protest within 200 miles, Bedelia is there. She is stocky built, with her hair parted down the middle; she wear jeans, boots, and lumberjack shirts, and she thinks I should write political manifestos, whatever they are, and that I should put a lot more social commentary in my stories.

"My motto is 'Piss in the ocean,'" Frank tell her when she start on one of her lectures.

In a joke shop one time I found a little button that say "Nuke the Whales" and that about turn Bedelia blue with anger. But she means well even if she's pushy. And she's a good friend.

People is sure odd. Soon as everyone knows where we're going, they start to say, "Why them?" and "Aren't there a lot of people who deserve to go more?"

"If people had their way they'd send two chicken dancers and a hockey player," says Frank. "And how come none of them ever thought of applying to go?" It is true that none of the three of us dance, sing, make beadwork, belong to a church, or play hockey.

To get to Pandemonium Bay we fly in a big plane to Yellowknife, then make about ten stops in a small plane, been made, I think, by glueing together old sardine cans. The plane feel like it powered by a lawn mower motor; inside it is as cold as outside, and there is cracks around the windows and doors let in the frost and snow. The pilot wear a heavy parka and boots, have a full beard make him look a lot like a bear. And he only growl when Frank ask him a lot of questions.

Pandemonium Bay is like the worst part of the prairies in winter, magnified ten times. Even though it is spring it is 30 below.

"Looks like we're on the moon," says Frank, stare at the pale white sky and endless frozen muskeg.

"Looks just like home," says Bedelia, sarcastic like, point to some burned-out cars, boarded-up houses, and dead bodies of Ski-Doos scattered about. There are gray and brown husky dogs with long hair, huddled in the snowbanks, puff out frosty breath at us, while a few ravens with bent feathers caw, and pick at the bright garbage scattered most everywhere.

Though the Government make a big deal out of our going, *pioneers* they call us in some of their handouts, and send about twenty pounds of propaganda to Pandemonium Bay, with copies to each of us, Chief Tom, Mr. J. William Oberholtzer, Premier Lougheed, and goodness knows who else, there is only one person meet our plane.

But when we see who it is, it explain a whole lot of things, like why Bedelia has told us at least a hundred times that we don't have to go with her unless we really want to, and that she could get a couple of her demonstrator friends to travel with her, or even go by herself.

"There won't be much for you guys to do up there," Bedelia said, like she wished we weren't going.

"Hey, we make our own fun. I never been arrested in the Northwest Territories," said Frank.

The only person who meet the plane is Myron Oglala.

Myron, he is the only man Bedelia ever been interested in. He is a social worker and she met him at a Crush the Cruise demonstration in Edmonton a year or two ago, and bring him home with her for a few days. Bedelia never had a boyfriend before, so that sure surprise us all. "A woman needs a man like a fish needs a bicycle," is one of Bedelia's favorite sayings.

Myron is soft and wispy, have a handshake like a soft fruit, and, though he claims to be a full-blooded Indian, is going bald. If you ever notice, 99 out of 100 Indians, even real old ones, have a full head of hair. That is something we is real proud of. We call Bedelia's friend Myron the Eagle, which we lead him to believe is a compliment, though Bedelia know the truth.

She was as proud of Myron as a mother cat carrying a kitten by the back of its neck. And she explain to us when we get too nasty with our teasing that her and Myron have an *intellectual communion* with one another.

"I bet you can't buy that kind at the Catholic Church," I say.

"Right," says Frank, "that's why you and him spend fifteen hours a day in your bedroom with the door closed."

Bedelia just stomp away angry. "No reason you shouldn't have sex like everybody else," we say. "But with *Myron?*" And we roll around on the floor with laughter.

Bedelia did admit one day not long after that that if she was ever to have a baby she'd name it Margaret Atwood Coyote.

We knew Myron was up north somewhere, but we didn't know where, or guess how badly Bedelia wanted to see him again.

"Well, if it ain't Myron the Eagle," says Frank. Myron stare at us through his Coke-bottle glasses, not too sure who we are. I sure hope he recognize Bedelia.

But we don't have to worry about that. Bedelia hug Myron to her, spin him around. She show more emotion than I ever seen from her, except when she's mad at someone.

Myron is expecting us. He have a Department of Indian Affairs station wagon and he drive us a few blocks to what look like a super-highrise apartment.

"What's that?" we ask. That huge, semicircular building sit on the very edge of this tiny village, look like something out of a science fiction movie.

"Pandemonium Bay is an accident," say Myron. "Somebody couldn't read their compass, so they built a weather station here when it was supposed to go 600 miles up the pike. By the time somebody pointed out the mistake they'd already bulldozed out an airport, there was so much money tied up they had to leave this town where it was. Bureaucrats from Ottawa, who had never been north of Winnipeg, hired a town planner from New York to build a town for 3000 people. He designed and built this . . ." What is in front of us is a ten-storey, horseshoe-shaped apartment building.

"There was supposed to be a shopping center inside the horseshoe, the stores protected from the wind by the apartments. But there's never been more than 150 people here, ever," Myron Oglala go on.

"I guess it ain't very cold in New York, 'cause the architect installed an underground sewage disposal system, so environmentally sound it would even make Bedelia happy," and Myron smile from under his glasses. It is the first hint we have that he has a sense of humor.

"The sewer system froze and stayed frozen. Indian Affairs spent a few million thawing pipes and wrapping them in pink insulation, but they stayed frozen. The big problem is the pipes are all in the north wall where it's about 60 below all year round," and Myron laugh, and when he do so do the rest of us.

"Folks still live in the first-floor apartments. They put in peat-burning stoves, cut a hole in the bathroom floor, put the toilet seat on a five-gallon oil drum, use the basement to store frozen waste."

"Native ingenuity," says Frank.

"Common sense," says Myron, "something nobody in Ottawa has."

Me and Frank get to stay in one of those apartments. The Danish furniture is beat to rat shit, but there are two beds, with about a ton of blankets on each. Four brothers with a last name sound like Ammakar share the next-door rooms. We find them sitting on the floor in a semi-circle around their TV set. They are all dressed in parkas and mukluks.

"Don't you guys ever take off those heavy clothes?" ask Frank.

"You don't understand," say the oldest brother, whose name is George, then he talk real fast in his language to Myron.

"George says the local people have evolved over the years until they are born in Hudson Bay parkas and mukluks."

All four brothers smile, showing a lot of white teeth.

These Indians seem more like Eskimos to me. They is wide-built and not very tall with lean faces and eyes look more Japanese than Indian. They are happy to see visitors though, and they bring out a stone crock and offer us a drink.

"This stuff taste like propane gas," say Frank in a whisper, after his first slug from the bottle. The four Ammakar brothers smile, chug-a-lug a long drink from the crock, wipe their chins with the backs of their hands. They speak their language and we speak Cree, so to communicate we use a few signs and a few words of English. The drink we find out is called walrus milk. And if I understand what the Ammakars is saying, after two swigs you likely to go out and mate with a walrus.

They sit on the floor of their apartment cross-legged, even though the place is furnished. Ben Ammakar bring out a bag of bone squares and triangles, got designs carved on them. He toss them on the blanket like dice. Him and his brothers play a game that is kind of a complicated dominoes. They play for money. Frank, he watch for a while then say to me in Cree, "This is easy. Boy I'll have these guys cleaned out in an hour. Which pair of their mukluks you like best? I'll win one pair for each of us." Frank draw his cash from his pocket and sign that he want in on the game. I put up a quarter twice and lose each time, though I don't understand the game the way Frank does. I decide to go back to our place. I've never liked games very much anyways. Frank has already won three or four dollars and is so excited he practically glowing. Bet his feet can feel those warm mukluks on them.

I watch television in our apartment. There is a satellite dish on the roof of the apartment and they get more channels than the Chateau Lacombe Hotel in Edmonton.

Earlier, when I mention the big, frost-colored satellite to Myron Oglala, he laugh and tell about how local people react to the television shows.

"*The Muppet Show* is the most detested show on TV," he say, "and the character everybody loathe most is Kermit the Frog. In local frog lore the frog is feared and hated. Frogs are supposed to suck blood and be able to make pacts with devil spirits."

"It really is no fun being green," says Frank.

"I bet the people who make *The Muppet Show* would sure be surprised at a reaction like that," I say.

"Up here they call the TV set *koosapachigan,* it's the word for the 'shaking tent' where medicine men conjure up spirits, living and dead. A lot of people fear the spirits of the TV are stealing their minds," says Myron.

"Just like on the prairies," says Frank.

About midnight I hear Frank at the door. He come in in a cloud of steam, take off his big boots and hand them out the door to somebody I can't see.

"I lost everything but my name," says Frank, hand my boots out the door before I can stop him.

"I only lost 50 cents," I say, feeling kind of righteous.

"Yeah, but I know how to gamble," says Frank.

To get our boots back Frank have to agree to do a day's work for Bobby Ammakar.

I don't like the idea of working. Just walking around Pandemonium Bay can be dangerous. Without no warning at all ice storms can blow up, and all of a sudden you can't see your own shoes, let alone the house you're headed to.

Bedelia and Myron spend all their time together. There ain't nothing for Frank and me to do except watch TV. This is about the worst holiday I can imagine. Also, nobody is interested in learn about our culture, and these Indians don't have much of any that I can see.

"They worship the Ski-Doo," says Frank. "At least everywhere you look there's a couple of guys down on their knees in front of one."

"You want to learn about our culture?" says Bobby Ammakar. "We take you guys on a caribou hunt."

And before we can say hunting ain't one of our big interests in life, the Ammakar brothers loaned us back our boots, and we is each on the back end of a Ski-Doo bouncing over the tundra until there ain't nothing in sight in any direction except clouds of frosty air.

Ben Ammakar is in front of me, booting the Ski-Doo across the ice fast as it will go, and, when I look over my shoulder, I see we lost sight of Frank and whoever driving his Ski-Doo. After about an hour we park in the shadow of a snowbank look like a mountain of soft ice cream. I think it is only about three in the afternoon, but it already dark, and once when the sky cleared for a minute, I seen stars. The wind sting like saplings slapping my face, and my parka is too thin for this kind of weather.

When I go to speak, Ben Ammakar shush me, point for me to look over top of the snowbank. Sure enough, when I do, out there on the tundra is a dozen or so caribou, grazing on whatever it is they eat among all the snow and rocks.

Ben take his rifle from its scabbard and smile. He take a smaller rifle from somewhere under his feet and offer it to me.

"I'd miss," I whisper.

If Frank were here he'd grab it up and say, "Fencepost has the eye of an eagle," then probably shoot himself in the foot.

Ben take aim, squeeze off two shots, and drop two caribou, the second one before he do anything more than raise up his head; he don't even take one step toward getting away. The other caribou gallop off into the purplish fog.

"You're a great shot," I say.

"You learn to shoot straight when your life depend on it," says Ben. "If you could shoot we'd have had four caribou."

"You speak more English every time I see you."

"We didn't know if you guys were real people or not. We thought maybe you were government spies." We have a good laugh about that. I tell him how, back at Hobbema, we been doing the same thing to strangers all our lives. "But if we'd of killed four caribou, how'd we ever carry all the meat back?" I ask.

"Where you figure the dead caribou is gonna go?" ask Ben. "And they don't spoil in this here weather."

"Polar bears?" I say.

"Not this time of year; they go where it's warm."

Ben climb on the Ski-Doo and turn the key, but all that come out is a lot of high-pitched whining and screeching, like a big dog been shot in the paw. At the same time one of them ice storms sweep down on us so we can't see even three feet away. The wind blow ice grains into our faces like darts. Ben take a quick glance at me to see if I'm worried and I guess he can tell I am. My insides feel tingly, like the first time an RCMP pulled my hands behind my back to handcuff me.

"Get down behind here," Ben yell, point for me to let the Ski-Doo shield me from the wind. He get on his knees above the motor, push a wire here, rattle a bolt there.

"I know some mechanics," I say. "I study how to fix tractors for two years now."

I get up on my knees and look at the motor. I take off one glove, but the tips of two fingers freeze as soon as I do. I think my nose is froze too.

"I think the fuel line is froze up," I say.

I wish Mad Etta was here. It hard to be scared with a 400 lb. lady beside you. Also Etta would be like having along a portable potbellied stove. Etta like to joke that if she was on a plane crashed in the wilderness that stayed lost for six months, everyone else would be dead of starvation but she would still weigh 400 lbs. It true that Etta don't eat like the three or four people she is as big as.

The wind get stronger. The Ski-Doo motor ice cold now.

"Are we gonna die?" I say to Ben Ammakar.

"You can if you want to," says Ben, "but I got other ideas." I don't think he meant that to be unkind. I sure wish I never heard of Pandemonium Bay and the Indian Nation Cultural Exchange Program.

"Come on," say Ben, stand to a crouch, move around the end of the Ski-Doo.

"We can't walk out," I yell. "At least I can't; my clothes are too thin."

"Be quiet and follow me," says Ben. I sure wish I had his leather clothes. I didn't even bring my downfall jacket; I didn't expect to be outdoors so much.

I grab on to the tail of Ben's parka and stumble over the uneven tundra. We aren't even going in the direction we come from. The wind is so bad we have to keep our eyes mostly shut. I don't know how Ben can tell what direction we're going in, but in a couple of minutes we stumble right into the first dead caribou. Ben whip a crescent-bladed knife out from somewhere on his body, carve up that caribou like he was slicing a peach.

I don't even like to clean a partridge.

In spite of the cold air, the smell of caribou innards make my stomach lurch. Ben pull the guts out onto the tundra, heaving his arms right into the middle of the dead animal, his sealskin mitts still on. I'm sorry to be so helpless but I can't think of a single thing to do except stand around freezing, wonder how soon I'm going to die. Ben clear the last of the guts out of the caribou.

"Crawl inside," he say to me, point down at the bloody cavity.

"Huh?"

"Crawl inside. Warm. Caribou will keep you alive."

"I can't," I say, gagging, and feeling faint at the idea.

"You'll be dead in less than an hour if you don't."

"What's the good? The caribou will freeze too."

"My brothers will come for us."

"How will they know?"

"They'll know."

"How will they know where we are?"

"They'll know. Now get inside," and Ben raise up his bloody mitt to me. I think he is about to hit me if I don't do as I'm told. All I can think of as I curl up like a not born baby is what a mess I'll be—all the blood, and the smell.

"Face in," says Ben.

"Why?"

"You want your nose to freeze off?"

I squeeze into the cavity, breathe as shallow as I know how, my stomach in my throat, I'm scared as I've ever been. Ben drape the loose hide across my back. It *is* warm in there.

"Don't move. No matter what," he says. "My brothers will come. I'm going to the other animal. Don't move."

And I hear his first few steps on the ice and rock, then nothing but the wind.

It pretty hard to guess how much time has passed when you freezing to death inside a dead caribou. I have a watch on, one of those $7.00 ones flash the time in scarlet letters when you press a button. But the watch is on my wrist, under my jacket and shirt, and I'm scared to make a move to look at it. I try thinking about some of the stories I still want to write, about my girl, Sadie One-wound, about some of the things I should of done in my life that I didn't. Still, time pass awful slow.

I'd guess maybe three hours. The more time go by, the more I know Ben has saved my life, even if it is temporary. Out in the open I'd be dead, and maybe Ben too, tough as he is.

Then from a long way away I hear the faint put-put-put of Ski-Doos. At first I'm afraid it is only the wind playing tricks, but the sound get louder, and finally a flash of light come through a crack between the ribs and the loose hide, hit the back wall of the caribou and reflect off my eye.

I try to move, but find I can't budge even an inch. I push and push. The caribou is froze stiff with me inside.

"Silas, Silas, you dead or alive or what?" I hear Frank yell.

"I'm here," I say. My voice sound to me like I'm yelling into a pillow.

There is a ripping sound as the hide pulled away from my back. Then Frank's hand shove a jug of walrus milk in front of my face, but I can't move to grab it and he can't position it so I can drink.

"Lie still." It is David Ammakar's voice. "We cut you out with a chain saw."

I hear the chain saw start. "Buzzzzz . . . rrrrr . . . zzz," go the saw. I know I ain't frozen when I can feel those blades about to cut into places all over my body. I sure hope Frank ain't operating it.

Eventually they cut the ribs away and somebody grab onto the back of my parka and pull me out onto the tundra.

Ben is there, smile his slow smile at me; his face is friendly, but his eyes is tough. We both look like we committed a mass murder.

"I told you they'd come," say Ben, slap the shoulders of his brothers with his big mitt. I tip up that jug of walrus milk, going down my throat it feel like kerosene that already been lit. But I don't mind. It great to be able to feel anything.

"Lucky they didn't leave the search up to me," says Frank. "Soon as we got home I borrowed five dollars from Andy Ammakar and was winning back my stake, when these guys, without even looking at a watch, all sit silent for a few seconds, listening, then Andy say, 'Ben ought to be back by now.' They get up, all three at the same time, right in the middle of a round, and head out to start their Ski-Doos."

"'Hey,' I said. 'Let's finish the game, and the walrus milk,' but they just get real serious expressions on their faces, and nobody say another word. We drive for miles through a snowstorm thick as milk, and find your Ski-Doo and you, first try. I don't know how these guys do it."

That night there is a celebration because me and Ben been brought back alive. An old man in a sealskin parka play the accordion. And we get served up food that I'm afraid to even think what it might be. A couple of men sing songs, unmusical, high-pitched chants, like the wind blowing over the tundra. A couple of other men tell stories about hunting.

Then Frank stand up and say, "Listen to me. I want to tell you a story of how I brought my brothers in from the cold." He then tell how he sensed we was in trouble, and how he convinced the Ammakar brothers to stop playing dice and drinking walrus milk, and start the search. When he is finished everyone laugh and pour Frank another drink.

"Come here," Ben Ammakar say to me. He carrying a funny little instrument, look something like a dulcimer, have only one string that I'd guess was animal and not metal. Ben pull at my arm.

"Why?" I say, holding back.

"You guys are here to learn about our culture. You and me going to sing a song to those two caribou, tell them how grateful we are that they saved our lives, ask them to forgive us for killing them before their time."

"I can't sing," I say.

"What kind of Indian are you?" say Ben. "When you open your mouth the song just come out, you don't have nothing to do with it." Ben pull me to my feet and we walk to the front of the little group.

He pluck at the dulcimer and it make a "plong, plong," sound, not musical at all. Ben sing a couple of flat notes, then make sounds in his throat like he imitating the call of some sad bird.

Frank staring around bold-faced, his black cowboy hat pushed to the back of his head. There are already two or three girls got their eyes bolted to him. "The best way to learn about any culture is to make love with their women," Frank said to me on the flight up. I bet he ain't gonna have to sleep alone for the rest of our stay here.

Ben Ammakar point at me and plonk on the dulcimer.

I've a truly flat voice and a tin ear. But it look like I've found a culture where everybody else have the same problem.

I've never felt so shy in front of a group of people. But I had a lot of time to think inside that dead caribou, and there no question it *did* save my life. I open my mouth and sing; the sound that come out is more high-pitched than I would of guessed, but flat as all the prairie. "Thank you, Mr. Caribou, for saving my life today. Please forgive me for killing you so I could go on living." After those first lines it is easy. Almost like when people get up and give testimonials at Pastor Orkin's church back home. Ben echoes my words, so do his brothers who sit in a circle on the floor in front of us. "Thank you, Mr. Caribou, for giving up your life," I sing, and as I do I raise the blood-stained arms of my parka towards the ceiling.

K MART

"The past is so melodramatic," my wife said to me not long ago. "I remember standing at the sink with a plate raised over my head," she went on, "screaming at my first husband, bringing the plate down on the pile of broken dishes already in the sink, screaming louder. I don't even remember what I was mad about. I've never done anything like that since we've been married. But then you don't goad me. I keep remembering all those terrible life-and-death situations when I was a teenager; you must have suffered the same kind: she loves me, she loves me not. If he doesn't ask me out I'll die. None of them were ever as disastrous as I feared they would be."

"Some are," I said.

"Name one," she said.

"Well . . ." I said, and remained silent, smiling wryly, letting her think she had me. But I was thinking of Cory.

"If we lived in the South we'd be white trash," my mother said as she stared around the living room of the dark, dilapidated house we were moving into. I was not quite fourteen and had spent all my life in a dreamy, small town called Onamata on the banks of the Iowa River, until suddenly, the hardware store my father had inherited from his father failed, and our big, old house with its wide verandahs and creaking porch swing was sold to pay off creditors.

We were not in the South but on the outskirts of a dingy factory town in Illinois, where a never-before-seen relative had found my father a job as a nighttime security guard at a tool and die plant.

There were dust demons on the scuffed floorboards. The previous tenants had left behind the skeleton of a chrome kitchen chair, scabby food particles dried on the legs. The chair glinted sickly under a single pale light bulb. We were, in my mother's no-nonsense way of speaking, "making the best of a bad situation." The year was 1949.

The cast of characters: Bronislaw Kazimericz, Edward Kleinrath, Corrina Mazeppa, and a character named Jamie (Flash) Kirkendahl who, when I look back, is less real to me than many of my fictional creations. The nickname, incidentally, was an irony, tacked to me because of my lack of speed on the basepaths, perpetuated because of my propensity to fall down while trying to get out of the batter's box after hitting the ball. Jamie Kirkendahl would say this is not a story about baseball. Perhaps I should let you be the judge of that.

"What are you lookin' at, Stretch?" were the first words Bronislaw Kazimericz ever said to me. It was noon hour on my first day at a cinder block school that looked more like a factory or a prison.

I hadn't been looking at anything. In fact I had been standing alone alongside a chain-link fence wishing I was almost anywhere else. I looked at the speaker, a squat, blond boy, heavily muscled. He had a wide, pink face, pale blue eyes, and a soft, flat nose like a baby's.

"Kaz beats up every new kid, just to show who's boss of the playground," said a thin boy with the face of a weasel, Coke-bottle glasses, and a shoelace of mud-colored hair that fell down on his forehead as fast as he flicked it back into place.

"So go ahead," I said, making no effort to defend myself.

"Aren't you afraid?" said the weasel. "Kaz is the toughest guy in Northside." Northside was both the name of the school and the district within the city where we lived.

"I guess I'm afraid," I said.

"You don't know?"

"If you bruise me or break something it will hurt and maybe I'll forget how miserable I am," I said. "Do your worst."

"Kaz doesn't usually beat up guys unless they want to take him on, or unless they try to get away," said the weasel.

"Shut up, Eddie," said Kaz. "You too good for us, or what?" Kaz said to me.

"If you're gonna kill me, get it over with," I said.

"Go ahead, kill him," said Eddie the weasel.

"I never met one like you," said Kaz. "You got a name?"

"Jamie," I told him.

"I'm Kaz; he's Eddie."

"His real name's Bronislaw," said Eddie, dancing backward in front of Kaz, staying well out of his reach.

"Let only fear and common sense stop *you* from calling me anything but Kaz," he said to me. "By the way, do you play baseball?"

"Yeah, I do," I said.

"Right after school," said Kaz. "Kitty-corner from the back door of the Railroad Hotel," he added, pointing across the gray schoolyard to where, a couple of blocks away, the hotel rose up rectangular and ugly. It was the only building over two stories for blocks.

"Bring your own glove," said Eddie.

I showed up at the baseball field. Baseball was my salvation, for it was the only real connection between my past and present. The game we played here in this dismal factory town with its constantly gray skies was exactly the same game I had played in the sweet, green warmth of an Iowa summer. Here, it was April and the snow was barely gone. If I looked closely I could just make out the fine green tendrils emerging from the earth beneath the brown fuzz of winterkilled grass.

There were some two dozen neighborhood boys from twelve to seventeen who played baseball from the time school was let out until dark, and all day Saturday and Sunday. In that strange way boys have of forming instant alliances, I was accepted by Kaz and Eddie, and because of that was grudgingly accepted by everyone else. Kaz cleared the way for me like a snowplow, for he was indeed a fighter to be reckoned with. He had been Eddie's protector, and now he was mine as well. By the end of the summer it was as if I had lived all my life in Northside. But buried deep within me were memories of a better place and better times and a determination to succeed at *something*. I hated the overcrowded, inferior school, the gritty rows of bars along Railroad Avenue, the meanness, the poverty, the myopia of almost everyone trapped in a hopeless cycle, dependent on the availability of work at the ugly factories. The most important thing in every adult's life was who was hiring workers and who was laying them off.

What did baseball mean to us? Why the daily ritual, the dawn to dusk devotion? We were not good at the game. Kaz could hit the ball a mile, but a good pitcher could make him look ridiculous. I was a sneaky hitter; I held out my bat and let the ball do the work. I hit dying quail Texas Leaguers to all fields. I was the only one who kept meticulous records of my batting average. My on-base percentage was over .560, but in a game where power hitting was everything, I was one of the least valuable players. Eddie had virtually no skills at all; his poor eyesight made him a liability both at bat and in the field, but he was never picked last because if Kaz wasn't a captain, he insisted that whoever picked him had to make Eddie their next pick.

Baseball held us together like glue. Kaz, Eddie, and I became known as the Three Ks, because each of us had a long, difficult name beginning with that letter. In science we had studied simple chemical compounds, and the diagrams of those compounds, dots joined by dark lines until they looked like constellations of stars, reminded me of our own attachments, and of the endless combinations we formed each day as the pickup game went on.

It was during that first summer in Northside that I met Cory Mazeppa, the fourth major character in this story, the pivotal character. If it wasn't for Cory, there would be no story. Her family operated a small grocery store across the street from the baseball field. We were in and out of the store two or three times a day all summer, and when she didn't have to work behind the counter, Cory would wander across Railroad Avenue and sit along one sideline or another watching the baseball game. She was a year younger but two grades behind me in school.

Mazeppa, Kaz informed me, was a Mongol name; he claimed there was some famous Mongol leader named Mazeppa. I often intended to look for confirmation in history books, but never have. The family claimed to be Yugoslavs who had crossed the border from Italy a century before. The parents had immigrated to America just before the Second World War. Cory would tell me a year later that she was conceived in the old country, born in the U.S.A. They belonged to a European church of some kind. It was housed in a sturdy building with a white steeple, formerly occupied by Lutherans who sold it after they built a flat, single-storey church covered in yellow California stucco. The signboard outside Mazeppas' church was covered in upside-down writing that Kaz said was Russian. At least four gaunt, bearded, and black-cassocked clergymen lived in the church basement, and could occasionally be seen walking single file, hands behind their back, down Railroad Avenue.

I would see the family file out the rear door of the small residence attached to the Mazeppa Family Grocery and head off in the direction of their church: the parents, Cory, her sisters, Mary and Pauline, one older, one younger, and a brother of about five who was always dressed in a replica of an adult suit and a tweed cap. The girls often wore billowing skirts and peasant blouses with brilliant embroidery patterns in vermilion, aquamarine, and kelly green.

Cory had soft brown eyes, chocolate hair, and a scattering of freckles across her cheeks and nose. She was shy and tended to look away if one of us tried to make eye contact with her at the baseball field. We were braver at the store and would tease her and try to confuse her change-making. None of us admitted any interest in girls that first summer, though I used to daydream of Cory when I came to bat, fantasizing myself in the big leagues, Cory my faithful sweetheart gallantly cheering me on against impossible odds. If I hit, I looked to where she sat, her skirt a tent floating about her on the grass. I was hoping for recognition, praise, a sign, knowing that if she did acknowledge me I would be the subject of unmerciful teasing, but I didn't care.

Baseball inextricably ties the four main characters together. But, as I've said, Cory is the important one, the fourth character. If Cory hadn't died there wouldn't be a story. But Cory chose to act, to end her life. If she had chosen not to act, to instead live out her days in the stifling cookie-cutter apartment, one in a complex of 250 identical apartments on the outskirts of Northside, apartments with gray stucco exteriors and close, airless interiors; if she had chosen to live that way, abandoned with her brood of children, she would have become only a passing memory to the Three Ks. To Kirkendahl she would have been a warm, grayish memory that would flit to the surface of consciousness every year or so on a honeysuckle-sweet summer evening, when fireflies glittered like sequins in the soft darkness. And she would have been even less to the other two.

But she did act, in her thirtieth year. Just as by thirty each of the others had acted. Kirkendahl quit his job as a sportswriter and lived off his wife's income while he researched and wrote *Murder's Blue Gown*, the re-creation of a sensational crime that had rocked a nearby

Illinois industrial suburb. The book had sex, mystery, and mutilation. It eventually sold eighty thousand copies and was made into a B movie starring Dean Stockwell that still turns up occasionally on the late, late show. The income from the book and movie allowed the author to pursue a full-time writing career. Kazimericz turned one used gravel truck into a small empire, then married into money. Kleinrath discovered his religious heritage. And Cory Mazeppa committed suicide.

My father was a confused, unhappy man, supervised by my mother. He had served as a medic in World War I, and his superiors told him he had the skill and temperament to be a doctor. But instead of becoming a doctor he did what was expected of him and returned to Iowa and the family hardware store.

"Don't ever let anyone talk you out of being what you want to be," he told me on more than one occasion. That was about the only advice he ever gave me, for we were awkward around each other, our time together full of clumsy silences. Father was pale and thin with a fringe of blondish hair. He spent his life doing a job he hated while Mother hovered behind him, bullying and cajoling. Grandfather, who retired to California, still sent long detailed letters in his large, vertical hand, offering advice, no, giving instruction, on pricing, inventory, and promotion. But Father had the last laugh, and I will always have a soft spot in my heart for him because of it. In spite of everyone's good intentions he managed to stay drunk on the contents of nefariously hidden bottles of vodka for over twenty years. He also flimflammed the books so my mother never suspected the insolvency of the business until the bankers arrived, padlocks in hand, to close the store. My father continued to drink; he would set off for his job as a security guard armed with a fifth of vodka and a heavy copy of *Gray's Anatomy*.

For all our bad times, we were better off than my friends. We had, if not a happy family, at least a relatively tranquil one. My mother would hiss at my father only long after I was in bed, supposedly asleep. I never heard exactly what she said, but I know my father never defended himself against whatever charges she made.

The time she made the remark about us being white trash my mother was about as depressed as she ever got. She rallied quickly and fixed up the house. She sewed bright curtains, scrubbed every inch of the place with Lysol, planted an extravaganza of flowers in the ugly front yard: poppies, pansies, heavy-headed white mums, sweet peas, cosmos, and hollyhocks. My bedroom reminded me of a coffin; my single bed filled the room. Mother put up a shelf alongside the bed and tacked a curtain to it to separate me from the bluish mildew that covered the wall.

She also made some quick alliances in the neighborhood: a Mrs. Piska, a Mrs. Hlushak, a Mrs. Hearne. "Misery loves company," she loved to say. The four of them would congregate for coffee each morning at the oilcloth-covered table in one of their kitchens. Mrs. Piska was roly-poly and always wore a black babushka festooned with blood-colored roses; she rolled her own fat cigarettes and in her heavy Polish accent stated that even though she had been married for over thirty years, her husband, Bronko, did not know she smoked. Mrs. Hlushak's only son was in jail for car theft; Mrs. Hearne, who had nine children, carried religious medals in her apron pocket and often gave the other ladies one when the coffee klatch broke up.

We at least had running water. Kaz lived in a cluster of shacks that didn't even have the dignity of being assigned a street address. His mother was dead; his father was a brutish drunk; he had one sister of about eleven who grew wild and untended. Kaz's father worked from four to midnight at the Firestone Tire plant. After work he would stop at one of the all-night bars along Railroad Avenue, drink himself into a rage, fistfight with whoever was handy, and often end up sprawled on the gravel behind the hotel. On more than one occasion I slipped out of the house deep in the night after Kaz tapped on the wall behind my head (my room had no window), and the two of us took turns pulling Kaz's metal wagon home from the hotel, his father face down, mumbling, cursing, his hands dragging on the street.

Eddie was the third of four children. His family lived in a shack with a slanted roof, and they had to carry water from a community water spigot four blocks away. Eddie's father, Isaac Kleinrath, claimed they were Hungarian Gypsies. Eddie said they were Jewish and called his father "The Rabbi" behind his back.

I don't think anyone ever realizes the best times of their lives while those times are happening. It's just as well, for if they did, they would realize that everything else is downhill, no matter how gentle and gradual the slope, and they would stop trying, stop striving. I suppose it was sometime in my twenties when I realized that my *baseball days,* those three summers I spent in Northside, had so far been the best days of my life. That time when baseball was like the sun lighting my days. I was through university, working my way up the ranks in the newspaper business, ambitious, acquisitive, when the first suspicions appeared. My suspicions, shadows, gray, disturbing, like animals skulking about the edge of a camp, came in the form of disturbing thoughts about Cory, mixed with pleasant reveries about baseball. I dreamed of the long, sunny afternoons on the field where our endless game went on from the time the dew left the grass until it was too dark to see the ball. We played a game called Eleven, where if either team was ahead by eleven or more runs after even innings the game was called; we either started over or broke up and chose new sides. I can still hear Eddie's shrill "Way to go, Flash," as I ran in on a fly ball that was going yards over my head, or as I crashed to the ground after connecting with the ball, taking precious seconds to get to my feet, turning a double into a single.

I loved those times, the tense, uncaring heat of August, the air thick, sweat drizzling into my eyebrows. I remember grabbing the bottom of my damp T-shirt, pulling it up and wiping my forehead, drying my eyes before heading for the plate. I remember squinting through a haze of perspiration from my spot in right field, the earth aerated by cheeky prairie dogs who peeked and chittered all the long, lazy afternoons.

I had been in the enclosed yard behind Mazeppas' store on more than one occasion. In that way boys have of exploring like animals, I had peeked through the caragana hedge, crossed the yard, peered through the window of the garage where Mr. Mazeppa stored a seldom used, pre-war Essex. The car was tan, all square angles, with a windshield that tilted forward. One day I helped Mr. Mazeppa, a grumpy man with a sharp tongue, unload boxes of groceries he had carried home from the wholesaler. I carried in crates of tin cans, boxes full of pungent coffee and exotic-smelling spices. The cottonwood trees were tall with broad leaves. The leaves deflected the sun even in midafternoon, so only a few white diamonds of light would dance on the spongy earth of the yard. A few bluebells grew in the mossy turf, a cool aster bloomed, its purple head bowed by the weight of its lush petals.

One afternoon, a skyful of black clouds stampeded in from the west, bringing heavy wind and rain with them. The game broke up quickly, some players running for home, some seeking shelter nearby. Cory had been sitting on the sidelines alone, as she almost always was; we both ran across the street, dodging the penny-sized raindrops.

"Come on in the yard," she said. I was planning to make a run for home, but I quickly took her up on her invitation. Cory was wearing a mauve dress, a hand-me-down of some kind, that clung to her body. We stood under the leaves for a moment or two. The wind whirled through the tops of the cottonwoods. The tempo of the rain increased but the yard remained dry.

"Do you want to see my rabbit?" Cory asked.

The storm made the yard darker than twilight. We peered through the wire mesh but all we could see were the rabbit's eyes, a phosphorescent amber in a far corner. I touched Cory's hand and my heart bumped as if I'd tripped and stumbled. But I didn't let go. The feeling I experienced was the most beautiful I'd ever known. Being an only child, I had never felt protective toward anyone. It never occurred to me that what I was feeling was sexual, though I considered kissing Cory as we walked slowly to the center of the yard and sat side by side on one of the gnarled roots of the largest cottonwood. Cory's fingers were slim and her hand so much smaller than mine. I couldn't speak, but I glanced at her. Her long hair was uncombed. There were water marks on her cheeks as if she might have cried earlier in the day. I let my arm circle her shoulder, my fingers barely touching the skin of her upper arm. Cory let her head lean against my shoulder. I was just about to turn to kiss her when I glanced down. Below our feet, in the bare dirt near the roots was a scuffle of twigs, feathers, and blood, where a small bird had probably fallen victim to a cat; there was a worm of entrails, an inch of pale yellow, scaly leg.

"What is it?" whispered Cory. I tightened my grip on her shoulder so she wouldn't look down. We were suddenly interrupted by pounding footsteps and loud voices. By the time Kaz and Eddie pushed through the hedge into the tranquillity of the yard, shaking themselves like dogs, Cory and I were sitting a couple of feet apart.

In the spring of my third and final year in Northside, on the opening day of the baseball season, my father died. In his typical way, not wanting to disturb anyone, he died in his sleep. Since he worked nights, it was midafternoon when my mother discovered his body. By the time I got home from school the undertaker had already removed the corpse, funeral arrangements had been made, she had called his employer to say he wouldn't be in again, and had contacted a branch of the insurance company which insured his life. Mother was so efficient that we were hardly inconvenienced at all.

Four months after my father's death, my mother married a man named Nick Walczak, a fifty-two-year-old dairy farmer, and we moved to Wisconsin in time for me to start school in September. Nick was a widower with a grown family. He wore a felt hat and a shiny blue serge suit. His face was windburned and he smelled of cattle. I hated Nick, the farm, Wisconsin, and the Bible Belt high school I attended in a holier-than-thou town called St. Edward. I have to admit that Nick was a good deal more tolerant of me than I would have been of him if our roles had been reversed.

My mother must have met Nick through the personal ads in our daily newspaper, or through a lonely-hearts club of some kind. I imagined his ad: Gent. 52, widower, farmer of some means, seeks marriage-minded woman. Box – – – .

"You're going to become Polish by marriage," Kaz teased me.

Nick claimed to be Estonian but Kaz taught me the vilest Polish curses he knew and Nick seemed to understand them. Someday I am going to write a novel about the year I spent on Nick Walczak's farm in America's Dairyland.

Cory is dead and her death stays with me, a stain on the canvas of my life. When I was a kid in Iowa, in our dark and unused parlor hung a watercolor painted from a photograph, a picture of my mother's older brother. It was a large head-and-shoulders view of what could have been either a boy or a girl: a pink-faced child with rouge cheeks and artificially blue eyes, staring sullenly from a mop of long, blond hair. Charlie had died at age seven from a bee sting to the eye. My mother, a year younger than Charlie, had been playing with him in the garden on a sunstruck afternoon when Charlie bent a tall hollyhock down to his face and the resident bee panicked and stung him on the eyelid. The poison went to his brain and he died a day later.

My mother, in one of the rare moments when she talked about her past, said that she blamed herself for Charlie's death, and that through-out the rest of her childhood she planned how, as soon as she was old enough, she would get pregnant and present her parents with a baby to replace Charlie. "I thought about it endlessly, but I never acted," she said. She was in her mid-thirties when I was born, and by that time both her parents were dead.

There is an Indian legend called "The Woman on the Rocks," and I can't help but recall it as I think of Cory and all the what-might-have-beens. The legend states that young warriors of pure spirit will, as they wander the forests, one day see a beautiful young woman sitting amid rocks at the top of a fearsome waterfall. The girl sees them, beckons to them seductively from behind the white spume of the falls. Each warrior who sees the young woman is immediately captivated, but each, for whatever reason, considers too long before going to her aid. Each one hesitates for a fraction of a second, taking his eyes from the beautiful face for an instant, and when he looks back the maiden on the rocks is gone, swept away to her death perhaps, or simply vanished because of the warrior's indecision. But the warrior is left forever with a memory pure and fresh, cut into his heart—a memory of what might have been if he had been quicker to act. No warrior ever reached the woman on the rocks. Elders interpreted the phenomenon as a moral statement, a truth. Carrying the leaden ball of what-might-have-been deep within us is not a punishment but a lesson. And the ache is not always unpleasant, but often warm and nostalgic, reeking of lost innocence.

But what of the woman on the rocks herself? What happens when she is not a spirit, a lesson, an abstraction, but real flesh and blood with a heart that breaks and a soul full of human longings?

I have tried on several occasions to write about Cory and how she touched my life. About ten years ago I got several pages into a story called "Who Can Eat a Gingerbread Man?" which was about Cory's last hours of life. But I was still too close to the material. I wrote a story about the Three Ks, called "Tough Guys." It is one of my few unpublished stories. What follows is the opening page of "Who Can Eat a Gingerbread Man?"

On a dismal afternoon in February 1967, Corrina Ann Mazeppa (her married name had been Kliciak, but she had taken back her maiden name after the divorce) bundled her three youngest children into their snowsuits, put them into a cab, gave the driver her last ten dollars and her mother's address, telling him to be certain and send the change in with the oldest child.

Corrina Ann Mazeppa, Cory to everyone, closed the door, shivered away the cold draft that had chilled her feet and ankles. She took a last look at the buried yard where snow sculptures like whitecaps sat stiffly in the sullen cold of midwinter. Cory made her way to the bathroom, where cheap plastic curtains covered the frosted glass of the single window. The room smelled of diapers, baby powder, and sour towels. She ran water into the scummy, avocado tub, took off her jeans and sweatshirt, slipped down into the very hot water. She picked up a safety razor, released the blade, rinsed dried soap and hairs from both edges, drew the blade harshly across the underside of her left wrist, changed hands, and cut her right wrist in the same manner. She slid deeper into the water until it touched the back of her neck. Suppressing an urge to vomit, she watched transfixed as her blood colored the water.

I abandoned that fiction, or *faction.* For though we know Cory put her kids in a taxi and later cut her wrists in the bathtub, no one can ever know her thoughts in those last moments.

I remember noticing, those first summers in Northside, how many of the boys at sixteen or seventeen suddenly began drifting away from the eternal pickup game. I couldn't imagine it ever happening to me. But during my final summer, after my father's death, life began interfering with baseball. I got a paper route; for six days a week, from three to six in the afternoon, I had to abandon the game. I also had to miss Friday evenings, which was collection time.

Kaz, the first of us to turn sixteen, got his driver's license and suddenly became obsessed with rebuilding a rusty skeleton of a one-ton truck that had languished in his father's yard for years.

Eddie, the most fearless and outgoing of our group, developed an interest in religion; he visited one of the two synagogues in the city to discuss his Jewishness.

"You circumsized?" he asked me one day as we slouched along Railroad Avenue.

"No," I replied.

"At the synagogue they asked me and I told them the truth. I wish I'd lied. I wonder if they really check your dong to make sure you've been cut?"

"I wouldn't know," I said.

And of course we all discovered girls. Some of us more than others. I was one of the others. Most of the girls I knew were shrill, giggling brats. Kaz suddenly started talking about one or two of the older girls who were reputed to put out; he talked as if he was speaking from experience. Eddie emulated Kaz, though I had more doubts about his claims. "What about you?" Kaz said one evening. "You're not cherry, are you?"

"I know my way around," I said defensively.

But Eddie was the one who talked, about anybody and everybody. "Oh, God," he'd cry as we walked away from Mazeppas' store in the twilight. "Did you see the knockers under that sweater of Cory's? I'd sell my right nut just to touch them. One touch and I'd die happy." He would fumble through his jacket pockets looking for matches to light his cigarette, his eyes bleary slits behind his thick glasses.

I was surprised one night when Kaz called Eddie on his wishful thinking. "You're all talk, Kleinrath," he said. "You're talking about Cory Mazeppa, for chrissakes. Anybody can do it with Cory."

Kleinrath was all ears and I, too, was silent as Kaz told us how Cory had taken him into the back seat of the square-fendered Essex. I knew Cory didn't come to the ballfield very often anymore. I'd seen her walking with a boy named Buck Johnson; he was white trash, a pock-faced kid who worked on the killing floor of the packing plant. He had a long, equine head and a greasy pompadour. Another time I saw her duck into her yard with Nick Kliciak, a thug who lived at the Passtime Pool Hall. He was short, and, even though he was only a year or two older than us, wore a charcoal-gray suit and pink shirt with an inch-wide black tie.

A week later, Eddie was echoing Kaz's story word for word.

"Come on, Kirkendahl," he said, "get in on the act. You've always had a thing for Cory, haven't you?"

I only smiled and changed the subject.

This is not one of those heartwarming stories of lasting friendships and lifelong loyalties. After I left Northside, we did not stay in touch. I finished high school in Wisconsin, moved to the warmth of California, and married a California girl. Now I seldom leave the state except to go on book promotion tours, which was what brought me to Illinois in the winter of 1967.

A few years after we left Northside, after my mother had been widowed for a second time—this time being left well off financially—she did a very strange thing. She moved back to Northside. She rented a modest apartment on the edge of the old neighborhood, and took up where she had left off with her old friends. The four of them have all been widowed for years and years. Among them they have the complete oral history of Northside in their heads. My mother can recite from memory the history of all the families who populated the district when we first moved there thirty-five years ago.

"You remember Heather Bratus," she'll write to me. "She married the youngest Dzuba boy, from the packing-plant Dzubas, not the lumberyard Dzubas—well, her daughter . . ." She will tell me a long, often pointless, story about someone I know only by name. I often remind her that I lived only about three years in Northside, but she can't seem to comprehend that, at least for more than a few minutes.

But it was through my mother that I knew what became of Kaz, Eddie, and Cory.

"Eddie, that nice boy with the bad eyesight, is an architect now. He turned Jewish. But then his name always was, wasn't it? He married the daughter of the founder of the firm he works for." She even went so far as to clip the bold-type listing from an outdated Yellow Pages directory: MOSER, SALTZMAN, GREEN & KLEINRATH, followed by a prestigious address in the downtown area of the city.

"Your friend Bronislaw is a millionaire," my mother reported. "Mrs. Piska says he owns a thousand trucks. But no one can figure how he got his money. Mrs. Hearne says he was doing something illegal to start with, drugs or stolen goods . . ." Kaz as Gatsby. Interesting. I've seen Kaz's trucks in southern California, golden transports and tankers, with Bronze Transport in swirling script on the doors and down each side, a small Polish flag beneath the curlicued *B* in Bronze. "Your friend Bronislaw married the ex-mayor's daughter. I guess two fortunes are better than one."

Once she mentioned Cory. "Pauline, the youngest Mazeppa girl— you remember the family has that little store on Railroad Avenue— got married over the weekend to a mining engineer from Chicago. A big splash at the Russian Orthodox Church and a huge reception at Northside Community Hall. I hope she's done better than the middle girl; she married one of the awful Kliciak boys and has had nothing but grief."

As my final summer in Northside moved into the heat of July, I found myself doing what I vowed I'd never do. I drifted further and further away from the continuous baseball game. My paper route took up my time; I had money to spend. I helped Kaz work on his truck. He taught me to drive.

One evening, as I headed home from Kaz's place, I found myself crossing the baseball field at twilight. There had been a heavy thunderstorm an hour or two before and the game hadn't resumed. The grass was sopping, the air fresh as an April morning. As I neared home plate, I saw someone leaning against the backstop.

The last red tines of sunset clawed across the field. I recognized Cory by her silhouette. She beckoned to me. I walked slowly toward her across the damp infield. She smiled shyly. "It's so fresh out here," she said. "I like the air after a storm." I didn't say anything. "You haven't been around very much this summer," she went on. I mumbled about being busy, about working on Kaz's truck. I became conscious that though I'd washed my hands I still smelled like solvent and had more grease on my clothes than I was comfortable with.

Cory didn't seem to notice. "Let's walk," she said. And she took my hand as if it were the most natural thing in the world for her to do.

"Pickup! Pickup!" screamed a couple of shrill voices from across Railroad Avenue as we started up the wooden sidewalk toward the edge of town. Though the words were directed at Cory, the girls yelling were schoolmates of mine, Ruthie Fontana and Cookie Brost. I realize now that Cory was doing what they didn't have the nerve to do. But what she was doing made her different, and there is no room anywhere for people who are different. "Pickup!" they screamed again, then went into a fit of shrill giggling.

"Don't pay any attention," whispered Cory.

Cory's father had made her quit school on her fifteenth birthday. For nearly a year, her life had revolved around the dark little store that smelled of coffee and oily floorboards. I didn't speak but I squeezed Cory's hand in a gesture of reassurance. I thought of Ruthie Fontana, pale, hatchet-faced, eyes quick as a bird's. Ruthie went steady with one of the Bjarnson boys, who lived down by the stockyards. They had a blanket stashed in the bushes behind a Coppertone sign way out at the end of Railroad Avenue; they went there every day after school and had probably spent half the summer there, too. But they were going steady.

There I was, walking up the sidewalk, the first hints of ground mist rising from the grassy gutters. Me, the clutch hitter, heart thrumming, tongue clotted in my mouth because I was holding the hand of a girl I'd known for three years and seen every baseball summer day that whole time.

We slowed and stepped into a gateway where tall, yellow caragana rose high above our heads. Cory turned to face me. I held her, my hands flat on the middle of her back, and we kissed. Cory was soft in my arms and she smelled sweet; her lipstick was slick against my lips. We clung that way for a long time. I remained totally silent. I kissed down the side of her face, across her cheek and back to her lips. They parted willingly. At the same time, I was as happy and as frightened as I had ever been in my life. Cory needed to be held. So did I. Fantasies of rescue flashed through my mind. Cory moved one hand to the back of my neck, twined her fingers in my hair, pulled my face closer to hers. She had none of the coyness of the girls I went to school with, girls who doled out half-returned kisses for favors real or imagined.

We walked on slowly, our arms now twined around each other's waists. The only sound was our shoes on the hollow wooden sidewalk. The sidewalk ended a block farther on. A single avocado-green house sat fifty yards back from the street, a cow grazing near it. In the distance a dog yapped.

We sat on the end of the sidewalk and kissed some more. Cory swung both her legs over my closest one. One of my arms braced her back. I kept thinking of what Eddie and Kaz said about her, of my seeing her with Nick Kliciak. What was expected of me? Wasn't instinct supposed to play some part in a situation like this? Wasn't I supposed to know what to do? I had no idea what to do. Cory was wearing a soft, pink sweater and a brown skirt. Her dark hair was restrained by pink barrettes shaped like kittens. I tentatively touched the sweater, let my fingers slide across to her breast. Cory didn't resist, so I cupped her breast gently, trying to convey affection through my touch. My throat felt cemented shut, like a useless plumbing pipe. I could say nothing. I tried once to speak her name, just her name, a whisper in a tone that would convey some feeling. What emerged was a helpless sound, like a shoe being extracted from mud.

"Your arm is shaking," Cory said, burying her face in my neck. My left arm, which supported her back, was trembling.

"I'm all right," I managed. Cory shifted her weight, wrapped her arms tightly around my neck, kissed me fiercely. I caressed her breast.

"Please, please, please," Cory murmured, holding on to me so hard her own arms trembled. We sat for several more minutes, kissing, touching gently.

"I have to get back," Cory said finally. "Papa will miss me." We walked back toward the lights of Northside, our arms still twined around each other's waists.

When we got to her door I cleared my throat and said, "Thanks, Cory." I felt like a fool the instant the words were out.

"For what?" She smiled, I think sadly, stood on her tiptoes, and brushed her lips across mine. "Do you like me?" she said suddenly, slipping her arms around me, resting her head against my chest.

"Yes, I really like you," I said.

"Will you come by tomorrow evening?"

"I will. I promise."

Cory slipped away, closing the screen door softly behind her.

My wife and I sometimes work as a team on journalistic assignments. She does the interviewing; I do the writing. I don't like interviewing people, because silence is still a problem in my life. Weeks after an interview I think of all the questions I should have asked. I relive the interview again and again even though it is water under the bridge. In the same manner I have spent a great deal of my life thinking about Cory. I feel like a wedding car with a tin can still traveling behind it, years and years after the event. I mean, I haven't been obsessed to the point where it has destroyed my life. I have a lovely wife and a grown daughter who has been a great joy to me. We live in a pleasant condo in La Mesa, California, with a cat the color of cinnamon, named Joy-Hulga. I have season tickets at nearby Jack Murphy Stadium where I watch the San Diego Padres perform. I have never mentioned Cory to my wife. In fact, I have never mentioned Cory to anyone, ever.

I have not done very many things in my life of which I am genuinely ashamed. But in the week following my evening with Cory I did three reprehensible things that will trail after me like pale ghosts all my life.

The first was that I did not go back to see Cory as I had promised. I wanted to. I planned to. But each evening as I made ready to walk over to Railroad Avenue, my throat tightened until I could barely swallow. Even away from her I could not think of a single word I could say. The anticipation of the long, crushing silences I knew lay ahead was too much for me. One day became two, three, six.

The second thing was worse and occurred a week to the day after our meeting. At midmorning I had to run an errand for my mother. I caught the bus downtown. The bus was small, painted red and cream, and held only about twenty people. It looked like a loaf of bread with windows and wheels. When I got on there were only three other passengers and one of them was Cory. She was sitting in a window seat just in front of the rear door. I lowered my eyes, took a seat at the front of the bus with my back to her. I rode the bus twenty blocks past the downtown, nearly to the end of the line, staring straight ahead, unseeing, my neck stiff as a railroad tie. When I stood up to leave I noted with great relief that Cory was gone.

What held me back? When I saw Cory why couldn't I have marched down the aisle and sat beside her? Why couldn't I have asked where she was going and then said something like "I guess we're both pretty shy, but maybe if we spend a little time together we'll get over the worst of it. Let's just walk around downtown for a while and window-shop. Maybe we'll get to be friends." And I would have taken Cory's hand, and she would have nestled her head against my shoulder. But then I've had nearly thirty-five years to compose that speech.

My third act occurred later that same day and made the other two forgettable. Eddie came by Kaz's place and the three of us tinkered with the truck. A couple of other sometime-ballplayers were hanging around.

"I hear you're travelin' with Cory Mazeppa," Eddie said to me.

"Where would you hear that?" I said.

"Cookie Brost saw you the other night. Nothin' happens in Northside that somebody doesn't see."

"So what?"

"Cory's hot stuff. Did you score?"

"What business is that of yours?"

"She took Kaz in the garage, more than once," said Eddie, leering, his mouth twisted. "And me." He danced backward a few steps. "So, what about you?"

Everyone was waiting. They were all watching me.

"She was easy," I said.

Northside and the city of which it is a suburb are not places where people buy books. They are rough, ethnically mixed, hard-working communities, distinctly lacking in imagination. I insisted the city be on my itinerary when I ventured out to promote *Murder's Blue Gown*. My mother had visited California once or twice a year, spending the money from Nick Walczak's dairy herd on airfare and hotels. I had not been back to Northside since the time about a month after my evening with Cory, when my mother sprang the surprise that she was marrying Nick and we were moving to Wisconsin.

I arrived the night before Cory's funeral. Coincidence? I suppose. A bitter wind drifted snow over the city. I bought a newspaper, found the ad touting my appearance at a bookstore the following evening, and scanned the obituaries, where I saw: "MAZEPPA, Corrina Ann (Kliciak). Suddenly, on Feb. 22; she is survived by . . ."

The names of her four children, her parents, and her sisters followed. The oldest child was named James. Another coincidence, I suppose.

Nick Carraway in *The Great Gatsby* states, "Everyone suspects himself of at least one of the cardinal virtues." His, he says later, was honesty. I wonder about my own. It certainly isn't honesty. Is hindsight a virtue? Where do vice and virtue blur together? How responsible are we for the lives of those we touch briefly? Is omission as much of a sin as commission? I tried not to think about it. But I couldn't help it. I decided to attend the funeral of someone I hadn't seen for sixteen years, half my lifetime, half hers. Yet I felt strongly that I had contributed to her death. At that point I didn't know for certain how she died, but I would have bet my own life that she was a suicide.

I arranged for my mother to take a taxi down to the hotel and have dinner with me. For once I was vitally interested in her oral history of Northside. I had only to ask "What's new?" to elicit more information than I wanted to know about Cory and her family.

"Lots of excitement," my mother said, leaning conspiratorially across the dark blue linen tablecloth. "You remember Mazeppas, the family had the little store on Railroad Avenue, their second daughter, Cory, the one who married badly, committed suicide Monday. The old folks still live behind the store, though it's not a store anymore; they closed up after Safeway opened across Railroad Avenue in the big shopping center. Well, the suicide isn't official or anything. Mr. Mazeppa went to the bishop of their church; they have to have the funeral at a funeral home and not at the church, but she can be buried in their cemetery." And she went on and on and on.

"Hey, Flash." It was Eddie at my shoulder, just as he used to be near me at my locker in high school and at the continuous baseball game. I was crossing the parking lot toward the door of the funeral home. Eddie punched my shoulder, just as he did a half lifetime ago, with a back-handed flick of his knuckles.

"Eddie." I turned and smiled down at him, his thick glasses revealing the same blue blur as in the past. His hair was styled now, the ever present shoelace defeated. He wore an expensive black overcoat, a maroon velvet yarmulke perched on his skull like a beanie.

"Did you come all the way back here for the funeral?"

"Coincidence," I said, "though I might have, if I'd known in time."

We talked quietly about our present lives. We didn't mention Cory.

"How long since you've been home?" asked Eddie.

"Years," I said. *Home.* What a strange word. *Where the heart is* kept flashing through my head. *Where the heart is.* Not so untrue. This miserable, cold, inescapable city may well be where my heart is, I thought. A heart never grown to full size, suspended in the humid summer evenings of long ago: the baseball field, Cory, home.

"You'll see a lot of changes," Eddie said.

"I don't recognize much. The downtown has been leveled and rebuilt."

"So has the old neighborhood. The Railroad Hotel's still there, but there's an auto dealership between the hotel and Mazeppas' store. There's a K Mart where we used to play baseball. Store's a block square, dropped right down on the old playing field like a circus tent. You wouldn't know the place."

At this moment Kaz appeared, getting out of a bronze limousine longer than the funeral cars parked at the side of the building.

"This guy's a wheel," said Eddie, grinning, displaying Kaz to me like a personal accomplishment.

"I guess none of us have done so badly, us three old ballplayers," I said, shaking Kaz's hand. Kaz looked every inch a millionaire: his hands were as soft and pink as his face, which was turning fleshy. In a few years he would look like a friendly bulldog.

We sat shoulder to shoulder on one of the varnished pews of the funeral home. The service was brief, the chapel less than half full. The coffin was closed. A relief. I could never have brought myself to walk by it.

"Those were the best of times," said Eddie, smiling sadly. We were back in the parking lot waiting for Kaz's limousine. He had offered to drop Eddie at work, me at my hotel. "God, I remember springing out of bed in the morning, wolfing down whatever I could find for breakfast, grabbing my glove, and heading for the field. I was almost grown up before I realized how poor we were."

"I always knew how poor we were," said Kaz.

"But what was it about baseball?" I said. "Why did we spend three or four years of our lives on that playing field?"

"It was something to do with the ritual," said Eddie. "There was a wonderful sameness, a stability. At that age you don't understand anything that's happening to your body or your life. Kids at that age think they're immortal; they don't want their parents' religion, if the parents have any . . ."

"There was something primitive about the game," said Kaz. "A closeness to the earth. The hardest part was waiting for the field to dry out after the snow melted. We'd try but we'd never make it, would we?"

"We'd be playing with the water over our shoes. Remember how clots of mud used to cling to the ball."

"I can still see the spray flying when I hit it square on."

"Let's drive by the field," said Kaz. And he gave the driver instructions, not giving Eddie or me a chance to object.

"Baseball is healing," I said. "I wish I could put it better, but the feeling I had, though I didn't know it then, is like I feel after being with a woman who loves me a lot, that dreamy lethargy, that feeling of well-being."

People stared at us as we got out of the limousine in the K Mart parking lot. Kaz and Eddie looked like Mafia hitmen; I looked like a poor cousin in my light jacket and slippery shoes. The sky was low, the air bitter; snow drifted around our ankles. Across the street Mazeppas' store sat forlorn and in need of paint. There were curtains drawn across the front windows, and what used to be the door to the grocery was drifted full of snow and street refuse.

Inside K Mart it was bright as summer noon. The ceiling was paved with white lights. There were few shoppers in the store. A bedraggled mother pushed a silver cart with two children in it. Another was tugging at her coat, whining.

"The backstop and home plate would be over there," said Kaz, pointing to the women's wear section, where circular dollies full of bright, cheap clothes were crowded together like a field of giant flowers.

"Left field would be out there in the furniture department," said Eddie.

We walked to the sporting goods section. There was little baseball equipment on display. But Kaz and Eddie found gloves while I took the only bat in sight. Kaz spotted baseballs, safely behind glass in a display case. He looked around. As usual in K Mart, there were no salespeople anywhere in sight. Kaz went behind the counter, slid open the case, and extracted a half-dozen baseballs. Kaz and Eddie took off their overcoats and laid them across the counter. We made our way to women's wear. I took a child's red dress from a dolly and dropped it to mark the spot where home plate would be. Kaz paced off the distance to the pitcher's mound, elbowing dress racks out of the way, clearing a path. Eddie sprinted for the outfield. "Hit me a good one, Flash," he sang.

I held the bat high, gripped tight at the end. I held it straight up and down, peeking over the crook of my left elbow. I have always prided myself that I was using a stance and grip remarkably similar to Carl Yastrzemski's, ten years before he first appeared in the majors. Kaz pawed the cheap white tiles where the mound used to be. Far back in left Eddie drifted among the sofas and loveseats.

"Burn it in there, Kaz," he hollered, shielding his eyes with his glove, blocking out the glare of an imaginary sun. A few people were staring at us, warily, as they passed in nearby aisles.

I wiggled the end of the bat and waited. As I did, the white light of

K Mart became summer sunshine. The store lifted away from us like a bell jar. The other players took their places on the field: tall, silent Ted Troy at first base, Peppy Goselin as shortstop, Pudge Green in center field. As the players took shape, the racks of pink and blue dresses, the women's and children's clothes, fresh as sunshine, smelling of ironing and starch, rose like mist. The grass was emerald-green, measled with dandelions.

"Burn it in there, Kaz," shouted Eddie.

Kaz fired the ball. I swung and fouled it off. Strange that it made a sound like breaking glass. Someone strange was walking in from right field, a young man, his face the color of maple, wearing a white shirt buttoned to the collar and a black-on-white name tag reading AHMED. He looked both puzzled and frightened. "Please not to do what it is you are doing, please," he said in a heavy accent. He raised his hands in a gesture similar to calling time in baseball, though I'm sure he had no idea what he was doing.

Kaz snarled several words at the intruder. He scuttled away.

"Come on, Flash, straighten one out," yelled Eddie.

"I lied about Cory," I yelled.

"Everybody lies about things like that," said Kaz.

"You?"

"Everybody." He made a gesture that encompassed us all.

All the players were in place now, my team along the sidelines, Kaz's team in the field. All the baseball boys. All the accountants and thugs and TV producers and packing-plant workers and railroad section men. And Cory was sitting on the grass a few yards behind the bench, alone as always, her black hair snarled about her face, her mauve dress spread in a wide arc about her.

There were two pinging sounds like a doorbell. "Security to Section 12. Security to Section 12," said a female voice.

"Burn it in there, Kaz."

Cory is dead and her death stays with me, trapped here with me, inside my own skin.

The maple-faced boy was back and there was someone with him. Someone larger.

"Please not to do what it is you are doing, please."

"Fire the ball."

"Security to Section 12."

What were these strange people doing on the field? The earth felt hard, my feet refused to dig in properly.

"Pitch the ball."

Kaz wound up; his thick arm and hamlike hand with the grease-stained knuckles snapped the ball toward me.

Cory smiled shyly. After the game I'd walk her to the end of the sidewalk, kiss her so gently in the lilac shadows.

The ball was one long laser of white connecting Kaz's hand with my bat. In the hairsbreadth of a second between the crack of the bat and the ball exploding into the sun above the outfield, I relished the terrible joy of hitting it square on.

For Lesley Choyce

THE FIREFIGHTER

It's Cal that I want to tell you about. But it seems there are so many other things I should get to first, like Delly and my baseball career. I just finished Rookie League up in Butte, Montana. The Butte Copper Kings. We finished 25-45 for the season, but I batted .337 and hit 30 homers in 70 games. Up in Montana winter breathes on you all year round; the grass was white with frost one morning before we left Butte on the last day of August.

It sure ain't cold where we are, headin' from Tulsa toward Oklahoma City, where we're gonna spend the off-season. The heat-gauge on this rattle-trap '71 Plymouth has gone clear out of sight and it must be a hundred outside the car. Delly's fanning her thighs with a baseball program from Kansas City, where we stopped off for three days to see how they play in the Bigs, a place where I'm gonna be in two, three years at the most. Delly grins and fans and don't mind lettin' me see there's a wet spot in the crotch of her denim cutoffs.

I'd pull off the road right now if there was anywhere to pull off to except sand dunes and red rock hot enough to fry steak. I know if I ever stop this rickety car it will just die and go to Plymouth heaven right by the side of the road.

We ain't actually headin' for Oklahoma City, but for a place called El Reno: twenty-two adobe buildings, five service stations, and an air-conditioned Taco Bell. Thirty-five miles past El Reno, out in the sage brush, is where Delly's family lives. Cal is Delly's father and he's the one I want to tell you about. There's an oil-donkey about every hundred yards on Cal's land, turnin' slow in the desert glare like big birds primpin' themselves. Cal don't own the oil rights so he ain't gettin' rich, but the oil company pays him so much for each land site.

I should tell you more about Cal being a firefighter and all, but I can't help thinkin' about this morning in the Blue Velvet Motel in Tulsa ($12.95 for two, day sleepers welcome), and how I was reading that same baseball program Delly's fannin' her thighs with, when I look up to see Delly come out of the bathroom. She don't actually come out. She just stands in the doorway, naked from the waist up, her titties pointing at the ceiling like they see something up there that I don't. Delly's got hair the same colour as the red desert sand and it's kind of mussed and casual like she just crawled out of the sack, which she did. She's wearing faded blue jeans not quite done up and she's leanin' against the door jamb starin' at me with her big, sleepy-blue eyes in a way that makes me toss the program on the floor and polevault over to her. Before we know it the maid is knockin' on the door tellin' us it's noon and check-out time for us was eleven.

Now it's Cal, and Eddie, and Regina, and Ma, who are Delly's immediate family, that I want to tell you about, and how they live so far back in the boonies, that, as they say on TV documentaries, they've hardly been disturbed by time or sanity.

"You ain't quite what I expected, but I expect you'll do," is what Delly said to me after the first time we was together in the single bed in the room she rented a few blocks from the university in Oklahoma City, where I'd come on a baseball scholarship. Delly was waitin' tables at a little bar patronized mainly by students. "I took a job here 'cause I figured I'd meet me a doctor or lawyer or maybe a dentist, 'cause they make the big money. I been poor the first eighteen years of my life and that's about long enough," is what she said to me, after we made love that was so sweet I couldn't have even imagined it. If somebody'd said to me, "Tell me about your wildest fantasy," I couldn't have dreamed up nothin' half as good as what Delly and me did that night.

I remember Delly comin' up to my table to take my order. She was wearin' blue jeans and a top the colour of green tomatoes, and I wondered if her titties had as many freckles on them as her face and arms. And the sound of denim rubbin' together as she walked away made me so horny that when I paid for my beer I held on to the dollar until our hands touched and I said, "I sure would like to know you better." And she said, "Where you from?" And I said, "Iowa." And she said, "That's a big state." And I said, "I'm like a fellow I read about in a story once. I'm not *from* a place, just from *near* a place. And if you ever heard of Onamata, Iowa, that's the place I was raised nearest to."

"I never," she said, and she frowned when I told her I was a Phys. Ed. major studying on a baseball scholarship.

"I ain't gonna be no Phys. Ed. teacher with a beer belly and a lot of might've-beens," I told Delly. "You come out and watch me hit the ball and see if you don't agree," and I guess she did, 'cause we been together ever since, and hasn't it been great.

"You let me worry about the money, Sugar," is what Delly said to me, and I let her. She banked her salary and tips and we lived off my scholarship money. When I graduated in the spring and got drafted by Seattle and then loaned to Butte for a summer in Rookie League, Delly said we could afford to get married.

Ballplayers in Rookie League ain't supposed to drag along wives or girlfriends. The scout who signed me looked at me like I was a pervert when I said I wanted to bring my wife with me. He arranged for one one-way airline ticket from Oklahoma City to Butte. Baseball club tried to make me take room and board with some solid-citizen baseball fans who would look after my *well-being* while I was in Butte. But Delly took care of things. She left two days before me on the bus and rented a two-bedroom basement suite. We took in one of the Panamanian outfielders to fill up that spare bedroom. Delly got a job waiting tables in a bar and she wasn't afraid to wear peek-a-boo blouses. "I can count your pussy-hairs through them jeans," I said to her one afternoon as she was getting ready for work.

"You bet you can," she smiled, "they're worth about a dollar each in tips. Look, Sugar, them drunkies are always gonna be tipping too much in sleazy bars and they'll never have a pot to piss in or a window to throw it outa. You just keep hittin' the long ball and let me worry about the money."

And you know what? We're comin' back to a condo all our own in a nice new building near downtown Oklahoma City. And the payments aren't any more than rent would be and Delly already rented the extra room to a student.

I've met Delly's family and except for her ma they'd make a great study for an anthropologist. This big company found oil on Cal's land about fifteen years ago, and Cal ain't worked since, not that he ever worked before.

"Pa used to run what he called an Underground Auto Wrecking business," Delly told me. "That means he sold stolen car parts. I went with him once or twice when I was a kid. We'd cruise into Oklahoma City and Pa would park behind a night club. 'Folks who can afford to drink can afford to donate to our livelihood,' he always said. Pa could strip four wheels, the spare, a couple of headlights and sometimes a grille off a pick-up in under four minutes. I seen him detach a mirror or strip a radio in broad daylight on the main street in about the time it would take somebody to sneeze."

Oil company pays Cal for the use of his land; they also pay him a thousand a month to stay the hell out of their hair, which he don't. They even appointed him head firefighter, whatever the hell that is. Delly says she don't remember there ever being a fire in that particular field. And anyway they only gave him a shiny new fire-engine-red pick-up truck with two pretty small fire extinguishers on the back. But that don't stop Cal from talkin' and actin' like he was Red Adair. Actually, Cal and Delly look a lot alike, only he's a man, about twenty-five years older and a hundred pounds heavier.

When they gave out looks and brains in Delly's family they clean missed Eddie and Regina, Eddie being her brother, who could be a basketball player if he knew what it was, and Regina being her sister, who looks like Eddie, poor Regina. Delly's Ma is the only other one in the family who has any sense. She should go around with a whip and a chair to keep the others in line.

We pull into the yard at Delly's folks' place. There's just a frame house that lists about three ways at once and ain't never seen a paintbrush even in its dreams, a couple of garages and out-buildings that list worse than the house, and about an acre of wrecked car bodies, used tires and faded appliances. The front of the house is hung with hub caps—when the sun shines you can see them glint like swords from a couple of miles away. That little red pick-up shines like an apple in front of the house. Delly goes directly inside to talk with Ma and Regina, while Cal walks around the truck and then around our shivering old Plymouth, kickin' tires as he goes, remarking on how shiny his truck is, puttin' his fingers on the hood of the Plymouth and pullin' them back quick, remarkin' on how it's a wonder such a wreck made it all the way from Montana and saying he'll give me fifty dollars for it if we ever want it taken off our hands. Delly says we can get four hundred dollars for a trade-in come January, when prices are low. Cal cracks us each a beer from a tub in the front yard that used to be Ma's washing machine until Cal tried to fix it. The beer bottle is wet but warm, and I figure Cal must have recently tried to fix Ma's refrigerator too.

I was all for buyin' a car, maybe a big one, with some of the money Delly had stashed away. "Cars depreciate. Land appreciates," she said to me. "We'll have a big car, Babe. You gotta hang in for a while." She was standin' by my chair and sort of kissin' at my ear while she was sayin' that. "You give me five years in the Bigs, and I'll see we own enough of Oklahoma City so's I never have to wait on another drunk and you don't have to take no job sellin' used cars the way them other retired ballplayers do." I can't fault that.

Cal's wearin' bib-overalls, a Minnesota Twins baseball cap with about eight ounces of oil worked into the crown and the bill, and for whatever damn reason, rubber boots that must have his feet broiled up to the colour of corned beef.

Cal eventually decides to take the shiny red pick-up truck and make a tour of the oilfield, "Just to be sure there ain't no dangerous situation developin' that I should know about." I beg off sayin' I've travelled enough for one day. When I get to the screen door I stop, for I hear Delly's voice rising: "What do you do with your money?" she says in exasperation.

"What do you mean?" says Ma.

"Look around you," yells Delly. "You got nothin' an' never *had* nothin'." I'd guess Delly has her left hand on her hip and her right hand open, palm up, sort of gesturing at the floor. That's exactly the way Cal stands when he's making a point. Delly'd be mad at me for a month if I ever pointed that out to her.

"I don't remember you ever goin' hungry," says Ma, her voice defensive.

"Hungry ain't the point," says Delly. "That oil company pays Cal a thousand a month up front and then rents the rig-sites, and he still sells lots of stolen parts . . ."

"Don't say that," says Ma in a harsh whisper. And I'd guess she's just looked at Regina, who must be sittin' on a kitchen chair, her hands folded in her lap, starin' off into space, her face blank as a dog's.

"Are you still pretendin' you don't know Cal steals anything that ain't bolted to the ground and a few things that are?"

"Your papa's a nice man . . ."

"I'm not sayin' he ain't nice. But he's thoughtless and shiftless and . . . and . . . why did you ever marry him?"

"Your papa has a winnin' smile," says Ma, with finality, as if her statement answers all the philosophical questions ever posed.

Delly huffs with indignation and bangs a handful of cutlery into the dishpan. "I'd like to manage your income for a few months; you'd be livin' in a nice place in Oklahoma City, and Cal could use this dump for a parts shack, like he's always done anyway."

The last time we were here there was a stripped-down motorcycle under the kitchen table and about two dozen generators sittin' around on the living room floor like a convention of alien pets.

"Oh, we couldn't move from here," says Ma. "Cal's on duty as a fire-fighter, twenty-four hours a day."

"For God's sake, Ma. They gave him that truck so he'd stay away from the oil-donkeys and rigs and stop sellin' booze to the roughnecks."

"You're too hard on your pa . . ."

I bang the screen door to let them know I'm here. Delly huffs a couple more times, but doesn't say anything. The motorcycle's still under the table, but Cal's found it a friend since we were here last. There's a dismantled trailbike keepin' it company.

"Where's Eddie?" Delly asks. "He in jail yet, or just workin' toward it?"

"Eddie's been working part-time on the rigs," says Ma. "He's goin' into El Reno tomorrow to buy his first new-to-him car."

"I should'a known," sighs Delly.

"Let's head into El Reno," Cal says to me after supper. I sort of glance at Delly to see how she feels about it. She ain't exactly been friendly toward her pa. She slammed his plate down in front of him so hard that some of the yellow beans jumped about a foot in the air and a couple came down in his coffee. When Cal deposited about a half-pound of butter in the middle of his grits Delly made a bad face. Then she suggested in no uncertain terms that Cal should buy Ma a new fridge, washer, dryer, stove, a TV that works, and that he should clear all his damn stolen parts outa the house.

At that point Cal says directly to me, "You know, boy, when a man comes home from a hard day's firefightin' or playin' with a baseball, or whatever, he don't want to be bothered with no women's stuff, you know what I mean?"

I said I reckoned I did. Delly looked at me like she'd just lifted up a rock and seen me for the first time. I wished right away I hadn't said it, and got busy eatin' my pork chops. I like sugar on my grits.

I don't exactly say that I'm goin' along but when Cal gets up from the table, belches, and heads for the door, I follow him. "Don't expect me to bail you out if you get in trouble," says Delly.

"I'll be fine," I say.

"As long as you know you're in bad company," she says.

"Pussywhipped," says Cal as he guides the car across the desert, spirals of red dust coiling out behind us. "Ain't nothin' worse than a pussy-whipped man," he mumbles. "If she'd said you can't go, you wouldn't be here."

I don't deny it, which don't please Cal very much.

"Don't take no crap from 'em, boy. She's my own little girl, but I don't know where she gets off bein' so feisty."

The Last Stand is located in a Quonset hut, surrounded by oilfield supply businesses on the far outskirts of El Reno. The building has one small window in the front, with two blue neon Coors signs bleeding down it. Inside there's a long bar down one wall and about twenty tables with scruffy kitchen chairs pushed under them, and a pool table at the very rear with one bright light above it.

"Bring us a coupla Coors and keep 'em comin'," Cal says and then he proceeds to tell anyone who cares to listen and a few who don't that he is the man taught Red Adair all about fightin' oilwell fires.

After about the third beer he spots a baseball sittin' on a shelf behind the bar. "Stanley here is a pro-fessional baseball player," he says real loud, and slaps my shoulder, practically makin' me bust a tooth on my beer bottle.

"Lefty," I say. "Nobody's called me Stanley since I started holdin' my baby bottle in my left hand."

"Bet that wasn't the only thing you used to hold in your left hand," laughs Cal.

"I reckon it wasn't," I say, and laugh with him.

"Where y'all play?" asks one of the roughnecks.

"Triple A," says Cal. "An All Star, goin' to be in the Bigs next season, you see if he ain't."

"What Triple A?" asks the roughneck.

"Hawaii," I say, not missin' a beat, and pickin' the team farthest away from Oklahoma City.

"Seen 'em three times in Honolulu this summer an' I don't remember you."

"I was out with an injury for about six weeks. Must have been then," I say. With my luck he'll have seen me in Butte, and remember me.

Cal winks at me, gathers up a handful of empty Coors bottles and walks to the end of the bar. He sets three of the squat empties at about one-foot intervals on the end of the bar. The empties are about the same colour as the bar wood and in the bad light they blend right in.

"I'm bettin'," says Cal, "that Stanley here can knock them three bottles off with three pitches of the ball," and he nods to where the baseball sits like a white tomato beside the cash register.

"Cal," I whisper, "how many people here know your full name is Calvin Washington Jefferson Coolidge Collinwood?"

"I'm bettin' my son-in-law, Lefty here . . ." and he repeats the proposition, flashing a wad of twenties.

"I'll take fifty," says one roughneck.

"Twenty says he can't hit three outa three," growls a guy built like a jeep, and with enough oil on his clothes to soak down a quarter mile of red dust.

"I ain't sure I can do it," I whisper to Cal.

"Cal here ain't never rowed with but one oar in the water," says the bartender, winking at me. "I'll take fifty of that."

"Put your money away," I whisper to Cal. "I ain't a pitcher."

"Hell, boy, you play way out there in the outfield, you told me so yourself. You got to throw two, three times as far as a pitcher. Can't be no more'n forty feet from one end of this bar to the other." And he waves the roll of bills again. "Duck soup," he says.

There's about $250 dollars riding on my arm. The bartender tosses me the baseball. "You know," he says, "one time Mickey Mantle came in here. Was just drivin' past, but the fellow drivin' Mick's 1956 scarlet Lincoln Continental convertible was sailin' her at about 125 mph. The sheriff hauled them over, but he brought them here instead of to jail. Mick bought a round for the house and he signed a baseball. It said, 'Best wishes to Sheriff McCall and everybody at the Last Stand,' and it was signed 'Your Friend, Mickey Mantle.' But somebody stole it right off the back of the bar."

They discuss whether I should get warm-up pitches or not and decide against it. It is awkward as hell to wind-up indoors, and I can barely see them little brown bottles at the far end of the bar. I let drive at the one on the left and hit the centre one dead on, sendin' it screamin' across the top of the pool table where it shatters against the back wall. All the people have been moved out of that part of the bar so it don't do no damage. There must be fifty people standin' around watchin' me.

I let fly at the left one again, and the ball bounces off the bar about two feet in front of the bottle but rises just enough to tip the rim, and the bottle topples off the bar.

"I told you he was a pro-fessional," says Cal. "He might even pitch this one from behind his back."

I give Cal one mean stare; he catches my drift and shuts up.

I take a big stretch and wing one at the last bottle. There's a stitch loose in the baseball from ricochetin' around the bar after my other pitches, and it makes a whirrin' sound and curves way more than I ever intended it to. Still it only misses to the right by about two inches.

"I be go to hell," says Cal, as people rush up to collect their bets. Somebody retrieves the ball and the bartender hands it to me, along with a pen. I sign it, 'Best Wishes to everybody at the Last Stand, your friend Lefty Brooks.'

"I need me some fresh air," says Cal, headin' for the side door. "I be go to hell," he's mumblin'. "Shoulda bet 'em two out of three."

"Cal keeps the whole town in spendin' money," says the bartender, grinning. "Brought in this little spit-lizard one day an' took bets he could eat it alive . . ."

After about ten minutes I figure I need some air too.

As I head out the side door I hear a little chink-chink sound off to my left. The moon looks like a slice of silver floatin' on its back in the sky.

"Pssst," says a voice that I know is Cal's.

I walk into the darkness to where there are five or six cars parked. Cal is just lettin' down his jack and the pick-up truck he's been workin' on is level to the sand. A wheel lays flat on its side beside where each axle rests on the ground.

"Give us a hand here," says Cal, pickin' up one of them wheels and layin' it on my outstretched arms. Then he stacks another wheel on top of the first one. "Take 'em to the truck," he whispers. "I'm gonna get me the grille and the front bumper."

I am only about halfway to the truck when a car switches on its lights, and I feel like a convict getting picked up by a search-light beam.

"Just stay right where you are," says a voice behind the light.

I do. There are footsteps comin' up behind me on the red shale. "Now where'd you get that armful of wheels," says the voice.

"Would you believe I won them from this guy in the bar?" I say. The voice steps around where I can see it, and it belongs to a man in a sheriff's uniform who is way taller than I am, wearin' a trooper's hat, and packin' a gun and a badge.

"Don't set 'em down," says the sheriff, noticin' my knees beginnin' to buckle under the weight. "Just carry these here wheels back into the Stand and we'll check out your story."

I take a couple of steps toward the bar before I have second thoughts. The wheels almost certainly belong to one of the roughnecks. Those dudes are so tough even their spit has muscles. And most of them have some pretty primitive ideas of justice. I figure I could be in a lot worse company.

"I was plannin' to pay for them when I could," I say.

"I'm sure you were, son. Now where did you put the jack?"

"I didn't use one," I say, settin' the wheels down and breathin' heavily.

"You reckon you can put them back without a jack?"

"No sir. They's easier to take off than put on."

The sheriff walks to the back of the black-and-white and opens the trunk. "Take out the jack," he says to me. "I don't want to get my hands dirty. I'll move the cruiser over and give you some light to work by, then I'll just write this up while you put the wheels back on."

While he's moving the patrol car I notice Cal's truck easin' off the lot and straight out into the desert, no sign of lights about it.

The sheriff stands with a foot on the bumper of the patrol car and writes on a clipboard, while I sweat the wheels into place and tighten the lug nuts.

"You come into town with Junkyard Cal, right?"

"Eeeyuh," I say, hoping the sound can be interpreted as either yes or no.

"All the way from Iowa, eh?" he says, looking at my driver's licence. "You must be the guy married Cal's good-lookin' daughter?"

"Eeeyuh," I say again.

"If I thought you were dumb enough to be courtin' the other one, I'da probably shot ya for a stray. That Regina Collinwood is the ugliest girl in six counties; she is gonna be a burden to Cal in his old age. There ain't much goes on around El Reno that I don't know about," the sheriff goes on. "Cal's not really a bad man. He usually steals from strangers, or at least people who can afford it. He sells reasonable, and his initiative keeps him off the county welfare."

At the jail the sheriff lets me wash up before he locks me in the second of two cells. The first one is occupied by a forlorn-looking Mexican who's playing "Streets of Laredo" on a plastic harmonica.

"We'll just wait for a while and see who comes to fetch you," says the sheriff, grinning. "I hope it's Cal. Doggone, but I love to listen to Cal lie.

Ain't nobody in these parts can do it better. I sure would like to know how he talked that oil company into givin' him that truck."

"Ain't I allowed a phone call?" I ask the sheriff.

"Call me Bud," he says, "an' sure, you're allowed a phone call; but who you figurin' on callin'? I reckon there ain't no phone out at Cal's place, unless'n he's tapped in on the oil company line again. Did that a year or two ago, but they got a little testy when he charged up a couple of thousand dollars' worth of long-distance bills. He was sellin' his car parts in about forty states there for a while."

I guess he can see I'm lookin' kind of worried.

"Also, if I let you use the phone I got to read you your rights, an' if I do that I got to book you, an' if I do that why things can get plumb out of my control, and you never can tell what might happen. So why don't we just wait around until somebody comes to get you. I suspect Cal will come pussyfootin' in like a coyote casing a hen house. Doggone, I never did look at the front of that truck; did he get the grille?"

"I don't know, sir."

"Magnets for fingers, that's what Cal's got. They should have a contest for strippin' down cars on *Real People* or *That's Incredible!* Cal could become a genuine celebrity if they did. Why don't you catch forty winks, boy. And let me give you a little advice: if you gonna steal, don't be dumb enough to get caught."

It wasn't Cal come to get me.

About 5:00 A.M. I hear the brakes on the '71 Plymouth singing from about a quarter mile away as Delly starts slowin' her down. The sheriff gets up from his desk and goes out to meet her.

"You holdin' Lefty here?"

"Sure am," says the sheriff.

"How much is he gonna cost me?"

"How much you figure you can afford?"

"Don't be cute. I just want to bail him out."

"You go have a word with him while I figure out the charges," he says.

Delly starts talkin' as she crosses into the room. "I woke up with a start about four o'clock and you wasn't there and I could hear Cal snorin' so I knew somethin' was wrong." All I can think of is how good she looks to me. She's missed the bottom button on her blouse so it's done up crooked all the way, and her red-rock hair is all tousled, one leg of her jeans is pushed into her boot the other is caught on the top and bunched up. She must wonder why I'm grinnin' as if I just hit a home run with a big-league scout watchin'. "I had to thump on Cal for about five minutes before he woke up. 'Where's Lefty?' I yelled. 'He got himself in a mite of trouble,' said Cal. 'Why didn't you tell me?' I screamed. 'You was sleepin' when I come in, and he'll still be there in the morning. I figured we'd all drive to town bright an' early, and I'd treat for breakfast at the Pronghorn Drive-in after we picked him up.' 'What'd he do?' I asked. 'Well, I don't rightly know,' said Cal. 'You know how these young fellas is, always lettin' off steam.' So what did you do? And what did Cal have to do with it?"

"I sort of got in a fight," I say. "This here cowboy mistook you for your sister and said I was married to the ugliest girl in six counties. Now I couldn't stand for that, could I?"

"I woulda bet money Cal was involved some way. Is he tellin' the truth?" she says to the sheriff.

"Yes, ma'am, he is," says the sheriff, and I breathe easy.

"Well, how much is the fine?"

"I reckon he's cooled down by now. I'll just let him off with time in custody. You take him home, Miss Delores, and take good care of him. I expect to see him in the Big Leagues next year. Y'all remember me to your papa, ya hear?"

The next day Delly ain't exactly happy with me or Cal. But, oddly enough, her anger kind of draws Cal and me together.

I guess Cal is a little sheepish about runnin' out on me, because he ain't got around to mentioning last night at all. We make a lot of small talk about the weather. Eventually he goes and digs for a while in a big metal box that has *Gulf Oil* stencilled on the side of it, and comes sidling over to me, one hand behind his back.

"I won this from a guy in a pool game a few years back," he says, producing a baseball. "You bein' a pro-fessional and all I thought you might appreciate it."

The baseball is brown and dry as if it's been baked in an oven. The inscription is still visible—"Your Friend, Mickey Mantle."

"I do appreciate it, Cal," I say. "I'll put it right on top of the TV in our new condo."

We are still makin' small talk and suckin' beer when we see a cloud of red dust puffin' up behind the closest sand ridge and a strange car comes barrelin' into the yard, screams straight through the chickens, and spins around with so much noise it brings Ma and Regina out onto the sloping wooden porch. When the dust settles downwind, givin' Cal and me a faceful, Delly's brother Eddie unwinds from behind the wheel and stands there like a smilin' hairpin.

"I be go to hell," says Cal, and then to me, "it's Eddie with his new-to-him car."

Eddie just stands grinnin' at us through the hole in his face where he got two teeth knocked out in a Chicano bar up to El Reno. We all walk around the car, which is a '57 or '8 Buick of a kind of winey-red colour, like we were doing some kind of ritual. We kick the three whitewalls and one regular tire and comment on how great she looks. I mean, what else can you say to a guy that's just got his first new-to-him car, except that it looks good, even if it's covered in dents and got about the same number of rods knocking, and has tailfins on which you could terminally injure yourself.

"Looks like she's puckered to shit," says Cal. And I know that Cal still likes to come home with a new-to-him car and take everybody for a ride into El Reno, where he parks in the Taco Bell lot right outside the dining room window. Then everybody goes inside where it's downright cold, orders Mexican food, and grins at the car through the thick, polished glass.

Eddie hops behind the wheel, kind of folding himself up like he was made of coathangers, taking two or three tries to get all of him into the car. Eddie was six-foot-eight the last time anybody measured him, which was a couple of years ago when he was in his third year of Grade 8.

"Ain't this just the best shitkickin' car you ever laid eyes on?" Eddie wants to know. And nobody's about to tell him it ain't true.

"Maaaa," he bawls, "come for a ride." Then he hollers for Delores to get on out of the house and see his new car, and for Regina to be careful as hell of the leopard-skin seat covers when she gets in the back seat.

"Come on, guys?" he says to us.

"Can't," says Cal. "I'm on duty." He says this with both thumbs hooked over the straps of his overalls.

"Ain't gonna be no *fire*," says Eddie.

"Never can tell," says Cal.

"You catch me next trip," says Delly, after she's admired the colour of the paint and the big plastic statue of Jesus on a spring that's held to the dashboard by a suction cup.

As soon as Ma closes the passenger door Eddie takes off spinnin' the wheels and scatterin' the chickens again. The force of his start tips Regina over backwards from where she was hangin' onto the back of the passenger seat.

After the dust settles Cal cracks us each another warm beer. Delly's gone in the house and I bet to the back bedroom that used to be hers. I remember that first night in Oklahoma City when Delly took me to her room. When I started to take her clothes off she helped me, and things have been gettin' better ever since. I'm kind of sidl'n toward the house but Cal is busy tellin' me all the things he knows about, like cam shafts and oil rigs. I let my mind wander until I hear him say something about, "What you reckon that is over yonder?"

When I open my eyes I see a streak of smoke risin' on the horizon. "Maybe it's an oilwell fire?" I say.

Cal looks at me like I was Eddie or Regina.

"Oilwells go BOOM, and shoot fire way up into the air, and any god-damned oilwell firefighter knows that," shouts Cal.

"You're the expert," I tell him.

"What's over the hill is likely only a brush fire," says Cal, then he goes on to tell me how Red Adair blasted sea water into the Big One in Alaska in '73. And he woulda told me about the whole ten days Adair worked on that runaway oilwell if I hadn't pointed out that someone is coming running up the road.

"I be go to hell," says Cal, "they is movin' right along."

"It's Ma," I say, 'cause I can see further than Cal even when he squints. "We better hop in the truck and go meet her."

"No use gettin' excited over nothin'," says Cal. "Let's just wait and see what she's got to say for herself." Cal is still squintin' down the road and is about ready to believe me that it's Ma runnin' toward us. Cal is rollin' a cigarette real careful, and asks me to fetch him another beer while he is strikin' a wooden match on the seat of his overalls.

Ma is yellin' at the top of her lungs. And as she gets closer we can hear that it's all about Eddie and his new-to-him car.

"Burnin', burnin' up," is what Ma is gasping. Then, "Couldn't you guys see me comin'? Why didn't you come meet me?"

"We didn't know for sure it was anything serious," says Cal. "Y'all just keep calm; you're in the company of a pro-fessional firefighter." All three of us are in the shiny red pick-up truck and Cal manages to do just about half a wheelie as we screech out of the yard, scattering them bedraggled chickens again. I'm pretty sure I seen Delly peeking out one of the curtainless windows as we roar away.

Sure enough, about a mile down the road, just overtop the first rise, is Eddie's car, hood up, burnin' like a spit-cat.

"I be go to hell," says Cal, as he swings down outa his truck and walks slowly around the burnin' car.

Eddie is bellowin' like a young moose that just lost its mama. "Where the hell you bin? Put out the fire!" and other stuff like that.

"I'm the firefighter around here," says Cal, climbin' up and takin' one of the shiny silver fire extinguishers off the back of the truck cab.

"Red Adair always takes his time," Cal says, trying to decide the best angle to shoot the flames. Cal gets all set, his boots braced as if he expects the extinguisher to kick like a rifle.

"Let her rip," shouts Cal, and pulls the handle on the extinguisher.

"Pffffft," says the extinguisher, and drops a couple of globs of foam on the road.

"I be go to hell," says Cal, and looks kind of puzzled.

Eddie is bellowin' so loud that if he'd do it on the fire he might put it out.

Regina just stands in the ditch wringin' her hands, and it's a good place for her 'cause she don't look anywhere near her six-foot-two standin' in the ditch.

And Ma, who's been watchin' cars burn up for thirty years, knows better than to say anything at all.

Cal heads back for the truck, mumbling about Red Adair always being prepared for any emergency. Somehow I see kind of a combination of Cal and Red Adair in a pair of Boy Scout shorts, and I laugh like hell.

Cal gives me a look like I just shit in one of his boots. He is up in the box of the pick-up trying to wrestle the second fire extinguisher loose from the truck. The extinguisher has a mind of its own. Cal gets both his pudgy hands around that extinguisher as if he was stranglin' it, and he braces his boots against the back of the cab and pulls with all his 225 pounds. Finally the extinguisher lets go and Cal crashes down on his back in the truck box and the extinguisher sails over his head and lands with a thunk in the dust.

Eddie pounces on it as quick as Eddie can pounce on anything, grabs it up, points it in the general direction of his burnin' car and fires it. It shoots like a dammer. Only the foam swishes right overtop of the car and hits Regina at about the spot where her boobies might be, if she had any.

"Looks like a cat just fell in the separator bowl," says Cal, picking himself up and relieving Eddie of the extinguisher.

"Gimme that thing, boy. Let a pro-fessional firefighter handle this."

Cal finally gets the foam pointed in the right direction. When he's finished the car looks like it's been sittin' in a blizzard for a week. It's totalled. After it's cooled off, me and Cal and Eddie push it into the ditch. Eddie is crying. And even Cal gives him a sympathetic slap on the shoulder. I mean you got to feel somethin' for a guy has just had his first new-to-him car burn up on the side of the road.

"Let's all go into town for a beer just the way regular oilfield fire-fighters do," says Cal. If Eddie'll stop cryin' Cal will let him drive the shiny red pick-up truck, providin' he promises to keep it on the road. "You can even have all the burritos you can eat at Taco Bell," offers Cal.

All four of them cram into the cab of that pick-up. I beg off ridin' in the truck box saying I'll just walk back to the house and keep Delly company. I figure by now she'll be over being mad about last night.

DR. DON

"How come you don't mind?" I ask Mad Etta our medicine lady.

"Hey, when you're young like you, Silas, you don't like nobody move in on your territory. But when you get old as me, you look forward to all the help you can get."

Who and what I been asking about is Dr. Don. His whole name is Dr. Donald Morninglight. He is an Indian and a doctor who come to the reserve about three months ago.

"He ain't as good as me. Never will be," say Mad Etta, as she laugh and laugh, shake on the tree-trunk chair in her cabin.

Must be ten years since we had a full-time doctor here on the Ermineskin Reserve. Maybe three times a year the Department of Indian Affairs doctors come around but they is all white and wear coats white as bathroom fixtures, smell of disinfectant, and to see them work remind me of a film I seen of assembly line workers who put cars together. Them doctors treat people as if they was cars need a new bolt or screw to be whole again.

But Dr. Don don't be like that. Guess being an Indian helps. One reason we never been able to keep a doctor here is they never like to live on the reserve. Even Indian Affairs can't get for them a fancy enough place to live. But Dr. Don when he come, just move into a vacant house near to Blue Quills Hall. He don't act like doctors we know, except that he make sick people better, and, as I say, even Mad Etta like him. And you got to be liked by Mad Etta if you is to get any respect around the reserve.

"Dr. Don he know which side his medical practice be buttered on," says my friend Frank Fencepost. And I guess Frank is right. Quite a few times in the first month Dr. Don was here, he come over to Etta's place in the evening, have a beer with her and tell her about patients he having trouble curing. Etta give him her advice. I don't know if he ever take it but it sure make Etta feel good. So good, that right now she would do just about anything for Dr. Don.

It is easy to tell by looking at Dr. Don that he is some kind of Indian. But he never say which kind.

"I'm a mongrel," he say when asked, and laugh. "If you went far enough back you'd find Cree blood in me."

Dr. Don ain't a handsome man at all. He is about 40, got short legs and a little pot belly. His hair be thin on top and what he got stand out like it never seen a comb. His eyes is dark and deep-set, his nose too big, and he got a thick black moustache that droop over his top lip. But he got such a friendly way about him that everybody like him. He ask a lot of questions and he already know how to make a good try at speaking Cree.

His wife is named Paula. She is an Indian, too, and as shy as anything. She have a new baby the doctor say is called Morning After Rain. I think it was a girl.

He only been here, I bet a month, when I see him walking across the reserve with Chief Tom. At least Chief Tom is walking, taking long steps with his head down. Dr. Don have to almost dance to keep up with him, and to get a bit in front so he can talk to his face.

I'm a long way behind them, but the words carry in the cold air. From

Dr. Don I hear words like clinic, Government Grants, nurse, disgrace, and about ten times, money.

Chief Tom only shake his head. We all know the Chief, being a Government MLA, could do lots of things for us if he really wanted. But he is more interested in sell off timber or give away land to make himself look good to the white people.

It don't take Dr. Don long to spot him for what he is.

"When is the next election for Chief?" he ask us.

"Next summer," we tell him.

"We'd better get an organization started soon. That Chief of yours needs to be replaced and fast."

We suggest he should run.

"Hey, I'm Indian, but not Cree. How about a woman Chief? Bedelia Coyote isn't afraid of anyone, and she's a very knowledgeable young woman where Indian problems are concerned."

Some of us get working on that right away.

I sure hope Dr. Don knows what he is doing. Chief Tom be a dangerous man to have as an enemy, 'cause he know lots of white people in high places.

At Christmas time, Dr. Don he stay right on the reserve. All the doctors in Wetaskiwin and Ponoka run off to Hawaii or someplace hot, but Dr. Don just pitch in and act like he is one of us. Funny thing is that a few sick white people who can't find their own doctors come to the reserve to see Dr. Don. Ordinarily, you couldn't get a white man to the reserve with a gun to his head unless he want to convert us to his religion or repossess one of our cars.

On Christmas Eve, Dr. Don emcee the Christmas Concert down to Blue Quills Hall. Boy, he can tell good jokes and everybody have a happy evening.

At the end of the concert he make a little speech to say how happy he and his family is here at Hobbema, and how he plans to work here until he retires and then still stay here.

It make everybody feel all warm inside.

Then he take from his pocket a sheet of paper, and what he read is kind of a poem. I couldn't remember it too good, so I went to see his wife just before her and the baby moved away and she gived it to me. It is the same copy he read at the concert, wrote in blue ink in real tiny handwriting. It seem to me it is both happy and sad at the same time.

> Words are nothing
> like pebbles beside mountains
> Deeds are all that count
> Watch and listen with me this Christmas
> For it is the small daily deeds of men
> that tell the heart what it needs to know
> Quietly, as you have made me welcome
> I will quietly go about my work
> But listen not to my words—wait and watch.

Everybody is silent for about 10 seconds after Dr. Don finish. And, as Frank Fencepost would say, you could have heard a flea fart. Then everybody break into clapping for a long time. Finally, Eli Bird start in soft on his guitar and Mary Boxcar join in on the piano, and we all sing "Silent Night."

One morning in January I meet Dr. Don walk down toward the General Store.

"You ever see anything this beautiful, Silas?" he say, and point at the pinky sky where two pale sundogs hang like grapefruit, one on each side of the sun. It is really cold and Dr. Don's moustache be froze white as if he dipped it in flour.

"That's what I want to be when I die," he say.

"A sundog?"

"A child of the sun—just floating in the morning sky, free as a balloon. Do your people have any legends about sundogs?"

It sure embarrass me but I have to admit I don't know.

"You should write one then," he say.

"Legends aren't really in my line," I say. I sure don't figure that in just a few weeks, I will be writing this story about Dr. Don.

It was Chief Tom's girlfriend, Samantha Yellowknees, who started up the trouble. Chief Tom ain't smart enough to do something like that himself. In fact, if it weren't for Samantha, Chief Tom would still be cutting ties for the railway.

What she done, she tell us one evening at Blue Quills Hall, was to phone the Department of Indian Affairs. "I told them to call the College of Physicians and Surgeons and check out this Dr. Morninglight. There's something not right about him. I can smell a phoney," say Samantha, glare at us, mean as a schoolteacher.

"If anybody know the smell of a phoney, it be you," says Frank Fencepost. That go right over Chief Tom's head but Samantha look ugly at us and square her chin. Her and Chief Tom been living together for a couple of years in an apartment in Wetaskiwin, ever since the Chief left his wife Mary. Samantha be a city Indian, been to the Toronto University to study sociology.

When we tell Dr. Don what been done he just smile kind of sad and say, "A man should be judged by his deeds." Then he stand silent for a long time.

It was about a week later in the late afternoon that the RCMP car pull up in front of the Residential School where Dr. Don hold his office hours in the Nurse's Room. It is Constable Greer, who be about the only nice RCMP I ever known. Constable Greer got grey hair and sad pouches under his eyes like a dog. But he got with him a young Constable who be about seven feet tall in his fur hat, and speak hardly nothing but French.

Constable Greer read out the charge against Dr. Don, only the name he read don't be Dr. Don's, but three long words that sound like Mexican names you hear on the television. He kind of apologize, but say he got to take Dr. Don to the RCMP office in Wetaskiwin. What he read out say Dr. Don is charged with "Impersonating a Doctor."

Dr. Don finish bandaging up the hand of Caroline Stick. Then he put on his parka and nod to Constable Greer. They is about to walk out when the French Constable step forward, pull out his handcuffs and snap them on Dr. Don's wrists. Then he sort of steer Dr. Don in front of him, look like a giant pushing a child.

Some of us stand around as Dr. Don duck his head and get into the back of the RCMP car. We still stand around even after the car is gone. It is a big shock to all of us. For me it is like that whole place where my stomach is, been empty for a long time.

But the shock is ten times worse the next day when the word come from Wetaskiwin that Dr. Don is dead. Hanged himself with his shirt from the cell bars is what everybody say.

All of a sudden the reserve is crawling with reporters. One of them big trucks from CFRN-TV in Edmonton get up to the school before we tear up the culvert in the road so the rest of them got to walk instead of drive.

Them reporters is kind of angry that we can't tell them anything they don't already know. They are waving a copy of the *Edmonton Journal* with a story that start out:

> HOBBEMA—Donato Fernando Tragaluz took his own life after he was unmasked as a medical imposter.
>
> Tragaluz killed himself in the Wetaskiwin RCMP lockup after police arrested him here Tuesday for impersonating a doctor. Using the medical documents of the real Dr. Donald Morninglight, the 42-year-old Tragaluz practised as the town's doctor for nearly four months.
>
> The *Journal* has learned that Tragaluz posed as a doctor under several aliases in communities in Canada, the U.S., and Mexico for about ten years, evading medical authorities, police and the FBI.

One group is interviewing Samantha Yellowknees.

"I knew there was something wrong with him," says Samantha, baring her upper teeth like a dog looking at you over a bone. "No real doctor in his right mind would start a practice out here."

"What about his funeral?" they all want to know.

Mrs. Morninglight said she guessed he was Catholic if he was anything. She get some of us to call on the Catholic church, but the priests shy away from the whole deal as if they get germs if they get too close. "He can't be buried by the church because he killed himself," they say. "People who kill themselves is going to hell for sure," is what they say. It seem to me the church do all they can to help them along.

Nobody know what to do for a while. Mrs. Morninglight, who always been silent, is even more now. She say she didn't know he wasn't who he said he was. They only been married a little over a year.

"All I want to do is go home," she say. Turn out home for her is South Dakota.

Then Mad Etta step in. Suppose with Mad Etta, I should say waddle. "We got to show we ain't as stupid as the white men, about a lot of things," say Etta and she get me to call a meeting of all the newspaper people who been creep around the reserve on their tip-toes for the last couple of days, take pictures and talk to anybody who even say they knew Dr. Don.

Etta can speak English good as me, but she just sit big as a bear on the tree-trunk chair in her cabin, arms fat as railroad ties folded across her big belly.

"This here is our tribal Medicine Lady," I tell them, squint into the glare of the lights that go with the TV camera. "You ask me questions. I'll translate them to Cree for her. She'll answer in Cree and I'll translate to English for you."

Things are pretty easy at first, except that Mad Etta she leave those easy questions for me to answer. She give a long speech in Cree that the white people think is her answer, but she really be saying things to make me and the other Indians laugh.

Like somebody ask how long she been Medicine Lady.

What she say to me in Cree is, "Look at that guy with the pointed face who ask the question. He got his hair stiffened up like it been mixed with honey. Try to imagine him naked, make love to a woman, or even a goat." She say this real serious.

"Forty-one years," I tell that weasel-faced man.

About two hours before, we buried Dr. Don after having our own service for him at Blue Quills Hall. Take Eathen Firstrider, Robert Coyote, and about a half-dozen other guys all morning to carve out a grave with pickaxes up on a hill where Dr. Don can look down on the town and up at the sky. Mary Boxcar play the piano and we sing the Hank Williams song, "I Saw the Light." A few people say nice things about Dr. Don, like Moses Badland, who tell about the time Dr. Don walk eight miles into the bush to sew up the foot he cut while splitting wood.

"He may not have been a real doctor, but at least he show us the kind of medical attention we should expect," say Bedelia Coyote and a few people applaud a bit.

I leave my ski-cap off as me, Eathen, Robert, Frank, Rufus, and Bedelia carry the coffin out of the hall. The wind chew at my ears with its little needle teeth.

"What do you think makes a man do something like that?" one of the reporters ask.

Mad Etta give a real answer to that question.

"Why shouldn't he? Here, if you or anybody else want to call themselves a doctor, it is okay. You just have to find people who trust you to make them better. Maybe he wasn't a doctor, but he had the call. There ain't very many who have the call."

"Then it didn't matter to you that he had never been to university or medical school?"

"People believed in him," growl Mad Etta. "He had the right touch and loving heart. If you like your doctor, you is halfway better. Most sickness is caused by what's between the ears . . ."

There was sundogs out this morning when we were putting the

coffin in the grave, shimmering like peaches there in the cold pink sky. I imagined for a second that I could see Dr. Don's face in one of them, but only for a second.

BROTHER FRANK'S GOSPEL HOUR

One of the weird things the government does for us Indians, not that everything the government does for us ain't weird in some way, is they provide money for us to have our own Indian radio station. The station is KUGH, known as K-UGH. The call letters were chosen a long time ago by Indians with a sense of humor. The white men are always a little embarrassed saying the name, so they call it K-U-G-H.

A year or so ago I read a letter in an Indian magazine, maybe it was the *Saskatchewan Indian,* where some woman was complaining, saying it was demeaning for it to be called K-UGH. One of the problems of Indians getting more involved in the everyday world is that they lose their sense of humor.

To tell the truth no one I know on the reserve pay much attention to the radio station. It originate in someplace like Yellowknife, which is about a million miles north of us, and instead of playing good solid country and loud rock 'n' roll, it is mainly talk, in a lot of dialects. It is a place for people to complain, which is the national pastime in Canada, the one thing whites and Indians, French and English, and everybody else got in common. And it seem like the smaller the minority the louder they whine.

It does have a news program called the "Moccasin Telegraph," where the title been stolen from a story I wrote quite a few years ago. People send messages to friends and relatives who are out on their traplines or who just live hundreds of miles from anywhere and they can't get to pick up their mail but once or twice a year.

"This here's to Joe and Daisy up around Mile 800. Cousin Franny's got a new baby on the eighteenth, a boy, Benjamin. Oscar wrecked his car, eh? We're doin' fine and see you in the spring. Sam and Darlene."

There would be an hour or more of messages like that run every night.

K-UGH would have gone on forever with only a few people noticing it, but somebody in the government get the idea that things got be centralized. That way everybody get to share in the money the government waste.

First we know of it is when one morning a couple of flatdeck trucks arrive at the reserve loaded down with concrete blocks. They followed by another flatdeck with a bulldozer and three or four pick-up trucks painted dismal Ottawa government green, full of guys in hard hats who measure with tapes, look through little telescopes and tie red ribbons to willow bushes and to stakes they pound in the ground.

That first night it is like a pilgrimage from the village to the construction site, which is on the edge of a slough down near the highway. By morning almost everybody who need concrete blocks have a more than adequate supply.

People got their front porches propped up, and I bet twenty families have concrete-block coffee tables. A couple of guys are building patios. I helped myself to a few pieces of lumber as well and my sister Delores and me made some bookshelves for the living room. Me and Delores each own about two hundred books at least, and until now they been living in boxes under our beds.

Nobody bother to tell the construction people that the place they planning to build on will disappear under about three feet of slough water when the snow melt in the spring or when we get a gully-washer of a thunderstorm, which happens about twice a week through the summer. But it is fall now and the grass is dry and crackly, and there is the smell of burning tamarack in the air, and the sun shines warm.

The construction men get awful mad about all the concrete blocks that disappear. They yell loud as schoolteachers, but we just stand around watching them, don't say nothing. A guy in an unscratched yellow hard hat say he going to send a truck through the village pick up every concrete block he sees.

Mad Etta, our medicine lady, stand up slowly from her tree-trunk chair, her joints cracking like kindling snapping. She waddle over to the foreman.

"You got a brand on your concrete blocks like the farmers over west of here have on their cattle?"

The foreman scratch his head. "No." And after he think a while he decide that collecting back concrete blocks ain't such a good idea. But that foreman have a long talk with someone on his cellular phone and the next load of concrete blocks have a big red R stamped on them that there is no scratching off.

"By the way," Etta say to the foreman, "what is it you're building?"

Rumors been going round that they gonna build public washrooms like they have at highway rest stops. Somebody else says the government going to build a Petro Canada service station, though the spot ain't within two miles of any kind of regular road.

"We're buildin' a twenty-by-twenty concrete-block building," says the foreman. "What they do with the building after we're finished ain't no concern of ours. Our department just build."

"I'm sure you do," says Etta, which the foreman take as positive.

The building seem too small to house anything important.

"I bet they gonna store nuclear waste, or a whole lot of these here PCBs," me and Frank say to Bedelia Coyote, knowing this will send Bedelia's blood pressure up about 100 percent. Bedelia belong to every protest group ever march with a clenched fist. She been out in British Columbia picketing the forest industry for cutting on Indian land, and down in southern Alberta trying to stop the dam on the Oldman River. Bedelia turn paranoid if you even hint somebody might be doing something not good for Indians or the environment.

"Her natural shade is green as I feel after partying all Saturday night," Frank say.

Bedelia kind of scoff but it's only a day or two until her and her friends is investigating like crazy, trying to find which government department is building the concrete-block building and for what.

"If you want something done all you got to do is delegate somebody to do it for you, even if they don't exactly understand that they been delegated," say Frank, smile his gap-toothed smile.

By the time Bedelia and her friends pin down what the building is for, a couple of flatdeck trucks is bringing in pieces of skeletal metal that eventually going to be a tall antenna with a red light on top to keep away airplanes.

"It's going to be a radio station," Bedelia shout as she crash through the door of the pool hall. "They're going to move the Indian radio station here to the reserve."

We didn't suspect it then, but those words were going to change the lives of me and my friends forever.

After the construction workers leave, a group of men in white coats arrive, unpack boxes full of electronic stuff. By peeking through the only window in the building we can see them with little soldering irons, hooking all this stuff together. There is a couple of snow-white satellite dishes set behind the building. The installers push some buttons, and the satellite dishes hum and turn, pointing their centers, which have a big stick like in the middle of a flower, at different parts of the sky.

There are boards full of flashing red, green, and blue lights that run the whole length of the building, which is divided into three cubicles, one big and two little, each one outlined by thick, clear-plastic walls.

One of Bedelia's "friends in high places," as she calls them, sends her a press release all about the Indian radio station K-UGH being moved to our reserve. It's part of a process of centralization of federal government and Department of Indian Affairs affiliates, whatever that might mean.

Painters turn up and paint the building all white on the outside (not a good sign, Bedelia says) with the call letters K-U-G-H in big green letters with red feathers, like part of a head dress, trailing off from each end.

At night we are able to receive K-UGH on our radios, but it still broadcasting from Whitehorse or Yellowknife, or one of those places with an Indian name. And it's still mainly talk and go off the air at 11:00 P.M., just when real radio listeners are waking up.

Frank, who is able to open doors by not doing much more than looking at them, let us into the radio building. Frank push every button he can reach, but nothing appear to be hooked up. We all go into the room with the microphone and Frank sit himself down in front of that microphone and pretend he is on the air.

"Good evening, all you handsome people out in radio land. This here's Frank Fencepost, a combination of whiskey, money, and great sex, all things that make people feel good, just waiting to make you happy."

"Makeup," say Frank's girl, Connie Bigcharles. "I need lots of makeup to be happy."

"A CD player," add my girl, Sadie One-wound.

"A credit card," say Rufus Firstrider.

"With no credit limit, and they never send a bill," say Rufus' big brother, Eathen Firstrider.

"And one of them Lamborzucchini cars that go about a thousand miles an hour," says Robert Coyote.

"World peace," say his sister, Bedelia.

"Boo!" we all say.

Then Frank ask the question that in just a few months will make him a little bit famous, and maybe gonna make him real famous.

"What do you need to make you happy? Tell Brother Frank, my friends. Brother Frank can make your dreams come true."

He repeat the question.

"I want you to pick up the phone, brothers and sisters. I want you to pick up a pen and write to Brother Frank in care of the station to which you are listening. I want all you wonderful people to let me know what it would take to make you happy."

"You're crazier than usual," we say to Frank.

"Thank you," says Frank. "But I think I'm on to something here. I sure wish I could figure out how to turn this equipment on. I really want to talk to people."

"Get a life," somebody says.

A few days later the radio station go on the air. One afternoon two cars pull up and park in front of the concrete-block building. A thin Indian with a braid, dressed in jeans and a denim jacket, get out of one, and a hefty Indian, look like he could be a relative of Mad Etta, get out of the other car.

"We been expecting you," Frank say, sticking out his hand to the thin Indian. "I am Fencepost, aspiring broadcast journalist. Me and my friends are at your service."

Both guys look at us real strangely. The thin one is Vince Gauthier, the announcer. The fat guy is Harvey Many Children, the engineer.

That's it. Takes just two Indians to operate K-UGH. Vince open the mail, decide which letters get read on the air. He do all the talking. Harvey make sure what Vince says gets out over the air. Other people, maybe in Edmonton or somewhere, sell advertising, fax in the commercials and the times when Vince is supposed to read them.

The station only open from 3:00 P.M. to 11:00 P.M. Monday to Friday.

"If there's a holiday, the station ain't open," Vince tell us. They can only afford two employees. When Harvey go on holidays, I have to do both jobs. You think that ain't fun.... When I go on holidays the station shut down for three weeks."

Vince and Harvey ain't very friendly at first, but Frank just study them and, as he says, figure their angles.

"Everybody wants something. Harvey's easy. We just bring him food. McDonald's, Kentucky Fried, chicken fried steak from Miss Goldie's Café. That will get us in the door. But Vince is the important one. I can't figure his angle yet."

It sure ruffle Frank's feathers some that I am the one Vince invite to be on the air.

"I know your name from someplace," he say to me the second day we hanging around while they is working.

"*America's Most Wanted*," say Frank.

Vince stare Frank into the concrete floor.

"I've written a few books," I say.

"Okay, you're *that* Silas Ermineskin. How about I have you on the show tomorrow? Bring your books in and we'll talk about them. I've always meant to read one of your books, but I never got around to it."

"That's what everybody say," I tell him.

"What about talking to me?" says Frank. "I'm the one inspired Silas to write. 'Sit down at your typewriter for three hours every day,' I tell him. Besides, I'm the one got him to learn to read and write. Also, I'm the handsomest Indian in at least three provinces . . ."

"This is radio," says Vince. "Girls think I sound handsome. And I never discourage them."

Now Vince is a scrawny little guy with a sunk-in chest and a complexion look like it been done with a waffle iron.

"I just figured me an angle," says Frank.

One thing that puzzles me is how many people actually listen to the radio. I mean *really* listen. We have the radio for background in the truck or on portable radios.

"Sometimes we have over twelve thousand listeners," Vince tell us. "For an area where trees outnumber people a hundred to one, that ain't bad."

We try to behave ourselves when we're at the radio station, and Frank coach Rufus Firstrider, who have a natural talent for electrical things, to see what it is Harvey do to make the station come on the air every afternoon and shut off at night.

One afternoon when I walk down to the station about an hour before opening time, I find Frank Fencepost sitting in the sun reading the Bible.

"Once you learn there's no telling what you'll end up reading," Frank say, smile kind of sickly. We've had lots of people who flog the Bible, from Father Alphonse, who come pretty close to being human, to Pastor Orkin of the Three Seeds of the Spirit, Predestinarian, Bittern Lake Baptist Church, who hate everybody who don't believe just like him.

"You know what I done?" Frank ask.

"Applied to have a sex change?"

Frank stare at me in surprise.

"A lucky guess," I say.

"I got out my Webster's dictionary and I looked up the word *gospel*. We think of it as all the 'you can't do that or you'll go to hell for sure' stuff. But it really mean 'good news.' I got me some really strong ideas. I just got to figure how I can get Vince to let me talk on the radio."

The day Frank got his Webster's dictionary, about a dozen of us go into the bookstore in Wetaskiwin. Everybody is looking at something different. I'm actually buying the new book by my favorite author, Tony Hillerman, who write about a kind old Indian policeman, Lt. Joe Leaphorn, who remind me of Constable Greer, the one really good RCMP in our area. Frank stuff a big dictionary with a rainbow-colored cover under the raincoat he borrowed from Mad Etta without asking and boogie right out of the store.

"I'm the one who needs a good dictionary," I say to Frank in the parking lot.

"Steal your own," says Frank. But later on he get softhearted, like Frank usually do, and let me keep the dictionary near to my typewriter, though Frank spend a lot of time at my place reading in it. Frank try to learn a new word every day, and use it in a sentence, which get pretty tiresome when he try to use words like *gleet,* which mean sheep snot, or *sutler,* which mean a person who follows an army and sells them provisions. Not words for everyday conversation.

Every night at suppertime, Rufus Firstrider make a run into Wetaskiwin and come back with lots of fast food. Those forays sure cut into our spending money, but we're willing to help Frank as much as we can. Harvey, when he's full of fatty foods, take Rufus under his wing, and in a week Rufus knows how to turn on the radio station and get Frank's voice out on the airwaves.

We watch the station close up at 11:00 P.M., wait an hour, then Frank open the door like he never heard of the word *lock.*

Before we turn on the lights we hang a heavy blanket over the window.

Rufus fuss with some switches. Then, from his glassed-in cage he signal Frank that it is okay to talk. A big red light come on over the door, say "In Use."

"K-UGH is going to present a special program one hour from now," Frank say. "'Brother Frank's Gospel Hour' will ask the question, 'What does it take to make you happy?' Be sure and tune in."

He make announcements like that every five minutes from midnight to 1:00 A.M. Then at one o'clock he cue up some music that he had me hunt up. The station have only about a hundred tapes. This one's some outfit with bagpipes playing "Amazing Grace."

"Welcome to 'Brother Frank's Gospel Hour.' Brother Frank wants everyone to feel as good as he feels, to be as happy as he is . . ."

And he's off and running.

"Silas," Frank has been telling me for weeks, "I'm gonna combine theology, mythology, history, ritual, and dream. Seems to me that covers everything. Got to have some Christian connection in order to get money, people will give to anything that they even suspect of being religious. And dreams is how we work in the Indian part."

Frank talk for a while about how everybody deserve to feel good, to be happy, to have enough to eat, a dry place to sleep, good friends, and happy dreams.

"Now, what I'm wondering, as I talk to this big, old microphone, is, is there anybody out there? If you're listening, call Brother Frank on the phone," and he give the area code 403, and K-UGH's telephone number. "We accept collect calls. Just let us know you're listening. Tell us what you need to make you happy. And if you got an idea, tell us how we could improve 'Brother Frank's Gospel Hour.' Remember, gospel means 'good news.' And Brother Frank is gonna make good news happen to you."

Frank sigh, and point to Rufus, who flip a switch and a trio start singing "Let the Sunshine In."

Frank has hardly lit up a cigarette when the phone rings.

"'Brother Frank's Gospel Hour,'" I say, in kind of a whisper. I'm betting it's either Vince or Harvey giving us five minutes to clear out of the station or they'll call the RCMP.

"Collect from Jasper, Alberta," say an operator's voice.

"Go ahead."

"Brother Frank is the biggest idiot I ever heard on the radio," say a man's booming voice. He apply a couple of unpleasant curse words to Frank, and a couple more to me, then he slam the receiver in my ear.

"Wrong number," I say. "They wanted a tow truck."

"Hey, I would of got them a tow truck," say Frank. "There is nothing Brother Frank and the power of prayer can't accomplish."

The record is about over before the phone ring again.

"Hello," say what sound like a young woman's voice.

"Go ahead," I say.

"If I tell you what I need to make me happy, what are you gonna do about it?"

"Maybe I should let you talk to Brother Frank," I say.

I nod to Frank. He nod to Rufus who got more music ready to go.

"What can Brother Frank do for you?" Frank ask.

"You really want to know what will make me happy?" say the girl.

"That is Brother Frank's purpose in life."

"I need a CD player and the latest Tanya Tucker CD."

"Don't we all," says Frank, with his hand over the receiver. "Why would that make you happy?"

"Because my parents belong to a religion that thinks music is sinful. I have to sneak my radio on under my covers after they're asleep."

"A day without music is like a day without sex," say Frank. "Give me your name and address and Brother Frank will mail you enough money to buy a CD player and Tanya Tucker." Frank write for a minute. "You start watching the mail. And when you get your own money, you make a contribution to 'Brother Frank's Gospel Hour,' so we can help somebody else."

The girl bubble with thank yous, and promise to send money when she is able.

"See, that wasn't so hard," says Frank.

"Only trouble is we don't have any money to send her," I point out. "All that's gonna happen is she'll watch an empty mailbox for a month or two."

"Never underestimate Fencepost Power," says Frank.

Frank launch right in. "Our motto is, 'Before my needs, the needs of others,'" Frank say, and he explain the girl who live in a house without music and ask listeners to send in a dollar or ten dollars to make other people happy.

Within an hour we got an old lady who need money to pay her heating bill. Another old lady need money to take her pet cat to the vet. And a woman who sound about thirty call to say her husband drunk up the welfare check and her kids is hungry, what will make her happy is a few groceries.

"Wow," says Frank. "I think we touched a nerve."

We get stupid calls, too. Smart-ass guys, sound like Frank just a few weeks ago, want money for beer, or a date with Madonna, or to touch the jockstrap of Mario Lemieux, the famous French hockey player.

Frank, without using any names, tell the stories of the people in need.

"Brother Frank going to see that those little kids don't go hungry, and that lady don't have to be cold, and that cat gets to the hospital. If I have to steal to do it, I will. But you can help. Send what you can, a dollar, five dollars, ten thousand," and Frank chuckle, "to 'Brother Frank's Gospel Hour,' c/o K-UGH Radio," and he give the station's box number in Wetaskiwin.

Frank stay on the air until 3:00 A.M.

"Brother Frank will visit with you again tomorrow. And may *your* Great Spirit, whatever that may be, never rain on your parade."

Rufus shut off the equipment and give Frank the thumbs-up sign like we seen Harvey give Vince.

"From now on, Silas, you pick up Brother Frank's mail every day. Wouldn't want all this money fall into the wrong hands."

We kept expecting Vince or Harvey to discover what we been doing, but Frank keep up his late-night broadcasting.

I check the mailbox every day, but there is nothing addressed to "Brother Frank's Gospel Hour."

People's requests all translate into money. The people who call in come mostly from a long way off. That girl without music live in a place called Blueberry Mountain, hundreds of miles up north.

Frank, doing some creative borrowing at a K Mart in Edmonton, acquire the CD player, but among us all we couldn't raise the postage to mail it.

Connie stand in line at a post office, ask for seven dollars' worth of stamps, then just pick them up and walk out. The clerk yelling like crazy, but not running after her.

"They wouldn't feel so bad if they knew they were contributing to making someone happy," says Frank, as he stuff the parcel into a slot at the main post office.

One morning me and Frank head off to Calgary in Louis Coyote's pick-up truck. Frank, he want to hear an evangelist on a Calgary radio station. This fellow he got a twang in his voice sound like the real Hank Williams used to.

"Entertainment, and touching the heart is what it's all about," says Frank. "I got to have the qualities of a good country singer, a striptease dancer, and . . ."

"A welder," I say.

"Damn right. A good entertainer melt solder with his bare hands. Look into that, Silas. See if there's a magic trick where I can pretend to melt metal."

We figure the place to listen to a radio in comfort would be at my sister's house up in the hills in northwest Calgary. It's been over a year since we visited.

I have to admit Brother Bob treat my sister pretty good, but he been insulting Frank and me ever since he first met us. He sic the police on us more than once, not that we are totally innocent. We one time wreck Brother Bob's new car, and another time we put live horses in his brand-new house. Last time here, Frank did a certain amount of damage to the computer system at the finance company my brother-in-law manage. Brother Bob McVey make it clear we ain't welcome at either his home or his business. But we figure time dim the bad things, and we make sure to arrive in the middle of the afternoon.

Only trouble is, he at home.

"How come you ain't off repossessing trucks from poor Indians?" Frank ask when Brother Bob answer the door.

Brother Bob don't look very good. He is wearing a bathrobe and ain't shaved in, I bet, half a week. I always figure Brother Bob woke up already shaved.

He just wave us into the living room, where my sister Illianna patching some of little Bobby's jeans.

"You sick or something, Brother Bob?" I ask.

Brother Bob just stare at *The Price Is Right* on TV. Illianna answer for him. "Bob's been out of work—almost nine months now. He's feeling kind of depressed."

Illianna explain that the big finance company Brother Bob managed went out of business. They loaned millions of dollars to companies in the oil patch, and since the price of oil been going down forever, those companies couldn't pay their loans. The finance company close up after they used up all the company pension fund trying to stay in business. Brother Bob don't get a dime in layoff pay for all his years with the company, plus he lose all his pension money.

"Why don't you get another job?" Frank ask.

"There aren't any jobs in Bob's field. In case you haven't noticed," Illianna answer, "the economy is really bad."

"Sorry," says Frank. "Being unemployed all my life, it's hard to tell."

"I've been trying to get a job," says Illianna, "but it's years since I worked, and then I was just waiting tables. All I could earn as a waitress wouldn't pay the mortgage. Silas, I don't know what we're gonna do."

"I got maybe sixty dollars," I say.

"And you got my good wishes," says Frank. "But I got a scam going that gonna make us all rich. Six months from now Fencepost will offer you a job. Fencepost might even offer Brother Bob a job." Frank consider that possibility for a moment, then say, "Nah."

After that we are kind of uncomfortable. We wait long enough to give little Bobby a hug when he get home from school, then we listen to the evangelist in the truck at a truck stop on Deerfoot Trail.

On the fifth day there are two letters addressed to "Brother Frank's Gospel Hour." I rush them back to the pool hall and Frank rip them open. One contain a two-dollar bill, the other a useless one-dollar loonie coin.

We is all pretty disappointed.

Frank is getting five to ten calls every night from people in need. It surprising how small people's wants are. A pair of eyeglasses, a toy, shoes, some dental work so someone can look passable when they go job hunting. Frank has written down everybody's requests along with their names and addresses in a notebook. There is close to forty and it don't look like we going to be able to fill none of them.

"If people could just see me in person," says Frank. "I could convince them to part with their money. We'd pay off the needy people and have a lot left over for us. Guess I'm gonna have to do like these real evangelists and beg hard."

Turn out the problem wasn't Frank, but our usual bad mail service. After about eight days, the mail box start to fill up. There is fourteen letters one day, total eighty dollars in cash and checks. The next day there is twenty-six letters, with over a hundred dollars. The lady from Drumheller get her grocery money. The lady from Obed get to pay her heating bill.

That night Frank thank people for their kindness, he get a tear in his voice as he say there is so much to do and so little time and money.

It take Bedelia and me and even Frank's girl, Connie Bigcharles, to talk him out of imitating that famous evangelist, I think it was Oral Robertson, who claim he going to be called to heaven if he don't get enough money donated from his followers.

"For one thing, we don't think you'd be called to heaven," we tell Frank. "For another, Oral Robertson didn't get all the money he craved, and he didn't die."

"All he got, I think, was a toothbrush named after him," says Connie Bigcharles.

"It would attract attention to me," says Frank. "That's what being a celebrity is all about. I read somewhere that unless you get caught in bed with little boys, all publicity is good publicity."

"Or unless, like that other evangelist, you get caught in the back seat of your car with a working girl."

"What's wrong with that?" says Frank. "I been in more back seats than a McDonald's wrapper."

Frank finally see things our way.

"Was that good, or what?" Frank say, after he is off the air. "I never knew I could get that catch in my voice. I figure I'm worth about a thousand dollars a tear from now on."

What Frank say is true.

In another week the requests are only twenty dollars or so ahead of the income. And the prospects are looking righteous. Unfortunately, whenever something is going good, something go wrong.

I only take the mail addressed to "Brother Frank's Gospel Hour." How am I supposed to know that people are writing to K-UGH to say how much they enjoy Frank's program?

One morning when I go to pick up the mail, Vince been there before me.

Vince and Harvey ain't mad. They just want a cut.

"Word will get back to the higher-ups eventually, but until then, you got a great scam going. We checked in on your broadcast last night. You, Mr. Frank, have got charisma."

"I hear you can get antibiotics for that," says Frank.

For 10 percent off the top, Vince and Harvey agree to be deaf, dumb, and blind to "Brother Frank's Gospel Hour." There was nearly four hundred dollars in that day's mail.

We have to open up a bank account for "Brother Frank's Gospel Hour" at the Bank of Montreal in Wetaskiwin. Frank and me and Bedelia Coyote are the ones who can write checks. Frank cut Bedelia in because she got the stamina to deal with government.

"There is ways for every dollar we take in to be tax-free, and I'm gonna research all those ways," Bedelia say.

Another month and Frank just keep getting better. Soon, there is actually money left over when the requests are filled.

"We put a definite five-hundred-dollar limit on what we pay out," Frank says. "I mean, no sex-change operations that ain't covered by medical insurance. No vans for the handicapped, no matter how worthy the cause. Three hundred dollars for bus tickets so Granny can see the daughter and new grandchild is what we're all about. That draw more tears than a $40,000 van for some guy who can only move two fingers and his pecker."

Things get complicated when the newspapers start coming around, wanting to interview Brother Frank. Soon as the stories run, the bigwigs at K-UGH start asking a lot of questions.

Since I am the worrier, I worry we been doing something illegal, and maybe all of us, or especially Frank, could go to jail.

But the bigwigs at K-UGH find that after only six weeks, "Brother Frank's Gospel Hour" draw more listeners at two in the morning than all their regular shows.

Frank get called in to K-UGH, and me and Bedelia go with him. There is three guys in suits, one come all the way from Toronto, which, they tell us, is where everything really happen.

"Then how come I never been there?" Frank ask. He live life like he got nothing to lose. And I guess that's true. Until now.

The suit from Toronto chuckle politely, then offer Frank a contract and the 9:00 P.M. to 11:00 P.M. broadcast time.

"We'd like to offer you a five-year contract at $60,000 a year, rising $5,000 each year, so by the end of the contract you'll be making $80,000 a year," the Toronto suit say.

"I bet that's almost as much as the guys on 'Stampede Wrestling' make," says Frank.

At this point Bedelia Coyote break into the conversation. Bedelia has studied accounting by mail, and she has studied business management by mail, as well as how to organize a demonstration and how to get your organization's name in the newspaper without committing an indictable offence.

"Mr. Fencepost will be happy with your salary offer," she say, "but we only want a month-to-month contract."

Bedelia have to pull Frank off into a corner and have a pretty loud whispered conversation to get him to agree to that.

"Plus," Bedelia go on, "'Brother Frank's Gospel Hour' manage all the money that is donated. We pick which people get their requests filled, and Mr. Fencepost hire his own support staff and pay them out of the donated money."

The suits argue for quite a while because they had their eyes on the income donated to "Brother Frank's Gospel Hour."

"We can take our program over to CFCW, the country-music station in Camrose. Bet they'd be happy to have us. Or, we might contact one of the big radio stations in Edmonton," say Bedelia.

The suits give in.

I can't believe how fast things move after that. What Frank talk ain't exactly Christianity, but he mention the Bible often enough that Christians like him. He throw in enough fictional Indian mythology, some of which I make up, to what Frank call "make us politically correct."

"Everybody loves the idea of an Indian these days. So look me up a bannock recipe, and I'll include it on tomorrow night's program," he say to me. "And saskatoon pie. We'll tell them where to pick the best saskatoons. The country will be overrun with berry-pickers."

Frank also talk about fulfilling dreams and positive thinking enough that the people who believe in crystal power and having conversations with rocks and trees like him, too.

By the time Frank get settled in his new time slot, Bedelia is negotiating with the big radio stations in Edmonton and some outfit would do something called "syndicate" the show, putting Frank on over one hundred stations, many of them in the United States, where, Frank say, the real money is.

Frank make Bedelia his business manager and me his personal assistant, and he find jobs for Rufus and Winnie Bear, Robert Coyote and his girl Julie Scar, and about ten other of our friends. My salary in a month is as much as I ever made in a year writing books.

One night I try to phone Illianna, but all I get is a guy with a deep voice tell me my call cannot be completed as dialed. After I pretend I'm Frank and get real pushy with Information, they tell me the number I'm calling been disconnected for non-payment.

The day I cash my first check at the Bank of Montreal, I put a hundred-dollar bill in an envelope and address it to Illianna.

At supper one night a couple of weeks later, Ma say, "Illianna phoned Ben Stonebreaker's store and left a message that she coming for a visit."

"That's wonderful," says my sister, Delores. "I just love Bobby."

Bobby is only a year or so younger than Delores.

"That's what makes me worried," says Ma. "She's bringing Bobby, and What's-his-name, and she ask Mrs. Ben Stonebreaker if maybe the

Quails' old cabin is available, 'cause they planning to stay for a while." After the Quails build themselves a new house, their old cabin sit vacant with half the windows knocked out and a few strips of what used to be bright green siding bulging loose under the front window.

Ma, over the years, has mellowed some toward Illianna's husband, Robert McGregor McVey. Now it's What's-his-name. She used to refer to him in Cree as He Who Has No Balls.

A few days later, Illianna and her family turn up on the reserve, and I can't help remembering the first time they visit after they been married. Brother Bob was driving a new car with racing stripes and silver hub caps, and we give him an Indian name, Fire Chief, just like the gasoline down at Crier's Texaco garage, and little Bobby was still a glint in Eathen Firstrider's eye.

Today they is driving what white people call an Indian car. It is a huge Pontiac, about a 1972, painted a pumpkin color, full of dents, sagging and clunking, with about a million miles on it, and a big U-Haul trailer with stuff tied all over the outside of it rattles along behind.

"They repossessed the house and the car and the boat and the snowmobile," Illianna say. Little Bobby start crying when he hear the word *snowmobile*. "Thanks for the money, Silas. I used it to put most of our furniture in storage, though I don't know how I'll pay the storage fees."

Brother Bob is, as they say, only a shadow of his former self. His suits hang on him like they was three sizes too big, and even his snap-brim hat seem to sink down over his ears. He hardly talk, and when he do he just sigh and whisper "yes" or "no."

The day we buy about a hundred yards of extension cord from Robinson's Store in Wetaskiwin ("Charge it to 'Brother Frank's Gospel Hour,'" Frank tell the clerk, and get a smile instead of a who-the-hell-are-you look) and run it across a slough and through a culvert from Blue Quills Hall so Brother Bob can hook up his TV to watch the soap operas and Illianna can plug in her microwave, Brother Bob mumble a couple of thank yous and grip both my hands the way an old person do.

Brother Bob used to look right through us like we didn't exist. And when he did see us, he make bad jokes about our large families, how run down our cars are, and how clean we ain't.

Within weeks word come down that "Brother Frank's Gospel Hour" going international on 112 radio stations. At the same time Bedelia sell a syndicated newspaper column where I write up some of the letters Frank get, and how he send money to those people for the one thing that will make them happy. I tell five stories in every column. Four serious and one that we find funny, one where Frank usually say no. Like the kid who want karate lessons so he can beat up on his teacher. Or the woman who claim she getting messages from Elvis in her back teeth and wants a radio transmitter so she can share the messages.

The number of radio stations expand almost every day and soon television want to get in on the act. One hour, once a week, where they fly in some of the people we been helping.

"I'm gonna be bigger than Oprah," say Frank, when Bedelia give him the news. "Let me rephrase that. I'm gonna have more listeners than Oprah."

"You wish," says Bedelia. "We're only starting in twelve stations. Besides, Oprah don't beg for money. But when you let that tear ooze out of your eye and run down your cheek, I can hear pens all over North America scratching signatures on checks."

Soon so much money come rolling in we rent Blue Quills Hall and hire Illianna to sort the cash and checks. When she need an assistant we hire my Ma, Suzie Ermineskin, full-time, and my sister, Delores, part-time.

Frank these days is dressing like Johnny Cash, frilly white shirt, black preacher's coat, western bow tie. He look a lot better than the time he wore a fuzzy green cocktail dress and won the Miss Hobbema Pageant.

The TV people want Frank to do a personal appearance tour.

"Forty cities," Bedelia tell Frank. "Starting in Calgary, working to Minneapolis and on to places I never heard of."

Bedelia arrange to buy a used bus, hire a lady sign painter with long red hair to paint tomahawks, eagles, and dream catchers all over the bus, and "'Brother Frank's Gospel Hour,' A Place Where Dreams Come True," down both sides.

The tour give me an idea. I argue loud and long with Frank, but I don't get anywhere until I take Frank for a walk around the reserve.

"What would make you happy?" I ask. "Pretend you could write a letter to 'Brother Frank's Gospel Hour.' What would you ask for?"

Frank stop and think.

"My biggest surprise is that some of the good things haven't made me as happy as I thought. Like renting that Lincoln Continental, and having more groupies than a rock star. The car is nice, but it's just a car. And it was more fun when girls told me to get lost and I had to impress them."

"I know what would make you happy," I say.

"What's that, Silas?"

"Revenge," I say, "against He Who Has No Balls."

I let that sink in for a minute. I wonder if Frank is gonna buy my idea, and what I'm gonna do to help Illianna and little Bobby if he don't.

There is the beginning of a smile on Frank's face. "There is an old saying in the Fencepost clan," Frank say. "Always kick your enemy when he is down."

"This is your chance to really get back at Brother Bob," I say hopefully.

"By golly, Silas, you're right. I can make him suck up to me. I'll make him wear a sissy uniform like a theater usher, and a visored cap with BRO. FRANK in silver letters across the crown."

He grab my shoulder, turn me around, and our pace pick up as we walk in the dark, spruce-smelling air toward Brother Bob and Illianna's cabin.

THE ALLIGATOR REPORT—
WITH QUESTIONS FOR DISCUSSION

A water-laden wind blows from the ocean over the Everglades. An unlucky black-tipped ibis slams into a palm tree, drops to the sand like a five-pound plastic bag full of liver, lies quivering, the wind furrowing its feathers.

> DO YOU SEE ANY SIGNIFICANCE IN THE DEAD
> BIRD BEING AN IBIS? LOOK FOR REFERENCES TO
> THE IBIS IN EGYPTIAN MYTHOLOGY. WOULD
> THIS PASSAGE HAVE BEEN AS EFFECTIVE IF THE
> BIRD WERE AN EGRET, HERON, FLAMINGO, OR
> ROSEATE SPOONBILL?

"Stay tuned to WTWT-TV," says Alvin Lee Wade, the anchorman, giving his audience a jowly, nearsighted smile. According to the latest ratings, Alvin Lee Wade smiles nearsightedly into 114,000 homes, bars, and motels in Talabogie County, Florida. "Right after this commercial break, we'll be back and have Buzz Hinkman with the sports, our own Charles Caulfield with the weather, and Carleen Treble with the Alligator Report."

> WHY DO YOU THINK THE AUTHOR HAS CHOSEN TO REPEAT HALF THE TITLE SO EARLY IN THE STORY? SINCE NAMES ARE OFTEN AN IMPORTANT COMPONENT OF A STORY, DO YOU SEE (SINCE THIS STORY IS SET IN THE SOUTH) ANY SIGNIFICANCE IN THE ANCHORMAN'S SECOND NAME BEING LEE? WHAT OTHER FAMOUS FICTIONAL CHARACER IS NAMED CAULFIELD?

Preacher Gore watches Alvin's red cheeks and alcoholic nose fade away into a used car commercial. Outside his apartment, the wind blows high and a broken shutter chatters against the siding. Preacher is not an avocation but a Christian name, though he is not often called Preacher. Before his accident, he was known as Foot-to-the-Floor Gore, when he drove in local demolition derbies, dirt-track stock-car races, and even once at Daytona Speedway.

> WHY DO YOU THINK THE AUTHOR CHOOSES TO USE THE WORD PREACHER TWICE, AND THE WORD CHRISTIAN ONCE IN SENTENCE THREE? THE WORD GORE HAS A NUMBER OF MEANINGS, ONE BEING "AN ANGULAR POINT OF LAND." SINCE FLORIDA IS AN ANGULAR POINT OF LAND, COULD THE NAME HAVE SOME SIGNIFICANCE?

While waiting to go on the air, Carleen Treble is munching sensuously on the tail of a two-foot chocolate alligator which was delivered to her anonymously at the front desk that very afternoon. She thinks of it as an anonymous gift, though she knows it is from Preacher Gore. Preacher Gore is in love with Carleen Treble and in the past few months has gifted her with: twenty-four varieties of candy (culminating with the chocolate alligator), a pink princess phone, a goldfish, a Doberman puppy, a tape deck for her car, a poster reading "Exonerate Shoeless Joe Jackson," a chrome cat with a clock in its belly, a pair of ice skates, a moped, a steamer trunk, a case of Saran Wrap, twelve pounds of pork chops, a microwave cooking course, a model kit of the Hindenburg, a case of Lipton's Chicken Noodle Soup, a *Star Wars* jigsaw puzzle, a cribbage board, his extra crutch, eight Willie Nelson records which he bought at a store owned by Burt Reynolds, and an alligator bowling ball bag which he made at physical therapy class. The doctors are worried that Preacher takes an inordinate amount of pleasure in making anything from alligator hide.

Although he didn't sign it, Preacher Gore left a note with the chocolate alligator. "If I'd listened to you," it said, "I'd be driving at Daytona, probably even in the Indy 500. I was watching the alligator report and I heard you plain as day say, 'There's alligators on the loose out around Old Sewanee Road and the Talabogie Swamp area. Now all you good ole boys be careful you don't get your Dingos bit,' and you smiled into that camera fit to break my heart."

THE CHOCOLATE ALLIGATOR IS A SYMBOL OF SOMETHING. CAN YOU GUESS WHAT? SINCE ALLIGATORS USUALLY EAT PEOPLE, RATHER THAN PEOPLE EATING ALLIGATORS, CAN CARLEEN'S ACTION BE SEEN AS SIGNIFICANT? WHO WAS SHOELESS JOE JACKSON AND FROM WHAT SHOULD HE BE EXONERATED? CAN PREACHER'S NOTE BE INTERPRETED IN ANY WAY AS A PARABLE? SINCE WILLIE NELSON IS AN OUTLAW, AND SINCE BURT REYNOLDS OFTEN PORTRAYS OUTLAWS, COULD THIS BE

SEEN AS FORESHADOWING AN ILLEGAL ACT BY
PREACHER GORE?

"Thus far, Hurricane Zoltan has dumped over four inches of rain on
Talabogie County, and at last report the wind was blowing at 80 mph, or
125 kph, whichever is greater," says Charlie Caulfield, the weatherman,
who for some reason is wearing a clown's red nose clipped over his
own, and a scarlet jacket with a small white alligator on the pocket. The
alligator is the symbol, mascot, and logo of WTWT-TV, *The Eyes of
Talabogie County.*

> SHOULD A HURRICANE EVER BE NAMED AFTER
> A MAN? OR IS THIS JUST A PLOY OF THE LIBERAL,
> COMMUNIST, DEMOCRAT, FEMINIST ALLIANCE
> TO DESTROY ALL THAT AMERICA STANDS FOR?
> AH HA! 125 KILOMETERS PER HOUR! ONLY
> COMMUNIST COUNTRIES USE KILOMETERS,
> METERS, AND UN-AMERICAN MEASUREMENTS
> LIKE THAT! NAME THREE OTHER SUREFIRE
> WAYS A CONCERNED AMERICAN CAN SPOT A
> COMMUNIST.

After another commercial for Mangrove Motors, and a promo for
the Miss Teenage Talabogie County Contest—following a trumpet
fanfare, the camera moves in on Carleen Treble. Carleen, as always,
is dressed like a cheerleader, with knee-high white leather boots,
a micro-skirt of red velvet, and a skimpy velvet halter with one
breast red and one breast white, the red one having a white alligator
embossed on it, the white one boasting a red alligator. As always,
Carleen stands at attention as if somewhere in the back of her rather
small mind the Star-Spangled Banner is waving in a gentle breeze.
Carleen stares straight at her cue cards, or cute cards as she calls
them, smiling vacantly, her grapefruit-colored hair cascading over

her bare shoulders. She has a tiny smear of chocolate in the corner of her mouth. Carleen's hazel eyes move from side to side as she reads the Alligator Report. Her voice is untrained and whining but no one seems to notice—WTWT-TV's ratings have shown a steady upward movement since the Alligator Report began.

Right now, in Tampa, the executives of a much larger station are preparing a six-figure contract in an attempt to lure Carleen away from WTWT-TV.

"We've had six sightings in the last twenty-four hours," reads Carleen, "and our $30 award for the Alligator Sighting of the Day goes to Mrs. J. D. Commings, of Bobwhite Road, in Talabogie, for getting right on the Alligator Line, 282-4117, out-of-county call collect, and reporting that an eight-foot-long gator et her dog, Hannibal. 'Jest chomped him right in half,' Mrs. Commings said. So y'all watch for your $30 in the mail, Mrs. Commings. Maybe you can buy yourself a new doggie."

DO YOU THINK THE AUTHOR IS TRYING TO COMPENSATE FOR THE COMMUNIST PROPAGANDA OF THE PREVIOUS PARAGRAPHS BY MENTIONING THE STAR-SPANGLED BANNER? SINCE GRAPEFRUIT IS A MAJOR PRODUCT OF FLORIDA, COULD THE COLOR OF CARLEEN'S HAIR IN ANY WAY BE A TOURIST PROMOTION? IS IT SIGNIFICANT THAT DOG SPELLED BACKWARDS IS GOD AND VICE VERSA? WHO WAS HANNIBAL AND WHY DID HE CROSS THE ALPS? DO YOU THINK MRS. COMMINGS' DOG WAS NAMED AFTER THE CARTHAGINIAN GENERAL OR THE CITY IN MISSOURI? WRITE A 500-WORD ESSAY JUSTIFYING YOUR CHOICE. SINCE MARK TWAIN THE FAMOUS HUMORIST AND DOG-HATER HAILS FROM HANNIBAL, MISSOURI, COULD THIS BE WHY THE AUTHOR

ALLOWS MRS. COMMINGS' DOG TO MEET SUCH
A HORRIBLE DEATH?

"Oh, Carleen, if I'd listened to you instead of letting Lester Griff talk me into going hunting in the Talabogie Swamp, I'd still have my right foot and still be driving professionally, probably in the Indy 500," says Preacher Gore, formerly known as Foot-to-the Floor Gore or just plain Foot to his friends. Preacher is speaking to the sizzling black and white TV set in his apartment. He notes the smear of chocolate in the corner of Carleen's mouth, and hope springs eternal in his bruised and battered breast, for Foot has lately had an encounter with the enemy. But in his passion, a passion so complete that he can picture Carleen in her white boots standing at a greasy stove cooking up his favorite chile and clam casserole, he decides to ignore the enemy and buy Carleen a foot-long vibrator with red eyes and a lolling tongue which he saw at Kinks and Things, and have it delivered to her at WTWT-TV, anonymously of course.

After the accident, his right foot (Adidas, sock and all) on the inside of a twelve-foot gator somewhere at the bottom of Talabogie Swamp, Preacher Gore had written to Carleen Treble to thank her for the warning he had disregarded and to tell her how sweet her smile was. Carleen read the letter over the air, then along with a camera crew went to visit the one-footed ex-stock-car driver at Talabogie County's City of Saviours Hospital: 22 stories, 626 rooms, the most modern equipment in all America, built as the result of a vision by Delbert Staggers, the blind giant.

Staggers, six feet nine inches, 330 lbs., slow moving, slow witted, his white eyes hidden behind blueberry-tinted, mirrored sunglasses, was formerly employed by The Mob as a collector of bad debts. He was driven to the scene of his assignments by Pico the Rat, the 98-lb. cousin of the presiding warlord. Pico would point out the debtor and guide Delbert Staggers forward until contact was made. Delbert would whack the debtor unmercifully with his white cane until he either paid up or fainted. He spent his days pummeling myopic Spanish fruit stand owners, and losers in shiny suits with stained fingers and ties who had blown their welfare cheques at the dog tracks.

Then, one afternoon when there were no collections to be made, Pico the Rat took Delbert Staggers to see *Rocky*. Delbert could only hear the movie. But he cheered Rocky in his final battle for the championship and several times shouted, "I'll loan ya my cane, Rocky! I'll loan ya my cane."

WRITE A COHERENT PARAGRAPH DEMON-
STRATING THE OBVIOUS RELATIONSHIP
BETWEEN THE FACT THAT DELBERT STAGGERS
CARRIES A CANE AND THE CORRECT ANSWER
TO THE RIDDLE OF THE SPHINX, MAN.

Behind his blueberry glasses Delbert had a vision. "If Rocky can fight for the heavyweight championship, then I can build a hospital." He reached over and put his large, red hand on Pico's birdlike arm. "Give me a hundred dollars or I'll give you a compound fracture," he said to Pico. And the rest is history.

The City of Saviours Hospital emerged from the Everglades, just off a secondary highway, a mile inside the Talabogie County line. At Delbert's instruction, Pico the Rat had a logo prepared showing Christ's head erupting in a blaze of heavenly light from the top of a 22-storey building. The stationery on which the logo appeared was thick and cream colored. Pico used his connections with The Mob to obtain the mailing lists of several TV evangelists and sent out 222,000 letters with Delbert Staggers' signature, demanding money for the City of Saviours project and suggesting that a certain vaguely defined plague would befall those who didn't contribute generously.

When the money began rolling in, Pico established, on paper only, his own medical supply wholesale firm, through which all equipment for City of Saviours passed, marked up 222%, a number which Pico considered lucky.

Only one minor problem surfaced. Talabogie County already had two major hospitals and was in no need of a third. Soon, City of Saviours boasted a staff of over 5,000—all hired through the P. R. Personnel Agency, president, Pico the Rat, which claimed six months' salary as its reward for placing the right person in the right job.

Only in the case of natural disasters like Hurricane Zoltan, or if someone like Preacher Gore was unlucky enough to get his foot bitten off in the immediate area of the hospital, did it ever operate at even 10% of capacity. The staff held daily Scrabble tournaments and the doctors played polo and miniature golf on the landscaped grounds. For rainy days, there were the five bowling alleys in the maternity wing.

After she and the camera crew visited Preacher Gore at City of Saviours, Carleen Treble was taken on a tour of the hospital and introduced to Delbert Staggers, who sat behind a wide chrome desk topped with blueberry-tinted glass. Although blind from birth, Delbert Staggers imagined he looked like Elvis Presley.

"Oh, Mr. Staggers, or should I say Reverend Staggers, I just love your blue glasses. I look so good reflected in them," said Carleen.

"I want you, I need you, I love you," said Delbert.

IN DESCRIBING DELBERT STAGGERS, DO YOU THINK THE AUTHOR WAS FAMILIAR WITH THE FOLLOWING BIBLICAL QUOTATION: "THERE WERE GIANTS IN THE EARTH," GEN. 6:4? NOTE HOW BLUEBERRIES ARE ASSOCIATED WITH STAGGERS. DID YOU KNOW THAT ALL BLUEBERRIES HAVE TEN—AND ONLY TEN— SEEDS? DO YOU THINK THAT HAS ANYTHING TO DO WITH THIS STORY? THERE IS A NERVOUS DISEASE OF HORSES AND CATTLE CALLED BLIND STAGGERS: CONSULT A VETERINARIAN AND LEARN THE SYMPTOMS. HOW DO THEY APPLY TO DELBERT AND PICO? IF YOU DON'T

ALREADY OWN ONE, ASK SOMEONE CLOSE TO
YOU TO BUY YOU A HORSE.

Carleen Treble and Delbert Staggers immediately became an item, as it
were. And while Foot Gore, the alligator-bitten, lovesick, ex-stock-car
driver showered Carleen with his dubious gifts, she was spending six
nights a week and Sundays after church with Delbert Staggers.

Pico the Rat often got to open the envelopes full of $100 bills which
poured in every day in response to the vaguely threatening letters of
Delbert Staggers—letters that intimated he was a minister of the gospel.
Pico knew a good thing when he was onto one, and ordered for Delbert,
by mail, several doctoral degrees ranging in scope from Divinity to
Zoology, all of which subsequently appeared on the letterhead and
under Delbert's signature. As the letters became more threatening, the
response from the lunatic fringe of Christianity to whom they were
directed increased in direct proportion to the nastiness of the request.

Delbert knew nothing about the changing tone of his letters or the
acquisition of degrees. He was only interested in Carleen. He had made
the earthshaking discovery that sex did not require 20/20 vision, and
rested easy in his excesses, confident that overdosing was unlikely to
damage his eyesight. Carleen loved it when he quoted from Elvis Presley,
and made Delbert leave his blue glasses on while they made love so she
could practice her various expressions of passion. For Carleen had no
intention of always delivering the Alligator Report for WTWT-TV, but
harbored ambitions of acting, singing gospel music, and being elected
to the state senate.

When Pico the Rat found out about Foot sending presents to Carleen
he immediately got on the phone.

"Listen, Foot," he said, trying to sound like 98 lbs. of menace, "it would
be very unhealthy for you to keep on sending unsolicited presents to a
certain female TV personality."

"So what are you gonna do, send another alligator to bite off my other
foot?" said Foot.

"Live in fear," said Pico the Rat, and hung up.

Foot Gore went out and bought a $200 gilt frame, inserted a photograph of his mother into it, and mailed it special delivery to Carleen Treble.

NOTE HOW A MAN NAMED FOOT LOSES A FOOT TO AN ALLIGATOR. IF YOU ARE NOT FAMILIAR WITH THE STORY OF OEDIPUS, ASK YOUR INSTRUCTOR TO TELL IT TO YOU. WHY DO YOU THINK FOOT MAILS A PICTURE OF HIS MOTHER TO CARLEEN? COULD IT BE THAT HE SUFFERS FROM AN OEDIPUS COMPLEX? OEDIPUS PUTS OUT HIS EYES. DELBERT STAGGERS IS BLIND. COULD IT BE THAT FOOT AND DELBERT ARE DIFFERENT SIDES OF THE SAME PERSONALITY? WHERE DOES THAT LEAVE CARLEEN? IS ELVIS PRESLEY REALLY DEAD?

The next afternoon, a Cadillac limousine pulled up in front of Foot's apartment and a weasel-faced runt in an oversized chauffeur's uniform guided a giant wearing mirrored sunglasses toward the door. When Foot answered the bell, he was first pushed back into the apartment by a poke in the belly, then struck sharply across the ribs by Delbert's white cane. Inside the apartment, Delbert whacked him into unconsciousness.

"Wait outside. I'll collect the money," said Pico.

"I've forgotten more than you'll ever know," Delbert said to Foot. Delbert thought he was punishing an ex-employee who had embezzled funds from the hospital.

"Stop annoying Carleen Treble or next time I *will* bring an alligator," hissed Pico into Foot's semi-conscious ear.

Today, the Alligator Report over, Carleen's vacuous smile fading into a feminine hygiene commercial, Preacher switches off the set, dons a yellow slicker, and exits, leaning into the bitter wind of Hurricane Zoltan.

He stumps along the beach on his cork, balsa-wood, and Styrofoam prosthetic.

A half mile up the beach he spots the dead ibis on the sand beneath a palm tree. He picks it up, examines it, decides (ignoring the pain in his ribs) that he will send it by special delivery parcel to Carleen at the TV station.

> IS IT LEGAL TO POST A DEAD IBIS IN THE U.S. MAIL? SUGGEST TO YOUR PRINCIPAL THAT HE ORGANIZE A FIELD TRIP TO THE NEAREST POST OFFICE.

The ibis has drawn one leg up into its feathers. Foot Gore carries it by the other leg, swinging it in time as he whistles the march from *The Bridge on the River Kwai*. Disguised as wild orchids, two postal inspectors follow at a discreet distance.

> HOW SIGNIFICANT IS THE IBIS APPEARING TO HAVE ONLY ONE LEG? COULD THE AUTHOR BE REFERRING TO THE FOOTLESS BIRD LEGEND? READ THE COMPLETE WORKS OF D. H. LAWRENCE AND TENNESSEE WILLIAMS TO FIND OUT.

The wind whips sand against Foot-to-the-Floor Gore's pant legs. As he walks, he pictures Carleen opening the box and finding the ibis. He wiggles the toes on his right foot. He can feel the sand collecting in his artificial shoe.

KING OF THE STREET

1.

A little buzzsaw of a wind chews at my ankles, whips dirt and sand up at my face, chases papers along the concrete until they flutter into storefronts like wounded birds. Though I'm over half a block behind him, I recognize King's strut as he hoofs along Hastings Street toward the Sunshine Hotel. He hesitates for just an instant at the door of the Sunshine's bar. I can see his lips curse as he glances around quickly to see if anyone has noticed. Two big whores wearing halters, shorts, and knee boots patrol the sidewalk. Neither looks at King. But I know, and King knows, that only cons and ladies wait for someone to open doors for them.

"Hey, King," I shout. "Wait up!" But he disappears into the Sunshine, probably heading to the back of the bar to find Hacksaw.

I lope after him. I'll catch up while his eyes are getting used to the cavelike darkness, while his other senses ingest the warm-sour odor of beer, the smell of smoky upholstery.

King has been in the slam for almost a year. I'm betting this is his first day out.

2.

It was Hacksaw I got to know first. Contrary to popular opinion, even bikers get lonely.

The Sunshine Bar is right in the heart of the drag, and is to the skid row area what the stock exchange is to the financial district. If you can't arrange to get it at the Sunshine, it can't be got. And, if you can smoke it, snort it, shoot it, fuck it, wear it, or drive it, Hacksaw, the head honcho of the Coffin Chasers, can get it for you.

Empty, the Sunshine is big enough to drive buffalo through, but it's never empty. The atmosphere of the Sunshine is like the inside of a bee-hive. The walls have faded murals of girls in grass skirts dancing against a background of blue sky and palm trees. The dancing girls have twenty years of accumulated fly specks on them, just like a lot of the clientele. The front half of the bar is for anybody, but the back door and all the tables around it are reserved for the Coffin Chasers.

I've been dropping in to the Sunshine a couple of times a week for years. I usually sit close to the bikers' section—it's called the Coffin Corner—but never in it unless I'm invited. If some stranger wanders in and goes to sit at one of their tables, one of the CCs ambles over and speaks without moving his lips. "If you want to live long and die happy, get the fuck out of this section," he says. Ordinary citizens, unless they have a death wish, tend not to argue with bikers.

I'm a voyeur when it comes to the bikers. I sit near their tables, eavesdrop as much as I can. I'm jealous of the women they attract. I'd give anything to behave as fearlessly as they do. But I never will. "There are only two kinds of men," Hacksaw said to me one night, "those who are bikers, and those who wish they were."

I agree.

"Come here," Hacksaw said to me one night. He was alone in the CCs' section, slumped down, sitting on his neck, looking like a denim bean-bag chair with a head. Hacksaw has been described as "300 lbs. of hate, with the disposition of a rhino."

After he beckoned to me, I picked up my beer and climbed the two carpeted steps to the Coffin Corner. Hacksaw motioned me to a chair; an honor in itself.

"I hear you write," he said. I was surprised that Hacksaw even knew I existed, let alone that he knew anything about me.

I nodded, swallowing.

"I could tell you some stories," he said. His voice emanated from somewhere near his four-inch-square brass belt buckle. He wore oil-splattered jeans, black biker's boots; what must have been a size 60 black tee-shirt covered his bulk. Gold lettering on the shirt read Harley Fucking Davidson.

"I'm probably not that kind of writer," I said, "but I'd be happy to listen any time you want to talk." It is a universal truth that *everybody*, absolutely *everybody*, thinks they have stories to tell.

"I don't understand what you're doin' here though," Hacksaw went on, waving his hand to show he meant not just the bar, but the area of the city, the street.

I shrugged my shoulders. Remained silent.

"Are you them or us?" When I looked puzzled he went on. "Are you straight or street?"

"I've been both," I said. "I didn't know I had to choose."

"You can't be both. Down there," and he pointed to the front of the bar, "you're swimmin' at the bottom of the barrel. This place is full of stumble-fucks, junkie-whores, winos . . . You stand out like a fuckin' wristwatch hippie . . ."

"Winos and whores are some of my favorite people . . . not necessarily in that order . . ." I said while Hacksaw stared coldly at me.

We talked for about an hour, until the Coffin Corner filled up with bikers and their ladies. The lot outside the back door looked like a chrome junkyard; the flashy motorcycles rumbled like guard dogs. Hacksaw, without ever coming right out and stating it, let me know that he was literate to some degree. Something he obviously didn't want his cronies to know, for he stayed on safe subjects—dope, sex and motorcycles, when any of them were within hearing. I remember thinking that if I had nerve enough to riff through the saddlebags on his chopper I might find a hardcover book or two stashed among his wrenches.

"You're droolin'," Hacksaw said to me at one point, grinning. I was staring too long at a lithe, dark-haired girl with amber eyes, who had tattoos from her wrists to the ragged edge of her cutoff denim vest.

"It shows?"

"I can fix you up no problem."

"Not tonight, thanks," I said with tremendous effort. There are iron strings attached to every favor a guy like Hacksaw performs. I wasn't ready to be in his debt.

<h2 style="text-align:center">3.</h2>

In that way outgoing strangers in a bar have of drawing people at nearby tables into their conversations, King reeled me in, like scooping a fish from a puddle. I'd seen him around the Sunshine for a month or two. He made it plain he was from the East and considered himself a cut above the locals, but he did it in such an ingratiating way that he offended no one. He'd scored himself two chicks, neither one very pretty, but diligent whores who stayed on the street until they turned as many tricks as King thought they should.

Some guys attract whores. King did. I wish I did. If a whore approaches me in a bar or on the street it is to ask if I want to go out: street talk for "Do you want to fuck and pay for it?"

When I stop to think about it I realize that I have never chosen a friend. I am always chosen. Male or female. My ex-wife chose me. Every lover I've ever had chose me. King chose me. Though you couldn't get him to admit it through torture, he likes me because I'm literate, introspective, shy, all the things King is not. We are friends though. He operates at the most primitive levels. But then everything on the street is at a primitive level.

The fall King took came after he scored a third chick, a sweet thing named Lannie; smoke-blond hair, a sensual mouth, no illusions about what she is or does. Her problem was too big a fondness for junk. King would have straightened her out. But Ginny, the number one chick, got jealous and set him up.

4.

"Even sociopaths need friends," Lannie said to King one evening. I noticed that she and I were the only ones who could tease King and get away with it.

"Hey, if you subtracted my I.Q. from the National Debt, the budget would be balanced," said King.

"He believes that," said Lannie.

"What can I say?" said King, smiling like he was accepting an award.

"King's never read anything longer than a street sign," said Lannie.

King is tall, raw-boned, moves like a sleek animal. He has dark, curly hair that floods over his collar and forehead. He *is* super-intelligent; he has total recall of conversations held months or years before. His eyes are a bitter blue, as if they're filled with metal filings. He always appears to be adding up unseen columns of figures, making calculations.

At his trial King's defense was "If she didn't give her money to me she'd have given it to somebody else," a premise that is completely valid on the street, but is not covered in any judge's manual. King drew 18 months for what was called Living Off the Avails of Prostitution.

Surprisingly, King was not bitter. "If you can't do the time, don't do the crime," he philosophized. But his eyes glinted like railroad tracks under moonlight as he was saying it.

I could have appeared at the trial as a witness for King. I was there the night he hooked up with Ginny. She came to him. I was at the next table when she sat down beside King, flashed a C-note she'd acquired by selling her services, and offered it to King, snuggling against his arm. "If you were my old man, there'd be a couple of these every day," she said, simpering, leaking smoke through her teeth.

I was practically exploding with lust at the thought. But King was cool as November. He let her sweat it out; he fingered the C-note, unfolded it, played with it, tucked it under a beer glass on the table instead of putting it in his pocket.

"How do you do it?" I asked him once.

"Never rush into anything with a broad, man. Let 'em know you don't fucking care a lick about them," he said. "Those kind of chicks know deep down they're not worth shit. It turns them on to have to crawl for a little attention. Listen, you fucking guys who read big books and don't know what's going down on the street got it all wrong about the relationship between whores and their old men. These chicks don't do anything they don't want to do; they never give away money they don't want to part with. Hell, most of them can't wait to give away their trick money. A good old man just keep his ladies happy, and keeps them from mainlining too much junk into their arms.

"You got to understand the psychology involved, and it ain't in your fucking books, man. I never roughed up a chick who didn't crave to be roughed up. Back East I had this chickie used to come to me with her belt in her hand, pull down her jeans and hand me the strap. Man, did we get it on when I was finished with her."

5.

About a month after King began serving his time, Ginny kept a date first with a hot cap (heroin about a hundred times stronger than the watered down shit that's usually on the street), then with the coroner.

"A tragic loss," drawled Hacksaw from under half-closed lids. "In the downward order of the universe there are cockroaches, slugs, shit, snitches, and bare pavement," and he smiled like a lion that had just eaten its fill of something less fortunate.

I was the one who introduced King to Hacksaw. King mentioned that he needed some wheels and had the bread to buy them.

"You're not gonna pay full price?" I said.

"Hey, what's money for?" said King, patting his vest pocket.

"I'll introduce you to Hacksaw," I volunteered.

"I don't know. I usually leave sleeping bikers lie." But he didn't stop me.

"You just put out the word on what you want and in a day or two it'll appear in the back parking lot. Two-thirds off retail. Hacksaw doesn't scoff it himself; he doesn't even hold; he just takes his cut."

I visited King in the slammer, twice. I went to tell him about Ginny, but of course he already knew.

"What can I say?" said King, grinning. "As you sow, so shall you reap.

"Like they say, man, the sun don't shine on the same dog's ass every day. By the way, I've joined the Bible Thumpers." He lowered his voice. "Hell of a P.R. move. Good for a couple of months off this gig."

The second time I offered to take Lannie.

"Nah," she said, "visitin' the joint always makes me sad."

When I told Hacksaw I was taking the bus out to the prison he said, "How much money do you make from writing stories?"

"I haven't made any yet," I admitted.

"For chrissakes," said Hacksaw, reaching deep into his boot and producing a plastic folder full of credit cards and I.D. "Rent yourself a car. Buy yourself some threads; you look like a bum. Go to the bank, go to seven or eight banks and get some cash. Then flush this stuff down a sewer."

What the hell! Being indebted to Hacksaw probably wasn't as bad as it seemed.

6.

"Hey, King, you leave your fucking hearing behind the walls?" I say as I catch up with him in the middle of the bar. A pathetic little half-breed girl is trying to dance on a tiny stage covered in green indoor-outdoor. She has a homemade tattoo on her butt reads: Property of Big Frank. Her sad little titties point at the floor.

King shakes hands, clasping my arm with his free hand. I think he is genuinely happy to see me. He is thinner, his clothes hang at odd angles.

"Come on," he says, "I'm goin' to see the Hacksaw. I need some new threads." He stares around the smoky beehive. "Place is still jammed with college graduates, I see."

We wait at the bottom of the steps until we catch Hacksaw's eye. It doesn't matter who you are, if you don't wear the club colors you don't go up the steps unless you're invited. Hacksaw's newest lady is squashed up next to him, a snubnosed chick with freckles and wheat-colored hair, must be at least sixteen. Up top she's wearing only a denim vest with the CC's colors on the back; she's busy licking Hacksaw's ear. He has his left hand all the way down the front of her jeans.

Hacksaw buys a round and we visit for a while. King lets his needs be known. "Who's boosting these days?" he asks.

"The Fox," says Hacksaw. "See the guy with the red hair and beard," and he points to the middle of the lower section where this laid-back lookin' dude has his chair tipped back and his Dingos parked on a table. "Works with a Black chick. They're cool. How long you been away?"

"Almost a year."

"I figured. When you want wheels you know who to see." King nods. "Make it within a week and I'll throw this in for a couple of days," and he uses his right hand to lift the kid's vest and show her little, freckled tits. "Nice, eh?"

"Nice, Hacksaw. You shouldn't do that to a guy who's only a few hours out of the slam."

"Take her back to the john for a few minutes. She sucks like silk."

"Maybe later," says King. We head down the steps toward the Fox's table.

Same old Hacksaw, wants to have everybody in his debt.

"Hacksaw sent me," says King, pulling up a chair backwards, straddling it.

"I seen you jawing with him," says the Fox. He is rightly named: only about 5'7", skinny, with a shag of red hair and a scraggily beard. His eyes are golden, and move around fast like a chicken's. King explains what he wants.

"I'll alert my boost," says the Fox, "back in two," and he signals the waiter to drop us a beer each.

Five minutes later the Fox is back. "Let's go shopping," he says, clapping his hands together. King picked a department store on Granville Street, in the high-rent district. We cruise the men's wear department and he picks out a complete wardrobe, topped by this nifty $550 suede suit. The Fox makes mental notes of types and sizes, tapping his head just in front of his left ear to show he has the information stored there. He takes the suede suit off the rack, holds it up to inspect it, puts it back with the hanger facing opposite to its neighbors.

"Where's your cannon?" I ask.

"She's around," says the Fox.

I look up to the mezzanine to where a coffee shop overlooks the business floor. A slim Black girl with tight, cornrowed hair and a long skirt sits staring down at us.

"Strong?" asks King.

"Can slap a table-model typewriter between her thighs and boogie out of the store like she was being chased."

"Class," says King. The Fox nods in agreement.

"Meet me back at the Sunshine at seven," he says to King. "We'll have everything for you by then," and he smiles though his thin, red mustache covers his upper lip completely.

7.

Outside the store, King and I part company. I am halfway back to my room when my teeth start to itch and I develop a feeling as if someone is staring hard at the back of my neck. Some guys claim they can tell when they enter a room if someone is carrying a piece. Other guys claim they can smell cops. To me there is something about the Fox that smells bad. Maybe it takes an outsider to spot an outsider. I circle around and head back to the store. Everything seems okay. The suede suit is exactly as we left it. I move to the mezzanine coffee shop and take a table with a view.

Two nervous hours later my hunch is rewarded. I watch as a sad-looking man in a brown-striped suit emerges from the dressing room area, takes the suede suit off the rack and carries it into the back. He has store-dick written all over him.

As I head back toward the Sunshine I wonder how I should handle the situation. The Fox and his lady are almost certainly undercover heat. They won't hit King or Hacksaw today. Sometimes these types make hundreds of deals before the ax falls. An operation can go on for a year or more, then in the dark of night the heat covers the drag like a sponge and slurps up every small-timer who ever custom ordered a five-finger-bargain or dealt an ounce of grass. But the Black chick, Cora, is supposed to be a junkie. That puts a whole new face on the operation. A lot of street people, Hacksaw included, could take a big fall. I'm clean, so I could warn the Fox that I'm onto him. If I did, he and his chick would disappear off the street fast as the steam that huffs up out of manholes. But they're not smart enough to leave well enough alone; they'd still drag the streets, use the evidence they've collected.

I guess I'm gonna have to decide if I'm *them* or *us*. "There's one law on the streets and one law in the suburbs. If the heat would only realize that it would be a lot better world." I realize that I'm quoting King. Well, maybe he's right.

At the Sunshine I head directly for the Coffin Corner. I don't wait to be invited up the steps. As I drop into a chair across from Hacksaw the corner gets very quiet.

"Get rid of the jailbait," I say, "we've got to talk."

A couple of Coffin Chasers are reaching for the shanks in their boots, but Hacksaw stops them with a movement of his head. He unwinds the blonde and pushes her away. "Bring Hacksaw fifty dollars," he says to the chickie. She pouts. He grabs a handful of ass and holds on. She yells as he gives her a push toward the back door. "And make it quick." She scuttles off like a dog that's just been kicked.

Hacksaw sniffs the fingers he's had down the front of Blondie's jeans, and smiles. "It better be important, my friend," he says to me.

"Could be," he says, after he's heard what I have to say. "The Man gets trickier every year.

"Be cool, I know how to handle this. Like that old joke, try to pretend nothing unusual is happening. All you got to do is what I tell you . . ."

8.

I disappear until about an hour before the deal is due to go down. King is with Lannie at her favorite table near the door. She is stoned, nodding into her beer, her neck whiplashing every thirty seconds or so. A john comes over, taps her awake; she gets up, walking like she has rubber ankles, takes his arm and they head for the door. She's wearing jeans and her sweater has stains on it.

"She's startin' to look like a whore," says King. "Guess I hit the bricks just in time.

"Lannie's a class chick," he goes on, "all she needs is an aggressive old man to keep her in line. What I like about Lannie is she can handle a john or a deal even when she's blissed to the gills. Her head clears when there's bread on the line."

When she come back to the table, King puts an arm around her shoulder, pulls her and her chair close up to him. "Later tonight," he says, "I'm gonna get me a room, some good smoke, a bottle of Three Crown and a lady who like to fuck up a storm. You know of a chick who might like to join me?"

Lannie blows smoke and licks her lips. "Why don't you cross the room off your list, we can use mine," and she rubs her nose against his shoulder.

"Suits me," says King, "but first some business. You know the Fox's woman?"

"Sure, Cora . . ."

"She a junkie?"

"Yeah. She buys . . ."

"You ever seen her fix?"

"She's on the stuff, man . . ."

"You ever seen the needle in her arm?"

"No."

He clues Lannie into the scene. She looks at me in a new light, actually seeing me; she smiles an off-center smile.

"Here's what I want you to do," says King. "Cora's on her way here. Go outside and get a couple of girls you can trust. The CCs want to talk to Cora but they don't want to be seen snatching her off the street. And make sure you keep her hands in sight, she might be carrying a piece."

Lannie is out the door a minute later.

"Blissed or not, she's a good lady," says King.

Seven o'clock comes and goes. I have purposely sat with my back to Fox's table, but every few minutes I sneak a glance at him. His feet are on the floor now, and he is nervous, doing a little dance. I bet he'd like to be up and pacing, but he's got to pretend to be cool.

Lannie comes in the front door, catches King's eye, winks, and goes out again.

He draws his index finger across his throat in a quick, slashing motion. "Fucking snitch," he says, without moving his lips.

9.

Following Hacksaw's instructions, I go and make a phone call on the single pay phone by the front door. I then accompany King over to Fox's table.

"Where's your cannon?" King says, standing close beside the Fox, giving him a pretend frisk, enough to establish he doesn't have a piece under his shirt. About his only chance right now is to haul out a piece, fire a shot into the ceiling, and wait for the management to call in the street cops.

"She's a little late, man. You know you can't trust junkies," and he gives us a little shark of a smile, though his eyes are blinking ten times a second. "What's with the frisk? You heat or something?"

"Or something," says King. "Fox, you and your lady have made a lot of people unhappy."

"I don't follow," says Fox. "Don't worry. Cora will be along with your stuff."

"No she won't." The Fox's skin is pale even under his beard and there are stains under the arms of his dark blue shirt. "They must have told you what happens to snitches, undercover, fucking pigs. You must know how a chick gets a few straightforward words carved into her body before she o.d.'s. You must have heard about how they find snitches with their cock and balls stuffed in their mouths. That's done while they're still alive, Fox. As a warning to the Man not to put any more snitches on the street. But they always do. Guys like you figure they're smarter than guys like us," and he stares at Fox, expressionless. I realize I'm looking at Fox the same way, not a trace of emotion on my face.

Fox is staring around in desperation. Hacksaw and most of the CCs are between him and the back door. A couple of Coffin Chasers, like leather-covered sides of beef, hang on each side of the front entrance.

"If you're a snitch, man, you got one chance, and that's to get to the pay phone and call your friends to come and get you." King picks a dime off the green terry-cloth table top and holds it out to Fox. He snatches it and darts toward the phone.

"Thanks," he mumbles.

"Luck," says King, then gives me a look. I nod.

He'll need it. I jammed the phone with a slug before we visited Fox's table.

WAVELENGTHS

Me and Brody driving north. We're four days into our trip home; southern Florida to Bellingham, Washington, over 3300 miles, five days if we push it, but neither of us are in the mood to push it. We've just finished our first summer of professional baseball, Brody and me. Neither of us is happy with how it turned out. The baseball was bad, at least for me. Our personal lives were worse.

We chug along in the beat-up Plymouth we shared in high school. I can see a map of the USA in my head, picture our progress, like a coloured bleep inching across the map.

More than anything in the world, I've always wanted to play in the Bigs, and until this summer I always believed I had a great chance. I still believe I have a chance, but my stock is way down. My fielding is okay; I play a mean second base, cover a lot of ground, turn the double play with the best of them, steal a lot of bases if I get on base. Getting on base is my problem. I batted .212, didn't walk as many times as I should have, swung at a lot of sliders in the dirt, and was always out in front of the changeup. As I've found out to my regret, there's a big difference between being a star on a high school team in Washington and being

281

one of twenty-five guys on a Rookie League team, all of whom were stars in high school.

I'm pressing management for an assignment to play winter baseball in Mexico or the Dominican Republic. If they give me the opportunity I'll take batting practice six hours a day. I'll learn to lay off the bad sliders, I will. I'll learn the strike zone, learn to be patient at the plate, practise bunting. I'll lay a towel about twenty feet up the third-base line. I'll bunt until I can stop two of three on the towel. I want to play in the Bigs so bad I'll do anything, I will.

Brody hit twenty-seven home runs, batted .276, and was okay in the outfield. The scouts liked his power, his bat speed. There was talk of him going straight through to Triple A after spring training next year.

It's odd the way life works out, isn't it? Brody's never going to play baseball again. He told the organization the day after our final game. After the interview, he gave away his glove to a twelve-year-old boy in the parking lot.

"I'm never going to attend a game again as long as I live, not even watch the World Series on TV," he said, as we made our way to our dusty old Plymouth, which was parked outside the house where we'd rented a basement suite, the back of the car already crammed with our clothes and equipment, Brody's stereo and weights. The long aerial was bowed back, casting a scythe-like shadow across the hood and windshield.

When we get home Brody's going to enrol at Western Washington State University in Bellingham, where he'll study chemistry, get a job teaching high school, and never leave Bellingham except to ski a little up in Snoqualmie Pass, or drive to Seattle for an afternoon at the Pike Street Market. Brody doesn't want any surprises. I can't imagine a life without them.

I feel obligated to report back to my family, but I'll be gone after a couple of weeks, a month at the most. Unlike Brody, I've got a few loose ends to untangle in Florida. If, in a couple of years, I don't advance toward the Bigs the way I feel I should—I've no plans to be a career minor-league player—I'll still head for a big city, Chicago probably, or

New York. I want to travel, see everything there is to see, live and work somewhere at the centre of the action.

"This whole summer's been all about growing up," says Brody. *"I grew up this summer,"* he's said, about once every hour during the whole trip, whether he's driving, or riding shotgun, or fiddling the radio to keep a fresh station blasting out music at us.

"If growing up involves getting your brains scrambled by a girl, quitting a career that would probably make you famous, would certainly earn you a million dollars, maybe even a million dollars in one year, just to study chemistry, teach at a local high school, and probably marry the girl next door and live a boring life ever after, then I'll stay the way I am, thank you. Not that I haven't got my problems."

"Not that you haven't," says Brody.

Brody is 6' 3" with reddish-blond hair, a wide, ruddy face, and pale blue eyes. He has arms big as furnace pipes, and size XL shirts are taut across his back and shoulders. I'm the opposite, 5' 9", 165 lbs., a bit stoop-shouldered from crouching at second base since I was five years old. I'm dark, with straight black hair, worried brown eyes and a crease between my brows that my summer girlfriend, Mary, thought was sexy, and my mother says she could plant petunias in.

Brody had the grades to go to college, but we both opted to play minor-league baseball as soon as high school was finished. Brody graduated. Me, I studied just enough to stay on the high-school baseball team. If I'm lucky I'll never have to crack a book again, except maybe my bank book. The bulk of my reading consists of checking the morning sports pages to see if I was mentioned in the write-up of yesterday's game.

It was Brody's folks who convinced him to skip college. They figured Brody would get to the Bigs faster that way. We've lived all our lives together, me and Brody, and his folks are the greatest. I remember when we were about six years old, Brody's mom was always the one who picked us up after school and took us to practice, and was right there cheering for us from the stands behind our bench. Oh, sometimes she'd get a little carried away, give the umpire a bad time, or bug the coach too much if Brody wasn't getting the playing time she felt he deserved. But she used to defend me, too. Boy, did I appreciate that. My own parents weren't much interested in my playing baseball. They'd have been prouder of me if I'd been an A student. Mom is a social worker and Dad teaches mathematics at Fairhaven College in Bellingham.

As we travel, the radio stations change every fifty miles or so. Whoever isn't driving has to search until something we like comes in clearly. Until a few minutes ago we had a dandy country music station; George Strait wailed, and Merle Haggard did some songs by Bob Wills and the Texas Playboys. But the station has faded away until it's only a shadow and something else is coming in all scratchy and tinny, some news and talk station. Radio stations can't be on the same wavelength unless they're a long ways apart. A lot like people, I figure.

I wish that just once in my life everybody could be on the same wavelength. But I guess that's not the way life is. See, if Brody and I could have traded parents, and then this summer, if we could have become involved with different girls . . .

Brody's dad is a huge, shaggy guy who works for the forest service and was away all week planting trees or cutting windbreaks, or whatever. But on the weekends he'd be out at every game, cheering Brody on, giving him an audience to perform for. But Brody never cared. He never tried. He was just so naturally good he was a star anyway. I performed for Brody's folks, and when they praised me it was better than a double chocolate malt, and I'd wriggle around like a pup being petted while they told me how good I was and offered pointers on how I could be even better. Brody never responded to their praise, except maybe to be a bit embarrassed.

Brody's dad was so great. He'd take us out on Saturday and Sunday nights and he'd hit Brody fly balls for a couple of hours. I'd cover the bases, after Brody's dad called out the situation, you know, "Runner going to advance from second to third on a run-scoring sacrifice fly," or "Single to centre with slow runner on second, play at the plate."

All my dad ever had to say was, "Have you done your homework?"

Then Brody would move to first base. "When a great hitting outfielder loses his speed they move him to first," Brody's dad would explain. But Brody complained, almost every time we practised, and sometimes he even acted like he'd rather be someplace else. Brody's dad would hit me grounders for an hour or so, and he'd coach me on playing second base, and Brody on playing first. On the best evenings Brody's mom would come out and play shortstop. She was a pretty fair fielder if the ball was hit right at her, and her being there allowed me to practise turning the double play.

"If you'd just hustle like C. J. here," Brody's dad said I don't know how many times to Brody. But Brody had one speed in the outfield, and that was dead slow. He had instinct though, and because of that he always got a jump on the ball and looked a lot faster than he really was.

While the Langstons sure wished Brody had my hustle, I wished they were my parents. I'm gonna have to spend a lot of time with them in the first week we're home. They're gonna be heartbroken when they find out what Brody's done, if they haven't already. I can't believe that the organization hasn't phoned to tell them Brody's quit professional baseball for good.

I figure three, four seasons at the most and I'll be in the Bigs. I'll send the Langstons free tickets; I'll invite them to be my guests wherever I'm playing. If I was doing what Brody's doing, my parents would be the happiest people in the world. And if Brody had half my desire to play in the Bigs his parents would be in pig heaven.

We made it as far as Atlanta the first night, which was too far to drive in one day, so we took it easier the second day, only drove as far as Nashville. We spent the night touring some of the country bars downtown after we discovered that the Grand Ole Opry was sold out for months in advance. Brody wanted to push on. I think he's actually looking forward to disappointing his parents.

We hit St. Louis in the late afternoon of the third day.

"I've never been to St. Louis before and the one thing I've got to see is Busch Stadium," I said.

"Why bother?" said Brody. "It's just another ballpark." I was parking the car on a dingy street across from the stadium. "It's empty," Brody went on. "I can't see sitting out here at dusk, in a drizzle, just to stare at a goddamned empty ballpark."

"Sit!" I said. "That's the bronze of Stan Musial," and I pointed far across the open area in front of Busch Stadium. "We'll have to get out in order to have a close look at it."

I had this crazy idea that I could still change Brody's mind. A forlorn hope that if he saw the way the light shone down on Musial's statue, casting a heavenly aura around his head, it would be like a visit to Lourdes for a dying Catholic, and Brody would say he was kidding, that the last few days had all been a bad joke. I believed there was a chance he'd laugh that deep, crusty laugh of his and say he was cured of his desire to quit baseball.

Though he accompanied me to inspect the bronze of Stan Musial, Brody didn't change his mind. We were damp and smelled like wet dogs by the time we got back to the car. We set out to find a cheap motel. The inside of the car was stale and smelled of apple cores and empty beer cans.

"So the guy could hit a baseball," Brody said of Musial, and shrugged, as we weaved through an industrial district of St. Louis. No matter how enthusiastic I was about what we'd just seen, Brody's mood stayed dark. We found an eighteen-dollar motel, where we parked the car close to the door of our unit so we could hear if anyone was tampering with it. The motel was located in a tampering neighbourhood.

Maybe if the Cardinals had been at home . . . maybe if we'd actually been able to see a game . . .

In Florida there was a bar called Clancy's, a place where a gang of us used to go after a game to relax. Clancy's was a quiet place, too quiet for most of the ballplayers. It had an old oak bar, one wall of booths upholstered in wine-red leather, and a black guy who played the piano, but had the courtesy not to sing.

There were five or six of us who were regulars; we'd pound a few beers, talk baseball, replay the game two or three times. After the baseball talk was exhausted we'd usually go to a nightclub and hope to meet girls. We were hardly ever successful.

It was at Clancy's, though, that we met Sheila-Ann and Mary. They came in together and were about to take stools at the bar, when Sheila-Ann looked our way, grabbed Mary's arm and pulled her over to our booth.

"We saw you guys play tonight," Sheila-Ann said to the group, though her eyes were focused on Brody as she spoke. If anybody had been listening they could have heard my intake of breath when I looked at Sheila-Ann. She wasn't gorgeous, but she was what my fantasies were all about, slim and blonde, her hair frizzed so that with the lights of the bar behind her she looked like an angel. Her brown eyes were deep-set, wise, ironic; her smile was controlled, almost insolent.

Brody, uncomfortable under Sheila-Ann's stare, mumbled his thanks.

"We've been to almost every game," Sheila-Ann went on. She then introduced herself, and Mary, who had remained silent. We invited them to join us. And though it was awkward, the five of us guys squeezed together so one girl could sit at each end of the semicircular booth. Sheila-Ann sat across from me. Mary sat beside me. And that's the way it was for the rest of the summer: Sheila-Ann across from me, beside Brody, and Mary beside me.

Eventually, the other players left so there was just the four of us in the booth, Sheila-Ann close beside Brody, telling him what a great baseball player he was, snuggling against him, talking right into his mouth. Because I was Brody's friend I stayed, and because some company is better than none, I offered to see Mary home. I hadn't said a dozen words all evening. I'd spent all my time looking at Sheila-Ann, wishing it was me she'd come on to. Mary was a stocky girl, in a grey skirt and maroon-coloured blouse. She had light brown hair and grey eyes.

At one point I almost had a vision. I glanced up from my drink to see Sheila-Ann in profile; the orangy light behind her was not kind. As she pulled deeply on her cigarette, her face looked drawn, her eyes hard. For a few seconds I could see how she'd look in twenty years, and I didn't like what I saw. But the vision didn't change my being in love with her. Hell, in twenty years I'd be a retired baseball player, probably nursing a gut and combing my hair forward to hide a bald spot.

We became a steady foursome. Brody and Sheila-Ann, because *she* chose *him*. Mary and I became a couple by default, something I should have run from because it was so unfair to her.

Mary was soft and compliant in my arms in the front seat of the car that first evening. We were parked along the ocean, a row of palms casting moonlight shadows on the white sand, but no matter how she tried to please me I only partially responded. I could sense she felt more strongly about me than I'd ever feel about her.

I didn't appreciate Mary, but there was a reserve outfielder named Becker who did. We called him "Beak" because of the size of his nose. He was a pale, gangly kid with shoelaces of black hair flopping across his forehead, who was never gonna advance beyond Rookie League, and who, that first evening, stared at Mary the way I stared at Sheila-Ann. And as the summer progressed, Becker told me a dozen times how he envied me finding a girl like Mary. Wavelengths.

What I can't understand is why life can't work out a little better. I'd sell my soul if I thought it would get me to the Bigs, I would. And I'll get there, too. Pete Rose was my idol, and like him I'm gonna put out, and put out, and put out. I'll make up with hustle what I lack in ability, and I've got stamina, and I'll practise twice as hard and twice as long as anybody else. I want to make the Show so badly, and I have only marginal ability, while without putting out any real effort Brody could hit thirty home runs every season, make a million dollars a year and be famous. All Brody wants to do is teach chemistry.

Sheila-Ann's deliberately setting out to marry a baseball player isn't as self-serving as it seems. She wants to improve herself, and for a girl raised by a single mother in the back streets of a small Florida city, there aren't that many options. Sheila-Ann has the same spark I have. I'm full of a terrible energy and I don't have any idea how to use it except to play professional baseball. That's why I can't consider failing, because if I don't consider it, it won't happen.

"Are you still in love with Sheila-Ann?" Brody asked suddenly, on the second day out. He hadn't said a word for a hundred miles, just sucked on a Bud and fiddled with the radio. The question surprised me, but I tried not to let on.

"Was it that obvious?"

"To me. I don't think Sheila-Ann noticed. And Mary was so in love with you . . ." he let his voice trail off.

"Yes. I'm still in love with her."

"Don't you see the kind of woman she is?"

"Yes."

Brody shrugged and the silence folded down around us like a comforter.

Why couldn't Sheila-Ann and I have latched onto each other? Instead, I reluctantly ended up with Mary, and aren't all four of us unhappy. What's more frightening is when I look five years down the line the only one of us I see being happy is Brody, and that's because he's willing to settle for so little.

I'll still be walking the blade. If I'm lucky I'll be in the Bigs, playing first-string for a bad team, or backup for a good one—getting in the lineup once a week, hoping the starter slumps or gets injured. Every time I think of Brody, I think how unfair it is when someone won't take advantage of the gift he's been given.

And Sheila-Ann, maybe now that she's been so close to fame and fortune, maybe she will, like an old egg-sucking dog that's had a taste of the forbidden, just keep on prospecting for a big-league ballplayer. But I wonder if she's a good enough judge of talent? Her odds of latching onto a star twice in a row aren't very good. The thing I'd hate most would be seeing her at twenty-five, still sitting in Clancy's, hustling a nineteen-year-old ballplayer who might have a shot at the big time.

I spend a lot of my time fantasizing about Sheila-Ann, about how, when I go back to Florida, I'll go after her, I'll win her respect, and she'll take a chance with me because she and I have the same kind of drive and ambition.

Mary will marry some local who sells insurance, or works with computers, someone who will appreciate her as much as girls like Mary ever get appreciated, and she'll stagnate, and get mousier-looking as time passes, and she'll think of me occasionally, and in her imagination what we had will be a lot more than it ever was. And if she really gets out of touch, she'll name her fourth or fifth kid Charles Jason, after me, and call him C. J. for short.

Brody will get his degree at Western Washington State, and he's already mentioned Dorinda Low, a girl he'd dated occasionally in high school, more than once. Dorinda is a girl who makes my skin crawl every time I think of touching her. She has lustreless black hair, big pores, and eyes that bulge just a bit. She has one of the most passionless mouths I've ever seen on a woman. She lives with her arms folded across her chest and belongs to one of those freaky churches that don't allow women to wear makeup.

At the end of our first month in Florida Brody's parents flew down and spent their entire two-week holiday with us. They watched us play seven games at home and then went on a seven-game road trip. Florida was the first time either of us had been away from home for any stretch of time.

"You guys jump up on us harder and are more affectionate than the dogs after we've been away a few days," Brody's mom said, as we each took a turn hugging her and swinging her off her feet. She was properly horrified at the basement we lived in so she bought us curtains, cleaned the bathroom, and stocked the shelves and refrigerator with a whole summer's worth of groceries before she left. They treated us both to dinner every night, and at the ballpark we could hear them cheering every time we came to bat or made any kind of a play in the field.

The two letters I had from my folks both discussed how I could make up my high-school credits with evening classes and start college in January.

It was Mr. and Mrs. Langston who landed us a sports agent and business manager. I'm sure they had to force him to take me in order to get Brody, but it made me feel good. Brody got a sizable bonus for signing, and I got a small one. Brody was always worrying about how to invest his. I just wanted mine to grow a little.

"C. J.'s got the right idea," Mrs. Langston said. "The reason athletes have agents and business managers and contract lawyers is to do your worrying for you. You boys just concentrate on baseball."

We should have. We really should have.

The scariest event of all was the night Brody and Sheila-Ann broke up. It was Brody's idea for the four of us to go to a fancy restaurant after our final game; we both had interviews with the organization scheduled for the next day. I knew something bad was up because Brody had hinted to me several times that he was unhappier than usual playing baseball, but I really had no idea how unhappy he was. I mean he was an All-Star, the press had honeyed him up all summer. They'd even nicknamed him "Bear" because of the deliberate way he played the outfield, and it looked like the nickname was gonna stick.

I felt like a monkey, all dressed up in my only suit and tie. There was dance music after dinner, and the first time I took Mary to the dance floor I spent most of my time watching over her shoulder as Brody and Sheila-Ann settled into a serious conversation.

"Sheila-Ann thinks he's gonna propose," Mary whispered as we danced. There was something so obvious in her voice that I pushed her back from me a few inches, hardly realizing I was doing it.

Brody and Sheila-Ann stopped their conversation and looked uncomfortable when we came back to the table, so as soon as the music started again I steered Mary toward the dance floor.

"What's Brody telling her?" Mary asked.

What I wanted to say was, "He sure as hell ain't proposing," but instead I said, "It may be her telling him something."

"Sheila-Ann was so happy she could have floated over here tonight," Mary said. "She's planning her wedding . . ." Mary looked at me in such a way that if I'd been in love with her, or even thinking about being in love with her, I had an opening a hundred yards wide to tell her I loved her, or to go ahead and pop the question. But I remained silent and the final number in the set seemed to last forever.

"Oh, don't apologize. I don't want to hear it," Sheila-Ann was saying as we returned to the table. "Just go away and leave me alone. I don't care what your prospects are outside baseball. I wasted a whole season!"

Choking with tears she shouted, "I wanted to marry a baseball player! I wanted to get out of this stinking little town! I wanted to be somebody."

What she said sounded selfish and bad-tempered, but I sympathized. And I wasn't entirely unhappy that Brody had done what he'd done, though I didn't know then exactly how far he'd gone. I was sad for what Brody was doing to Sheila-Ann but I was also elated. I wanted Sheila-Ann almost as much as I wanted to play Major League baseball. Watching the tears splash out of her eyes, watching her face turn blotchy, her mascara run, I had never loved her more. There was nothing I wouldn't have done for her at that moment.

Brody got up and walked slowly out of the restaurant.

I wanted to shout to Sheila-Ann, "Look at me! Look at me!" I thought those words over and over, trying to make them pierce Sheila-Ann's unhappiness. "Look at me! *I'm* a baseball player! I'm going to make it!"

But Sheila-Ann stared right through me as if I was perfectly clear glass. It never crossed her mind to consider me.

And that frightened me. Sheila-Ann always had a hungry look about her. I had studied her real close on more than one evening, when she didn't realize I was watching her. She wasn't nearly as pretty as she seemed at first glance. She'd studied all about makeup and how to style her hair to her best advantage, and what colours to wear. Mary told me that Sheila-Ann once went all the way to Tampa to take a three-day course on how to smile and what to do with her hands when she walked.

"You know what she said to me?" Brody asks, fiddling with the radio. The tone of his voice makes it clear that *she* refers to Sheila-Ann.

"What?"

"She said she picked me out because I was not only the best player on the team, but because I was gonna end up a superstar. Her and Mary had watched us play fifteen times before they introduced themselves. They planned the meeting with us at Clancy's; they'd followed us there before."

I was surprised Brody had to be told that. I knew it the first time I saw Sheila-Ann smile. Neither Mary nor I ever mentioned the meeting being planned. What good would it have done?

"Seems to me that's the kind of things guys do to girls all the time, follow them around, set up an accidental-on-purpose meeting."

"'What if I'd been a jerk?' I asked her. 'Would you have fallen in love with me anyway? A lot of guys who can hit a baseball a long way or throw a strike to the plate from the right-field corner have about the same IQ as their equipment bag, and not only are they stupid, they aren't even nice. What if I'd turned out to be one of those?' And you know what she said, C. J.? She looked at me in that insolent way she has, like she was talking to a teacher she didn't like very much, and she said, 'I'd be willing to make certain adjustments.'

"Then she tried to cuddle up to me, tried to move her chair around

293

beside mine, but I wouldn't let her. 'Listen!' she went on. 'I checked you out pretty thorough—I can tell a lot about a guy by the way his teammates treat him. Mary and I, we came into Clancy's two nights running and we sat in the booth behind you, and we followed you home once to see what part of town you lived in. We could tell both of you were smart and nice by the way you talked to your friends.'

"'But what if the only guy on the squad this year who was going to make it to the big time was mean, and ugly, and dumb as a baseball bat?'

"'Then I reckon a man with all those handicaps might need some-body to organize his finances for him,' she said, smiling every inch of the way."

At least Brody had the courage of his convictions. I didn't exactly break off with Mary. I promised I'd write. I promised I'd phone. I knew I was lying as I made each promise, but I couldn't cut myself off from the possibility of seeing Sheila-Ann again. The last night in Florida, Mary and I engaged in some of the saddest lovemaking ever imagined. Mary tried to ingest me, her lips were soft, her tongue wild, she opened herself to me in every way possible, and though my body responded, my heart was somewhere else. To be exact, my heart was in the next bedroom where Sheila-Ann was alone, a Willie Nelson tape crying softly through the thin walls.

Before we left Florida, I had an interview with the manager, the Florida-Texas-Louisiana scout for our organization, and a guy from the head office, an accountant type, called a player development officer.

"I want to play winter baseball," I said to them before they could say anything to me. But they didn't give me a yes or a no.

"The computer ranks you 38th among second basemen in profes-sional baseball not on a Major League roster, the player development type said to me.

That was bad. We all knew that.

"The computer can't measure desire," I countered.

"If we took desire into account," said the scout, "there'd be a lot of sixty-year-old men with active imaginations in the Bigs."

"You know what I mean. I'm willing to work. I'll hone the skills I have, develop the ones I lack. I'm gonna make it, if not with this organization, then another one." That raised a couple of eyebrows.

The scout smiled.

"What we'd really like to do," he said, "is give your friend Brody Langston a transfusion of whatever gives you your get-up-and-go."

For a minute I considered trying to make a deal. I suspected what Brody was going to do, and I think they did too. If I could convince Brody to keep playing they'd have to carry me with him every step of the way. I'd be like that goat that keeps the high-strung race horses calm.

I think they were hoping I'd ask for a deal too. But while it might get me up a couple more notches toward the Bigs, it would take the edge off. I know from experience I'd have to earn everything.

When we parted they said they'd call me at home next week about winter ball, and about an assignment for the spring. I think they're going to keep me for at least a year, and that's all I ask. Just a chance to prove myself.

"I asked her to marry me, anyway," Brody says out of the blue. We're a few hours from home.

"Who?" I say before I can stop myself.

"Who do you think? I asked her to come back to Bellingham with me. I've got a good solid future. I thought she would. I really did."

"I'm sorry," I stammered. "I had no idea you cared that much."

"I know," said Brody.

Whoever isn't driving has to constantly adjust the radio. Stations fade away, become staticky, and have to be replaced by new ones. I'm always pleased when I hit on a new, strong wavelength. But they don't last; it's something about us travelling over the edge of the earth, while radio waves shoot straight ahead.

Me and Brody driving north. Silent. On totally different wavelengths.

DO NOT ABANDON ME

I don't really know what my husband, Richard, does for a living. I do know that because of his occupation he is one of the loneliest men on earth. The reason I don't know is not for lack of interest, but lack of understanding. Richard, never Ricky, Rick, or Dick, is employed by Harvard as a sort of one-man think tank. He spends his days in a quiet office in front of a clean desk thinking about mathematics. He has made some breakthroughs in the echelons of higher calculus that only two other men in the world are capable of interpreting, of telling him whether he is right or wrong. One is in Japan, the other in one of those countries, Honduras, Ecuador, Bolivia, where magical thinking is part of the national psyche, a country where it is unreasonably hot and humid and the political situation is terminally volatile.

I know it sounds cruel, but Richard is such a bore. I am so sick of him. He is totally predictable. I know I am being unfair to Richard because, ten years ago predictable was what I wanted. I was 22, had just come out of a two-year, knock-down, drag-out relationship with a 6'8" tackle for the New England Patriots. Sex so intense I often felt I'd explode, or at the least cause myself irreversible bodily harm if we continued for one more minute. The bad times were equally intense, to summarize all our difficulties, Karl had no concept of the word fidelity. Women flung themselves at him as if he were a rock star. I traveled with him one fall, road trips to Dallas, and Los Angeles. He received FedEx packages and letters at the front desk, hand-delivered letters slipped under his door. Panties, bras, photos, gifts, some purchased, some handmade, each accompanied by primitive, pitiful letters full of misspellings and pornographic suggestions. I'll always remember one from a girl who in her arcade, three-for-a-dollar photo looked about eighteen, she had a long pimply face and lank black hair. The accompanying note read in part: "I like to due a good blowjob so there's no chance I should get pregnate."

I met Richard at a book signing. There is a monster bookstore in Worcester and a girlfriend convinced me to accompany her there one Sunday afternoon where a young author, whose name I had never heard, and can't recall, was signing his book, which had something to do with philosophy and the cultural revolution. I read, but I enjoy love stories and mysteries, and like to be scared by Stephen King. While we were waiting in line to get her book signed, Richard walked by. My girlfriend's brother had roomed with Richard at Harvard, where Richard had attended from freshman to PhD, and then gone into their esoteric think tank. He looked like a sad puppy. I wanted to cuddle him and pet him and wipe those laces of black hair off his forehead. We went for coffee after the signing, and Richard was shy and looked into his coffee whenever he spoke. My girlfriend was the one he should have been interested in, she had a degree in psychology from Smith and was about to set up her own practise; she was as close to an intellectual equal as Richard might find. She was trying to impress him, but it apparently didn't work, for the next week Richard phoned her brother and asked him to call his sister and get my last name and phone number.

After my tumultuous relationship with Karl, Richard was peace, tranquillity, stability. Richard would never have groupies.

We dated for several months. Movies, dinners, concerts, lectures. I had to seduce him. Undoing my bra while he was tentatively touching my breasts, after about our seventh date, gave him a clue that I was ready. I compared this to Karl, who moments after we met, clutching me in an elevator on the way to the parking garage, asked me if I enjoyed a number of activities, all connected with oral sex. I was too stunned not to reply. I panted that I did. "Just laying it on the line," said Karl. "There are actually chicks who think they can impress me by holding out."

When we did make love, Richard was surprisingly passionate. I hadn't expected much from this slight, sink-chested man with his uneasy smile and small, pale hands. Eventually, Richard asked me to marry him. I said yes. I longed for stability. But not boredom.

Let me give you an example. This is what Richard considers a significant activity for the two of us. I'm sure he's read somewhere in a magazine that married couples should do things together in order to keep their marriage fresh. He enrolled us in a course on Navigational Codes and Signals.

"We don't own a boat," I protested.

"That's not the point," Richard said. "This is something new to us. I'll bet none of our friends have done this."

"And with good reason," I said, but under my breath.

We do occasionally go out for a Sunday afternoon on a friend's boat, but if they have any navigational flags I've never noticed them, and I certainly don't recall anyone ever flashing them signals. After the first class, held in a musty room in some kind of privately funded community center not far from Harvard Square, I said to Richard, "These flags aren't even applicable anymore. They're obsolete."

We had to put a one-hundred-dollar deposit on each text, a book published in the 1930s, and long out of print. The elderly instructor loaned us each a copy that was held together by glue, tape and fingerprints. "These flags were used by commercial vessels. That kind of communication has been almost completely replaced by radio, radar, sonar, computers. And who is this guy teaching the course? He looks like he's old enough to have sailed on the *Pequod*." The signals themselves were mainly commands. T: Keep clear of me. U: You are running into danger. Y: I am dragging my anchor. I joked that many of the commands could apply to personal relationships as well as seagoing vessels. Richard stared at me as though I had spoken in a foreign language. His sense of humor is minimal to say the least.

We attended every Thursday for six weeks. We wrote a final exam, received a little certificate stating that we were qualified in the Communication Aspects of Practical Navigation.

"I'll put this on my resume," I said. I laughed. Richard smiled slowly. I have no resume. My degree certificate reads *Artus Generalis* or something foolish; I took a few literature courses, some theater, art history, basic psychology. I'm qualified to work as a part-time clerk in an art gallery, which I do when I'm totally bored.

West travels. On a moment's notice he flies off to Cairo, Budapest, Peking, Madagascar, Zanzibar. He told me a story about being associated with clove smugglers in Zanzibar who risk death to sneak sacks of contraband cloves into Kenya, from where they eventually make their way to the gourmet chefs of Europe, who use them to create exotic sauces.

"My business," says West, "is dangerous antiques and artifacts."

His life is full of intrigue. Albania has only recently become accessible. Last month, he smuggled a dozen silver goblets from the 1300s out of Albania, each encased in a garishly painted plaster statue of a saintly looking monk. I helped him unpack them from their bed of cedar shavings and shredded newspapers.

"Part of my business is to circumvent bureaucracy," says West, a smile crinkling the lines at the corner of each eye. "Countries make unacceptable rules concerning cultural artifacts. It is my job to stretch, bend, or even break the rules. I can bribe my way through customs anywhere except the United States, Canada and sometimes Great Britain. One has to be patient, in some countries it takes a long time to reach a bribable official."

West has golden hair, the body of a very good tennis player which, at 42, has widened until his step has slowed enough that he only plays doubles of a Sunday morning, and only for fun. He has a golden aura of danger about him. I have to admit, I have a fascination with dangerous men.

"I want us to travel together," West said over the phone yesterday, as we were finalizing this date. West has been married once, has a child to whom he is very good. "My ex," he says, "lost her spirit of adventure."

"Perhaps we could introduce her to Richard," I say. We giggle like children.

I met West at an antiques show. "I don't usually do this," he said, after I'd stopped to admire a jade dragon, seamless, seeming to glow with an inner light. "But sometimes rich people go slumming, and they assume that I'm selling at below my regular prices because everything else in the show is so tacky. I usually work by appointment only."

I inquired about the dragon. "Because you're such a beautiful woman I could let you have it for $80,000."

"I'm afraid only tacky is within my price range," I said. West was wearing khakis with many pockets; he looked like a scientist in a Tarzan movie, the one who warns the expedition leader, "The natives are restless, I don't think it's safe to travel any further up this river."

"I'll give you my phone number," West said cheerfully. "Call me, I'm sure I have any number of artifacts within your price range." He handed me a business card centered with a W in sweeping calligraphy. His hand held mine for a few seconds as the card, and jolt of sexual energy, passed between us.

I called him the next day. I went to his shop on antiques row, where customers are admitted only after ringing a bell, stating their purpose, and sometimes showing ID. "I deal in coins, precious gems," said West. "Browsers aren't welcome here. There are many extremely devious men in my profession."

We went for lunch, three hours with good wine, and food I don't even remember. I spent my time staring into West's aquamarine eyes and longing to touch him. As we slid from the booth in the now empty restaurant West faced me, put his right arm around me, lifted me right off the floor and kissed me. I never wanted him to stop.

Whatever guilt I had drifted away as his tongue filled my mouth and I grabbed the golden curls that extended over his collar and returned the kiss as passionately as I knew how.

Still, I put off consummating the affair.

"I have to be certain," I told West, "about our feelings, about my lack of feelings for Richard. I think it would be sinful to just have an affair. That would be tacky."

We've had lunch almost every afternoon for three weeks. I've lied to Richard about working at the gallery. I've actually told the owner I won't be in for the next few weeks, maybe never again. We've done everything but have actual intercourse. I have only to say the word and West will get us a hotel room for an afternoon, because I can't figure a way to stay out overnight.

One afternoon in his office, after kissing passionately for a long time, West sat me in the huge leather swivel chair behind his desk, knelt in front of me, slipped my panties down and loved me with his tongue until I shrieked and thought I might faint from ecstasy. We traded places and I found myself, still trembling from my own climax, letting myself go completely. I was so anxious to fill my throat with him, to please him, that for a moment I knew what those football groupies (Karl referred to them disdainfully as cum garglers) must have experienced, the chance to give the gift of passion, with a hope, no matter how slight, that it would be received meaningfully, that something like love might follow.

In the evenings, whenever Richard retires to his study to read his texts and treatises on mathematics, I phone West, who lives some fifty miles out of Boston. The calls will appear on our phone bill. I don't know how I will explain them. I don't care.

I think of Richard in his study perusing documents in a language only three people in the world understand. Richard once considered a hobby. "I think I'd like to get a little lathe and put it in the garage," he said. "I thought I could make wooden coat hangers."

I think opulent might best describe the hotel room where I will shortly give myself completely to West. There are fresh flowers, champagne, a fruit basket, a wooden bowl of those delicious, foil-wrapped chocolates that are mysteriously placed on your pillow in the late evening. I eat one without even realizing what I am doing. Its taste is so intense I eat another.

I have been in this hotel room once before, this elegant, impersonal space, or at least an identical room on this or a nearby floor. The room was engaged by Harvard, and from it we were able to see the finish line of the Boston marathon. The Japanese genius was visiting Boston, and Harvard had booked the room months in advance because the Japanese mathematical prodigy, a Mr. Nakagawa, postulated that there was a possible mathematical formula that would explain the muscular coordination of trained athletes, something to do with the way they pumped their arms when running.

It was an eerie feeling watching the progress of the race on television where, every so often they would cut to the finish line, which we could see below our window. In fact, once they showed the hotel and if they'd held the shot another few seconds we could have picked out our window. The view was remarkable in that we could read the numbers of the runners, chests heaving, as they crossed the line, and we could see the journalists shoving microphones into the faces of the sweating athletes. I felt disoriented, like a kitten in a room filled with somber monkeys in business suits, their arms folded in privacy across their collective chests.

At 10:00 A.M. a FedEx courier arrived at my door with a large, colorful envelope. It contained one of those coded plastic cards for opening a hotel room door. There was a hotel business card with the room number scrawled on the back along with the word Noon, and West's large calligraphed W, his signature, the same W that appears on his shirts, in gold on a ruby pinky ring, his key chain.

The ringing phone jars me back to the present. Oh, no. West is going to be late. Worse yet, West can't make it. Some European count is desperate to purchase a Ming vase.

"Madame, it is the Concierge. Madame is requested to glance out the window of her suite."

"What on earth for?"

The Concierge has a heavy French accent. All American concierges have heavy European accents. He's probably lived all his life in Worcester. I wonder if European concierges have heavy American accents?

"I can only repeat the message supplied to me, Madame. I am informed that if you glance out the window of your suite you will see something interesting."

I hang up.

It can be only one of two things. West is doing something wonderful and extravagant, a banner on one of the nearby buildings that says I LOVE YOU, ESME. A huge floral arrangement: I picture a horseshoe-shape, ten feet high, like those at the Kentucky Derby, or a gangster's funeral, sculpted of white carnations, with my face centring the interior, my cheeks and lips red roses, my eyes blue hydrangeas.

On the other hand, what if Richard has followed me? I can't imagine him doing that. He's never missed a day at his job in the ten years I've known him. I've been so happy the past few weeks, since I've been spending time with West, perhaps Richard has noticed. Has he shown any signs of suspicion? Nothing comes to mind. He left for work at his usual time; he always leaves the house at 7:30 A.M.

I make my way across the room to the window, slowly, as if I am walking in something congealed, each step an effort.

Oh, it is worse than I thought. It is Richard. He is standing across the street, about where the runners crossed the finish line of the Boston Marathon, staring toward me through his thick glasses. He looks so helpless. His colorless slacks are rumpled, he wears a brown windbreaker, a slight breeze blows unruly laces of black hair down across his fore-head. His right shoulder droops so unhappily. He is holding a flag. It is on a tiny flag pole. Where in the world would he find such a little flag pole? It is one of the flags from our text book. I can picture Richard in his study, thinking about, instead of mathematical formulas too complicated for even extraordinary mortals, something he can do to rekindle my interest in him, to make me love him again.

The flag he holds displays the letters CXL. I have to admit I only did a halfhearted job of learning the signals, and after we passed the test, Richard with 100%, me with 55%, a bare pass, I let many of them drift way like notes of music disappearing forever. This is information I will never use again, I thought. Let's see: A=I am undergoing a speed trial. K=You should stop your vessel instantly. What do these combinations mean? CXL sounds like the acronym for a football league.

Oh, my. Oh, my. It comes to me. And I place my hands, palms flat to the glass, arms extended above my head as if there is a burglar with a revolver standing behind me. Tears well up, overflow. I snuffle. Richard looks so intense, so vulnerable, so lonely.

CXL is a command: Do not abandon me. DO NOT ABANDON ME! It is the perfect flag. Richard sees me, raises the flag a little higher with his right hand, waves diffidently with his left.

West's knock sounds at the door. Cheerful, full of energy. My heart flutters. I remain at the window. West knocks and knocks.

Marco in Paradise

Marco Ferlinghetti spends his life getting picked out of police lineups. The police collar Marco nearly every day. He is not hard to find for he is never more than two blocks from the corner of Hastings and Main in Vancouver at any time in his life. Marco stands sullen in the middle of the lineup, eyelids drooping, while behind two-way glass victims and witnesses scrutinize. On one especially productive day Marco was positively identified as a flasher, a hit-and-run driver, a burglar, and a peeping Tom.

The rationale of the police is that if a potential witness can pass over Marco for someone else, then the identification is likely to stick. The reason that Marco is such a popular choice is that he looks exactly the way people think a criminal should look. He has scraggly, receding hair, protruding eyes, no chin to speak of, and is always in need of a shave. His teeth are yellow, his nose hooked; he wears a dirty trenchcoat, baggy pants and sneakers. Marco Ferlinghetti is the middle-class idea of a child molester, pimp, pusher, and petty thief.

Marco did indeed do time a few years ago for the innocuous crime of selling a marijuana cigarette to an undercover cop. While he was in prison (Marco was treated rather harshly, partly because of his looks and partly because the undercover cop was standing outside an elementary school when he made the buy), he decided to learn a trade. Behind the walls he learned to be a cannon (a professional pickpocket) and practices his trade with a solemn efficiency. His stall (an assistant who distracts the intended victim, usually by bumping into them) is his girlfriend, whom he calls Jackson, a bedraggled little hype in jeans, boots, and a halter that exposes most of her breasts. Jackson always looks as if she is about to ask someone for directions.

The police know of Marco's profession but live and let live as long as he keeps himself available for daily lineups.

A few weeks ago, Marco, in all his grimy splendor, crabwalked into a Toronto-Dominion Bank on Granville Street, several blocks from Hastings and Main, and presented the teller with a note which was clearly printed but poorly spelled and punctuated. Marco, the proud holder of a B.Com. from the University of British Columbia, walked away with several thousand dollars.

The police pulled in an assortment of known bank robbers; they also pulled in Marco Ferlinghetti.

"That's him!" said the robbed teller.

"That's him!" said the assistant bank manager.

"That's him!" said an elderly lady who had been in line behind Marco.

The police politely thanked them for their trouble.

A few days later Marco limped into the Main Street Police Station and approached the sergeant in charge of police lineups.

"I'd like to take a little time off," he said deferentially. "I think I picked a rotten pocket, if you know what I mean. Came into a large amount of bread, but the empty pocket belonged to the Mob. There are nasty rumors on the street."

"You go ahead, Marco," said the police officer. The sergeant had a soft spot in his heart for petty criminals like Marco. He didn't like the Mob either. "Just be sure you settle around here when you come back. You're very valuable to us."

Marco and Jackson caught the next flight for Honolulu. But even in paradise, dressed in a Hawaiian shirt, with a lei of waxen orchids around his neck, Marco Ferlinghetti looked like a criminal. His third day on Waikiki, Marco was picked up and displayed in a police lineup. Late at night, wallets, picked clean as fish skeletons, glow whitely in the alleys of Honolulu.

OUT OF THE PICTURE

I have the privilege of doing most of my writing in a sunny, corner office overlooking the Pacific Ocean. On the long back wall of my office are a number of oil paintings, mostly by the famous Cree artist Allen Sapp. Sapp paints his memories of reservation life in rural Saskatchewan a half century ago. His paintings are realistic. Though I sometimes write of magical happenings, I have little tolerance for abstract art, something I believe I inherited from my Grandfather Drobney, though I never called him Grandfather in any language. He was simply Drobney, to one and all. A few days ago I rearranged the oils on my wall to make room for a new acquisition, though the painting was not new to me, for it hung in my home when I was a child.

My family have always been secretive. The past was treated as something to be discarded, like out-of-style clothing, something once disposed of, never to be thought of again. Family history was seldom discussed. Baba Drobney told me she was the seventh daughter of a man who owned a small winery near Dubrovnik in Yugoslavia. Other than that and the oil painting I know little about either side of my family. And I realize I have been equally uninformative. I have withheld from my daughters what little I know about my parents and grandparents.

Drobney died before I was old enough to start school. I was an adult before I visited his grave and saw his tombstone—ARON DROBNEY 1847–1939—where I learned both his first name and the fact that he lived to be 92. I remember him sitting in a rocker in the kitchen of our drafty farm house, a bright afghan around his knees. He had a full head of iron-gray hair, a walrus mustache of the same color, and flashing black eyes.

After the Depression ended, and with the advent of World War II, prosperity slowly returned to Canada, and it was my vivacious Aunt Lichta who got custody of the family portrait. Lichta was my mother's sister and lived with us until I was seven years old, as did the rest of my mother's family, along with the portrait, an oil, painted by an artist who Aunt Lichta named as one of the Canadian Group of Seven, which meant nothing to me at the time.

The artist did not ordinarily do portraits, Aunt Lichta said, but Drobney, my grandfather, when he wanted something could be very persuasive, and over one thousand pre-Depression dollars was a great deal of money for a struggling artist in the 1920s. In those halcyon days before my grandfather became like everyone else in North America, more or less insolvent.

Aunt Lichta's second marriage was to a man who became a federal member of parliament for Alberta, and who, when his career was over, was appointed to the senate. The Canadian senate has no political power and is a dumping ground for political hacks, faithful fund raisers, and defeated incumbents. But the pay was excellent, the duties non-existent. Aunt Lichta and her husband lived out their lives in Ottawa where she became famous as a hostess.

I remember, in the late sixties, seeing a photo in *Maclean's* magazine, taken at some diplomatic function, where the Senator, sleek and gray as a Rolls Royce, was flanked by his wife, *Lucille*.

Aunt Lichta was in her sixties then, a tall, striking woman with hair the pure white of hoarfrost. In spite of always having an extravagant European accent, she somehow must have thought Lucille a more Canadian name than Lichta. Foreignness has not always been a virtue in Canada, though a recent Prime Minister's wife delighted in acknowledging *her* Yugoslavian ancestry.

Once, when I was quite young, I remember my Baba Drobney being very angry with my grandfather. He had gone to a neighboring farm owned by a Czech named Weisocovitch, and they had gotten into the dandelion wine. Drobney, as everyone called my grandfather, could be heard singing loudly in his own language, as he crossed the meadows toward our home. Drobney was unsteady and mumbling when he entered the kitchen.

"Go to bed, you old fool," Baba barked at him in English. Everyone except me and my father spoke several European dialects, Slovenian, Serbo-Croatian, German, Romany. Though I never noticed, Aunt Lichta told me years later, at Baba's insistence only English was spoken when either I or my father was present.

Drobney stared at us bleary-eyed.

Baba Drobney rearranged me on her ample lap.

"In his family was Gypsies," she said, the foreboding dripping down her chin. Then, after a pause to let the gravity of that situation sink in, "Worse, was Rumanians." She paused again to let me reflect on how bad that must be. "In Sarajevo we had a cat. He named it Nistru," she went on. "'For that river used to run by my door as a boy,' he said. Nistru is a *Rumanian* river," said Baba Drobney ominously.

Apparently Yugoslavians and Rumanians did not hold each other in high regard. "If I'd only known," said Baba Drobney, shaking her head. She and Drobney spent sixty-two years together, and as far as I know, were extremely happy.

The portrait: by the time I was old enough to comprehend, one person was already gone from it. My first memories of the painting are of it hanging on the bulging calcimined wallpaper in the dark inner hallway of our farm house. The house I grew up in was made of logs, the cracks chinked with white plaster by my father, who was a plasterer by trade. The upstairs was unfinished, and the wind whistled eerily through the gaps between the unpainted boards at each end of the attic. A colony of bats lived in that attic, oozing out at dusk on summer evenings to hurtle about the farmyard like black clots in the feathered twilight. Baba Drobney, who when her coiled braids were combed out, had waist-length yellowish-white hair, refused to set foot beyond the screen door after sunset in summer, and strongly warned my mother and my aunts not to venture outside for fear of getting a bat in their hair.

"A bat in the hair prophesies an early death," Baba said darkly.

In the portrait, Drobney had one arm across his chest as if he were clutching something unseen, the other hand, fingers spread, was poised above his right leg, a colorful vest was visible beneath his dark suit.

"Drobney once owned a thousand taxis in Ontario. Your mother grew up in a stone mansion before everything went poof," Baba confided in me, as she patched the knee of my overalls. "We had servants before everything went poof."

Drobney stared at the artist as if it were offering him an insultingly low price for something. Beside him on an ice-blue love seat sat Baba, looking more benign than in real life, smiling secretly, perhaps pleased by the expensive, peach-colored gown she wore. To the right of them, my tiny mother sat on a red-velvet chair with insect legs. She was very beautiful in a pale blue dress, her cheeks rouged, her blond hair coiled in a French braid. Though an adult, her feet did not even come close to touching the floor. Behind her stood my curly haired Irish father who was destined to die young.

Behind the love seat, my tall, beautiful Aunt Lichta, smiling as if the portrait had been her idea. Next to Lichta was a younger sister, Rose, looking slightly scared. On the left stood my uncles Waldemar and Jaroslaw, and Jaroslaw's wife Katarinka. Uncle Wald looked exactly like Drobney, only younger.

Everyone knew about the empty space in the portrait, except me. And because everyone knew, the space was mentioned occasionally, sometimes seriously, sometimes in a joking manner. I came to understand, without ever being officially told, that in the original painting someone named Percy had been beside Aunt Lichta.

When Drobney said "Percy," there were many cees between the r and the y.

The women were more tolerant, wondering sometimes, when Drobney wasn't present, where Percy might be now. My uncles punched each other on the shoulders and snickered when Percy's name was mentioned.

I came to realize that Percy had been Aunt Lichta's husband, someone she met in Ontario, when the family was still prosperous. Before everything had gone poof, and they had, with my father's help, purchased one-way train fare to Alberta. Percy was what was called a remittance man, someone who had brought some kind of embarrassment to his wealthy family in England, so was banished to the colonies with an allotment which allowed him to live well but not regally.

After Percy had, as Drobney sometimes said, let his bristles grow, a reference to Percy being a pig, and after he and Aunt Lichta were divorced, Drobney took the painting back to the original artist and insisted that Percy be obliterated from it.

"He is no longer part of the family," Drobney raged. "I can no longer look at his snout without wanting to burn the portrait. The others I love," shouted Drobney in his extravagant European way. "*Him*, I want OUT!"

So Percy had been painted into oblivion.

When I was a little older, just before Aunt Lichta left the farm to live in Edmonton, where she met her second husband, I begged her to tell me what Percy looked like.

"I can do better than that," said Aunt Lichta, "though you must promise never to mention this to Drobney." Going to her closet, which smelled of dried rose petals, she produced a small photo. Percy was younger than I imagined; dressed in a variety of tweeds, he had straight blond hair slicked back off a high forehead, a long, thin nose with a pale mustache beneath it, thin lips and a receding chin. My mother had let slip once that Percy wore a monocle, but it was nowhere to be seen in the photo.

"He did," said Aunt Lichta, smiling sadly as she answered my question, "but it wasn't an evil monocle like the Germans wear. I believe even Percy's mustache was tweed," she added, and laughed prettily.

One evening when we were seated around our large oilcloth-covered kitchen table, eating supper by the light of two coal-oil lamps, someone mentioned the portrait. Drobney congratulated himself for having Percy painted out of the picture.

"I suppose if I died you'd have me painted out," said Baba, not entirely joking.

"Of course I would," shouted Drobney. "Everything should be as it is," and he stared around the table hoping, I'm sure, that someone would contradict him. Aunt Rose scurried to the stove to fetch more turnips.

"Then everyone in the picture should be wearing overalls, like we are now. And why aren't I in the picture?" I asked.

Everyone in the room wore bulky sweaters and bib overalls, a far cry from the finery of the portrait. I didn't realize until years later just how poor we were. That winter we lived on turnips from the root cellar and eggs preserved in stone crocks of alum. What must my father have thought when he suddenly became responsible for seven members of my mother's family, when the stony and worthless quarter-section of land he farmed produced barely enough for our own livelihood? If one of the chickens looked as though it was definitely going to expire of natural causes, it was killed and we enjoyed chicken soup, liberally laced with turnips for a meal or two.

That night, after I was put to bed, there was a heated discussion, parts of which drifted to me where I lay bundled in a down comforter, in what had once been a pantry attached to the kitchen. The discussion was about whether, when there was money, if there would ever again be money, should I be painted into the portrait.

"Jerry and Kitty," Baba Drobney said, referring to my aunt and uncle, "will have children. Wald and Rose will marry. What if Mariska has ten brothers and sisters for Jamie? Children, no. Future in-laws, maybe," she declared with some finality. There was argument, especially from Aunt Kitty for her future offspring. But Baba stood fast, won her point, and the subject of my being painted in, when and if prosperity returned, was never broached again.

I tried to learn why Baba and Drobney had chosen to immigrate to Canada.

"Drobney thought it was a good idea," my mother said.

"I heard the streets of Canadian cities were paved with gold. Ha!" Drobney barked, when I got up the courage to ask him.

Once, when Baba was rocking me to sleep, at a time when I was almost too big to fit on her lap anymore, she hinted that Drobney had been in some kind of difficulty with the Yugoslavian government, and that large sums of money were involved. I share a birthday with Josip Broz, code name Tito, the man destined to rule the conglomeration that became Yugoslavia. Apparently Baba was hell-bent on my being named Josip Broz O'Day.

"If your grandmother had been here when you were born you'd probably be Marshal Tito O'Day," my father said several times over the years, "but she was in Toronto then, and she's not as persuasive by mail as she is in person."

The Drobneys were not poor when they came to Canada. They settled in Toronto in a large stone house close to the University of Toronto. The house still stands, long ago converted into a warren to house students. Not many years ago, on a visit to Toronto, I drove my wife past the property. "That's where my grandparents lived when they first came to Canada. It's where my mother was living when my father came to patch the plaster in the upstairs bathroom."

Drobney, who had been a horse trader in the old country, became a used car dealer in Toronto, one of the first. Then he discovered the taxi business. It is said that at one time fifty percent of the taxis in

Toronto bore a white line down each side with Drobney Taxi in fat white letters on each door. Drobney's mistake was that he believed in his new homeland. In Dubrovnik he had kept his wealth in a money belt, under the floorboards beneath his and Baba's bed. In Canada, he decided to trust his wealth to a bank. When the Depression came, not only did people stop riding in taxis but the bank failed. Drobney lost everything.

My father and mother, Baba and I, were the last to leave the farm. Lichta was the first. She got a job in Edmonton as governess to the children of a wealthy lawyer. She married the lawyer's younger brother, the aspiring politician.

After the war, Uncle Waldemar went back to Yugoslavia and after a few years stopped writing. I suspect Uncle Wald was gay. I always meant to ask Lichta about that. Jerry and Kitty moved to Winnipeg, where he became a bus driver. Timid Aunt Rose married a timid Alberta farmer named Stefanichan.

And one fall, while we were still on the farm, Drobney announced that he was going to die, and sixty days later he did. In his final days he lay in bed, his hands raised in front of him, braiding imaginary rope for the horses he had long ago led through the streets of Dubrovnik.

On golden Indian Summer days Baba helped Drobney to a rocker on the sunny south side of the house, where fist-sized marigolds glowed along a path bordered with whitewashed stones.

Drobney sat in the sun, his right hand poised as it was in the portrait. He mumbled the word, "Nistru, Nistru."

Whether he was referring to the river or the long dead cat I never knew.

After her second marriage, Aunt Lichta wrote asking if she could have the portrait. It was Baba's decision. No one offered any objection, so she agreed.

Baba wrapped the portrait in a blanket, tied it with binder twine and drove by horse and cart eight miles to the highway where she put it on board the east-bound Western Trailways bus. That was the last time I saw the portrait for over forty years.

Aunt Lichta turned out to be the only member of the family I kept in close touch with, other than my parents. I visited her whenever business took me to Ottawa. My parents produced no brothers or sisters for me. Aunt Rose and the timid Stefanichan had several children, as did Jerry and Kitty in Winnipeg.

One of Rose's daughters dropped in on us a few years ago. She was a dark, sullen girl of nineteen, named Lily, who had decided to call herself Desiree and become an actress. She was disappointed that, as a writer, I didn't know any movie stars, more disappointed that I didn't know anyone who could get her into local TV or radio. She departed after a few days. Aunt Lichta says she became a hairdresser and married a boy who was training to be an auto body repairman.

About a year before she died, I received a letter from Aunt Lichta, her beautiful handwriting suddenly spidery and uneven, asking that I be certain to call on her the next time I was in Ottawa.

"Do you remember the portrait that used to hang in the hallway at the farm?" Aunt Lichta asked me.

"The one your first husband had been painted out of?"

"You remember."

"That was what made it memorable."

"I've kept up the tradition," Aunt Lichta said.

"Having people painted out when they . . ."

"Die. Or lose contact like your Uncle Wald. Drobney was a very strong personality. You have no idea. Even now I don't recall him as Papa or Father, but as Drobney."

"Baba was no slouch herself when it came to a strong personality. She was the one who made me a writer. Remember her stories, 'Knocks at the door a stranger'?"

"The messages of childhood are strongest," said Aunt Lichta. "They are engraved," and she touched her head, her hair still the purest of whites, but cottony now, not healthy-looking.

"My children think I'm crazy," she went on. She had two sons with her second husband, one a corporation lawyer, the other in the diplomatic service in Finland. "But they weren't there . . ."

"And I was?"

Aunt Lichta smiled. She stood up slowly from the antique settee in her living room.

"No one knew about what I was doing until after your mother passed away two years ago. After she was gone I had her removed. Clyde handles my finances now and he had a fit when he got the bill. I had to confess."

Aunt Lichta kept the portrait in an expensive leather carrying case. It was a shock to see it again. It was smaller than in my memory, but still large. The furniture was dominating now, the settee, the red-velvet insect-legged chair where my mother had posed. A youthful Aunt Lichta was the only human figure left in the portrait.

"Take it with you, and finish the job when I'm gone," Aunt Lichta said.

I promised I would. "Childhood messages," I said, kissing her frail cheek.

I have the privilege of doing most of my writing in a sunny, corner office overlooking the Pacific Ocean. There are a number of oil paintings on the walls of my office, all realistic, I have little patience with abstract art. Most of my paintings are by the famous Cree artist, Allen Sapp. One wall is dominated by a winter scene of a grave-side service. I am attracted to Sapp's landscapes because they portray a harsh and desolate rural world similar to the farm where I grew up.

Now, among the landscapes is an interior scene, a studio, a blue love seat in the foreground, a rose-colored chair with insect legs to the left. The room is finished in dark panelling, several gas lamps burn in the background. There are old-fashioned oil paintings on the wall of the studio.

A few months after she died, I had Aunt Lichta painted out of the picture. I also had the portrait X-rayed to confirm something I had long suspected. The artist in Vancouver who did the work charged enough that he didn't feel the need to ask questions, after I assured him the artist's name was a coincidence, that he was a relative of mine and certainly not one of the now world-famous Group of Seven.

The picture of the empty studio is quite astonishing. Visitors often remark on it because it is the only one of my paintings that doesn't have at least one human figure in it. When I stare at it, Drobney's words, "Everything should be as it is," echo over a half century of my life.

Sitting, writing, at my large oak table, watching the fog-colored waves of the Pacific, I feel happy and secure. I am delighted that my family are gathered in the room while I work, not just in memory, not hidden the way dead people usually are, but available if I choose to make them so. Baba, Drobney my coal-eyed Gypsy grandfather, my parents young and beautiful, and all the rest should I choose to resurrect them, even Percy the remittance man, who I feel more sympathy for as I grow older. The Drobneys were not an easy family to marry into.

And, finally, if I decide to, I may reveal the secret of Drobney's raised hand, for the demise of Percy was not the first alteration to the painting. The X-ray revealed that under Drobney's hand was a large orange cat. Nistru, named for a river in Rumania.

They are all there, sturdy and smiling, in case I need them.

THE LIGHTNING BIRDS

That summer it was impossible to get a job. Things was so bad I end up working on a farm for a guy named Wilf Blindman. He got a big farm down to the south end of the reserve and I bet he is the richest Indian in the area, in money anyway.

I don't like to work on a farm. I been taking courses at the Tech School in Wetaskiwin on how to fix tractors, but I never even sniffed a job doing what I been trained for. Working for Wilf Blindman I get to cut clover with a team of horses and a mower, and after it's cut I get to make coils of hay in the field with a shiny-tonged pitch fork.

It is pretty lonely work. Wilf is the kind of guy who says "Yep," or "Nope," after you ask him a question. And if he strains himself and says, "Looks like rain," that amount of conversation likely to last him for two or three days. I miss my girlfriend, Sadie One-wound, and my friends, Frank Fencepost and Rufus Firstrider. Wilf's farm is too far off the beaten track to walk anywhere of an evening, and usually I'm too tired anyway. Wilf only let me off on Sundays, and then on the condition, "You don't have none of your useless friends hang around steal everything that ain't nailed down."

Wilf may be an Indian, but he think like a white man. I guess you have to do that to be successful. Wilf left his bank book sitting out on the table one evening and I seen he got enough money in the Bank of Montreal in Wetaskiwin to last somebody like me a couple of lifetimes. He could afford farm equipment if he wanted. But then horses work for food and I practically do too. Coal oil lamps and a wood stove is cheaper than electricity. Maybe Wilf ain't got the wrong approach after all.

About two weeks after I got there, while I'm eating supper with Wilf, canned Campbell's Soup, with bread and margarine—Wilf sure don't waste any money on food, for either him or me—Wilf say to me, "Kid's comin' to visit."

"What kid?"

"Brother's kid. Girl. His wife's dead." That about broke Wilf's record for speaking words in a row.

Next morning Wilf open up the door to a small bedroom off the kitchen.

"Clean it up," he says.

Take me most of the day. There is a single bed, an old dresser with a mirror so yellow and spotted it like staring into rippling water. The room is filled with junk. Boxes might have come from an auction, some full of old magazines, other got dead flashlights, parts from vacuum cleaners, cracked dishes. There is harness strewn around, some coyote hides in the corner. Whole place ain't been dusted in my lifetime.

Wilf is a tall, ungainly man with a slight stoop. He have bushy eyebrows, and a square, clean-shaven face, look like polished oak. He shave every morning with a shaving mug and a straight razor, after he pump a washbasin full of cold water from the cistern under his house.

His house is tall and unpainted, gaunt windows stare across the prairie. Coming down the road toward Wilf Blindman's place, if I didn't know someone lived there I'd think the house been vacant for years.

The child that arriving must have something to do with a letter Wilf got the second day I was working for him. The mailman, one of the Dodginghorse boys, is probably a cousin of Wilf's if you was to check back far enough. Instead of leaving the mail in the mailbox at the end of what must be a quarter-mile driveway, he drive his Canada Post car right to Wilf's door, give letters to him in person if he's there, otherwise put them under a rock that sit on the front porch.

Wilf sat at the kitchen table what covered in a gray oilcloth, got black squiggles all over it, fit right in with the darkness of the whole place, and read the letter by the wavery light of a gas lamp, again and again. Wilf could afford light, but I think he enjoys living a dark life like a mole.

There was a good old Alberta thunder and lightning storm raging outside, lightning zippering across the sky, now and then frying a tree somewhere not far away, thunder rattling the window panes. Didn't look like Wilf was one to make quick decisions. Look to me like he is as stolid and silent as the land he farms.

"What do you know about Wilf Blindman?" I ask Etta our medicine lady the next Sunday when I'm back at Hobbema.

Etta don't waste any words either.

"Got his heart broke twenty years ago. Lives like a hermit. Don't want anyone to forget he got his heart broke. Better at feeling sorry for himself than anybody I know. Probably gone bushed from living out there alone for so long."

"How'd he get his heart broke?"

"Same as anybody else. He loved a girl; she married somebody else. Only difference everybody else sulk around for a week or two, or a month or two, then get on with their lives. Wilf still sulking."

"Must have loved her a lot?"

"Hmmmph!" says Etta. "He enjoy being a victim. Made a career out of it. Listen, unless you being held hostage, or got a terminal illness, what you got in life is pretty much what you want."

I'm gonna try to remember that.

"Yeah," I say. "Kitchen floor at Wilf's is so dirty people wipe their feet when they get outside."

But I changed all that. I sluiced out the kitchen, washed down the walls. I took the bedding off the bed and the curtains off the windows in what I think of as the guest room. There is no kind of washing machine on the place so I get permission to drive Wilf's truck to the laundromat in Wetaskiwin, and reluctantly, a ten-dollar bill to change into quarters.

The blankets and sheets wash up okay, but the curtains, which was made from what look like yellow lace, break up in a thousand pieces in the wash, look like I been laundering Kleenex.

I price some curtains at Field's Department Store.

Back at the farm, Wilf stare at me like I'm trying to rob him. But I remembered to toss a double-handful of what was left of the curtains into the truck box.

"Look like mush I could feed the chickens," Wilf says and almost smile. He pull out a sweaty-looking roll of twenties and peel off money for curtains.

I would have liked to suggest a toy or a doll or something bright for a little girl. Everything around Wilf's farm is in black and white. But, I figured I inconvenienced Wilf enough already. I get bright blue curtains, with pink kittens running all across them. Bet the bedroom is in shock to have so much color in it at one time.

"Hello, I'm Jennifer Chickadee," the little girl says, soon as she step down out of the mouth of the north-going bus.

She is thin with gangly arms and legs, at the age where she's growing new front teeth; she is about as ugly as she's ever gonna be, and that's still pretty. Her hair is in a long braid, tied with a blue ribbon; her skin is the soft, light color of buckskin. Her nose is straight, her eyes hazel, and in spite of her missing teeth she have a very beautiful mouth. In five years she's gonna drive a lot of boys crazy.

"Hi, I'm Silas," I say.

If I hadn't been there I don't know what Wilf would have done. He stand back about twenty feet from the front of the bus, look like he got the worries of the world on his shoulders.

The bus driver hand me Jennifer's suitcase from underneath the bus. We walk back toward Wilf.

"Hello, I'm Jennifer Chickadee," she say to him.

"Hyuh," says Wilf, don't make to hug her or even shake her hand.

"You look just like my father," the little girl says.

Wilf grunt again and turn to walk toward the truck and parking lot, leaving me with Jennifer.

I ain't gettin' paid enough for this, I think.

I do have a young sister, Delores.

"You like Barbie dolls?" I ask after she climb up on the seat between me and Wilf.

That get her started. She tell me all about her dolls, and if her suitcase wasn't in the truck box she would have showed me the one she brought with her.

What I'm wondering is if she's Wilf's brother's child, how come she's named Chickadee and not Blindman?

Wilf sit behind the wheel like he's frozen, concentrate on shifting the gears, glance quick at Jennifer a few times, but never say even one word.

"Brother changed his name," Etta say to me. "Decided he didn't want to be Indian no more. Al Lindman used to be Alphonse Blindman. Hear he's a big car dealer in Calgary."

"How come her name's Chickadee?"

"Why don't you ask her? In case you ain't figured it out, was her mother broke Wilf Blindman's heart. Her mother was Sylvia Born With Long Hair. She was Wilf's girlfriend. Wilf's old man, Seymour Blindman, when he knew he was going to die, called both boys together, said there wasn't enough farm for both of them. Wilf wanted to stay on the farm, so he did. Alphonse took the money from a little life insurance policy, worth way less than the farm, and head off to Calgary.

"He buy himself a couple of old cars, fix them up, paint them, and sell them. Pretty soon he rent a lot on a main street, have Al's Premium Used Cars. It was about that time he cut off his braids, dress like a white man, change his name to Al Lindman.

"Al come back to the reserve one Christmas, take off back to Calgary after a week or so with Sylvia.

"Like I said, Wilf been sulking ever since. Al just keep getting more and more successful. He supposed to have his fingers in a dozen or so pies, besides his Chrysler/Plymouth dealership, like insurance companies, and I hear one of his companies build highrise apartment blocks.

"About three years ago Sylvia up and died. That's when Wilf go from just being an old bachelor to being a hermit and a strange one at that.

"I went out to the farm once, you know. I get Rider Stonechild to drive me there. I try to tell Wilf that feeling sorry for yourself is a pretty poor way to spend your life. But he blames Al for Sylvia dying. He thinks he didn't treat her right. Says he's gonna get even, whatever that might mean. The Blindman brothers was never close, but I don't think they spoke a word in the fifteen years since Al stole Wilf's girl.

"Wilf ain't near as old as he looks. You should see Al, looks like he could be Wilf's son. Al ain't a bad guy. Word around is he offered Wilf a good job, but Wilf turned him down. Then he offered Wilf an interest-free loan to develop the farm. All Wilf said was, 'Got my own way of doin' things.' What I can't figure out is why a rich man like Al Lindman send that poor little girl for Wilf to look after. You got to stick around there, Silas, make sure that she's okay."

I been complaining all evening I wish I could find any kind of a job so I could get away from Wilf and his farm.

If I ever seen a little girl dying for somebody to like her, it is Jennifer Chickadee. But Wilf is perfect at ignoring her. It is like she hasn't arrived yet.

One lunch time when me and Wilf comes in from the hay field, Jennifer has added wood to the fire box, heated up Campbell's Chicken Noodle Soup, and made us each a bologna sandwich. She even set the kettle to boiling tea water.

Because Wilf don't say nothing, I go overboard praising her cooking. I stare at Wilf, my look telling him to say something nice. All he do is wipe the sweat off his forehead with his hand, dry his hand on his overalls, give Jennifer a longer than usual glance, as if he trying to decide exactly what it is of his she's stolen.

I read where someone said that dealing with Indians is like trying to play catch with someone who won't throw the ball back. Wilf won't even catch the ball let alone throw it back.

Another few days and I get around to talking to Jennifer. "Is Chicka-dee your real name?"

"I figured if I was coming to live with a real Indian, I should have an Indian name," is what Jennifer says. "I thought about being Blind-man like Uncle Wilf, but Chickadee is prettier. My Daddy used to say I was like one of those bouncy little black and white birds. I wish I could remember more about my mother. I was five when she died, and she is kind of like a character in a TV show I watched a long time ago. I have a picture of her, but I can't remember her actually touching me.

"Daddy's told me a hundred times at least never to mention I'm Indian. He says we're Irish, Black Irish. And I heard him tell one of his friends that Mama was from Quata-malla. I don't understand what's wrong with being Indian. Daddy says people won't like us if they know we're Indian.

"Do people not like you, Silas? I guess people don't like Uncle Wilf. He sure doesn't seem to have any friends."

This summer there are a record number of thunder and lightning storms. Almost every night the huge black cloud billow up out of the west like black ships and the lightning crisscrosses the sky like gold chains. The wind swirls, the trees bend and the rain begins with a few plopping drops that make quarter-sized impressions in the yard dust, then the rain turns to a torrent, slams against the windows and beats the dandelions flat to the ground. Thunder shakes the whole house, and we can hear the whine of lightning and the crash and screech as it strikes. Once it hit a lone aspen out by the county road, split it almost in two. Sometimes we can't do much work the next day because everything is so wet. There are storms in the afternoons too. Me and Wilf have to come in from the fields and we sit and watch the windows steam up. We play three-handed Snap, and Books, and Hearts. Wilf don't act like he enjoying himself. Soon as the rain stop he pulls on his rubber boots and slogs off toward the barn.

Another week passes. There is something weird going on here. I wish I knew what it was, and if I should be worried enough about it to tell Etta or somebody else. I sure would hate for something to happen to that little girl.

Frank Fencepost come by to visit one evening. He take a shine to Jennifer right away.

"Guess who gives the orders in a cornfield?" says Frank. "The Kernel," he answer before Jennifer had a chance to think about the question. She smile showing the big gaps between her teeth.

"I have a photogenic memory," Frank says, showing Jennifer how he can read something once, even upside down and then repeat it all back. The joke goes over her head, but I laugh and explain it to her.

"The bank's looking for teller," Frank says.

"I thought they just hired one last month," I say, playing along.

"That's the one," says Frank, slap his thigh. Jennifer giggle and bounce around the kitchen like she was on a pogo stick. Wilf sit at the kitchen table, glare into a three-month-old copy of the *Western Producer*.

Jennifer is a city girl all the way. She at first can't believe we don't have indoor plumbing. She never even guessed there were outhouses. Or wood stoves. Or houses without electric light. I'm guessing she don't even know her mother was Indian, or that she have maybe a dozen relatives with the same name as her mother, Born With Long Hair, on the reserve, and I bet hundreds of cousins in Southern Alberta on the Blood Reserve, where her mother's family come from originally. Etta says Sylvia Born With Long Hair was light skinned and had gray eyes. I'm afraid if I tell Jennifer she has relatives on the reserve Wilf will fire me and I won't be able to keep an eye on Jennifer.

A few days ago Wilf started talking. First he ask Jennifer if she'd like to ride on the cultivator with him, and she act like he's taking her to Disneyland. She spend all day with Wilf, while I'm mending fences. She come in sunburned and covered in black dust. She lines up behind Wilf to wash her hands in the white enamel washbasin sit on a upturned apple box over by the cream separator.

"Uncle Wilf told me stories all day," she says later on while we're sitting on the front steps. "But he says they're secret stories, and I can't even tell them to you, Silas."

I don't figure Wilf for the kind of guy to know any stories.

There is a weeping birch sit about a hundred yards south of the house, on a knoll in the pasture, alone like it been abandoned. One morning early I see Jennifer in front of the kitchen window, hands on hips, studying the tree, a scowl on her face.

"What?" I say.

"Uncle Wilf says that tree is where the lightning birds live. I've never seen any, have you?"

The tree is broken in several spots where it been struck by lightning before. If the tree were a man it would be walking on crutches.

I don't answer Jennifer's question. I've never heard of a lightning bird.

The next day Wilf and Jennifer go into town for a couple of hours. They come back with plain groceries—I'd been hoping for some gingersnaps, or Oreos, maybe a carton of ice cream we could sit right down and eat before it melted. What Wilf has sprung for is a yellow slicker and rainhat for Jennifer. She can't wait to try them on.

"Boy, I wish it would rain," she says, staring at the high, blue sky. She look like a giant cowslip running in circles around the weeping birch in the pasture. Wilf also bought her a child-sized broom which she wave like a weapon.

"Soon as it rains I'm gonna put a scare into those lightning birds," Jennifer says.

I don't say anything.

"You ever heard of lightning birds?" I say to Etta soon as I get back to the reserve that Saturday evening.

"Uh-oh," says Etta. By her tone I know something is wrong. "That son of a bitch," says Etta. This from a big lady who hardly says anything stronger than oops!

"Tell me," I say. "Should I be worried? Jennifer's full of secrets these days," I say.

"Hard to know what he's up to. But I don't figure it for good. There's a legend, more a story. I don't know where it come from. Might even be a white man's story. There's these birds with silver and gold tails the color of lightning. When they set in a tree, or roost on the roof of a building the lightning finds them. I think the story is they got to be shooed away so the tree or house or building won't get struck."

"It's clouding up," Etta says to me, pointing out her window to where a thunderhead is peeking above the western horizon like a mountain.

"I seen something this morning," I say. "I can't believe I saw it, is why I wait so long to tell you. Just as the sun was coming up, I seen Wilf walk out to the weeping birch, stab a crowbar into the ground at the base of the tree. I can't believe Wilf would do something like that, send a little kid out in a lightning storm?"

"If he was mad enough at her father. If he didn't know what I know. I think you better run over to Louis Coyote's and see if you can borrow the truck."

"What is it you know?" I ask Etta, as we struggling to make a ramp with a couple of planks so Etta can make it up into the truck box.

The wind is picking up, the leaves are silverbacked, rustling dangerously. A dust demon whirls around my boots.

"I made a few inquiries," Etta say mysteriously. Etta makes these inquiries without ever leaving her cabin where she don't have a phone or a FAX or a computer. "Al Lindman's dying. Maybe he knows, maybe he don't, but he senses it, that's why he's sent his girl to Wilf. The old saying's right, blood is thicker than anything else."

"I can't find the tarp," I say, as Etta and I try to wrestle her tree-trunk chair into the truck box. Etta is too big to fit in the cab.

"I been wet before," says Etta, ease herself down into the tree-trunk chair, both her and the truck sighing heavily.

"If Al Lindman senses trouble how come Wilf don't? Blood don't seem to mean much to Wilf."

Etta motion for me to drive.

The first big drops are plopping on the hood and I start the truck down the hill from Etta's cabin toward the highway. I drive like mad over the greasy country roads, the truck fishtailing in spite of Etta's weight in the back. It begins to storm in earnest, the wipers only partially clearing the windshield. The thunder is loud enough I can hear it over the roar of the truck, lightning zap across the sky in silver and yellow streaks.

The ditches are rivers. About a mile from Wilf's I have to slow down to pass the mail delivery truck which stopped on a piece of high ground, I guess waiting for the worst of the storm to subside. I catch a glance of Etta in the rearview mirror. She look like a muskrat just poke its head above water.

There is more trouble when I try to turn into Wilf Blindman's driveway. He have a sort of cattleguard made of poles, and the rushing water moved the poles apart enough for the front wheels to drop through. We come to a sudden stop. Etta's chair crash against the back window, teeter as it bounce back, look for minute like it might tip over.

The road for about half the distance of the driveway is under water. Up by the house on higher ground, I can see the old weeping birch, and through the wind and driving rain I can see Jennifer in her yellow slicker and hat, broom in hand, moving in among the tall grasses, standing guard against the lightning birds.

I open the door and step out into the deluge.

Etta is standing in the truck box.

"Run!" she hollers. "Get that little girl away from the tree."

I start out, take about ten strides when I hit a slippery spot, my feet shoot out from under me and I land right on my back in about a foot of running water. It take a few seconds for me to cough out the water, decide that nothing is broken, get to my feet and slither on. I slip to my knees one other time. I try hollering but sheets of rain and wind absorb the sound of my voice.

Jennifer is turned toward the tree so there's no chance of her seeing me.

I'm about halfway there when Wilf Blindman burst from the door of the house come down the steps in one leap, a sheaf of papers flying from his hand and blowing away in the wind as he do. Wilf don't see me either. He scramble up the side of the ditch into the field, covering himself in mud in the process. He take a dozen long steps, sweep Jennifer up in his arms and turn away from the crippled tree. He cross to the ditch, Jennifer's little yellow hat falling and disappearing into the wind-blown grasses, and leap right into the flowing water making a big splash just as the lightning shrill across the sky again, kind of scream as it strike the base of the weeping birch, splitting it even worse than it was before.

The air is full of the stink of lightning. Thunder rattles the earth and the house seems to vibrate.

I get there in time to brace my feet extend a hand and help Wilf and his armful out of the ditch.

Jennifer is the only one of us laughing. She's got her arms locked around Wilf's neck. He is nuzzling her cheek, and both of them is so wet it hard to tell if the water on Wilf's cheek is rain or tears. He holds Jennifer tight and strokes her wet hair. He looks at her like he finally realizes what it is she's stolen from him. I'd guess it is something he can get along without.

PUNCHLINES

Pascoe and Martinez came to visit me at Vancouver General Hospital the day after I picked up forty-one stitches from running through the glass wall next to the front door of my girlfriend's apartment building.

Pascoe is black, but beside Martinez he looks gray. Martinez is new to the team; his home is in the Dominican Republic; he comes from that famous town where they have a factory that turns out iron-armed shortstops who gobble up ground balls like they were Pac-Man. Martinez speaks only about ten words of English, so he's happy to have anybody pay any attention to him. He has worried brown eyes and is so black his round cheeks and wide forehead give off a glare in bright sunlight. Martinez doesn't know he's getting himself in the manager's bad books, making himself an outcast by hanging around with me. Pascoe does.

My name is Barry McMartin. Reporters describe me as the Vancouver Canadians' designated flake. The team bad boy. A troublemaker. Most of my teammates don't like me very much, in fact most are a little afraid of me. Some of them think I'm on drugs. There's more than the usual hassle about athletes and drugs in these post–Len Bias days. But I've never done drugs. I have some common sense, even if most people tend to think the amount I have is minimal.

At the hospital, Pascoe stuck his head around the doorjamb and when he saw me he said, "How the hell did you get all the way to Triple A on one fucking brain cell?"

I smiled, though it hurt like hell. Nine of those stitches were in my hairline. Martinez grinned his greeting, showing off his white eyes and teeth. He said something in Spanish, ending by clapping his hands once and doing a little dance step. I assume he was wishing me well.

"How long will you be out of action this time?" Pascoe asked. He is our first baseman. This is his third year in Triple A, and he's not likely to go any higher. He is six foot seven and shaves his head to resemble Otis Sistrunk, the football player; he looks mean as a boil, but one of the reasons he's never had a shot at the Bigs is that he lacks the killer instinct. He plays an average first base, but for such a big man he has only warning-track power as a hitter.

"Management put me on the fifteen-day disabled list. I'll be ready to go in less than that. The doctors said I was real lucky. 'You are very lucky you're not dead,' is what the doctor in emergency said to me as he was sewing up my cuts. 'A couple of guys get killed every month by doing what you did tonight. You must have a guardian angel; it's a miracle you didn't permanently disable yourself. You'll be back playing baseball inside of two weeks.'"

I pulled up my hospital gown and showed the guys the rest of my stitches. The cuts made a primitive mark of Zorro on my chest. None were deep, not even close to a tendon or a vital artery. What did scare me almost to death at the time was that a shard of glass clipped off the tip of my right earlobe and I bled like a stuck pig. When I recovered my senses, I was lying in a pool of blood and broken glass in the entranceway to Judy's apartment building. I thought I was a goner for sure.

"Well, what are we gonna do to cheer our friend up, Marty?" Pascoe says, with a smile that goes halfway to his ears.

"Si," says Martinez.

"Tell me a joke," I say.

"We know he can't play baseball, lady. We want to use him for second base," says Pascoe, and we both break up, while Martinez watches us, mystified. My laughter lasts only a few seconds before pain from my stitches brings me up short.

One night last season, soon after I became Pascoe's roommate, we stayed up all night telling jokes. We were sitting in a twenty-four-hour café called the Knight & Day, and we just kept drinking coffee and telling stories until the sun came up. We both agreed that we'd told every joke, clean or dirty, that we both knew. And as we got to know each other better we decided that instead of retelling a whole story we'd just shout out the punchline. We both knew the joke so we could both laugh. To give an example, there's a long shaggy-dog story about a white man trying to prove himself to the Indian tribe he's living with. The Indians give him a list of acts to perform that will establish his courage. When he comes back to camp looking happy but torn to rat shit, one of the Indians says to him, "You were supposed to *kill* the bear and *make love* to the woman." So now instead of retelling that story we just shout out the punchline and both of us, and anyone else who knows the story, have a good laugh. But it stymies some of the other players and doesn't go over well when we're out on dates.

"The trouble was the pilot was gay," I say, and this time Martinez laughs along.

Martinez is so congenial we are genuinely trying to teach him English. Not like some of the Spanish-speaking players. We've been known to take them to restaurants and have them say to the waitress, thinking that they're ordering a hamburger, "I'd like to eat your pussy, please."

"What did management have to say?" Pascoe asks, changing the subject. There is genuine concern on his face.

"When you get to my balls try to act as if nothing unusual is happening,"

I reply. That's a punchline from a joke about Sonny Crockett going undercover, dressed as a woman. "Hey, the nurses here are terrific, there was this one last night pulled the screen close around my bed . . ."

"I'm serious," says Pascoe.

"So am I."

"Goddamnit, Barr. How much trouble are you in?"

"Well, Skip didn't come down. As you know, Skip hates my guts. Skip wanted to fire my ass. Or so says Osterman. But I'm too valuable for them to do that. Milwaukee's going to call me up inside of a month— see if they don't. So it was Old Springs came down himself."

Springs is what we call Osterman, the general manager of the baseball team. He is one of these dynamic guys who walks like he's got springs in his shoes, and he's read all these inspirational books like *How to Fuck Your Friends, Rip Off Your Neighbors, and Make a Million by Age 30*. He's always talking to us ballplayers about long-term investments, five-year plans, and networking.

"You're an asshole, McMartin," he said to me. "You're a fuck-up, you're an asshole, you're a jerk. You're also a criminal. If it wasn't for baseball, your ass would be in jail in some town out in the Oklahoma desert, or you'd be in a psych hospital, which is where *I* think you belong. Skip said he'd personally kill you if he visited you himself. So he sent me. For some reason he figures I have more self-control. Skip says to tell you he wishes you'd cut your troublemaking throat when you fell through that window, or whatever you did."

"Yeah, well, you tell Skip his wife's not bad in bed. But she's not nearly as good as your wife."

I was sorry as soon as the words were out. I knew I'd gone too far, again. I don't really want these guys to hate me. I just want to make it clear that I don't take shit from *anybody*.

"You really are pure filth, McMartin," Springs growls. "The front office personnel voted unanimously not to send you flowers or wish you a speedy recovery. Unfortunately, in Milwaukee they don't know what an asshole you are; they think you might be able to hit thirty home runs for them next year. They'd let fucking Charles Manson bat cleanup if they thought he'd hit thirty homers. But just let me remind you, the minimum wage in Oklahoma is about three-fifty an hour, and out of a baseball uniform you're not even worth that."

"Try to imagine how little I care," I said.

"We're going to tell the press you were being chased out of the apartment by an angry husband," said Springs. "It will fit your image and make you look less like a fool. But let me tell you, Milwaukee is fed up with your antics, too. This is absolutely the last time."

"Did management suspend you, or what?" asks Pascoe.

"Naw, I told you, I'm their fair-haired boy. I'm on the D.L. for fifteen days. I'll be out of this hospital tomorrow morning. So while you guys fuck off to Portland and Phoenix and get your asses whipped eight out of nine without your favorite cleanup hitter, I'll be sitting in Champagne Charlie's pounding a Bud and drooling over the strippers."

"I should have that kind of luck," says Pascoe. "I don't know, Barry, you got to stop acting so . . . so external, man," he added, shaking his head sadly.

I should treat Pascoe better. He's a decent guy. I don't know why he hangs around with me. Lately everything I touch seems to turn to shit. Pascoe's really a good friend. When I first arrived he showed me around Vancouver, which bars and clubs to visit, which to stay away from.

"Stay away from the King's Castle," he said to me as we walked down Granville Street one evening, heading toward Champagne Charlie's strip joint. "It's the biggest gay bar in Vancouver. Stay away from the Royal Bar, too. Bikers and Indians; half the people in the bar have shivs in their boots—and those are the women." There were flamingo neon bars above the entrance to the King's Castle and a dozen young men were standing in groups or lounging individually against the walls near the entrance, all caught in the pinkish glow of the neon.

"Fucking queers," I said as we passed, not caring if I was heard.

"Behave yourself," said Pascoe.

The first real *incident* happened the second week of the season. I have to admit I am naturally a loud person. I tend to shout when I speak; I walk with a bit of a swagger; I keep my head up and my eyes open. I've never minded being stared at. I like it that girls often turn and stare after me on the street.

The incident: there is a play in baseball called a suicide squeeze. A manager will call for it with a runner on third, and none or one out. As the pitcher goes into the stretch, the runner breaks from third; it is the hitter's duty to get the ball on the ground anywhere in the ballpark, though they usually try to bunt it between the pitcher and third or first. The idea is that by the time the ball is fielded, the base runner will have scored, the fielder's only play being to first. If, however, the hitter misses the pitch, the base runner is dead, hence the term suicide squeeze.

We were playing Phoenix in Vancouver, at Nat Bailey Stadium, a ballpark that, like the city of Vancouver, is clean and green; the only stadium in the Pacific Coast League that can compare to it is the one at the University of Hawaii, where the Islanders play part of their schedule. I tripled to lead off the second inning. Pascoe was batting fifth and he popped up weakly to the shortstop. The manager put on the suicide squeeze. The pitcher checked me, stretched, and delivered. I broke. The batter, a substitute fielder named Denny something, bunted, but he hit the ball way too hard. It was *whap! snap!* and the ball was in the pitcher's glove. He fired to the catcher, who was blocking the plate, and I was dead by fifteen feet. But I'd gotten up a real head of steam. I weigh 217 and stand six foot two, and I played a lot of football in high school back in Oklahoma. I hit the guy with a cross block that could have gotten me a job in the NFL. He was a skinny little weasel who looked like he was raised somewhere where kids don't get fed very often. I knocked him about five feet in the air, and he landed like he'd been shot in flight. The son of a bitch held on to the ball, though. The guy who bunted was at second before someone remembered to call time. They pried the ball out of the catcher's fingers and loaded him on a stretcher.

I'd knocked him toward our dugout and had to almost step over him to get to the bench. What I saw scared me. His neck was twisted at an awkward angle and he was bleeding from the mouth.

The umpire threw me out of the game for unsportsmanlike conduct. The league president viewed the films and suspended me for five games. The catcher had a concussion, a dislocated shoulder, and three cracked ribs. He's still on the D.L. as far as I know.

The next time I played against Phoenix, I got hit by a pitch the first time up. I charged the mound, the benches cleared, but before I even got to the pitcher, Pascoe landed on my back and took me right out of the play. Suddenly, there were three or four guys wrestling on top of us.

"Behave yourself," Pascoe hissed into my ear, as he held me pinioned to the ground, while players milled around us. Those have become Pascoe's favorite words as the summer has deepened, and I keep finding new ways to get into trouble.

Pascoe was happy when I started dating Judy. Word even got back to Skip, and he said a couple of civil words to me for the first time since I coldcocked the Phoenix catcher. Judy was a friend of a girl Pascoe dated a couple of times. She was a tiny brunette, a year younger than me, with dancing brown eyes, a student at the University of British Columbia, studying sociology.

"You're just shy," she said to me on our second date.

"Ha!" cried Pascoe. He and his girlfriend were sitting across from us in a Denny's.

"It's true," said Judy. "People who talk and laugh loudly in order to have attention directed to them are really very shy."

"You are, aren't you? Shy, I mean," Judy said later that evening in bed at her apartment. Our lovemaking had been all right, but nothing spectacular.

"I suppose," I said. "But I'd never admit it."

"You just did," said Judy, leaning over to kiss me.

The next thing that got me in bad with management was far worse than just coldcocking a catcher with a football block. Pascoe, Martinez, and I had been out making the rounds after a Saturday night game. I had several beers, but not enough that I should have been out of control. We closed up Champagne Charlie's, decided to walk home instead of taking a taxi. When we crossed the Granville Street bridge, the predawn air was sweet and foggy. We were near Broadway and Granville, swinging along arm in arm, when the police cruiser pulled up alongside us.

The passenger window of the police car rolled down and an officer no older than Pascoe or me said, "Excuse me, gentlemen, but I'd like to see some identification."

Pascoe was reaching for his wallet when I said, "What the fuck are you hassling us for? We're minding our own business."

The officer ignored me, but he opened the door and stepped out, accepting the piece of ID Pascoe handed him.

Martinez, coming from a country where the police do not always exhibit self-control, stayed behind us, looking worried.

The officer returned Pascoe's ID. "And you, sir?" he said to Martinez.

"Leave him alone," I said. "He doesn't speak English."

"I'm not addressing you," the officer said to me.

"Fuck off," I yelled. "Leave him alone." I stepped in front of Martinez.

"Behave yourself," said Pascoe, and grabbed my arm. But I shoved him away, and before he could recover his balance, I shoved the officer back against the car. As the driver was getting out I leapt on the hood of the police car.

What happened next is a blur. I remember screaming curses at the police, dancing madly on the hood of the police car, feeling the hood dimple under my weight, dodging the grasping hands of the police and Pascoe.

I remember hearing Pascoe's voice crying out, "Oh, man, he's just crazy, don't shoot him." Then there was a hand on my ankle and I toppled sideways to the pavement. My mouth was full of blood and someone was sitting on me and my arms were being pulled behind my back and the handcuffs fastened.

I missed the Sunday afternoon game because management let me sit in jail until my court appearance Monday morning. The police had charged Martinez with creating a disturbance, but when a translator explained what had happened the prosecutor dropped the charge. I faced a half-dozen charges, beginning with assaulting a police officer.

The judge looked down at me where I stood, unshaven, my shirt torn and bloodstained, the left side of my face scraped raw from where I landed on the pavement. He remanded me for fourteen days for psychiatric evaluation.

"I'm not fucking crazy," I said to no one in particular.

The Vancouver Canadians' lawyer got on the phone to Milwaukee, and the Milwaukee Brewers' high-powered lawyers got in on the act. Before the end of the day, they struck a deal. If I agreed to spend an hour every afternoon with a private psychiatrist, the team would guarantee my good behavior, and my sentencing would be put off until the end of the baseball season.

Management had me by the balls. "You fuck up again and you're gone, kid," Skip said to me. "It doesn't matter how talented you are, you're not worth the aggravation."

I saw the shrink every afternoon for the whole home stand, weekends included. I took all these weird tests. Questions like "Are you a messenger of God?" and "Has your pet died recently?" I wore a jacket and tie to every session and talked a lot about what a nice girlfriend I had and how much I respected my parents.

"Well, Barry," the doctor said to me after about ten sessions, "you don't appear to have any serious problems, but I do wish you'd make an effort to be more cooperative. I am here to help you, after all."

"I thought I was being cooperative," I said innocently.

"In one sense you have been, but only partially. I find that you are mildly depressive, that you're anxious, under a lot of stress. Stress is natural in your profession, but I sense that there is something else bothering you, and I wish you'd level with me. To use an analogy, it is said that with a psychiatrist one tends to bare the body, scars and all, tear open the chest so to speak, and expose your innermost feelings. However, to date, you have scarcely taken off your overcoat."

"Look, I'm okay, honest. I had too much to drink, I got out of control. It won't happen again."

"Suit yourself," said the doctor.

My life leveled out for almost a month. We went on a road trip. I continued to hit well; I watched the American League standings, studied Milwaukee's box score in each day's newspaper, watched them fade out of the pennant race. I wondered how much longer it would be before I got my call to the Bigs. Once in Tacoma, Pascoe had to keep me from punching the lights out of a taxi driver who said something insulting about ballplayers, but other than that incident I stayed cool. I phoned Judy almost every night. I found myself doing with her what Pascoe so often did with me; I analyzed the game, dissected my at-bats pitch by pitch. I knew what I was saying wasn't very interesting for her, but it was a release for me, and not only did Judy not seem to mind, she gave the impression she enjoyed it.

I can't understand why I continue to fuck up. Judy brought two friends to a Sunday afternoon game. It was a perfect blue day and the stands at Nat Bailey Stadium are close enough to the field that I could look over at Judy and smile while I stood in the on-deck circle swinging a weighted bat. Her friends were a couple, Christine, a bouncy blonde with ringlets and a sexy way of licking her lips, and her husband, a wimpy guy who wore a jacket and tie and looked like he was shorter than Christine.

Although I had three hits and two RBIs, I wasn't in a good mood after the game. We went to one of these California-style restaurants with white walls and pink tablecloths, where everything is served in a sauce, and they look at you like you just shit on the floor if you ask for French fries. To top it off, I didn't like Trevor, and he didn't like me. I pounded about three Bud and then I drank a whole pitcher of this wine-cooler slop that tastes like Kool-Aid.

What really threw the shit into the fan was when the three of them decided the four of us would go to a movie, something called *Kiss of the Spider Woman,* about a couple of queers locked up in a prison in Argentina or someplace. Trevor gave us a little lecture about the *eloquent statement* the director was trying to make.

"There's no fucking way I'm going to a movie like that," I said, standing up to make my point.

"Barry, don't you dare make a scene," said Judy.

"No need to be boisterous about it," said Trevor. "You've simply been outvoted. We'd be happy to let you choose, but I don't think *The Texas Chainsaw Massacre* is showing in Vancouver at the moment."

I didn't say anything. I just grabbed the tablecloth and pushed everything across the table into Trevor's lap, then turned and stomped out.

I was surprised when Judy caught up with me a half block down the street.

"You were only half to blame for that scene," she said. "I'm always willing to go halfway," she added, taking my arm.

"I'd rather you went all the way," I said.

But things didn't go well back at her apartment.

"For goodness' sake, Barry, relax," Judy said. "You're still mad. Nobody can make love when they're mad."

But I was thrashing about the room; I'd pulled on most of my clothes by the time I got to the door. Ignoring the elevator, I ran down the stairs, realizing about halfway that I'd abandoned my shoes in Judy's apartment.

I crossed the lobby running full out, and it felt to me as if I was on one prolonged suicide squeeze, the catcher twenty feet tall, made of bricks, waiting with the ball, grinning. I didn't even slow down as I hit the wall of glass next to the door.

In spite of my bragging about spending my time in the strip joints while the team was on its road trip, I actually stayed out of downtown the whole time. Last night I met this chick at a club over on Broadway, near the University of British Columbia. She was with a date, but she knew who I was and made it pretty plain she liked me. I made a late date for after the game tonight. I'm supposed to meet her at some white wine and fern restaurant in the financial district downtown, in the same building as the American embassy. Vicki is her name. She's tall with red-gold hair and freckles on her shoulders. Last night she was wearing a white sundress that showed off her tan.

"Bazoos that never quit," I said to Pascoe. "You should see her, man." I made a lapping motion with my tongue.

The game ended early. I took right up where I left off before the accident; I hit two dingers, a single, and stole a base. After each home run, I toured the bases slowly, my head erect, trying to look as arrogant as possible; I have a lot to prove to Skip, to management, to the self-righteous bastards I play with.

Sometimes I can't help but think about a note that was shoved through one of the vent slats in my locker at Nat Bailey Stadium. It was written on a paper towel from the washroom, printed in a childish scrawl. "Management pays Pascoe 300 a month to be you're freind," it said. For an instant my stomach dipped and I thought I might vomit. I quickly crumpled the towel and stuffed it in my back pocket. I glanced around to see if I could catch anybody watching me. No luck. I'd never ask Pascoe. What if it was true? I hate to admit it, but that note got to me. I think about it more than I ever should.

"Let's the three of us stop by Champagne Charlie's," I said to Pascoe and Martinez in the locker room. "We can pound a few Bud and eyeball the strippers. There's a new one since you guys have been out of town. You should see the fucking contortions she goes through. Someone there said she licks her own pussy during the midnight show."

"I thought you had this red-hot date," said Pascoe.

"Fuck her," I said. "Let her wait. They like you better if you treat them like shit."

We headed off, three abreast, just like old times. Me in the center, Pascoe to my left, Martinez linked to my right arm.

"Just like a fucking airplane," I said, walking fast, watching pedestrians part or move aside to let us pass.

"Punchline!" I shouted, as we loped along. "So I stood up, tried to kick my ass, missed, fell off the roof, and broke my leg."

Pascoe laughed. Martinez grinned foolishly.

"The nun had a straight razor in her bra," said Pascoe, the bluish streetlights reflecting off his teeth.

"Fucking, right on," I said.

We swaggered into Champagne Charlie's, got seats at the counter, right in front of the stage, ordered a round of Bud, and settled in.

"This Canadian beer tastes like gopher piss," I said, drawing a few ugly stares from the other customers. But we knocked back three each anyway.

The stripper was named La Velvet and was very tall and black. She took a liking to Pascoe, winked, and crinkled her nose at him as she did the preliminary shedding of clothes. When she was naked except for red high-heeled shoes, she dragged her ass around the stage like a cat in heat. Then, facing us, with her hands flat on the floor at her sides, she edged toward us, braced her heels on the carpet at the edge of the stage, spreading her legs wide until her pussy was about a foot from Pascoe's face.

"Way to go, baby," I yelled. "Hey, Marty, how'd you like to eat that for breakfast? And lunch? And dinner?"

Martinez grinned amiably, pretending to understand.

I stood up and clapped in rhythm to her gyrating body.

"Behave yourself," hissed Pascoe.

"Way to go, baby. Wrap those long legs around his neck. Show me a guy who won't go down on his lady, and I will."

The bouncer came over and tapped me on the shoulder.

"Sit down," he said.

I was holding a bottle of Bud in my right hand. For half a second I considered smashing it across his face. He was obviously an ex-fighter, with a nose several times broken and heavy scar tissue across his eyebrows. Then I felt Pascoe's huge hand on my arm.

"Sit down, Barry," he growled. "Why do you always have to act like an asshole, man? Why do you have to be bigger and tougher and raunchier and more rough-and-ready than everybody else?"

I sat down. La Velvet was gathering up her robe and heading down some stairs at the back of the stage. I noticed that her nails were painted a deep, dark red, the color of a ripe cherry.

"Sorry, I just get carried away," I said lamely.

Pascoe glared at me.

"You spoiled my chances, man. Why do you have to act like a fucking animal?"

I didn't have any answer for him. I suppose I could blame it on the summer, the pressure of playing pro ball, being a long way from home for the first time.

La Velvet, wrapped in a scarlet robe that matched her high heels, appeared from a door on Martinez's side of the counter. As she walked behind us she leaned close to Pascoe and said in a throaty voice, "My last show's at midnight. You plannin' to be here?"

"Somebody'd have to kill me to keep me away," said Pascoe, grinning like a maniac.

"Don't you have a date?" he said to me as soon as La Velvet was gone.

"Yeah," I replied.

"You don't seem very excited about it anymore."

"Why don't you guys walk over to the restaurant with me? Just to keep me company."

"Naw, I want to sit here and dream about that midnight show and what's comin' after it," said Pascoe.

"You want to come for a walk, Marty?" I said.

Martinez stared at me, smiling, uncomprehending.

"Walk. Hike. El tromp-tromp. How the hell do you say *walk* in Spanish?"

Martinez continued to look confused. He glanced from me to Pascoe, as if seeking advice.

"Walk with me!" I howled, standing up, my beer bottle clutched in my hand. Out of the corner of my eye I could see the bouncer start in our direction.

"Behave yourself," said Pascoe urgently, standing up, too. "We'll come with you, just stop acting like a jerk." To the bouncer he said, "We're just leaving. Two drinks and my buddy here thinks he's Tarzan."

"Pound that Bud," I called out as Pascoe pulled me toward the exit. People were staring at us as we made our way across the nightclub and up the stairs to the street.

The movies were just out and Granville Street was teeming as we walked along three abreast, arms linked. I forged ahead, the point of the wedge, the pilot. Pascoe relived that night's game, every at-bat, every play he was involved in.

"Man, if I'd just laid back and waited for the slider," he was saying. "He struck me out with an off-speed slider because I was guessing fast ball—"

"Punchline!" I shouted. "If you can get up and go to work, the leasht I can do ith pack you a lunch."

I guffawed loudly. Martinez grinned, jigging along beside me. Pascoe, however, continued to analyze the game.

As we rolled along, we passed the shadowy entrance to the King's Castle. One door was open, but it was too dark to see inside. A fan expelled the odors of warm beer and cigarette smoke onto the sidewalk. There were several men in the entranceway. Two of them stood near the doorway, touching, talking earnestly into each other's faces. Pascoe talked on, looking neither right nor left. A tawny-skinned young man in tight Levis, his white shirt open, tied in a knot across his belly, leaned insolently against a wall.

"Fucking queers," I yelled, pushing on faster.

"Behave yourself," snapped Pascoe.

Beyond the King's Castle I breathed easier. As we were passing, my eyes had flashed across those of the tawny-skinned boy and I had felt that he knew. As I know. That it is not a matter of will I or won't I, but only of how long before I do.

"Punchline!" I wailed. "Trouble was, the pilot was gay."

"Ha, ha," cried Martinez, thinking he understood.

THE LAST SURVIVING MEMBER OF THE JAPANESE VICTORY SOCIETY

I fell in love with Kimiko because she was a happy person. It was easy. Happy is contagious, especially to me, after a lifetime of too little pleasure. Kimiko was not what I would ordinarily have considered attractive, but joy makes the plain beautiful, as their aura of cheerfulness expands to encompass all around it.

I met Kimiko at the plant nursery she operated. I had recently taken up gardening; I asked her advice; she was very helpful. I found myself returning again and again, telling myself that the trips were necessary. Asking questions just to interact with her, leaving each time with my station wagon crammed with new acquisitions.

I was one of those 50-something men, recently divorced after a long unhappy marriage, on my own in an ancient Victorian home in an older area of the city. I have no money worries having practised law for over 30 years. My ex-wife lives alone in what was our million-dollar home. She was and is a terribly unhappy person, something I should have realized immediately on meeting her, had I not been blinded by her beauty, her model's figure, her honey-colored hair, her large, brilliant blue eyes. If I had not been so enthralled I would have noticed her lack of passion, her critical tongue, her negative attitude toward everything and everyone except me. A concept that changed dramatically after a few months of marriage. My business success that allowed me to provide the best of everything including world travel was never a consolation. I watched beauty become bitter.

What could I have done differently? I tried for most of thirty years, experimenting, failing, blaming myself for failing.

Finally, I asked Kimiko out. I did it badly because I was truly scared. I had been on my own for a year. My friends were eager to find me a new partner; I tired quickly of the frail women in expensive clothes, swathed in clouds of perfume, birdlike, anxious, talking too much about their ex-husbands. Kimiko was not like other women who I would ask for a casual date to dinner, the theater, or a charity function.

Kimiko was totally different, probably no more than five feet tall, muscular from wrestling tubs of plants and saplings about the nursery every day. Her father, who had started the business, was dead. Her mother, who appeared to speak no English manned the cash register. There were no employees, it was a summer business that closed from November to April. Her nose was wide, flat as a baby's, her eyes a hazel blur, behind rimless, Coke-bottle glasses.

She smiled up at me. If she was surprised she didn't show it. "So, you like Japanese chicks?"

"Uh, no," I stammered. She wore her usual work clothes, black jeans and a flowered smock, today one decorated with pink geraniums.

"Don't tell me you didn't notice I was Japanese?" She laughed prettily, the sound like the burbling of a meadowlark.

"What I'm saying badly is that I've known a number of Japanese women but have never asked one for a date, until now."

Everything about Kimiko was joyful. She smelled tangy, like lemons. Our first date was at a Greek restaurant. Kimiko ate like what she was, a hard-working woman. It was such a pleasure to watch her devour a fried cheese appetizer, moussaka, a rice pudding, then a baklava with our coffee. I was used to women who ordered salad, then pushed it around their plate, pretending to eat.

"What you see is what you get," said Kimiko, her eyes sparkling behind the thick lenses, as she finished an after-dinner drink. "I'm a big girl, I eat like a stevedore, and I've never watched my weight. Most men find that a problem."

"No me," I said. "I'm successful enough that I can afford to feed you." Kimiko laughed. "I asked you out because you're funny, and happy, and not the least pretentious. All night I've been longing to put my arms around you."

"Well, let's take care of that right now," said Kimiko. She stood up, walked around the table, and as I stood up, she put her arms around me, stood on her tip toes and kissed me. She was warm, and soft, and tasted lemony.

We never looked back. In the car we couldn't keep our hands off each other. She spent the night with me at my place. My bed was in a spacious upstairs room, a brisk wind rubbed birch limbs against the side of the house. The blind was up, tines of moonlight spangled the bed. She was everything I dreamed of, sexual, sensual, loving, anxious to please and be pleased.

"You're a very passionate woman," I said, breathless, as we rested, her head on my shoulder.

Kimiko laughed her wonderful laugh. "When people do something that on the surface appears so ridiculous, it would be a terrible shame if everyone involved didn't enjoy a great deal of pleasure."

That was Kimiko; she felt that everything in life should provide a great deal of pleasure, even work. Particularly work. I had a weakness for annual flowers, brilliant begonias, pansies. Marigolds, which reminded me of a trip to India where in some rural areas, rivers of marigolds ran beside the roads, their spicy odor masking the unpleasantness of poverty. It was Kimiko who wrestled the tubs of pampas grass, the potted roses, the flats of brilliants, to my station wagon. "I love customers like you," she said. "Everything but the roses and pampas grass will die in the fall, then you have to replace it all in the spring. You're like a trust fund for my business."

I had guessed I was twenty years older than Kimiko. I was fifty-two.

A few months later I suggested that since I essentially had more money than I knew what to do with that she could sell the nursery if she wanted to, we could travel a lot, do whatever we wanted. She wouldn't hear of it.

"I love my job," she said. "I'd go to fat if I didn't work. I wrestle hundred-pound bales of peat moss, huge tubs of trees and plants. I'm 190 pounds of solid muscle. So if you don't treat me right you better live in fear." And she laughed as she threw her arms around me, and pushed me back onto our sofa. I never again mentioned selling the plant nursery. It was about that time that Kimiko first suggested I carry her. She was being facetious, but there was a certain longing I sensed. "I'm 58 years old, I'm 6' tall and weigh 150 lbs. Do the math," I said in a jocular tone.

"Maybe you should take up weight lifting?" said Kimiko.

As lovers do, we exchanged life stories in monologues. Mine was very short, and as I told my story, I realized I had spent a small lifetime, repeating the same mistakes, expecting different results, trying unsuccessfully to please a woman who couldn't be pleased, though I didn't realize my mistakes until I was distanced by divorce from the situation.

Kimiko's story was much more interesting.

"My father grew up in Hawaii, the island of Maui. But he was the youngest son, their farm was small, there was no life for him there, so he married my mother when she was sixteen, and they had the bad luck to immigrate to Canada a year before Pearl Harbor. They were interned, my father's recently purchased land, in Richmond, outside Vancouver, where he was establishing a market garden, was seized and sold without compensation. It was part racism, part fear of the unknown. Japanese Americans were treated equally badly, but in Hawaii things went on as normal, because a third of the residents of Hawaii were of Japanese descent, there were just too many of them.

"Virtually all Japanese immigrants were loyal Americans or Canadians, the way they were treated was so unfair. That unfair treatment made many of the Hawaii Japanese choose sides. In all of the Hawaiian Islands there was not one act of sabotage during World War Two, but that doesn't mean there wasn't great resentment, but they were too subtle for sabotage.

"They realized any resistance would be small and futile, and put everyone in danger, so they established an underground. The Japanese Victory Society. Mama says it started with my father's family, and some members of her family, and other neighbors on Maui. Eventually, there were cells on every island; they believed without reservation that Japan would win the war. They decided to wait and watch and be prepared. They established a shadow government, had it all in place, ready to take over as soon as the Japanese took control of the islands. They believed that as soon as Japan won there would be a massive exchange of prisoners. On that rationale my father, Hiro, was to be Secretary of Agriculture in the occupation government.

"Mama said he joked that he would be Secretary of Pineapples, for they communicated through pineapples. Incoming mail to the internment camps was censored, outgoing letters too. But a crate of pineapples could be shipped from Hawaii. The paperwork was always immaculate, the attached letters innocuous in the extreme, but inside the pineapples lay sedition.

"I had a brother, Norbu, born in the internment camp in Alberta. After the war when my father came back to B. C. and started over, my brother was known as Knobby, and was rebellious, hating what had been done to him and his family but not quite knowing how to take revenge. He hung out with rough white boys in East Vancouver. When he was sixteen he drove his first car into a lamppost and died, at a time when my mother was pregnant with me.

"Mother's small revenge was to refuse to learn English. My father spoke fluent English with just a trace of an accent. Mother claimed her refusal was so I would have to speak Japanese, and would not forget it as many teenagers did when they assimilated in white society. I taught her the only word she knows in English. Ask. When my father was alive, no matter what anyone said to her as she tended the cash register, she replied, 'Ask Hiro.' After my father died it became 'Ask Kimiko.' She may not speak English but don't ever try to cheat her at the cash register, she makes change better than a bank teller.

"The Japanese Victory Society did not die with Hiroshima and Nagasaki.

"They could not believe that Japan lost the war.

"The secret meetings continued, at least on Maui, at least within my father's family. Japanese society was highly patriarchal, but because she was a prisoner, mother was considered a member of the Japanese Victory Society. At the camp, the crates of pineapples came addressed to her—what harm could a teenage wife, with a tiny baby, do with a box of pineapples?

"Once, when I was a teenager, mother went back to Maui for a visit. She was guest of honor at a meeting of the Japanese Victory Society. 'Aging men,' she said, 'with unrealistic dreams of Japan ascending to power again, and a box stuffed full of rising sun flags, folded politely, stored in a dry place, sleeping until insurrection or conquest called.'

"My uncles are all dead now, and I'm not far from middle age. Mother must be the only surviving member of the Japanese Victory Society."

Her mother was another story. Kimiko introduced us. I bowed clumsily, called her Mrs. Shibayama, tried to smile a lot. The old lady stared stonily at me, with small black eyes, glaring as if I was attempting to shortchange her.

"Mother is hard to get to know," Kimiko said, smiling. "We'll just play around her, as if she's a tree in our yard. By the way, she refers to you as 'White Devil,' not a white devil, but THE white devil. She advises me not to play with you."

"How can I win her over?"

"You can't. But I'm a big girl, I can choose my own friends."

We were married in the winter, at city hall on a day of alternating squalls and sun showers. Her mother, who pretended I didn't exist, refused to attend. We went to Hawaii for three glorious weeks. Kimiko found some cousins on Maui, but though they were hospitable I sensed they weren't comfortable with me, and when Kimiko brought up the Japanese Victory Society, her cousins politely changed the subject.

Kimiko moved in with me in my spacious Victorian home, once again suggesting that I should carry her over the threshold. "And if I put my back out, what good would I be as a husband?"

On another occasion I said, "Your mother is welcome to live with us. She can have the back bedroom on the ground floor; she'll scarcely have to see me. There's even a Japanese market two streets over."

Before we married, Kimiko and her mother lived in a drafty cottage/ shed, at the back of the nursery. It was immaculate in its sparseness.

"Mother says she would rather die than live with THE white devil. She can still look after herself. Here, she'd slip around the house like a ghost, cleaning things that don't need cleaning, putting her mark on everything like a cat spraying its territory. She'll be happier alone."

I was persistent. "She's had a hard life," I said. "I could make things easier for her." But she continued to live behind the nursery for a number of years until she took a serious fall. Luckily it was in July when Kimiko worked every day, so she only lay unattended for a few hours. Her hip was broken, she was in hospital, then in a rehab center for several months. She could no longer live alone so, against her will, we moved her into our first-floor bedroom. I peeked in one day. The floor was covered with tatami mats, a pallet for a single bed, a wooden pillow with a thin pad for comfort. The closet door was closed. I assumed everything she owned was inside the closet. I would go weeks without seeing her. She moved about the house like a spirit, emerging to eat only when she was sure I was away or in some other part of the house.

I would sometimes hear her high-pitched voice speaking rapidly in Japanese, like bursts of gunfire and then Kimiko's softer slower speech, but sometimes even Kimiko grew frustrated and her voice would rise, then she'd emerge from her mother's room, shaking her head in frustration.

"She says, if something happens to me, you will throw her onto the street."

"Can't you reassure her? First, I'm 22 years older than you, I'll die first. If it would comfort her, I'll open a bank account for her. I'll give her a pillowcase full of money that she can hide in her closet. I know the only thing we have in common is you, but there must be something that will ease her mind."

There was not.

But the old lady was more perceptive than I. It was she who first noticed that Kimiko was losing weight and energy. I had noticed the dark circles under her eyes, the constant tiredness, but we had both been lucky health-wise, our years together had been blessed. I had gone into old age quite gracefully, scarcely noticing that I was grayer, slower moving, more forgetful. Kimiko was shrinking before my eyes and I had scarcely noticed. I simply thought she too was slowing down.

That was not the case. There were treatments, but they were stop gap. Our world was turned topsy-turvy, it was always a foregone conclusion that I would die first, but it was not to be the case.

Even Kimiko's good nature could not forestall the foreboding that seemed to drip from the walls. The nursery was sold within days of being on the market. We waited, none of us quite knowing what to do with ourselves. Kimiko and I shared a love seat in the living room where we watched TV in the evenings. She was always cold, needed to be swathed in a blue afghan quilt, I sat close to her those evenings so she could draw from my warmth. She was still cheerful, still joked that I should carry her to bed. Now, she had to take my hand and lean on me as we walked down the hall and the stairs up to our bedroom.

Sometimes, I watched surreptitiously as the old woman moved about the kitchen, her sandals and cane clicking ominously on the tiles. What was she going through? She had lost her son, her husband, and now she was about to lose her daughter. She would be left to share a house with someone she mistrusted.

One evening after Kimiko was in bed, I made a pot of the thick green tea that Mrs. Shibayama liked. I had seen Kimiko pour it in a bowl and take it to her hundreds of times. I did what I could, I knocked lightly on her door, waited a few seconds before opening it, I cupped the heavy little bowl with both hands. She was sitting cross-legged on her pallet. How could someone so old sit that way? It would be an impossibility for me, as would sleeping on a pallet on the floor.

I bowed awkwardly, holding the bowl of tea out to her. She stared at me for several seconds. It was her chance to humiliate me as she had seemingly longed to do for all the years I had known her. Then she held out her own hands and accepted the tea. I thought there might have been something like the start of a smile on her face, but it quickly vanished. She drank the bowl of tea, while I stood by awkwardly. When she was about to return the bowl to me I motioned for her to set it on the mat by her bed. I held my hands out to her in a universal gesture. Again, she stared at me for several seconds before letting me take hold of her dry, aged hands and help her to her feet.

"I love Kimiko," I said. "I love her so much." I placed my hands gently on her shoulders and moved her toward me. "I love Kimiko," I said again, my voice breaking. My body shuddered and tears dripped down my cheeks. She remained rigid, her arms at her sides, like sinewy old brooms. She smelled of tea and something like fresh cut grass. Suddenly, I felt her fingers on my back just above my waist, her old hand patted me a few times, very gently, like a cat tapping at a new toy.

As Kimiko's time lessened, we still spent our evenings on the love seat, but several times Mrs. Shibayama joined us, sitting on an oak chair near us, though there was a large comfortable sofa across the room.

Tonight, the TV show is over. The three of us have finished our tea. I stand in front of Kimiko, offer my hand to help her up from the sofa.

"I'm so tired," she says, "I think you'll have to carry me."

Our standing joke.

But this time, as I look at her strained face; I scoop her gently into my arms, afghan and all, her cheek against mine, an arm tight around my neck. She weighs scarcely more than her clothes. I carry her for the very first time, down the hall, resolutely toward the stairs, my heart so full of love, but bleeding with each step.

For Barbara Turner Kinsella
April 6, 1956–December 24, 2012
Ever Loved, Sorely Missed

THE JOB

The building was in the warehouse district, brick long ago painted white, freckled now, paint curling like untended fingernails. The door said merely PERSONNEL. No company name. The ad in the newspaper read *Person with driver's license,* followed by the address.

Inside, the building was like a hangar, three stories high, with windows at the second and third levels suffering from occasional broken panes. In the ceiling were skylights muffled by years of cobwebs. The whole place smelled of oil and bird droppings. There were perhaps two dozen motorcycles of various makes and models scattered about. Toward the back of the building a fleet of vans was parked in a long row, their windshields like the sad eyes of children. The motorcycles and vans were all past their prime.

Part of the cement floor was turning back to gravel, the remainder was cracked and oil-stained. I heard the sound of a mechanic's dolly, and a man in soiled pin-striped overalls bumped from beneath a van, arms flailing as if he were swimming. A pigeon fluttered in the rafters.

When I stood up, I saw he was fortyish, with a ragged crewcut, a cigarette dangling from his pouty lower lip.

"I came about the job," I said, in reply to his questioning glance.

"Oh yeah," he said. "Lemme see your driver's license."

I showed it to him. He turned it over a couple of times with oily fingers, compared the photo to my face, then said, "You'll do. Wanna start tonight?"

"What is it I do?"

"You ride a bike," he said, pointing at the congregation of motorcycles.

"To where?"

He looked at me as though I were stupid. Perhaps he had recently explained the intricacies of the job to someone who looked like me. Exasperated, he walked to one of the bikes, an elderly Harley, leapt on and started it up. It didn't appear to have a muffler and was out of tune.

"I'll assign a four-square-block area," he yelled over the rumble of the bike. "From nine in the evening to three in the morning you just ride around those streets on your bike. Stick to your assigned area and everything will be fine. There's a pump out back to gas up. You sign in and out over there," pointing to a greasy, black, ledger-like book lying among tools on a workbench.

"But why?" I asked. "What's my job?"

He shut off the Harley. "You live in a residential district?" he asked.

"Yeah."

"Well, isn't there a motorcycle without a muffler that travels around your neighborhood?"

I stopped to think for a minute before I replied. "Yeah, there is," I finally said.

"Well, you don't think those things happen by accident, do you?"

"You mean you supply motorcycles to drive around and keep people awake, make them mad, disturb their TV reception?"

"You got it. In the winter we use vans. The drivers sit them at the curb, work their wheels into the ice until they're stuck, then spin their wheels and roar their engines for an hour or so."

"Always outside my house," I said.

"Right. Probably they're three or four doors away, but if we do a good job, everybody thinks it's in front of their house."

"I've never driven a bike before," I said.

"I could give you an ambulance," he went on. "We have a couple, but you have to cover a twelve-block-square area. The consolation is you get to turn the siren (he pronounced it "si-reen") up to full wail."

"Are you a government agency?"

"We're not sure. It's all very hush-hush. My paycheck comes from a holding company; it would take twenty years to find out who owns it. Personally, I think we're sponsored by the Southern Baptist Convention—there are thirteen million of those suckers, did you know that?—or maybe Oral Roberts. Duke—he's the night man—thinks we're CIA or FBI, but I don't think so. You'd have to be religious to want to make *everybody* miserable."

"Just driving, that's all?"

"Well, you burn a lot of rubber, make quick stops and starts. Just try to remember how the driver in your area does it. Now, you want it or not? I got a muffler to tear off and a couple of motors to get out of tune before the nightshift."

"I think I'll pass. Thanks anyway."

"Suit yourself. You can't change your mind though. If you come back tomorrow, you'll find a sash-and-door plant here."

I've often wondered if that was true. Every time a motorcycle roars past my bedroom window, or a stuck van screams at the curb, I make a mental note to go back and check. But in the morning it all seems like a dream.

Risk Takers

1969. Jee was not her real name. And I never knew her last name, though it was Van de something, or Vander something, for she was from a Dutch immigrant family. "Never mind," she used to say, "you couldn't pronounce it anyway."

The valley east of us was farmed by established Dutch immigrants who came to Canada after WWII, the fertile delta land was used for dairy farming and for market gardening. However, Jee told me she had come to Canada only five years ago, when she was twelve. She said her father had been in some kind of trouble in Holland and that relatives had paid the family passage to Canada so they could make a new start.

"Ha," Jee said derisively at that point in her story. Her father had worked on a dairy farm, but apparently lacked whatever skills were required for such work, and was fired.

"He was lazy and stupid," Jee said. He then stole a cultivator, but was not even a good thief, for the RCMP caught him towing the cultivator behind his ragged pick-up truck, only a mile from his former employer's farm.

"Now, the asshole's in jail," Jee said.

We were both new arrivals in a community of tiny, rundown cottages and shacks about a mile outside a small city east of Vancouver. It was a rural slum occupied by the poor and the shiftless, designations that were not interchangeable, my mother insisted.

"There is nothing wrong with being poor," she said, "it can happen to anyone, Cathy," by which she meant us. Until a few months before, our family, my mother and father, myself and a younger brother, lived in a small rented house in a quiet neighborhood in East Vancouver. Then one Sunday afternoon in March my father died of a heart attack, after which Mother explained that while we had lived comfortably, we had lived month to month.

There wasn't even enough money to pay the next month's rent. There was an insurance policy with my father's union, but the company and union were stalling, the union rep said it could take another year before Mother saw a dime.

Mother got a part-time job with a janitor service in this small city and we moved into a basementless, mildew-smelling cottage, amidst a cluster of shacks and cabins outside the city limits. The rent is twenty dollars a month. We have no indoor plumbing, a wood-burning stove, and we carry water from a community spigot two blocks away.

"Her name is Markje," a market gardener's daughter told me on the school bus one morning. "She's stuck up. Thinks she's too good for the rest of us," the girl hissed into my ear. "And her living out in Darktown." She stopped, embarrassed, realizing that I, too, lived in Darktown.

I was surprised the market gardener's daughter even talked to me. The area we lived in *was* called Darktown, because the original inhabitants had been a few black people who came to the coast from an all-black town in Alberta and set up their own community in the 1920s. Over the years most of the blacks and their descendants found employment with the railways and integrated into Vancouver, it is said some of them are the landlords who collect rent on these dilapidated buildings, occupied now by the really poor and truly shiftless.

Jee's long, lemon-colored hair touched the back pockets of her jeans, which were faded to an existential blue and held to her wide hips by an expensive black belt with a heavy buckle sporting an embossed marijuana leaf. The principal spoke to Jee about the marijuana leaf, saying it was unacceptable, just as it was unacceptable for her to carry her cigarettes in the front pocket of her jean jacket, the top of the red cigarette pack peeking out like a pocket handkerchief.

"Fuck him and his creepy rules," said Jee. "He's from the valley, everybody from the valley is Dutch Reformed Church, like Christian Fundamentalists, only stricter and creepier. My mother reads her Dutch Bible as if it's going to put food on the table, and my old man, when he's home, and when he isn't using one of the family as a punching bag, puts on a suit every Sunday and acts so pious shit wouldn't melt in his mouth."

Jee was everything I was not. She was pretty and sexy, with almond-colored eyes and full lips. I have plain black hair and a very dark complexion with a few seed-like freckles on my cheeks and nose.

"There were black Russians in your daddy's family," Mother said. "Your grandfather had the blackest eyes I've ever seen."

It doesn't matter how little I eat I'm still plump. I'd look better if I could afford to dress like everyone else, but I won't ask Mom for clothes money, I take whatever she scrounges at the Goodwill store. I've tried for an after-school job, but there aren't many, and I live so far from civilization.

Jee had arrived in Darktown only a few weeks before I did.

"Second day I got on the school bus, that big bastard Cory DeJong sat down beside me. First he grabbed my tits and I told him to fuck off. He sat back and looked surprised like these little Christian girls in their skirts and sweaters let him twist their nipples every morning. Then the son of a bitch leaned across me, pinning me to the wall of the bus, and shoved his hand down the front of my jeans, pushed my panties aside and had a finger inside me all in one motion. I shrieked, but nobody paid any attention except his friends who were all staring.

"Maybe these plain-looking Christian girls do let him fuck with them, I thought. I wiggled like I was getting off on it. 'You don't need to hold me down,' I said. 'Move your arm and I'll do you, too.' He did.

"I reached over and unzipped his fly, his erection was just dying to escape his jeans. His buddies across the aisle were watching and drooling, their eyes glazed with lust. I took hold of his cock, nice and gentle until I got a good grip on it, then I bent and squeezed and pulled and he screamed like he was being fucking murdered. He leapt into the aisle, screeching and tears running down his cheeks, trying to stuff himself back into his pants. 'Anybody else want a turn?' I said to the boys across the aisle. That was the first and last time any of them fucked with me."

That story was true; it was confirmed to me by several other students. I wondered, though, about some of the other things Jee told me.

"I steal," she said, "five-finger bargains, all my clothes." We were walking the back roads after school on a sunny, lazy spring day, there was calm water in the ditches while crocuses and daffodils spangled the right of way and the smell of warm tree sap filled the air. Jee took a deep drag on her cigarette.

"You know you don't have to stop and give yourself up just because some security creep tells you to. Like the day I grabbed this belt," she fingered the heavy buckle with the marijuana leaf, "just as I stepped out the door of the store this old lady lays a hand on my arm and says, 'You better come with me, young lady.'

"Well, I gave her a push and beat it across the parking lot. For an old lady she could move right along, but I got away with no sweat. Unless the security staff catches and holds you the police don't put a high priority on shoplifting calls. You don't see a police car, siren wailing, on the way to chase down a kid who snatched a lipstick and ran. You ought to come with me sometime," Jee said. "You need some cool clothes."

She was right, I wore a plastic belt that was cracked and falling apart, and my jeans were the on-sale kind, with plain pockets and no rivets or sexy inseams.

"There's nothing I ain't seen," Jee said on another occasion. "On that fucking dairy farm the five of us lived in one room with a bathroom tacked on as an afterthought. It came furnished with a few sticks and a picture of Jesus on each wall. Living in a place like that you learn about sex quickly, not that I didn't know before. Our place in Holland wasn't much larger. They'd wait to have sex until they were sure us kids were asleep. But I'd outwait them. For all her Bible reading and all she said about Papa being lazy and stupid, when he'd go down on her she'd fucking freak. I felt sorry for her because she couldn't scream out the way she wanted to. She'd take a mouthful of pillow to keep from yelling. Then she'd go down on him, for like hours, and he'd sigh and groan and say the sweetest, sexiest things to her. Seeing them like that made me realize what kept them together."

I had little idea of what she was talking about, sex education in the schools was only a rumor, and there were no red-hot videos to watch on a VCR after school. While my parents, when my father was alive, were civil with each other, they did not show affection in public, my presence, or my brother's, being considered public, and it had never occurred to me that they might actually engage in sex at their advanced ages. What went on in the night behind their closed bedroom door was never a subject of speculation for me.

Many of the things Jee said shocked me, though I tried not to let on, though I felt my face blush furiously. I was not quite able to picture the sex acts she described, they were just out of my vision like animals hidden in a thicket.

But there were apparently some things Jee didn't share with me. A girl at school told me that Jee's father had been out of jail for some time, had not come back to his family, was rumored to have returned to Holland, perhaps had been deported because of his imprisonment. The girl said she thought that Jee and her family, as non-citizens would be scheduled for deportation, too. And maybe the authorities didn't know where they were.

In the washroom at school I commented on Jee's new lipstick, on the fact she always had cigarettes. "I got to fend for myself," she said. "The old lady doesn't have a dime. The church pays the rent, gives her a few dollars for food. Everybody else in Darktown is on welfare but she's afraid, and maybe with good reason, to get involved with the government in any way."

I'd seen Jee in the hall at school talking animatedly with a boy, one of the hoody types with a car that he drove at high speed up and down in front of the school at noon hour, wheels churning dust. Jee had her fingers on his bicep, leaning in allowing her knee to rub his leg. When she left him she had a pack of cigarettes three-quarters full. We went to the washroom, locked ourselves in a booth and lit up. "Those creepy types are the easiest to con," Jee said, "they're not shy, they think they're God's gift to horny girls. 'Come for a ride,' he said to me. 'Give me your cigarettes,' I said, and rubbed my tits against him, just one touch to let him know I was serious. Easier than taking candy from a baby. I got bus fare from him, too. We'll go into Vancouver after school. You need some clothes and I need some makeup. The great thing is I can con him again tomorrow, and the next day, these creeps who think they're irresistible, who think every chick who makes eye contact with them is dying to suck their cock, are the easiest to rip off."

"Don't they catch on and become dangerous after you rip them off a few times?"

"Not likely," she said, "They're marks. Their egos are too big, they consider being ripped off foreplay. Steve, the guy I was talking to today, is cute in a James Dean kind of way. I'd trade him a blow job some noon hour for a carton of cigarettes and bus fare for a week."

We strolled through a department store while she pocketed a lipstick that I'd admired, stashed some perfume for herself and eye shadow for both of us. She was brazen about stealing, never skulking, or looking suspicious. She never glanced around to see if someone might be watching her.

"This is something you'd look really good in," she said in the clothing department, a few minutes later. She took a bomber jacket of soft brown leather off its hanger and held it up in front of me; it had silver buckles on the sleeves and shoulders. The price tag was astronomical.

"Go wait at the bus stop two blocks over," Jee said as we rode an escalator toward the first floor. Outside, she handed me the cosmetics.

"That jacket's got an electronic gadget on it, it'll shriek like a dying rabbit when I hit the street, but I'll be running full out when I activate the detector. I'll see you about the time the bus is due."

"Jee, you don't have to . . ." I began, but she was swallowed up by the lights of the store.

I paced around the bus stop for what seemed like forever. Just as the bus was pulling up and as I was trying to decide whether to catch it or wait for Jee, the bus only ran every two hours, she came bounding out of the park across the street, and pushed into line in front of me.

"Everything's cool," she said, "I think I lost them. There was a young guy chasing me, but I hid under a parked car. She pointed to an oil stain from the thigh to the knee of her jeans. When we were settled at the back of the bus she produced the bomber jacket from under the bulky sweater she was wearing.

"We'll take a rock and smash that tag off it," she said.

"I can't take it home," I said. "How would I explain it?"

"Say I gave it to you. Something I've outgrown. I'll come by if you want and show your mother how much taller and broader across the shoulders I am now. I'll tell her I've grown six inches in the last year."

Jee had an answer for everything. The explanation worked. My mother was on her way to work and wasn't really interested in what kind of jacket Jee was giving me, just one less item for her to worry about.

It was after school let out for the summer that we met Frank and Angie. We were hanging out at the local cafe, spinning around on the counter stools, nursing Cokes and smoking, when they came in. They got out of a telephone company truck, one of those big white ones with blue lettering, with a hydraulic ladder on the back.

"I'm on call twenty-four hours," Frank explained later. "If there's a storm I have to get up at 3:00 A.M. and repair the lines after trees fall on them or the wind blows them down."

Frank and Angie walked into the Drop Inn Cafe and took one of the two tables in the center of the room. There were four booths down the outside wall and ten counter stools. They ordered large Cokes with ice. We could feel Frank staring at us. He was stocky with a red complexion, heavy red hair to his collar and a walrus mustache the same color. His eyes were a deep-set green-brown. Angie was very slim, wearing tight jeans and ankle-high black motorcycle boots, and a well-worn denim jacket. Her hair was a shining bay color, worn very short in a pixie cut. Her features were delicate, her skin clear and pink, she had blue eyes and a pinprick of a dimple to the left of her mouth.

Jee glanced over her shoulder a couple of times, once she spun slowly on her stool, boldly returning Frank's stare. As they were lighting cigarettes she stepped off her stool, her long hair swishing side to side making a quiet sensuous sound, and moved toward them.

"Got a cigarette?" she asked

"Sure," said Frank, taking the pack from his shirt pocket and holding it out to her. As Jee took a cigarette, Frank said to her, "Why don't you and your friend join us?" We did.

"I see you're a collector," Frank said, staring at Jee. She shrugged her shoulders, not understanding. "You've got cigarettes right in your pocket there," he pointed at her jean jacket, "yet you're smoking mine."

"Yeah," said Jee, smiling easily. "Other people's taste better. I like to stock up. One of my great fears is that I'll run out of cigarettes."

"Used to be mine, too," said Angie, "then I met Frank, and now he takes care of me."

I realized when Angie spoke, she had a breathy, childlike voice, that she was barely older than us, maybe eighteen. Frank was twenty-five at least, maybe closer to thirty.

"How long have you two been together?" Jee asked.

"Couple of years," said Frank. "I found her hitching on a back road out near Agassiz Prison; she looked to me like a dangerous escaped prisoner so I picked her up, took her captive and we've been together ever since. We got married three months ago, the day she turned eighteen. We got ourselves an A-frame way back in the foothills, no neighbors for two miles. We're renting but we've got an option to buy if it stays private. Privacy's very important to us."

I didn't really like Frank, though Jee seemed to, and Angie did little but smoke and smile her little tic of a smile when someone said something that interested her. I didn't like the way Frank looked at Jee, or at me for that matter, there was something commanding about his stare, something vaguely frightening, yet I wondered if I could resist it if it were turned full on me. I also didn't like the way he treated Angie, as if she were his personal property, something bought and paid for.

"I do most of Angie's thinking for her," he said at one point, while Angie nodded agreement. "She pretty well does as I tell her."

I kicked Jee's foot under the table but she scarcely glanced at me, her eyes were locked on Frank's face, as she pulled smoke deep into her lungs.

"You should come visit us some time," Frank said as we were leaving.

"I thought you liked privacy?" I said.

He scowled at me, and I felt my heart rate increase.

"We make exceptions." He gave us directions, drew a little map on a napkin. "Or you could visit Angie during the day. She gets a little lonely up there sometimes, and she's got all the latest records. I set up a charge for her at the record store, and he pointed across the street at the blinking sign The Platinum Disc.

"There's something creepy about them," I said to Jee, as we walked out of town. "I didn't like the way he stared at us, at you."

"I think he's sexy," Jee said.

"Well, I do, too, in a kind of dangerous way."

"And imagine being like Angie, having your own house, getting to stay home all day and play records, being looked after, not have to rip people off for bus fare, or bum cigarettes."

"Everything has a price," I said, but left it at that, not adding that I wondered what price Angie was paying.

We did visit though, a couple of afternoons later. It was nearly a five-mile walk. As we traveled the bush got denser, the sky more sheltered, the public road turned into a trail which ended when a private road began, the only visible tracks were of Frank's telephone company truck. The private road was heavily posted. NO TRESPASSING. NO HUNTING. PRIVATE PROPERTY. PATROLLED BY SMITH AND WESSON.

The private road was damp and mossy, willows grasped at our hair as we walked. Ferns plucked at the legs of our jeans; the road narrowed. Ropes of moss dangled from cypress branches. Cheeky columbines, Indian paintbrush, and some waxy yellow flowers grew in the center of the road. We came round a sharp bend into a clearing and there was the A-frame, brown as sand, its windows running from floor to the pointed peak of the building, gave off a bluish light, a cloud reflected in the topmost triangle of glass.

We were at the back of the building. There was a large deck, newly stained, furnished with white wooden chairs and a white picnic table. We walked up the four stairs to the deck, crossed it and peered into the living room through the sliding glass doors. We had to put our hands on either side of our faces to deflect the light. An expensive black leather sofa faced us. There was a stone fireplace in the background. The deck narrowed and continued around to the front of the house where a new red Datsun was parked, and the spot where the telephone company truck usually rested was clearly defined. In front, a heavily forested hillside rose at a harsh angle. The front was also glass panels with a large cedar door in the middle, the kitchen was to the right of the door. We found Angie at the sink doing dishes and listening to music at high volume from a new hi-fi set in the living room.

She started when we tapped on the glass until we attracted her attention, but she seemed happy to see us. Inside, the smell of cedar prickled my nose. Angie offered us coffee, or a choice from an assortment of soft drinks in a startlingly large refrigerator, but before we could make a choice she interrupted to say, "No, why don't I make us drinks? There's this drink Frank taught me, a daiquiri, it has lime it in. I'd never seen a lime until Frank came home with them. It's delicious."

Angie got out three small glasses and a glass pitcher into which she measured white rum, lime juice, stirred in sugar, then took the pitcher to the fridge, which on command dispensed crushed ice into the pitcher. A minor miracle to us, in Darktown an apple box nailed to the wall outside a north window served as ice box, fridge and food storage unit.

"Take it easy," Angie said, after Jee drained half her glass in a swallow. "It tastes like fruit juice but it's got a kick to it." It was my first taste of liquor and maybe Jee's, too, though she would never admit it if it was. The three of us smoked and sipped daiquiris.

"Do you get lonely out here, so far from everything?" Jee asked.

"No. Frank takes good care of me. We need to be off by ourselves. Sometimes we get . . . pretty noisy."

She smiled her tic of a smile indicating with an upward movement of her head, the upstairs bedroom. Earlier we had been given a tour of the house which stopped at the foot of the stairs.

"I haven't cleaned up there yet," Angie said, "besides, there are things up there you guys shouldn't see," and she smiled mysteriously. "At least until we get to know each other better."

We had two daiquiris each and listened to Angie's records. The drinks seemed to make Angie more talkative. Jee's cheeks flushed and she laughed more loudly than usual. For me, the room seemed occasionally to fall off its axis, instead of feeling happy, I felt anxious and a little depressed.

"You're welcome to stay until Frank gets home," Angie said. "He'll be here about five."

"No. I have to get home," I said, before Jee could argue, though it was a lie, my mother would be at work until midnight.

"I should start dinner," Angie said. "Frank's teaching me to cook." She laughed. "I've had some real disasters. Frank gets . . . annoyed when that happens, and," and she smiled her curious little smile again, and bent to pull an orange mesh sack of potatoes from a cupboard drawer.

Jee dawdled on the walk home, hoping, I'm sure, that we'd meet Frank. I walked fast, breathing the ferny air, often getting a half block or more ahead of Jee.

"There's something eerie about both of them," I said to Jee later in the evening. We were sitting on the rickety steps outside the cottage where I lived. My mouth was furry and I had a slight headache.

"I think they're great," Jee said. "Imagine having a sexy guy like Frank to take care of you. It would be like heaven."

"There's something mean about him," I said.

"Guys are like that," Jee said. "I wonder what's upstairs that she wouldn't show us? Fuck movies? Sex toys. There's this whole store in Vancouver sells crotchless panties, oils, creams, and fucking dildoes big as your arm. One of the DeJong twins brought a catalog to school full of pictures of vibrators, leather panties and bras, and photographs of naked girls with their hands tied, giving blow jobs. I wonder if . . ." but Jee's voice trailed off.

"Whatever it is I wouldn't want to see it," I said, which wasn't really true, but I felt somehow obligated to argue.

"You're sure a spoilsport, Cathy. You'll never take a risk, you'll live in a slum like this for the rest of your life. You're not a leader, you're a follower, actually you're not even a good follower."

"Thanks a lot. But what's any of that got to do with whether I like Frank and Angie?"

"It's your attitude. You go with me when I steal smokes, makeup, clothes. When do you ever risk anything? Frank's a risk. All guys are risks. Angie took a risk and now she's taken care of for life."

I couldn't articulate my fear, and I told myself that maybe that was all it was, fear. So I said nothing more.

At Jee's insistence we visited Angie again a few days later.

"Frank was real pissed off I didn't insist you guys stay for dinner," Angie said. "He must have just missed you. He even drove back to look for you and we went into town that evening hoping to see you guys at the cafe."

Jee and Angie had daiquiris again. I drank Orange Crush over a full tumbler of ice cubes. It was while I watched them laughing, chattering, smoking, or rather when Angie went to the fridge for the pitcher of daiquiris that I noticed what it was about her that made me uneasy. It was the way she walked with an exaggeratedly correct posture, like an old person with fused discs. She moved carefully as if she was in pain, something that thrilled me as much as it frightened me. However, Angie showed no signs of pain when she threw herself into Frank's arms when he came through the door. She had been barefoot when we arrived, but after a while, in preparation for Frank's arrival she put on her black boots and a creamy satin blouse that tucked into her jeans, showing off her tiny breasts. I noticed that she made a point of not inviting us up to the bedroom while she changed.

"Frank likes me to look a certain way when he gets home," she said, "and he doesn't ask that much for all he does in return."

After leaping into his arms, Angie kissed him passionately, wrapping her legs around his waist. Frank gripped her denimed ass with his stubby-fingered hands that had little tufts of red hair at each knuckle. Frank did most of the cooking. He was mildly impatient with Angie's ineptness in the kitchen.

"Can you cook?" he asked Jee at one point, after Angie had sliced a tomato up and down instead of crossways.

"Try me," said Jee ambiguously, a little drunk, as was Angie.

We ate on the deck. Frank had changed into Bermuda shorts and as I watched, the red hair on his legs was turned golden by the sun. Afterwards, we sat around drinking coffee and smoking. Frank brought out a bottle of Southern Comfort, along with thimble-sized glasses. I refused because I didn't like the aftermath of the daiquiris on the previous visit, plus I knew liquor made me lose some control, and I didn't feel this was a situation when I could afford any loss of control.

Later, as the sun was setting into the forest, as Angie returned from the washroom, Frank pulled her into his lap in the big, white deck chair. He kissed her for a long time, arranging her body, his left hand gripping a breast, not fondling but clutching, his right caressing her satin blouse, the belly of her jeans, before settling into the crotch of her jeans, his big hand spreading her already open legs.

I felt terribly uncomfortable. Like a spy. I glanced at Jee, who, a forgotten cigarette burning uncomfortably close to her fingers, stared at them as if conjured. I could see that Angie was responding; she had one of her small hands down the front of Frank's shorts. They were kissing ferociously now, Angie thrusting her pelvis against Frank's big hand.

I scraped back my chair and stood up. Frank broke the kiss, smiled at us past Angie's head as she melted into his neck.

"I was going to offer to drive you ladies back," he said, "but it appears we have a situation here."

He stared boldly at us while continuing to rub Angie's crotch. Jee took a deep drag on her cigarette. "How about if we see you early evening tomorrow at the cafe? Unless, of course, one or both of you would like to join us upstairs?"

He heaved himself up out of the chair, Angie nestled in his arms, licking his neck. He stared searchingly at us as he walked into the house. I took Jee's hand and pulled her away.

"No, thank you," I said, speaking for both of us. Jee frowned at me as I led her down the steps to the grass and in the direction of the road.

Jee was sullen on the walk home.

"You could have gone if you wanted to," I said.

"And leave you sitting, or to walk home by yourself."

"Would you have if I wasn't there?"

"I think so. The idea's so scary, and so exciting. And Frank's so sexy."

"I don't think so."

"Different strokes," said Jee.

"What would three people do?"

"If you have to ask you've got no business being there."

"You're so experienced," I said nastily. "Seriously, how could you know?"

"Instinct," said Jee. "Instinct, and willingness to take risks."

Frank and Angie were at the cafe next evening.

"Sorry about last night," Frank said, "but a call from nature always takes top priority."

Angie smiled her little tic of a smile. Frank treated us to sundaes, pineapple for me, chocolate for everyone else. Then we walked around the small shopping district.

"Let me buy you each a little present of apology," Frank said. He seemed to know exactly what pleased us, a carton of cigarettes for Jee, eight packs of twenty-five, an expensive lipstick for me. I almost went for a shade called White Peach that would have set off my dark complexion, but at the last moment I remained traditional and chose Ripe Raspberry.

A few nights later, the Saturday of the Labor Day weekend—we'd begin our final year of high school on Tuesday—Jee and I hung around the cafe until closing, both hoping that Frank and Angie would show up, at the same time I was scared that they would. We walked off into the night, breathing the cool, damp air, hearing the gravel crackle under our shoes, the occasional scuttle of an animal in the underbrush. An almost full moon illuminated our way. We giggled, smoked, walked, drawn it seemed to Frank and Angie.

As we neared the clearing the glow was like a sunrise, a forest fire.

"Do you think it's a fire?" Jee asked. This was not our first night visit, but on the two previous occasions the building had been dark, the moon reflected off the topmost triangle of window. We had walked around the building. The Datsun and the telephone company truck were cold and dewy. Once, a raccoon had clacked across the deck while we stood statue-like on the lawn, staring. We watched the house for a long time, imagining we heard things, groaning, crying, the more violent sounds of love.

Tonight, the house was totally illuminated, and the sounds ensuing were not like anything we'd heard, or imagined. We stopped just out of view of the house. I thought the sounds were of a bird, or birds, clattering, flopping, crying out to escape. Jee gripped my hand. We advanced across the lawn to the edge of the deck. The night was yellow and black. Every light in the A-frame was on. Music was playing on the hi-fi, Donovan, Rita Coolidge, loud enough to carry to the edge of the deck but not overpowering.

We glanced at each other, inched up the steps to the deck, straining forward trying to make out what was happening. The glass doors were wide open. Frank had his back to us. Angie was bent over the arm of the black leather sofa. She was naked from the waist up, her face against the leather seat cushion.

Her arms were tied behind her back. Frank was wielding a belt or a length of leather strap, bringing it down hard across Angie's ass, the backs of her legs. Her ankles were tied with a leather thong. It became clear as we watched that this was not a punishment inflicted in anger, for the strokes of the strap were often a half minute even a minute apart.

Frank was talking to her, constantly, though we couldn't quite make out what he was saying, for he was speaking in a measured, almost conversational voice. There was the sound of the strap striking Angie's denimed ass, her cries and whimpering, the soothing music, the unintelligible words Frank spoke, then the strap again.

After we'd watched five or six strokes, Frank talked for a longer time, as if he were making a serious argument, as if Angie was in a position to do something, anything. He bent close to Angie to hear something she said. He nodded. He set the strap down, and reaching under her undid the zipper on Angie's jeans. He pulled them down a few inches at a time until they were bunched about her knees.

Still talking to her, he picked up the strap, and at that moment the record ended and suddenly we could hear Frank's voice clearly, even though he was speaking toward the interior of the building.

"Let me hear it, baby. Tell me how much you want it. Show me how much you want it."

Angie was crying, whimpering, babbling, but I know I saw her raise her ass an inch or two in response to Frank's words.

"That's it, baby, that's it," he crooned, then brought the strap down twice in succession, once across her bare ass, the second across the backs of her legs.

Angie screamed, and we could make out, "No more. No more," as Frank began talking to her again.

Jee let go of my hand and strode across the deck toward the open door. I followed, my heart hammering. But they were so involved they didn't see or hear us until Jee tapped loudly on the glass wall beside the door.

"What's going on?" she said, her voice ragged.

When Frank turned I expected the worst. I thought he might begin flailing at us with the belt. If he was surprised he didn't show it. He gave us a sly, knowing, half smile.

"Everything's cool," he said. "We play a lot of games. We get off on it."

But it was Angie's reaction to our arrival that stunned us. Eyes wild and swollen from crying, her face pushed into the leather of the sofa cushion, she screamed, "Get away from us!"

Her voice was shrill and full of tears, like a child throwing a tantrum.

"Get away from us!" she shrieked again. "You've spoiled everything. This is why we live so far from people. You've spied on us. Get away, leave us alone."

We retreated to the deck. Frank followed us to the door.

"It's cool," he said, the strap still dangling at the end of his arm. "You best go now. Everything will be cool tomorrow. She'll be okay. I'll have a talk with her. Maybe we'll see you at the cafe."

As we walked into the darkness the music came on again. Donovan singing about San Francisco and flowers. For a long ways we'd hear the strap like a car backfiring, we heard it until we were so far away it must have been only memory.

"Wow!" said Jee.

"It's sick," I said.

"I've never seen anything so incredible," Jee said. Her breath was shallow and I'm sure I could hear her heart beating. Her step slowed as she lit a cigarette, and even over the sound of our footsteps I could hear the force with which she pulled the hot smoke into her lungs.

Later, as I recalled the scene on the deck, I wondered if Jee had been alone, would her purposeful stride toward Frank and Angie have been to intercede or to join them?

"I don't want to see them again," I said to Jee the next afternoon. "Surely they won't have the nerve to show up at the cafe."

But, as we walked toward the cafe after school, Frank's truck was parked at the curb.

"Wait here," Jee said. I did, though I should have gone with her. She straightened her back, walked to the window of the truck, she was wearing a raspberry-colored sweater, leaned in, her breasts on the window ledge. A moment later she stepped back, opened the door and got in. The truck eased away from the curb. She didn't even wave.

"I said to him, 'Whatever you do with her I want you to do with me.'"

We were in a cubicle in the school washroom. Jee lit cigarettes for each of us.

"You didn't."

She smiled. She unbuckled her jeans and moving cautiously sat down. I saw all that I needed to. I thought my heart would burst from my chest. "I stayed overnight," Jee said. "I'm gonna like work for them."

"Work?" I echoed stupidly.

"Like housekeeping. That's what I told my old lady. What she don't know won't hurt her."

There were so many questions I couldn't bring myself to ask. I refused to go with Jee to the cafe in case we ran into them. I was the outsider now, they couldn't be themselves around me. They had too many secrets.

Jee relayed an invitation to dinner from Frank and Angie.

I couldn't make myself say the words. I just kept shaking my head.

Then they were gone. Jee was spending at least three nights a week with Frank and Angie and often missing class. Frank dropped her off at school on the mornings she did attend.

She didn't come to school on Friday or again on Monday. Monday night I walked the lonely miles to the A-frame, only to find it scary and silent. Leaves crunched under my shoes as I walked across the empty deck and peered into the vacant living room. The empty house creaked ominously in the night, in a light wind tree branches dragging against the eaves frightened me.

"Acht, gone nord. Work. Work housekeep," said Jee's mother, shrugging her shoulders.

A few days later I saw a telephone company truck parked by a house under construction. I leaned in the passenger window, the way Jee did with Frank.

"Do you know what's become of Frank?" I asked. "Stocky guy with red hair, big mustache," I added. The driver was dark and thin, eating a lunch of fish and chips, wrapped in newspaper.

"Took a transfer way up north, place called Hundred Mile House, way out in the wilderness."

I hoped Jee might write, or even Frank. I'd visit if they asked.

Last week I took the bus into Vancouver. In a clothing store on Robson Street I stole a pair of Levis. From our darkest closet I took a worn out black shoulder bag of my mother's, one she would never use again. I filled it with empty cartons, newspapers, junk. Leaving my old unstylish jeans and my purse behind in the changing booth, I admired the fit of the new ones in the mirror. "I want to see how they look in daylight," I said. No one stopped me as I stepped into the street and kept going. Jee would have been proud of me.

THE LIME TREE

It didn't surprise Fitz that McGarrigle, even though at seventy-eight he was a year younger than Fitz, was beginning to lose it. Yes, Fitz decided, carrying on conversations in the courtyard with long-dead relatives was a definite sign. McGarrigle was out there now, crouched by the lime tree, even though it was well after midnight. Though both men were used to turning off the TV after the ten o'clock news, and heading for bed, they had become positively nocturnal in the past few weeks, McGarrigle out in a corner of the moon-blue courtyard talking to his dead wife and daughter, Fitz pacing, worrying, keeping an eye on McGarrigle.

"A couple of old women." That was how Fitz had heard himself and McGarrigle described by a young man in their apartment complex, Lime Tree Courts. McGarrigle had just passed by the pool, limping in from the parking lot, a sack of groceries in the crook of his left arm, his rubber-tipped cane helping him keep his balance.

"Queer as three-dollar bills," another young man, dangling his feet in the azure-blue water of the swimming pool, had added.

"I heard they were both football players about a hundred years ago," the first young man said. The speakers didn't realize that Fitz was standing on his balcony two floors above the pool. Voices travelled clearly through the dry, early evening air.

"They're not queer, at least in the way you mean it," a girl in an orange bikini contributed. "They're just old. I talked to them once. They both had wives and families. And it was baseball they played, though you're right it must have been a hundred years ago."

The group around the pool all laughed.

Fitz didn't hear any more because McGarrigle was thumping at the apartment door, probably having misplaced his keys again. They should have seen us in our prime, Fitz thought. We could have licked the whole lot of them, their friends and relatives, and the box they came in. Bull McGarrigle was like a raging bull in them days, alright. Saw him almost single-handedly whip six Boston Red Sox in a barroom brawl after a Saturday doubleheader. "Them Red Sox always choke in the clutch," McGarrigle wheezed as he and Fitz walked away from the bar, McGarrigle shaking beer and blood and broken glass off himself like a wet dog emerging from a river.

He's always been larger than life, Fitz thought, and he fumbled the door open. "What took you so long? Tangled up in yer knitting yarn again, Granny," said McGarrigle, ducking his head, crowding into the apartment like an oversized sofa.

Though pushing eighty, Fitz held himself ramrod straight. He walked slowly, his full head of porcelain-white hair contrasting his healthy pink complexion. His eyes were a clear, aquamarine colour. He did not wear glasses or a hearing aid. McGarrigle, on the other had, looked every bit of his seventy-eight years. He had taken on a bulldogish appearance in his later years, his large ears emphasizing the huge size of his head, his potato-like face blotched and mottled. His huge catcher's hands were gnarled and arthritic. He walked with his legs spread wide, guided by a redwood walking stick.

Lime Tree Courts consisted of seventy apartments built around a swimming pool and shrub garden. Most of the units were studios and one-bedrooms. Fitz and McGarrigle shared one of the only two-bedroom units.

Fitz had been widowed most recently. Pegeen had been gone seven years. At first he'd puttered around the big house in Gardena, taking little pleasure from the landscaping and house repairs that seemed to occupy most of his time. He and McGarrigle golfed year round and had season tickets to California Angels' games. When the Angels were on the road they often drove to Chavez Ravine in McGarrigle's little Buick, to watch the Dodgers.

McGarrigle's wife, Mary-Kaye, had been dead for almost twelve years. Their marriage had not been as happy as Fitz and Pegeen's. Neither McGarrigle nor Mary-Kaye had ever been the same after they'd lost their daughter.

Fitz and McGarrigle talked of moving to one or the other's house; McGarrigle's was grander, with an ocean view, and he could afford to hire a gardener and a part-time maid. Eventually, the empty space became too much for McGarrigle, even with the thought of company. So both houses were sold, and together Fitz and McGarrigle bought a unit in a new and luxurious singles complex, Lime Tree Courts.

Neither would have admitted it publicly, but what prompted their particular purchase was what Fitz had heard referred to as the vanity of the athlete, the hubris that kept thirty-five-year-old pitchers, hitters, quarterbacks, and tennis players hacking away long after their bodies had ceased to react promptly to the commands of their brain.

Fitz and McGarrigle each harboured a secret fantasy that a young woman in Lime Tree Courts would find them attractive. That a young Pegeen or Mary-Kaye would see through the erosion of time to the magnificence that had been, and each harboured an even more forlorn hope that the young woman's youth would somehow transform them, even for a short time, into what they had once been.

Friends for almost sixty years—McGarrigle from New York City, Fitz (Elwood Joseph Fitzgerald on formal occasions) from a Kansas farm—they'd met playing baseball in Louisville in the first years of the Great Depression. Both had up and down careers in the Bigs, McGarrigle catching for the Browns and the Senators, Fitz playing second base and shortstop for five clubs, with a few stops in the minors in between. His longest stint was a full season at second base for the Pirates in 1933. Fitz had played part of twelve seasons, and he was quick to point out to McGarrigle that his career had been longer, even if he hadn't played as many games.

"I was still turning the double play when you were hammering 2x4s in California," Fitz would crow.

After baseball, McGarrigle started a construction company in Los Angeles; he cashed in on the post-Second-World-War building boom, moved later to apartment construction during which time his company had built several complexes similar to Lime Tree Courts.

Fitz and Pegeen had settled briefly in St. Louis, until at McGarrigle's insistence they visited California and, again at McGarrigle's insistence, stayed.

McGarrigle offered to take Fitz into the construction business. "I don't have the temperament to be a boss," Fitz said. "I like to leave my job behind at the end of the day and head home to Pegeen and the kids."

McGarrigle found Fitz a job as a representative for a large building supply firm.

Fitz never regretted his choice. He and Pegeen had four children, two boys, two girls, all settled now. There were grandchildren galore and by the size and beauty of a couple of his teenage granddaughters, he guessed he might live to be a great-grandfather.

McGarrigle had not been so fortunate. His marriage to Mary-Kaye was good enough; they both enjoyed fighting, one minute flinging plates and curses at one another, the next making up, putting the same amount of passion into reconciliation.

"Don't you try any of that aggressive behaviour with me," Fitz told

McGarrigle when they made the final decision to move in together, "or, by God, I'll pin your ears back like Mary-Kaye could never do."

Mary-Kaye and McGarrigle had had one daughter, Maggie, as beautiful and sweet-tempered a girl as ever lived. In her senior year of high school, as she was riding her bicycle to a babysitting job a few blocks from her home, she'd turned to wave to a friend and steered her bike into the side of a passing car. One second she was alive, the next dead.

McGarrigle muddled through. Mary-Kaye didn't. She became at first a secret, and later a not-so-secret drinker. She withdrew from everyone, including McGarrigle, refused help, and McGarrigle spent the last fifteen years of her life essentially alone.

It was his long-lost daughter, Maggie, McGarrigle was talking with now, out under the lime tree in the dew-fresh hours before dawn.

"We have such a lot to catch up on, Fitz," McGarrigle had said, after the first episode, a week ago.

Neither man had ever been nocturnal, so Fitz, when he'd heard the outside door latch snap at 4:00 A.M., had gotten up to investigate. He'd caught McGarrigle, not going out but coming in, shoes in hand, like a guilty husband.

"Let me guess," said Fitz. "It's one of the flight attendants in #27B. I noticed the one with green eyes staring at you last week."

"It's my cane that enthrals them," said McGarrigle. "None of these sweet young things have ever dated a man with a cane. Of course, the symbolism of the cane doesn't escape them either."

"Could I interest you in telling me the truth?" Fitz said. "I gather you've been outdoors for some time. You've got the cool smell of the night on you, and your shirt is wilted."

"I believe I'd rather lie," said McGarrigle.

"At least give me a hint," said Fitz. "You're not one to miss your sleep without good reason. Is it animal, vegetable, or mineral?"

"Eternal," said McGarrigle.

"You're having an experience with *Himself*?" said Fitz, nodding toward the ceiling. Neither he nor McGarrigle were of a spiritual nature.

"Not so you'd recognize," said McGarrigle. "What's happened to me is my fondest dream come true. It's what I've wished for in my heart every moment of the last twenty-seven years. Out there, under the lime tree, I've been talking with Maggie."

"To your Maggie?"

What with all the publicity given to Alzheimer's Disease, both Fitz and McGarrigle kept a wary eye on each other, kidding each other about Oldtimer's Disease when they forgot names, put their eyeglasses in the refrigerator, or walked about with their zippers undone.

"Just trolling," McGarrigle would say, zipping his fly, but every joke was tinged with worry.

"Yes, my Maggie," McGarrigle said, after a pause, while he gazed around the living room as if trying to remember where he was.

"What did she have to say?"

"She relieved me of my fear of death. Not that I had a great fear."

"I see," said Fitz. "And Maggie, is she still a girl, or is she a middle-aged lady?"

"Well, now, I didn't ask. Her voice is as I remember it though. Sweet, and with a little catch just before she laughs."

"So why here? Why now? Why you? You're not the only old ballplayer hungry for loved ones lost. What did you do that no one else has done? Do you belong to the right organization? Did you give to the right charity?"

McGarrigle looked startled, as if he'd just been awakened.

"It's way past my bedtime, Fitz. Yours, too. It's the lime tree, Maggie told me, the way it scents the air, it . . ." McGarrigle tottered off toward his bedroom leaving his statement unfinished.

———

So it had been for several nights: McGarrigle pacing the living room, clock-watching, waiting for midnight, waiting for the pool lights to go out, waiting for the last stragglers to leave the poolside area.

"I want to spend every precious moment I can with her, Fitz. She says she doesn't know how long she'll be able to come to me."

Was McGarrigle really losing it? Fitz wondered. Was it possible to appear coherent in most respects, yet be loony as a bedbug? Fitz sat alone in the living room for a long time. "You're not the only one has lost someone you loved," he said, rising slowly, the low-slung sofa taking its usual toll on his back, and heading outdoors.

Fitz padded slowly around the pool and, ducking his head, walked the concrete block path through oleander, bougainvillea, what may have been hibiscus, past orange trees, a lacy-leafed olive tree, until he came to, off in a corner next to the concrete-block wall, a lime tree.

The earth was dry, even dusty. Lovers walked to the end of the sidewalk and turned around. As Fitz left the sidewalk, a few fallen leaves crisped underfoot.

Soon after he and McGarrigle had moved into Lime Tree Courts, they had explored the outback, as McGarrigle had called it.

What had drawn McGarrigle out here in the dead of night to this isolated corner, to this small lime tree?

Fitz remembered as a boy in Kansas planting an orange seed in a soup can full of dirt, watching the plant grow day by day, being amazed when his mother squeezed the small deep-green leaves, unleashing the heavenly scent of oranges in the middle of winter.

Fitz pressed gently on a leaf of the lime tree, inhaled the pure perfume it emitted fresh as a dash of cold water, obliterating the exhaust fumes, seeming to quell the sound of traffic from nearby streets.

"Oh, Maggie, I hope you're here, dear," Fitz whispered. "I hope you're talking with your daddy, that it's not just old age, a failing mind and terminal wishful thinking he's suffering from."

Another evening, as they waited, Fitz kept pressing McGarrigle for details: Did he see Maggie? If so, did he touch her? If he touched her, was she there in reality, or just a shade?

"Fitz, do you remember telling me the story of how you tricked your sainted mother?"

"I remember," said Fitz. "It was a dry, hot Kansas day when the wind teared my eyes and chafed my skin. I was about eleven, and I ran home from the nearest neighbours, two miles away, and told my mother the Parson was there at the Sonnenberg's, and would be along to our farm as soon as he finished his tea and fruitcake.

"A terrible dirty trick, it was. Poor Mama near had a fit. I'm sure she developed an extra pair of hands as she cleaned and scrubbed the house and us children, all the time cooking a noontime meal that a chef would have been proud of. It was such a simple lie, a teasing lie, but when Mama turned into a whirling dervish of a housekeeper-cook, it became a lie I was afraid to undo. Mama wasn't even very mad when I finally confessed as she was standing on the porch staring into the white afternoon glare, squinting down the road looking for the Parson's buggy.

"'Well,' she said. 'I've done me a week's worth of work in under two hours. I believe I'll take the rest of the day off.' Which she did. But what has that story got to do with anything?"

"Now, Fitz, do you remember once in Yankee Stadium, about 1935, when you were with the Browns. It was 8–1 for the Yankees late in the game, at least 40,000 fans roaring at every Yankee hit and every Brown error. Two on, two out, and Tony Lazzeri hit a little inning-ending pop-up behind second base. A can of corn. You camped under it; the sky was cloudless, no wind. Yet the ball passed between your hands, hit the bill of your cap, scraped your nose, then bounced over behind first base, while the runners galloped around the bases, and the fans booed the Browns, cheered the Yankees, and rejoiced at your inept play."

"Are you saying the two events are somehow related?"

"You figure it out, Fitz. You've never been slow on the uptake."

"My own sainted mother would do such a thing to me?"

"Only in a game that was already decided. My Maggie says such acts aren't revenge. Just a trick here, a harmless joke there. A little soup down the front of a tuxedo might be a mother evening up the score for a three-year-old puking during a bus trip."

"I don't think I believe you," said Fitz.

"My Maggie says that's the way things are. And you know Maggie wouldn't lie. No one seems to think folks laugh on the other side."

"If I came out to the lime tree, would I be able to hear Maggie? Would I be able to see her?"

"Well, now, Fitz, I doubt it."

"Then there's no reason for me to believe that it's not your hardening arteries sending you these messages?"

"You believe what you like. But there's something better coming." McGarrigle moved closer to Fitz, whispering.

"Maggie tells me she's like a scout. She's sizing things up. Seeing if conditions are right. Some night when everything's perfect Mary-Kaye will be there instead of Maggie."

"You really believe that?" said Fitz.

"Even if it's a combination of old age and wishful thinking, I don't want it to end. I've talked to my little girl, Fitz. Tonight I held her hand. And she hugged me and kissed my cheek the way she used to do."

"Can I get in on this good thing? I'd trade any two of my remaining faculties to feel Pegeen's hand in mine, to hear her sweet voice one more time. For one single kiss sweet as a dew-covered rose."

"I don't know," said McGarrigle.

What good would it do me to argue, to push him further, Fitz thought. He patted his old friend on the shoulder and wished him well.

In the deepest part of the night, while McGarrigle was again out by the lime tree, Fitz sat alone by the silent swimming pool, a single light turning a section of the black water a beautiful turquoise. The scent of blooming flowers, of fruit trees, hung in the air.

As he waited, Fitz imagined he had passed back over sixty years in time to a dusky summer evening at a sandlot baseball game. To a moment when the ball hit the sweet spot on his bat and disappeared far beyond the right fielder. He could hear Pegeen's startled cheer, her voice rising above the few fans scattered along the baselines.

As he loped around the bases he caught a whiff of the first essence of dew rising from the evening grass; he knew the game was over and Pegeen would be waiting for him, her sun-blonde hair on her shoulders.

He would walk her home. He could already smell Pegeen's perfume, the sweet and sour of it, and he could feel her in his arms in the shadows of the hedge beside her home, her lips parted for him.

Somewhere a cat yowled, startling Fitz back to the present. He stood and began to make his way slowly down the path toward McGarrigle and the lime tree. His steps were awkward at first, his joints snapping.

Before he even reached the lime tree, he heard gentle noises, and soft scufflings. He recognized the sweet breathless sounds of love, and for just an instant he saw the moonlight-filtered silhouette of the lovers, McGarrigle and Mary-Kaye, beneath the lime tree.

Fitz turned slowly and tottered back toward Lime Tree Courts, his heart full of hope.

DOVES AND PROVERBS

If you wait on the bank of any river long enough the
body of your enemy will float by.

—Chinese Proverb

My friend Frankie should not drink. Because, when he ingests alcohol
he turns into a dove. Other men, when they drink, grow boisterous,
sullen, or imagine themselves to be Sugar Ray Leonard. Some, after a
few drinks, become great lovers. Frankie becomes a dove. The sad truth
is that a dove is only a glorified pigeon. It would take the Birdman of
Alcatraz and Peter, Paul and Mary, to distinguish a dove from a pigeon.

You cannot get a three-base hit by swinging a banana.

—Biblical Proverb

Synthesizing himself into a 160-lb. dove is Frankie's business. I mean,
I have some idiosyncrasies too. However, it is when Frankie develops
the peaceful disposition of a dove that the trouble starts. Would that he
instead developed little black fists and a winning smile.

A wet bird never flies at night.

—A Comedic Proverb

We are at a cocktail party.

"Hello," coos Frankie.

I notice that his spur is sticking out the back of his oxford. He is wearing shorts that may well be made of feathers. His legs are the color and consistency of yellow floor tile, and about as thick as a pencil. As Frankie takes another swallow of gin his purplish-gray feathers grow before my very eyes. *His* eyes are now orange. His beak is tan.

The Chicago Cubs will win the last pennant before Armageddon.

—A Milwaukee Proverb

Like Gilbert and Sullivan, I keep a little list of those who won't be missed. Frankie is accompanied by one of those near the top of my list.

People who think they know everything sure piss off those of us who do.

—A Romanian Proverb

"I've decided you guys should be friends," whooshes Frankie, his wing nestled around a cocktail glass. My enemy hulks beside Frankie, shaggy as a timber wolf. In Alberta, timber wolves often grow to a height of six feet, and, if they wear contact lenses, are allowed to teach in community colleges, though not in high schools.

"Rowl," says my enemy.

Sheep have short memories.

—The Politician's Proverb

Frankie attempts to flash the peace sign with his feathered fingers. I can tell Frankie is still struggling, but he is losing the battle with his uncontrollable desire to make peace. Frankie's beak turns from tan to yellow; his feathers sprout so rapidly I might be watching a time-lapse camera.

> I was only taking my girlfriend for a drive in the country.
> —Charles Starkweather's Proverb

"You have so many common interests, you shouldn't be enemies," says Frankie, though I'm sure I am the only one who can understand him. To anyone else it sounds as if Frankie is saying, "Coo, cooo, trrrrr, trrrr, cooooooo."

My enemy stares at me through bloodshot contact lenses. He teaches a seminar on *elastic* at a progressive community college. We have about as much in common as Mother Teresa and Idi Amin.

"Rowl," says my enemy, shrugging Frankie's wing off his hairy shoulder.

> In Texas it is illegal to carry concealed wirecutters, or
> for a bachelor to own sheep.
> —The Rio Grande Proverb

"Blessed are the peacemakers, for they shall become late-evening snacks," I say to my enemy. A small glint of primordial intelligence appears in his eyes. Salivating, he turns his long, hairy jaw toward Frankie, whose metamorphosis is now complete. He is a 160-lb. pigeon.

> A foul ball hit behind third base is the short stop's play.
> —Proverbs 2:27

"Those who never attempt the absurd never achieve the impossible," coos Frankie. I am the only one who understands him.

My enemy has a mouthful of feathers.

The aim of literature is to create a strange object covered
with fur, which breaks your heart.
—Donald Barthelme's Proverb

"Rowl," says my enemy, feathers, like snowflakes, drifting in the air.

WAITING ON LOMBARD STREET

There is an old-fashioned IHOP on Lombard Street in San Francisco, probably one of the originals, blue roof, A-Frame, from the days when they were known as International House of Pancakes.

Driving south on a hot afternoon, fresh out of both air conditioning and Diet Coke, we decided to stop for refreshment. A pleasant young woman greeted us and escorted us to a booth, my red-headed lady and I, brought us water and menus and an assurance that a waitress would soon be with us. She may have even supplied us with a name, "Barcelona will be your waitress this afternoon." I prefer waitresses who don't have names, I prefer an arm clutching a pencil with a yellow pad at the end of it.

It was about 3:30 in the afternoon, Bermuda Triangle time in restaurants: the last of the lunch crowd has lurched out, belching martini fumes, time to wash the floors and scrape the food off the windows.

We decided on what we wanted, I chose a chocolate malt, my red-headed lady decided on iced tea, then we visited the washrooms one at a time so in case the waitress came one of us would be there to give her the order.

The waitress did not appear. She never appeared.

There came a point when we simultaneously realized we had been waiting an extraordinarily long time for service. We stared around. There was only one other occupied table, far away. The silence was eerie. It reminded me of the *Mary Deare*. Food steaming on some tables, but no one in sight, especially a waitress.

We waited a few more minutes. We finished our water.

I really wanted a chocolate malt. No one came or went.

"In another dimension, in another IHOP, perhaps in Sacramento, or San Luis Obispo, or maybe even Honolulu, a tall, blond man and his red-headed lady have just been served a chocolate milkshake and an iced tea," I said. "They've drunk them up, received their check, and are now going to try and sneak out without paying. Look furtive," I said, standing up. "I'm going to walk sideways down the aisle. Try to look as if you have a sugar dispenser in your purse.

We walked out, silence clinging to us like lint. No matter how suspicious we tried to look, no one paid the slightest attention.

I leafed through the San Francisco newspaper the next day to see if perhaps a waitress had been kidnapped from an IHOP on Lombard Street. Or if maybe there was a story of the entire staff of an IHOP being locked in a walk-in cooler at the rear of the restaurant by a drug-crazed robber. Or, if perhaps an IHOP had been found abandoned, floating down Lombard Street like the *Mary Deare*, food still warm but all humanity vanished into the ether without a trace.

Several months have passed. I wonder if in some other dimension, my red-headed lady and I are still seated in that IHOP on Lombard Street in San Francisco, spectral, ghostly, playing with our ice cubes, waiting for service.

SHOELESS JOE JACKSON
COMES TO IOWA

My father said he saw him years later playing in a tenth-rate commercial league in a textile town in Carolina, wearing shoes and an assumed name.

"He'd put on 50 pounds and the spring was gone from his step in the outfield, but he could still hit. Oh, how that man could hit. No one has ever been able to hit like Shoeless Joe."

Two years ago at dusk on a spring evening, when the sky was a robin's-egg blue and the wind as soft as a day-old chick, as I was sitting on the verandah of my farm home in eastern Iowa, a voice very clearly said to me, "If you build it, he will come."

The voice was that of a ballpark announcer. As he spoke, I instantly envisioned the finished product I knew I was being asked to conceive. I could see the dark, squarish speakers, like ancient sailors' hats, attached to aluminum-painted light standards that glowed down into a baseball field, my present position being directly behind home plate.

In reality, all anyone else could see out there in front of me was a tattered lawn of mostly dandelions and quack grass that petered out at the edge of a cornfield perhaps 50 yards from the house.

Anyone else was my wife Annie, my daughter Karin, a corn-coloured collie named Carmeletia Pope, and a cinnamon and white guinea pig named Junior who ate spaghetti and sang each time the fridge door opened. Karin and the dog were not quite two years old.

"If you build it, he will come," the announcer repeated in scratchy Middle American, as if his voice had been recorded on an old 78-rpm record.

A three-hour lecture or a 500-page guide book could not have given me clearer directions: dimensions of ballparks jumped over and around me like fleas, cost figures for light standards and floodlights whirled around my head like the moths that dusted against the porch light above me.

That was all the instruction I ever received: two announcements and a vision of a baseball field. I sat on the verandah until the satiny dark was complete. A few curdly clouds striped the moon and it became so silent I could hear my eyes blink.

Our house is one of those massive old farm homes, square as a biscuit box with a sagging verandah on three sides. The floor of the verandah slopes so that marbles, baseballs, tennis balls and ball bearings all accumulate in a corner like a herd of cattle clustered with their backs to a storm. On the north verandah is a wooden porch swing where Annie and I sit on humid August nights, sip lemonade from teary glasses, and dream.

When I finally went to bed, and after Annie inched into my arms in that way she has, like a cat that you suddenly find sound asleep in your lap, I told her about the voice and I told her that I knew what it wanted me to do.

"Oh, love," she said, "if it makes you happy you should do it," and she found my lips with hers, and I shivered involuntarily as her tongue touched mine.

Annie: she has never once called me crazy. Just before I started the first landscape work, as I stood looking out at the lawn and the cornfield wondering how it could look so different in daylight, considering the notion of accepting it all as a dream and abandoning it, Annie appeared at my side and her arm circled my waist. She leaned against me and looked up, cocking her head like one of the red squirrels that scamper along the power lines from the highway to the house. "Do it, love," she said, as I looked down at her, that slip of a girl with hair the colour of cayenne pepper and at least a million freckles on her face and arms, that girl who lives in blue jeans and T-shirts and at 24 could still pass for 16.

I thought back to when I first knew her. I came to Iowa to study. She was the child of my landlady. I heard her one afternoon outside my window as she told her girlfriends, "When I grow up I'm going to marry . . ." and she named me. The others were going to be nurses, teachers, pilots or movie stars, but Annie chose me as her occupation. She was 10. Eight years later we were married. I chose willingly, lovingly to stay in Iowa, eventually rented this farm, bought this farm, operating it one inch from bankruptcy. I don't seem meant to farm, but I want to be close to this precious land, for Annie and me to be able to say, "This is ours."

Now I stand ready to cut into the cornfield, to chisel away a piece of our livelihood to use as dream currency, and Annie says, "Oh, love, if it makes you happy you should do it." I carry her words in the back of my mind, stored the way a maiden aunt might wrap a brooch, a remembrance of a long-lost love. I understand how hard that was for her to say and how it got harder as the project advanced. How she must have told her family not to ask me about the baseball field I was building, because they stared at me dumb-eyed, a row of silent, thick-set peasants with red faces. Not an imagination among them except to forecast the wrath of God that will fall on the heads of pagans such as I.

He, of course, was Shoeless Joe Jackson.

Joseph Jefferson (Shoeless Joe) Jackson
Born: Brandon Mills, S.C., 16 July, 1887
Died: Greenville, S.C., 5 December, 1951

In April, 1945, Ty Cobb picked Shoeless Joe as the best left fielder of all time.

He never learned to read or write. He created legends with a bat and a glove. He wrote records with base hits, his pen a bat, his book History.

Was it really a voice I heard? Or was it perhaps something inside me making a statement that I did not hear with my ears but with my heart? Why should I want to follow this command? But as I ask, I already know the answer. I count the loves in my life: Annie, Karin, Iowa, Baseball. The great god Baseball.

My birthstone is a diamond. When asked, I say my astrological sign is "hit and run," which draws a lot of blank stares here in Iowa where 30,000 people go to see the University of Iowa Hawkeyes football team while 30 regulars, including me, watch the baseball team perform.

My father, I've been told, talked baseball statistics to my mother's belly while waiting for me to be born.

My father: born, Glen Ullin, N.D., 14 April, 1896. Another diamond birthstone. Never saw a professional baseball game until 1919 when he came back from World War I where he was gassed at Passchendaele. He settled in Chicago where he inhabited a room above a bar across from Comiskey Park and quickly learned to live and die with the White Sox. Died a little when, as prohibitive favourites, they lost the 1919 World Series to Cincinnati, died a lot the next summer when eight members of the team were accused of throwing that World Series.

Before I knew what baseball was, I knew of Connie Mack, John Mc-Graw, Grover Cleveland Alexander, Ty Cobb, Babe Ruth, Tris Speaker, Tinker-to-Evers-to-Chance, and, of course, Shoeless Joe Jackson. My father loved underdogs, cheered for the Brooklyn Dodgers and the hapless St. Louis Browns, loathed the Yankees, which I believe was an inherited trait, and insisted that Shoeless Joe was innocent, a victim of big business and crooked gamblers.

That first night, immediately after the voice and the vision, I did nothing except sip my lemonade a little faster and rattle the ice cubes in my glass. The vision of the baseball park lingered—swimming, swaying—seeming to be made of red steam, though perhaps it was only the sunset. There was a vision within the vision: one of Shoeless Joe Jackson playing left field. Shoeless Joe Jackson who last played major league baseball in 1920 and was suspended for life, along with seven of his compatriots, by Commissioner Kenesaw Mountain Landis, for his part in throwing the 1919 World Series.

"He hit .375 against the Reds in the 1919 World Series and played errorless ball," my father would say, scratching his head in wonder.

Instead of nursery rhymes, I was raised on the story of the Black Sox Scandal, and instead of Tom Thumb or Rumpelstiltskin, I grew up hearing of the eight disgraced ballplayers: Weaver, Cicotte, Risberg, Felsch, Gandil, Williams, McMullin, and always, Shoeless Joe Jackson.

"Twelve hits in an eight-game series. And *they* suspended *him*," my father would cry, and Shoeless Joe became a symbol of the tyranny of the powerful over the powerless. The name Kenesaw Mountain Landis became synonymous with the Devil.

It is more work than you might imagine to build a baseball field. I laid out a whole field, but it was there in spirit only. It was really only left field that concerned me. Home plate was made from pieces of cracked two-by-four imbedded in the earth. The pitcher's mound rocked like a cradle when I stood on it. The bases were stray blocks of wood, unanchored. There was no backstop or grandstand, only one shaky bleacher beyond the left field wall. There was a left field wall, but only about 50 feet of it, 12 feet high, stained dark green and braced from the rear. And the left-field grass. My intuition told me that it was the grass that was important. It took me three seasons to hone that grass to its proper texture, to its proper colour. I made trips to Minneapolis and one or two other cities where the stadiums still have natural grass infields and outfields. I would arrive hours before a game and watch the groundskeepers groom the field like a prize animal, then stay after the game when in the cool of the night the same groundsmen appeared with hoses, hoes, rakes, and patched the grasses like medics attending wounded soldiers.

I pretended to be building a little league ballfield and asked their secrets and sometimes was told. I took interest in their total operation; they wouldn't understand if I told them I was building only a left field.

Three seasons I've spent seeding, watering, fussing, praying, coddling that field like a sick child until it glows parrot-green, cool as mint, soft as moss, lying there like a cashmere blanket. I began watching it in the evenings, sitting on the rickety bleacher just beyond the fence. A bleacher I had constructed for an audience of one.

My father played some baseball, Class B teams in Florida and California. I found his statistics in a dusty minor league record book. In Florida, he played for a team called the Angels and, by his records, was a better-than-average catcher. He claimed to have visited all 48 states and every major league ballpark before, at 40, he married and settled down a two-day drive from the nearest major league team. I tried to play, but ground balls bounced off my chest and fly balls dropped between my hands. I might have been a fair designated hitter, but the rule was too late in coming.

There is the story of the urchin who, tugging at Shoeless Joe Jackson's sleeve as he emerged from a Chicago courthouse, said, "Say it ain't so, Joe."

Jackson's reply reportedly was, "I'm afraid it is, kid."

When he comes, I won't put him on the spot by asking. The less said the better. It is likely that he did accept some money from gamblers. But throw the Series? Never! Shoeless Joe led both teams in hitting in that 1919 Series. It was the circumstances. The circumstances. The players were paid peasant salaries while the owners became rich. The infamous Ten-Day Clause, which voided contracts, could end any player's career without compensation, pension, or even a ticket home.

The second spring, on a tooth-achy May evening, a covering of black clouds lumbered off westward like ghosts of buffalo and the sky became the cold colour of a silver coin. The forecast was for frost.

The left-field grass was like green angora, soft as a baby's cheek. In my mind I could see it dull and crisp, bleached by frost, and my chest tightened.

Then I used a trick a groundskeeper in Minneapolis taught me, saying it was taught to him by grape farmers in California. I carried out a hose and making the spray so fine it was scarcely more than fog, I sprayed the soft, shaggy, spring grass all that chilled night. My hands ached and my own face became wet and cold, but as I watched, the spray froze on the grass, enclosing each blade in a gossamer-crystal coating of ice. A covering that served like a coat of armour to dispel the real frost that was set like a weasel upon killing in the night. I seemed to stand taller than ever before as the sun rose, turning the ice to eye-dazzling droplets, each a prism, making the field an orgy of rainbows.

Annie and Karin were at breakfast when I came in, the bacon and coffee smells and their laughter pulling me like a magnet.

"Did it work, love?" Annie asked, and I knew she knew by the look on my face that it did. And Karin, clapping her hands and complaining of how cold my face was when she kissed me, loved every second of it.

"And how did he get a name like Shoeless Joe?" I would ask my father, knowing full well the story but wanting to hear it again. And no matter how many times I heard it, I would still picture a lithe ballplayer, his great bare feet, white as baseballs, sinking into the outfield grass as he sprinted for a line drive. Then, after the catch, his toes gripping the grass like claws, he would brace and throw to the infield.

"It wasn't the least bit romantic," my dad would say. "When he was still in the minor leagues he bought a new pair of spikes and they hurt his feet; about the sixth inning he took them off and played the outfield in just his socks. The other players kidded him, called him Shoeless Joe, and the name stuck for all time."

It was hard for me to imagine that a sore-footed young outfielder taking off his shoes one afternoon not long after the turn of the century could generate a legend.

I came to Iowa to study, one of the thousands of faceless students who pass through large universities, but I fell in love with Iowa. Fell in love with the land, the people, with the sky, the cornfields and Annie. Couldn't find work in my field, took what I could get. For years, each morning I bathed and frosted my cheeks with Aqua Velva, donned a three-piece suit and snap-brim hat, and, feeling like Superman emerging from a telephone booth, set forth to save the world from a lack of life insurance. I loathed the job so much that I did it quickly, urgently, almost violently. It was Annie who got me to rent the farm. It was Annie who got me to buy it. I operate it the way a child fits together his first puzzle, awkwardly, slowly, but when a piece slips into the proper slot, with pride and relief and joy.

I built the field and waited, and waited, and waited.

"It will happen, honey," Annie would say when I stood shaking my head at my folly. People look at me. I must have a nickname in town. But I could feel the magic building like a storm gathering. It felt as if small animals were scurrying through my veins. I knew it was going to happen soon.

"There's someone on your lawn," Annie says to me, staring out into the orange-tinted dusk. "I can't see him clearly, but I can tell someone is there." She was quite right, at least about it being *my* lawn, although, it is not in the strictest sense of the word a lawn, it is a *left field*.

I watch Annie looking out. She is soft as a butterfly, Annie is, with an evil grin and a tongue that travels at the speed of light. Her jeans are painted to her body and her pointy little nipples poke at the front of a black T-shirt with the single word RAH! emblazoned in waspish yellow capitals. Her red hair is short and curly. She has the green eyes of a cat.

Annie understands, though it is me she understands, and not always what is happening. She attends ball games with me and squeezes my arm when there's a hit, but her heart isn't in it and she would just as soon be at home. She loses interest if the score isn't close or the weather warm, or the pace fast enough. To me it is baseball and that is all that matters. It is the game that is important—the tension, the strategy, the ballet of the fielders, the angle of the bat.

I have been more restless than usual this night. I have sensed the magic drawing closer, hovering somewhere out in the night like a zeppelin, silky and silent, floating like the moon until the time is right.

Annie peeks through the drapes. "There *is* a man out there; I can see his silhouette. He's wearing a baseball uniform, an old-fashioned one."

"It's Shoeless Joe Jackson," I say. My heart sounds like someone flicking a balloon with their index finger.

"Oh," she says. Annie stays very calm in emergencies. She Band-Aids bleeding fingers and toes, and patches the plumbing with gum and good wishes. Staying calm makes her able to live with me. The French have the right words for Annie—she has a good heart.

"Is he the Jackson on TV? The one you yell, 'Drop it, Jackson,' at?"

Annie's sense of baseball history is not highly developed.

"No, that's Reggie. This is Shoeless Joe Jackson. He hasn't played major league baseball since 1920."

"Well, aren't you going to go out and chase him off your lawn, or something?"

Yes. What am I going to do? I wish someone else understood. My daughter has an evil grin and bewitching eyes. She climbs into my lap and watches television baseball with me. There is a magic about her.

"I think I'll go upstairs and read for a while," Annie says. "Why don't you invite Shoeless Jack in for coffee?" I feel the greatest tenderness toward her then, something akin to the rush of love I felt the first time I held my daughter in my arms. Annie senses that magic is about to happen. She knows that she is not part of it. My impulse is to pull her to me as she walks by, the denim of her thighs making a tiny music. But I don't. She will be waiting for me and she will twine her body about me and find my mouth with hers.

As I step out on the verandah, I can hear the steady drone of the crowd, like bees humming on a white afternoon, and the voices of the vendors, like crows cawing.

A little ground mist, like wisps of gauze, snakes in slow circular motions just above the grass.

"The grass is soft as a child's breath," I say to the moonlight. On the porch wall I find the switch, and the single battery of floodlights I have erected behind the left-field fence sputters to life. "I've shaved it like a golf green, tended it like I would my own baby. It has been powdered and lotioned and loved. It is ready."

Moonlight butters the whole Iowa night. Clover and corn smells are thick as syrup. I experience a tingling like the tiniest of electric wires touching the back of my neck, sending warm sensations through me like the feeling of love. Then, as the lights flare, a scar against the blue-black sky, I see Shoeless Joe Jackson standing out in left field. His feet spread wide, body bent forward from the waist, hands on hips, he waits. There is the sharp crack of the bat and Shoeless Joe drifts effortlessly a few steps to his left, raises his right hand to signal for the ball, camps under it for a second or two, catches the ball, at the same time transferring it to his throwing hand, and fires it into the infield.

I make my way to left field, walking in the darkness far outside the third-base line, behind where the third-base stands would be. I climb up on the wobbly bleacher behind the fence. I can look right down on Shoeless Joe. He fields a single on one hop and pegs the ball to third.

"How does it play?" I holler down.

"The ball bounces true," he replies.

"I know." I am smiling with pride and my heart thumps mightily against my ribs. "I've hit a thousand line drives and as many grounders. It's true as a felt-top table."

"It is," says Shoeless Joe. "It is true."

I lean back and watch the game. From where I sit the scene is as complete as in any of the major league baseball parks I have ever attended: the two teams, the stands, the fans, the lights, the vendors, the scoreboard. The only difference is that I sit alone in the left field bleacher and the only player who seems to have substance is Shoeless Joe Jackson. When Joe's team is at bat, the left fielder below me is transparent as if he were made of vapour. He performs mechanically, but seems not to have facial features. We do not converse.

A great amphitheatre of grandstand looms dark against the sky, the park is surrounded by decks of floodlights making it brighter than day, the crowd buzzes, the vendors hawk their wares, and I cannot keep the promise I made myself not to ask Shoeless Joe Jackson about his suspension and what it means to him.

While the pitcher warms up for the third inning we talk.

"It must have been . . . It must have been like . . ." but I can't find the words.

"Like having a part of me amputated, slick and smooth and painless, like having an arm or a leg taken off with one swipe of a scalpel, big and blue as a sword," and Joe looks up at me and his dark eyes seem about to burst with the pain of it. "A friend of mine used to tell about the war, how him and a buddy was running across a field when a piece of shrapnel took his friend's head off, and how the friend ran, headless, for several strides before he fell. I'm told that old men wake in the night and scratch itchy legs that have been dust for fifty years. That was me. Years and years later, I'd wake in the night with the smell of the ballpark in my nostrils and the cool of the grass on my feet. The thrill of the grass . . ."

How I wish my father could be here with me. He died before we had television in our part of the country. The very next year he could have watched in grainy black and white as Don Larsen pitched a no-hitter in the World Series. He would have loved hating the Yankees as they won that game. We were always going to go to a major league baseball game, he and I. But the time was never right, the money always needed for something else. One of the last days of his life, late in the night while I sat with him because the pain wouldn't let him sleep, the radio dragged in a staticky station broadcasting a White Sox game. We hunched over the radio and cheered them on, but they lost. Dad told the story of the Black Sox Scandal for the last time. Told of seeing two of those World Series games, told of the way Shoeless Joe Jackson hit, told the dimensions of Comiskey Park, and how during the series the mobsters in striped suits sat in the box seats with their colourful women, watching the game and perhaps making plans to go out later and kill a rival.

"You must go," he said. "I've been in all sixteen major league parks. I want you to do it too. The summers belong to somebody else now, have for a long time." I nodded agreement.

"Hell, you know what I mean," he said, shaking his head.

I did indeed.

"I loved the game," Shoeless Joe went on. "I'd have played for food money. I'd have played free and worked for food. It was the game, the parks, the smells, the sounds. Have you ever held a bat or a baseball to your face? The varnish, the leather. And it was the crowd, the excitement of them rising as one when the ball was hit deep. The sound was like a chorus. Then there was the chug-a-lug of the tin lizzies in the parking lots and the hotels with their brass spittoons in the lobbies and brass beds in the rooms. It makes me tingle all over like a kid on his way to his first double-header, just to talk about it."

The year after Annie and I were married, the year we first rented this farm, I dug Annie's garden for her; dug it by hand, stepping a spade into the soft black soil, ruining my salesman's hands. After I finished it rained, an Iowa spring rain as soft as spray from a warm hose. The clods of earth I had dug seemed to melt until the garden leveled out, looking like a patch of black ocean. It was near noon on a gentle Sunday when I walked out to that garden. The soil was soft and my shoes disappeared as I plodded until I was near the centre. There I knelt, the soil cool on my knees. I looked up at the low grey sky; the rain had stopped and the only sound was the surrounding trees dripping fragrantly. Suddenly I thrust my hands wrist-deep into the snuffy-black earth. The air was pure. All around me the clean smell of earth and water. Keeping my hands buried I stirred the earth with my fingers and I knew I loved Iowa as much as a man could love a piece of earth.

When I came back to the house Annie stopped me at the door, made me wait on the verandah, then hosed me down as if I were a door with too many handprints on it, while I tried to explain my epiphany. It is very difficult to describe an experience of religious significance while you are being sprayed with a garden hose by a laughing, loving woman.

"What happened to the sun?" Shoeless Joe says to me, waving his hand toward the banks of floodlights that surround the park.

"Only stadium in the big leagues that doesn't have them is Wrigley Field," I say. "The owners found that more people could attend night games. They even play the World Series at night now."

Joe purses his lips, considering.

"It's harder to see the ball, especially at the plate."

"When there are breaks they usually go against the ballplayers, right? But I notice you're three for three so far," I add, looking down at his uniform, the only identifying marks a large S with an O in the top crook, an X in the bottom, and an American flag with 48 stars on his left sleeve near the elbow.

Joe grins. "I'd play for the Devil's own team just for the touch of a baseball. Hell, I'd play in the dark if I had to."

I want to ask about that day in December, 1951. If he'd lasted another few years things might have been different. There was a move afoot to have his record cleared, but it died with him. I wanted to ask, but my instinct told me not to. There are things it is better not to know.

It is one of those nights when the sky is close enough to touch, so close that looking up is like seeing my own eyes reflected in a rain barrel. I sit in the bleacher just outside the left-field fence. I clutch in my hand a hot dog with mustard, onions and green relish. The voice of the crowd roars in my ears like the sea. Chords of the "Star-Spangled Banner" and "Take Me Out to the Ballgame" float across the field. A Coke bottle is propped against my thigh, squat, greenish, the ice-cream-haired elf grinning conspiratorially from the cap.

Below me in left field, Shoeless Joe Jackson glides over the plush velvet grass, silent as a jungle cat. He prowls and paces, crouches ready to spring as, nearly 300 feet away, the ball is pitched. At the sound of the bat he wafts in whatever direction is required as if he were on ball bearings.

Then the intrusive sound of a screen door slamming reaches me, and I blink and start. I recognize it as the sound of the door to my house and, looking into the distance, I can see a shape that I know is my daughter toddling down the back steps. Perhaps the lights or the crowd has awakened her and she has somehow eluded Annie. I judge the distance to the steps. I am just to the inside of the foul pole which is exactly 330 feet from home plate. I tense. Karin will surely be drawn to the lights and the emerald dazzle of the infield. If she touches anything, I fear it will all disappear, perhaps forever. Then as if she senses my discomfort she stumbles away from the lights, walking in the ragged fringe of darkness well outside the third-base line. She trails a blanket behind her, one tiny fist rubbing a sleepy eye. She is barefoot and wears a white flannelette nightgown covered in an explosion of daisies.

She climbs up the bleacher, alternating a knee and a foot on each step, and crawls into my lap, silently, like a kitten. I hold her close and wrap the blanket around her feet. The play goes on; her innocence has not disturbed the balance.

"What is it?" she says shyly, her eyes indicating that she means all that she sees.

"Just watch the left fielder," I say. "He'll tell you all you ever need to know about a baseball game. Watch his feet as the pitcher accepts the sign and gets ready to pitch. A good left fielder knows what pitch is coming and he can tell from the angle of the bat where the ball is going to be hit and, if he's good, how hard."

I look down at Karin. She cocks one sky-blue eye at me, wrinkling her nose, then snuggles into my chest the index finger of her right hand tracing tiny circles around her nose.

The crack of the bat is sharp as the yelp of a kicked cur. Shoeless Joe whirls, takes five loping strides directly toward us, turns again, reaches up, and the ball smacks into his glove. The final batter dawdles in the on-deck circle.

"Can I come back again?" Joe asks.

"I built this left field for you. It's yours any time you want to use it. They play 162 games a season now."

"There are others," he says. "If you were to finish the infield, why, old Chick Gandil could play first base, and we'd have the Swede at shortstop and Buck Weaver at third." I can feel his excitement rising. "We could stick McMullin in at second, and Cicotte and Lefty Williams would like to pitch again. Do you think you could finish the centre field? It would mean a lot to Happy Felsch."

"Consider it done," I say, hardly thinking of the time, the money, the backbreaking labour it entails. "Consider it done," I say again, then stop suddenly as an idea creeps into my brain like a runner inching off first base.

"I know a catcher," I say. "He never made the majors, but in his prime he was good. Really good. Played Class B ball in Florida and California . . ."

"We could give him a try," says Shoeless Joe. "You give us a place to play and we'll look at your catcher."

I swear the stars have moved in close enough to eavesdrop as I sit in this single rickety bleacher that I built with my unskilled hands, looking down at Shoeless Joe Jackson. A breath of clover travels on the summer wind. Behind me, just yards away, brook water plashes softly in the darkness, a frog shrills, fireflies dazzle the night like red pepper. A petal falls.

"God, what an outfield," he says. "What a left field." He looks up at me and I look down at him. "This must be heaven," he says.

"No. It's Iowa," I reply automatically. But then I feel the night rubbing softly against my face like cherry blossoms; look at the sleeping girl-child in my arms, her small hand curled around one of my fingers; think of the fierce warmth of the woman waiting for me in the house; inhale the fresh-cut grass smell that seems locked in the air like permanent incense, and listen to the drone of the crowd, as below me Shoeless Joe Jackson tenses, watching the angle of the distant bat for a clue as to where the ball will be hit.

"I think you're right, Joe," I say, but softly enough not to disturb his concentration.

WHERE IT BEGAN: *SHOELESS JOE*
W. P. Kinsella

The book came first. Actually, the story came first. I wrote a twenty-page short story that eventually became chapter one of my novel *Shoeless Joe*. The story was published in an anthology, and a young editor at the publishing house Houghton Mifflin in Boston, Larry Kessenich, read not the story but a review of the anthology in *Publishers Weekly*. On the strength of that, he wrote to me at Desolate U. in Alberta, where I was teaching bonehead English, to suggest that if the story was part of a novel, he wanted to see it, and if it wasn't, it should be.

I wrote back to say I would need guidance, as I had published four collections of short stories but had never written a publishable novel. We worked well together, and *Shoeless Joe* was just like a baby—it took nine months. I wrote it under the title "The Kidnapping of J. D. Salinger." Houghton Mifflin chose the title "Shoeless Joe," though they considered "Dreamfield." When finished, it was awarded the Houghton Mifflin Literary Fellowship and was published in 1982.

Shoeless Joe was optioned by a small independent movie company that kept it in development for two years before the option expired.

Paramount Pictures then optioned it and hired Phil Alden Robinson to write the screenplay. Phil was absolutely in love with my book and kept in touch all through the adaptation—though I had no input, nor would I have wanted any. Phil explained that there was no way to fit a three-hundred-page novel into an hour-and-forty-minute movie. He explained that marvelous characters like Eddie Scissions had to be cut, and that time had to be telescoped in many sequences.

I replied that to me, writing a novel was akin to a baker baking a loaf of bread: So long as the buyers pay for the bread, they were free to do with it as they chose. If they made dainty sandwiches, fine. If they fed it to their gerbils, fine. I realized that most books optioned for movies became gerbil food. I've never understood authors who are proprietary with their work, fighting any changes of plot or character. All I care about is being properly paid.

Field of Dreams was a stunning exception. I wept when I read the finished screenplay. "This is my own work doing this to me," I said. "How can this happen?"

When Paramount read the script, it said, "This is a wonderful script. However, it is a SMALL movie, and this year we are not making small movies."

A disappointed Phil Robinson asked, and was granted permission, to shop the screenplay to other studios.

Eventually, Universal Studios took over the option.

Robinson and his associates accepted a lower budget in return for Phil being hired to direct the movie, something he felt was essential to protect the integrity of the script. Even so, he had his battles. Studio executives, when they read the ending, loved the idea of father and son playing catch so much that they insisted on moving it forward and have father and son travel across America together, searching for writer Terence Mann and Moonlight Graham. Phil was appalled and stood his ground, pointing out that it would nullify the sweet surprise of the father's resurrection. Executives reluctantly conceded the point.

In the novel, the reclusive writer was the real life J. D. Salinger. Why was he not a character in the movie? The answer involves both moxie and cowardice. Houghton Mifflin had their lawyers analyze the manuscript word by word. The lawyers said to the effect that "the only thing Salinger could sue for was under a little-known definition of libel called 'false light.'" They went on to say that in order to advance his case, he would have to appear in court in person, something he definitely would not want, and he would have to say: "I have been portrayed in this novel as a kindly, loving, humorous individual. In reality, I am a surly son of a bitch who lives in a bunker on the side of a hill and shoots at tourists when they drive by my house. Therefore, I have been portrayed in a false light."

Houghton Mifflin's lawyers did receive a grumbling letter from Salinger's lawyers stating that he was outraged and offended to appear in the novel and would be very unhappy if it were transferred to other media. They didn't say that he would do anything, just that he would be unhappy.

The cowardice involved was that studio executives were afraid Salinger would launch a nuisance lawsuit just as the movie was being released, and it would cost them time and a lot of publicity money to get rid of it. The moxie appeared when the executives pointed out that on a good opening weekend, the movie would be seen by ten times the number of people who had read the book. The change would be noticed by only the literate few, people who are not valued by movie executives.

For once, the movie people were right. Over the years, most people I have met have no idea that J. D. Salinger was the original reclusive author. Also, many who read the novel have no idea that Salinger was a real person, not my fictional creation.

Why Ray Kinsella? The choice of name for my protagonist had little to do with me personally, and everything to do with Salinger. While researching the novel, I found that Salinger had used two characters named Kinsella in his fiction: Richard Kinsella, an annoying classmate in *The Catcher in the Rye*, and Ray Kinsella, in the short story "A Young

Girl in 1941 with No Waist at All," originally published in *Mademoiselle* magazine. I decided to name my character Ray Kinsella so he could turn up on Salinger's doorstep and say, "I'm one of your fictional creations come to life, here to take you to a baseball game."

After scouting locations from New Mexico to Ontario, the movie was filmed near Dyersville, Iowa, primarily on Don Lansing's farm. The movie site has become a major tourist attraction in Eastern Iowa. The Lansings have recently sold to a conglomerate, with ex-baseball great Wade Boggs as an investor.

I spent a few days on the movie set. I am a person who stays in the background and observes, so few of the cast or crew knew I was there. Making movies requires tons of patience, which I don't have. The endless setups, the persnickety lighting, the repetitive retakes are not something I can tolerate. My theory of movie making is you get two chances. If you screw up the first take, then you'd better get it right the second time. I'd always come in under budget if nothing else.

I was present for the filming of the feed store scene, shot at an actual store in Dyersville. I sat just out of range of the cameras, finally was tired and completely bored after about eight takes, and went back to our motel. My wife and I were part of the audience at the PTA scene. We were trapped there for a full day of sweltering retakes, and we never appeared in the final cut.

I met Kevin Costner and Amy Madigan, and Gaby Hoffmann, who played their daughter. The most interesting person I met and spent time with on the set was Hoffmann's mother, Viva, the former Andy Warhol movie star of the 1960s. She was a charming, articulate woman who was also a writer and painter of note.

When we were informed the movie was going ahead, we, of course, talked casting. We were informed they were recruiting Kevin Costner. I had never heard of Costner, so my choice for Ray Kinsella was Bo Svenson, who I thought looked a little like me and the imaginary Ray, and whose work I had admired in *Walking Tall*. I rented *No Way Out* and agreed that Kevin would be perfect for the part. James Earl Jones was the obvious choice for Terence Mann, and I was delighted when he was available.

I am told that the Voice that speaks to Ray in the cornfield was, though not credited, Ed Harris, Amy Madigan's husband.

I loved the movie. Novels and movies are entirely different art forms. I don't see how Phil Robinson could have done a better job of successfully transferring one to the other.

How have things changed in the past twenty-five years since the release of the movie? Fathers and sons still bond playing catch, still attend baseball games together, still share warm and luminous memories of games and players gone but not forgotten.

I have received letters from every part of the world, mainly from younger men, about how the ending of the movie affected them. Moved by those final scenes, men traveled, often thousands of miles, to take their fathers to baseball games, or just to have a catch in the backyard.

When the movie went into wide release and came to my then-hometown of White Rock, British Columbia, I set up a table in the lobby of the local theater to sell books as the crowd exited. But before that, each evening, I stood at the back of the theater as Kevin Costner and Dwier Brown, Ray and John Kinsella, played catch; and as I did, I came to realize the absolute power of the great movie that Phil Robinson had created. For every night, one could hear the sniffling and snuffling of the audience, and the unabashed and unashamed tears that flowed as the universality of the father-son dynamic touched even the most indifferent hearts. I realized that my writing coupled with Phil Robinson's genius had made that happen.

Still, after twenty-five years, the saga that began with my recalling my own father's recollections of a disgraced baseball player undeserving of his fate is not over; *Field of Dreams* the musical is out there in the cosmos, ethereal as Brigadoon, lurking, waiting patiently, being groomed for the stages of the world.

ABOUT THE AUTHOR

W. P. (William Patrick) Kinsella (1935–) was born in rural Alberta, Canada. Kinsella was homeschooled until the age of ten by his mother, Olive, through correspondence courses. He attended school for the first time when he and his parents moved to Edmonton. By the age of five he had already begun to write fantasy stories. His father John, a semi-professional baseball player, instilled a passion for the game in his son. At fourteen, young Bill Kinsella won a YMCA writing contest with his short story, "Diamond Doom," a tale of murder in a baseball stadium.

As a young man, Kinsella had many occupations, including taxi driver, claims investigator, restaurant manager, and civil servant. In 1970, he decided to take creative writing courses at the University of Alberta, receiving a B.A. in 1974. He continued his education at the University of Iowa, receiving an M.F.A. from the prestigious Iowa Writers' Workshop in 1978. He taught at the University of Calgary from 1978 to 1983, until he began to write full time after the publication of *Shoeless Joe*.

Baseball has had a lasting influence on Kinsella. In addition to his several baseball-related short-story collections, including *The Last Pennant Before Armageddon* and *The Dixon Cornbelt League*, Kinsella has written other baseball-related books, including *The Iowa Baseball Confederacy*, *Magic Time*, *If Wishes Were Horses*, and *Butterfly Winter*; two novels on prairie life during the Great Depression, *Box Socials* and *The Winter Helen Dropped By*; he edited *Diamonds Forever: Reflections from the Field, the Dugout & the Bleachers*, and he co-wrote *Ichiro Dreams*, a nonfiction book on the Japanese pitcher Ichiro Suzuki.

Kinsella has also earned critical acclaim for his satiric short-story collections that focus on the members of a fictionalized Native Canadian tribe from the Hobbema reservation in Alberta. These collections include *Dance Me Outside* (adapted for the CBC television series *The Rez*), *The Fencepost Chronicles*, *Brother Frank's Gospel Hour*, and *The Moccasin Telegraph*. Kinsella's characters, such as Silas Ermineskin and Frank Fencepost, provide a window into the difficult, frequently dark, yet also comedic juxtapositions between Native and Caucasian Canadian modern life. Kinsella was occasionally criticized for some of his portrayals, and once responded, "It's the oppressed and the oppressor that I write about. The way that oppressed people survive is by making fun of the people who oppress them. That is essentially what my Indian stories are all about."

Other books by Kinsella include two collections of poetry co-written with Ann Knight, and several works of nonfiction, including a biography of Cree painter Allen Sapp. "Lieberman in Love," a short story from the book *Red Wolf, Red Wolf*, was adapted for film, which won an Oscar for Best Live Action Short Film at the 1996 Academy Awards.

Kinsella is best known for his bestselling novel *Shoeless Joe*, which was later adapted into the movie *Field of Dreams*. The hugely popular film featured Kevin Costner, Amy Madigan, Ray Liotta, and James Earl Jones. The famous expression from the movie, "If you build it, he will come" (often misquoted as "If you build it, they will come"), and the very phrase "field of dreams," continue to be used affectionately in the American vernacular.

Shoeless Joe won the Canadian Authors Association Prize, the Alberta Achievement Award, the Books in Canada First Novel Award, and the

Houghton Mifflin Literary Fellowship. Kinsella won the Leacock Award in 1987 and in 1993 was made an Officer of the Order of Canada. In 2005, he was awarded the Order of British Columbia, and in 2009, he was awarded the George Woodcock Lifetime Achievement Award. He has been presented with honorary degrees from Laurentian University, University of Victoria, and the Open Learning Institute.

In 1997, W. P. Kinsella suffered brain damage from being struck by a car while walking near his home. He was unable to produce any fiction until 2011, when he published *Butterfly Winter*, winner of the Colophon Prize. Kinsella continues to publish nonfiction, is a noted tournament Scrabble player, and lives in Yale, British Columbia.